Choir Boy

Choir Boy

Charlie Anders

Soft Skull Press

Brooklyn, NY • 2005

Choir Boy

©2005 by Charlie Anders
Cover Design by Rachell Sumpter

Published by Soft Skull Press
71 Bond Street, Brooklyn, NY 11217

Distributed by Publisher's Group West
www.pgw.com | 1.800.788.3123

Printed in Canada.

Library of Congress Cataloging-in-Publication Data

Anders, Charlie.
  Choir boy / by Charlie Anders.
       p. cm.
  Summary: As his home life deteriorates, twelve-year-old
Berry decides to remain a choir boy forever and, after try-
ing to perform surgery on himself,obtains testosterone-
inhibiting drugs from a clinic, leading to huge,unexpected
consequences.
  ISBN 1-932360-81-6 (alk. paper)
  [1. Choirboys—Fiction. 2. Singing—Fiction. 3. Voice—
Fiction. 4. Sexual orientation—Fiction. 5. Transsexuals—
Fiction. 6. Family problems--Fiction.
7. Cathedrals—Fiction.] I. Title.
  PZ7.A51876Ch 2005
  [Fic]—dc22
                              2005001108

for Annalee and Kelly

Acknowledgments

I had an amazing amount of help and advice on this book, but of course any excesses and abscesses are all my doing. Feedback is always welcome at choirboymail@charlieanders.com.

Annalee Newitz and dgk goldberg both provided invaluable feedback on early drafts of this novel, and helped make it what it is. Tim Krol helped make sense of my musical ramblings. Rebecca Hensler cast an experienced eye over the kids' dialogue and behavior. And Mark Stanger helped with my liturgical references. I also received invaluable feedback from Scott Heim, Miek Coccia, Sam Stoloff, Liz Henry, and Tennessee Jones.

I found some wonderful resources on the Web, including Kai Wright's excellent article, "To Be Poor and Transgender" (*The Progressive*, Oct. 2001.). I was lucky enough to find tons of web postings and journals by transgender teens and their parents as well. The Sylvia Rivera Law Project has some great information on the difficulties TG people are having getting Medicaid to cover hormones on its web site. Though somewhat out of date, the GLBT Health Access Project's study "Access to Health Care for Transgendered Persons in Greater Boston" has some good info as well.

Choir Boy

1.

Berry dreamed of bloodshed and smoke, or churches that collapsed around him as he tried to sing. Disasters nearly choked his voice, or sheet music turned to nonsense. But even in his dreams Berry remembered his training: he kept the sweetness in his voice and the Hosanna in his eyes no matter how he suffered. One image lodged between fantasy and memory like a repeating nightmare: Berry severing a finger in church and singing through the pain. Berry saw himself holding the finger in place with another finger and using every other finger to hold up his music. Sometimes, Berry was so sure this had happened, he'd swear one of his fingers still crooked the wrong way. There was no scar, but maybe that was because when things happen to you at a young age, they sometimes heal really well.

• • •

Berry wept the day he became a choirboy.

It was his earliest memory. His atheist parents abandoned him on the steps of St. Luke's Episcopal Cathedral and raced back to their car. Marco, Berry's dad, yanked his car door shut as if the church was chasing him. Then Marco had to wait for Berry's mom to air-kiss and arrange herself. Marco swatted the steering wheel, his mustache torqued with annoyance. His stockbroker blazer fit too tight over his football sweatshirt. Berry's mom, Judy, fussed with the seatbelt over her magnolia bosom. Red hair fell from her headscarf over her eyes as she smiled at Berry. Then Judy closed her door and Marco tore the Toyota away.

The five-year-old Berry waited on the steps of St. Luke's for someone to collect him. He stared up at the granite spires and stained glass, which looked black on the outside. He'd begged his parents to spare him this. But Judy wanted Berry to learn music. Most music classes charged money, but St. Luke's paid choirboys a stipend. Marco, meanwhile, remembered pranks and transcendence from his choirboy days.

Nobody from the choir came for Berry. Instead, he perched on the church steps for half an hour or so, watching cars pass through teary distortions. The cathedral's ridges and crags made Berry think of a stegosaurus, his favorite dinosaur. Eventually, he tried the cathedral's front door, but couldn't open it. Boredom beat out Berry's fear. He hopped down the leg-high stone steps one by one, then walked around the cathedral to the small alley that separated it from its office building. At the alley's end, he heard sounds.

It didn't sound like human music. It confused Berry's ears. He walked down that alley to a back door in the cathedral, where the vibration thrummed the most. The voice of an alien invader who felt guilty joy over the terror its face inspired, it drew Berry. He opened the hole in the cathedral's shell. Inside, a hallway led to a curtained doorway and beyond that was the area behind the altar. Berry glimpsed gritty stonework lit by rainbow threads of light. He'd never been inside a church before.

The hallway had doors to Berry's left and his right. The left door led to a dirty crawlspace and a spiral staircase that rose forever into a funnel of stone. The right door led to the alien chorus.

When Berry pushed the right door open, he found people instead of the monster he'd half expected. Up close, the choir almost deafened Berry, who couldn't separate voices or identify the notes each person sang. Harmonies clung and wrapped Berry as he walked into the center of the swell. He almost ran away.

The long room was half church, half gym. The outer wall glistened with stained glass windows set in stone, but the inner wall had concrete and lockers filled with Playstation games and sneakers. A corner of the room had pasteboard walls forming an office, with a small desk and swivel chair inside. A few dozen chairs clustered in rows around a grand piano. In front of each chair stood the source of a voice, his face warped with what looked like rage. The biggest singers mostly had beards, and furious mouths a mile above Berry's head. The closer Berry got to the piano, the smaller the people became, but even the smallest dwarfed Berry. Many of them wore blue blazers like Marco's.

About the time Berry reached the piano at the center of the semicircle, the music stopped. Someone spoke to him. Berry turned to face a wild man at the piano. His first impression was of a porcupine beard and eyebrows, then he noticed the round glasses that magnified the man's eyes to the size of Berry's hands. The caveman wore a shirt and tie, but his hairy hands jerked like a demon's. The creature asked Berry's name, and he gave it. Somebody handed Berry his own blue blazer, with a patch that showed the stone dinosaur. It hung to Berry's knees and swallowed his hands, but it was the smallest jacket they had.

Berry found a chair just as the music started again. The others pretended to include him, but it was a long time before he tried to add his voice. By the time the notes made sense to Berry, they had already claimed him on a level beneath reading and counting. He'd grasped the difference between a dotted quarter note (three quick leaps) and a triplet (three beats in two). He learned a thousand anthems by heart, but more than that, he understood something about the patterns of music. You could count on music to change but return to its starting point, which made it more dependable than people.

• • •

Berry turned thirteen on a Sunday in June. Marco glanced at the calendar, swore, and flung granola and butter into a frying pan that was nearly a wok. Judy wasn't home, as usual. "Don't bother," Berry said. He already wore his choir blazer, white shirt, and gray pants. Shower dew dribbled in his eyes. He'd traded up blazer sizes seven times in the past eight years. The latest blazer had bleach stains along the rear right shoulder from its previous owner, Roddy, who'd dropped out of the choir after his voice had changed. Berry's wrists had started poking from this blazer's sleeves six months ago. A label inside the blazer's scruff read Haddock & Lange, Men's Clothiers.

"I don't want to be late for choir." Berry stared at the dream-catchers and mandalas Marco kept on the walls for the spiritual advice clients he sometimes entertained at the apartment. He tried not to watch Marco savage the pan with a spatula. The hot butter smelled of tar babies. The granola leapt and flecked Marco's mustache. Marco scooped the fried granola into an ice cream cone: "A birth-day treat." Then he excavated a tie from his stockbroker days and wrapped it in Sunday funnies. Berry looped the tie under his choir blazer and sat through Marco's half-assed birthday chant, cocked to run for the downtown bus.

The bus came late. Berry found a seat up front near the old and legless people and perched, legs quivering with so much voltage his butt barely sat. "What's with you?" asked the large old man next to him.

"Going to church," Berry said mid-twitch.

The bristles around the man's chops rearranged into a scowl. He rose and found another seat.

Berry got to the cathedral just as the choir warmed up. He ran down the alley to the side door. From the alley's end, he heard scales and grace notes, voices waking. Berry ran into the cathedral and through the right door, into the choir room. A few basses and tenors turned to glare at the latecom-er. Berry ignored them and found his chair at the center of the front row of trebles. Berry felt a jab in the arm as Teddy, the head choirboy, punched him. "Late," Teddy whispered. Teddy wore the same blazer, but with low-hanging baggy pants. He kept his eyes on Mr. Allen, the choirmaster.

Mr. Allen didn't bother to chew Berry out for lateness. The director's hair and beard had only gotten wilder since Berry had joined. He still wore the wine-bottle glasses; rumor among the younger boys whispered Mr. Allen was blind but could read thoughts.

That morning, Mr. Allen threatened to cancel church if the choir didn't pull its shit together. Staring into his cloudy eyes, Berry didn't doubt Mr. Allen could abolish religion for-ever if he chose. Berry imagined Mr. Allen walking out into the cathedral, its brownstone vaulting already pregnant with

Charlie Anders

the congregation's chattering, and announcing: "Show's over—go home and worship your own way, folks. We got nothing for you here." Dean Jackson and Canon Moosehead might jump out of their carved seats, tripping on their golden robes to protest. But Berry couldn't see them arguing with the choirmaster.

Berry's stomach clenched around fried granola. He tried to concentrate on the notes and clear the bracken out of his voice.

"This is the strongest this choir has ever been," Mr. Allen told the semicircle around him of terrified men and boys. "We have twenty polished trebles and a dozen experienced altos, tenors and basses—there's no excuse for you to sound like the Akron Tourettes symphony chorus."

The choir kept mauling the day's anthem, Ireland's "Greater Love Hath No Man." Berry kept singing too loud at the wrong moment, or coming in too soon. This time, he watched Mr. Allen carefully and tried to see the changes coming. The piece started as a lullaby about love undrowned by floods, and then it thundered like Marco on too many pills. Berry let the score and Mr. Allen's hands guide him to its ending, which was all about cleaning yourself from the inside out. George, the choir's solidest treble, held down the solo.

"I guess that won't drive anybody to the druids." Mr. Allen shut the piano, threw a black robe over his sweater, tie, and jeans and disappeared. A moment later, Mr. Allen played something by Bach on the organ.

The choir ditched blazers and wriggled into floor-length cassocks and white surplices, with white frilled collars that served up the choirboys' heads like John the Baptist's on a platter. Just as Mr. Allen's organ prelude started, Berry's best friend Wilson ran in. He gave Berry a cupcake with one candle. The pleated paper jagged Berry's hand. "Thanks," Berry said. Wilson had sandy hair and freckles and lived in the suburbs. Teddy, herding the other choirboys into the hallway, gave Wilson's scruff a yank for lateness.

"Shit sorry late late late." Wilson tugged his robe so hard from the locker that his cassock fell on the muddy floor. "My parents fought all night. My dad is the only person whose vocabulary improves when he gets drunk. Get some liquor in him, he turns into a walking thesaurus, only without the walking part. It makes me glad I only have a few years left to live."

"Why do you always say that?" Berry asked. They lined up as the men filed two by two ahead of them into the cathedral's stone embrace.

"Stone fact," Wilson whispered. "If I live to eighteen, I'll shit myself. I'm marked for death, like JFK or Jesus."

Canon Moosehead stepped through the red velvet curtains that shielded the hallway where the choir assembled from the cathedral's nave. A white-bearded soft-faced man in silk, the Canon spared none of his trademark smiles for the choir. "I just wanted to let you know that some members of the Downtown Association have agreed to pay us a visit today. I just spotted a dozen or so of them in the congregation. As I'm sure you know, the association has some concerns about our cathedral."

"What, like we feed junkies and street people, and sometimes they crash here," muttered Marc audibly. He stood on Teddy's other side in line. For years, Marc had tried to hide the fact that his parents visited the cathedral's Hungry Souls soup kitchen.

"I heard that," Canon Moosehead said. He looked straight at Marc, his eyes hard behind puffy lids. "And sure. There's no way to deny it, our cathedral brings the wrong element to the neighborhood. Not the sort of people who will help to bring our downtown back as a destination. They also have problems with choirboys disrupting local merchants before and after rehearsals. So I came to tell you all that if you have any stunts planned for today's service, you'd best postpone them. I'm sure you know there are already plenty of people who'd welcome a smaller, simpler chamber choir. I wouldn't give those viewpoints any more ammunition."

The Canon withdrew through the curtain. Marc hissed.

"For real," Teddy told Marc. "We don't start shit today. Another time."

Marc nodded.

Bach died. A hymn started and the choirboys lifted their music. By the time the cue to sing came, the first few boys had already parted the curtain and started up the cathedral's aisle.

As soon as Berry's voice left the outer passage and entered the rafters, it gained majesty. These were the moments Berry believed in God, despite all the stuff his mom and dad said. Berry kept his eyes cast upward in rapture that was only partly for show. He tranced and channeled music. He almost tripped over the boys in front of him once, and he had to glance down at his hymnal every now and then. But he tried to keep his gaze Heavenward—presentation is all. Berry especially avoided eye contact with the congregation. The cathedral looked like a big gingerbread house, with its brown walls surging to meet overhead. The only non-gingerbread parts were the back-destroying pews, the lily altar, and the stained glass windows.

The choir reached the front, the hymn ended, and Berry's mind screen-savered. The Collect for Purity rang out. Liturgy curled Berry's tongue and itched the space under his fingernails with its tuneless seriousness, imploring and blessing and confessing and psalming. Every week Berry's life led up to this hour, but he spent at least half of it trapped in his own head waiting to sing.

Mrs. Gartner, a doughy woman in plaid, got up and read a passage from the Old Testament about toads or honey or something. Mrs. Gartner's daughter Lisa watched her mom from near the front, wheat-colored hair catching the light. It was the first Sunday of Pentecost, the season that starts in early June and ends in late November. Someone read from the Bible about the apostles and then the choir sang a hymn, "Dear Lord and Father of Mankind." Someone else got up and read about Jesus.

Then Canon Moosehead rose to read his sermon. Berry heard Marc hiss two seats away. The Canon started by reading the ledgers of the cathedral's Bell Tower Restoration Fund, which had fallen behind target. He talked for twenty minutes about assets and liabilities, interest-bearing CDs and municipal bonds. "How can we give witness from a high place if it crumbles below our feet?"

"Fucker," Marc muttered. "Baby eater." Canon Moosehead heard noise from the choirstalls and turned to glare. The Canon's eyes narrowed and his mouth opened in a clear threat. Teddy whacked Marc, who looked away from the Canon and went silent. The Canon talked about tithing. "Show you're a witness. Make this pillar of worship strong and a strut to the community."

At last it was anthem time. Mr. Allen smiled briefly from behind the organ, as if to say it would be all right after all.

Charlie Anders

The St. Luke's choir thundered, entreated, and extolled as one. Where Berry wandered, Teddy or Marc steadied him, and they all bolstered the younger boys. The weave of music that had terrified the younger Berry now held him. Berry's mind stilled and time stretched.

Then it was time for George to take his solo, to beg the people to offer themselves, clean, to God. The choir stilled. Berry imagined laying himself bare to show the frills and vestments inside his body, displaying an acceptable sacrifice to the Lord. George's pale round face ignited with passion, and he opened his mouth to beseech.

A roar came out. No, a braying. It sounded like one of the goat impressions Teddy did before rehearsals. But George didn't laugh. He looked scared of the noise coming from his own mouth. Mr. Allen scowled, and Berry feared he'd stop playing and cancel church after all. But Mr. Allen just plowed through the wreckage. The choir held its breath as George hit a few notes in his lower range, then lifted back into bagpipe-land. Berry covered his face, then uncovered it just in time for the return to full chorus. George clapped his mouth as soon as his solo ended. In between reading the music and watching Mr. Allen, Berry stole glances at George, who blinked scarlet.

As soon as the boys filed out of the cathedral and reached the side entrance out of sight of the congregation, Teddy grabbed George by the scruff of his cassock and slammed him into the wall. "What the fuck?" Teddy hissed. "What were you trying to do, motherfucker? Was that some kind of joke?" The rest of the choir stood in the side entrance of the cathedral singing verse three of the recessional hymn. Wilson gestured to Teddy to shut up. Teddy slapped George so hard he yelped in his goat voice. That only made Teddy slap him again. His cheeks looked extra rosy.

The hymn ended. The choirboys waited for Mr. Allen to come and kill George. But Mr. Allen had to play some Scarlatti piece as the postlude, so the boys had time to stoke George's terror.

Wilson tugged Berry's sleeve. "Cookies," he muttered.

Berry followed Wilson across the alley to the cathedral's office building. The big auditorium just past the main door had plates of butter cookies on one table, with little cocktail napkins in lieu of plates. Urns of coffee and punch left wet rings on trays. The congregation already buzzed around the cookies, but Wilson and Berry grabbed a few with no trouble. After the first half cookie, Berry craved punch.

He scooted to the urns, but a livery mountain blocked his path. Canon Moosehead squeezed Berry's shoulder. "Whoa. Somebody is moving much too fast in an adult space, and creating commotion."

"I'm sorry." Berry tried to shrink away. "I won't come here again."

But the Canon didn't let go of Berry. "You'd best not." Still clenching Berry's collarbone, he turned to face a group of men and women in crisp suits. "This is one of our choirboys. Benny, say hello to Mr. Finch and—" Berry squirmed while Canon Moosehead introduced him as "Benny" to thousands of people in suits. "It's so important," Canon Moosehead told the wool-and-cotton spiral, "to nurture the children and give them a role in our community here at St. Luke's. I believe that children have so much to teach us. Tell me, Benny, what did you think of my sermon?"

Berry wriggled and tried to ease the pain of the Canon's nerve pinch. He wanted to say something brilliant about the duty of the church to the least among us, or quote a smack-down from scripture. Instead he mumbled that the sermon had been okay, he guessed, but that he didn't really think financial statements belonged in church.

The Canon laughed, which had the effect of shaking Berry. "That's why we need the young among us. Here, Benny. Why don't you help yourself to some punch and then run off to your choir friends?" Berry filled a Styrofoam cup and then dashed back to Wilson.

"That was painful to watch," Wilson said.

"He wanted to toss me out a window," Berry said. "Good thing he couldn't get away with it."

"He's seen choirboys come and go," Wilson said. "He doesn't need a window."

They walked down the main stairs of the cathedral office building, ringed with pictures of bishops. Back in the alleyway, they looked around but didn't see the other choirboys. "I can't believe about George," Berry said.

"It happened so fast," Wilson said. "Usually they crack before they croak."

Teddy and some of the other choirboys clustered around the closed door to the choir room. Teddy had his ear against the thick wood panel. "Mr. Allen's in there with George," Teddy told Berry and Wilson. "Some flaying going on after that performance."

"What's the worst he can do?" Berry asked. He thought George must already be suffering enough as it was.

"Yo, Mr. Allen can flay with a look," Marc said. He pulled his ear away from the door just before it opened.

George and Mr. Allen walked out together. George looked both crushed and relieved. Mr. Allen looked resigned to a friend's death. The boys parted to let Mr. Allen pass, but he stopped in front of the group and said, "George's voice has broken. Happened faster than expected—but there's no way to put off the inevitable. George will move to the men's section and sing alto from now on." Then Mr. Allen walked out into the parking lot to see if any homeless people had peed on his car today.

"A man," George said through phlegm. "I'm a man now." Everybody looked at him as if he were an alien.

Berry poured his punch all over the tie Marco had given him. He glanced down at the spreading stain on tie and white shirt. "Shit." He pointed the mess out to Wilson, who was too busy watching Lisa Gartner walk past.

"There are still things to look forward to," Wilson said without taking his eyes off Lisa. Her church skirts formed lacunae around her slender legs, almost down to her sandals. Wilson's gaze followed her until she reached her mother's car. "So like happy birthday."

"Thanks," Berry said. He sipped punch dregs and thought about manhood.

2.

The station wagon loaded with ruckus crawled up the winding mountain roads. The boys in the back seat heckled the driver, a bass named Maurice, to speed up. They made revving noises and called Maurice "feather foot." A large man with a pointy beard, Maurice turned up his Puccini tape to drown the commotion. He'd given up on drawing his choirboy crew into a game of "name that anthem" with a different tape.

In the Dodge's "way back," Berry hunched between backpacks and gym bags. He watched the road twist downward and tried to forget his soul-shriveling summer. The full choir had just sung together for the first time in six weeks, to thank the congregation for raising money to send it to camp. Every August, the choir rented the Peterman School, three hours from the city. The choir had use of Peterman's dorms, soccer fields, swimming pool, and most importantly, chapel for a week.

Berry pretended he was a prisoner of war, his will broken by torture. He'd spent the summer break alone, since Marco and Judy couldn't afford to send him to any other camps. Berry'd had the whole summer to contemplate George's voice-dive. He'd wandered his parents' crumbling neighborhood, kicking garbage and singing to himself. Every day, he'd done vocal exercises and monitored every notch in the scale for blemishes. Treble voices die from the middle and the decay spreads both ways. The bottom of the upper "head voice" range is the first to go. Promoting George to alto only showcased how bad his mid-treble had gotten, since that was the peak of the alto range.

That summer had scorched away Berry's hope. Berry had looked at his life to come and had seen boredom and revulsion. Marco had broken the television in May, and Berry's allowance could handle only one or two movies a month. So he'd read any books he could find at the library or in his parents' bookshelves. He'd listened endlessly to the same dozen or so used CDs: *Choral Fugue State, Blissed Out Boys Sing Britten,* etc.

And he'd locked his door. He'd ignored his mom saying things like, "The only reason you don't physically abuse me is it would require concentration." And his dad saying, "Your animal guide told me to burn all your pantyhose." Berry had gotten so strung out he'd considered getting a job. Somewhere in the middle of that awful asphalt-cracking, benzine-scented, sandmouthed permanent headache of a summer, Berry had come across the phrase in a book: "Boredom is a valid reason to kill yourself." He knew it was true.

On the road to Choir Camp, Berry forgot the summer's details. What stayed was bleakness he couldn't investigate. It was tarmac-flat pain with a choral soundtrack, two months without ritual, companionship, or the sung word in person.

The road leveled and forest became meadow. Finally, Maurice pulled up in front of the Peterman School with a sigh. Berry jumped out of the back of the station wagon and lay on the grass comparing the country sky with the city sky. All around Berry, pebble pathways sliced the tree-specked grass into triangles and rhomboids. It felt good to bust out of the POW cage. The country sky looked bluer and wider.

The buildings reached with pillar hands and brick legs to embrace Berry.

Teddy and pals started an Ultimate Frisbee game on the biggest grassy space. Some of the girls went for a nature walk. The men cracked beers. The choir had an hour and a half before Mr. Allen drilled it on Hindemuth and Handel.

Wilson sat next to Berry on the grass. "I want to go to a high school like this," he said. "Seems like a good place to spend my last few years."

"What made you decide on seventeen?" Berry snared one fat cloud with his eyes and held it.

"It's an estimate. I'm all shroudy, like mortality is my jockstrap. Seventeen is the oldest I can imagine living to. It sucks: I get one year when I can drive. I'll probably be stuck with mom's ten-year-old Geo. I want to die behind the wheel of a black Monte Carlo like Dale Earnhardt."

Lisa Gartner passed. Death and cars fled Wilson's mind. So thin she wafted instead of walking, she was all long brown hair and linen. She hadn't joined the other girls on their nature walk.

Berry waved at Lisa. Wilson just stared. "Hey, you guys. How's it going?" she said.

"Good to be back," Berry said. "I hate summer break. Wilson was just telling me which car he'd like to die driving. How about you?"

"Some miracle flying car, decades from now."

"Optimist," Berry said.

After dinner, the choir had another chance to explore the Peterman campus before bedtime. Berry wanted to be rested for rehearsals, which would start at eight AM and continue all day when the choir wasn't playing or swimming.

Charlie Anders

One change from the previous Choir Camp became obvious the first night. George had become an authority figure. He paid a special visit to the room whose bunks Teddy, Berry, Marc, and Randy occupied. "Okay, you fuckin' worms. Last year, you just had those pushovers Maurice and Tony watching you. Tony's only a tenor, for fuck's sake, and Maurice thinks Puccini is some macho shit. This year it's gonna be different. You've got me to deal with. I know all your little tricks and schemes because I planned most of them last year. This year, no bra-huntin' on the girls' floor, no midnight rock climbing, no skinny dipping in the pool or anywhere else. And no talking after lights out. Is that clear?"

Nobody said anything.

"Next year, you'll all be in my shoes, or most likely not in the choir at all," George reminded the four of them, then killed their lights.

Teddy yawned. "Won't be as much of a prick as you."

The next day everyone swam after morning rehearsals. Lisa refused to swim, so Wilson stayed out of the pool too. They sat in folding chairs, her in tennis clothes and him in swimwear like everyone else. She never explained, and people stopped asking. Wilson brought her Cokes and chips, and even used his body to block splashes. Randy and Marc tried to drown Maurice, who clutched a beach ball from their game of keepaway. "Somebody else get on his head," Marc shouted. "We can't keep him down by ourselves!"

Wilson courted Lisa hard because she was too popular to talk to him at the Quaker day school they both attended in the burbs. "She's the hot favorite for student body president this year," Wilson explained to Berry in the boys' locker room after swimming. "If I don't get bouncy with her at camp, I'll be stymie boy at school for sure."

"I never talk to popular people," Berry said. "That makes it easy."

As soon as Berry had his clothes on, Teddy, Marc, and Randy grabbed his arms and legs. They jogged him back to the pool and tossed him in. They laughed. Berry sloshed. Three times he climbed out, and each time they plunged him back in. Finally he stayed in the water until they left.

Berry still got dry and dressed for the next rehearsal. Mr. Allen hauled them through Herbert Howells's "Like As The Hart," full of melancholy quavers. Berry had always hated this piece, but now it made sense. The parched deer wanders the desert or dry glade. If the deer found water, it would throw itself in up to its neck and soak, inside and out. Howells's piece never finds water, it just fades in the desert.

After dinner the second day, Wilson and Berry joined the cool boys for cigarettes. They sat on an old porch out back of the big brick building with the auditorium and cafeteria, watching the evening sun on the football field. "We shouldn't really be smoking these," said Wilson between drags. "They fuck your voice."

"Yeah," said Teddy. "We bad. Paranoia self-destroya."

All five boys on that porch were some flavor of thirteen. Wilson was thirteen and a third, Teddy nearly fourteen.

"So I say blow off rehearsals tomorrow and head into town," said Randy. "We need porn and booze. Bet Teddy here looks old enough. The used bookstore off the main strip sells porn to anyone."

Shock singed the roof of Berry's mouth worse than tobacco. "How can you skip rehearsals at Choir Camp?"

Marc laughed. "Hey, it's our last summer here as boys. You want to spend it singing?"

Berry snuffed his unsmoked cigarette and wandered off. He ran into Lisa in the least well lit part of campus. The darkness in that spot felt different than city or suburb darkness. It ate faces and colors in a way gloom around malls or convenience stores couldn't.

"You enjoying camp?" Berry asked.

"I guess. The girls' choir is kind of a joke. You guys rehearse till you drop. We learn a few chants."

"So you get to hang around campus more. Play sports. Go swimming." He realized his mistake. "Oh, sorry."

"It's okay. Hey, you read a lot. Ever hear of Roland Montreux?" She spelled the last name.

"No. Why?"

"No reason. Just curious."

That night, George came to the room Berry shared with the cool kids while they huddled and listened to Outkast. "I know what you're planning. Everything you're thinking," George told them.

"Mind reader, huh." Randy clucked.

"Thinking of ways to fuck with Canon Moosehead. He arrives in a couple days," said Marc.

"Oh," said George. "Oh. In that case, I'm in. I thought you were up to something bad."

The guys brainstormed late. They sent two of the younger boys out for sodas. Marc shot down lame ideas like whoopee cushions, exploding crucifixes or Tabasco communion wafers. "Fuck this," George said. "Shoulda known you guys would have boy ideas. This needs Man Thought."

"Wait. I got it," said Marc. "I brought something with me on the off chance. Stole it from my dad." He rummaged his gym bag until he found an amber pill bottle. He handed it to George. "This too boyish for ya?"

"Fuckin' A." George squinted at the label. He scratched his buzz cut. "What you bring this for?"

"Come in handy."

"What is it, G?" Teddy asked.

"See for yourself." George tossed the bottle to Teddy. He read the label and laughed so hard he blew snot. He swatted his bunk bed in two/four time.

Wilson crawled on the bed and looked over Teddy's shoulder. "Viagra. Food of the limp-dick gods."

"So like, we slip two or three or four of those into his coffee an hour before he officiates at Wednesday's Evensong. Then we watch the fun," said Marc.

"I thought you already had to be turned on for that stuff to work," George said.

"Dunno," Marc said. "My cousin's boyfriend got paralyzed from the waist down in a car accident. She says it's rocket fuel, even if he still doesn't feel much. Besides, just makes it more interesting if he takes it and it works."

Every boy and George swore secrecy. They used a thumb tack to prick each finger and rubbed it on the same stolen tampon. "Nobody better have AIDS or I'ma kick your ass," Teddy said. Then George went back to menacing his former comrades with whoopass if they screwed around. Wilson and the other boys went back to their rooms.

The next morning, four boys missed rehearsals. "Prolly got caught in traffic," Mr. Allen joked. But when Teddy, Marc, Randy, and Wilson turned up at lunch, Maurice grabbed Teddy's collar with a huge hand. "Get your shit. We're going back to the city." Maurice and George made a big show of herding the four boys to Maurice's station wagon until they promised not to blow off any more rehearsals.

That afternoon, Berry joined Lisa and Wilson poolside. They all wore bathing suits, even Lisa. They ignored the chlorine smell and pool violence. "So, like, which is worse: losing real innocence or just losing the look of innocence?" Berry asked.

Nobody answered for a while.

"Depends," Lisa said. "There's, you know, more than one kind of innocence."

"Innocent people don't see themselves as innocent," Wilson said. "But people who look innocent know it. So maybe losing an innocent mask is way worse than losing the real thing."

"I've never been innocent," Lisa said. Neither had the two boys.

"Think fast!" Teddy and Marc cannonballed at once into the pool right in front of the three dry holdouts. Wilson tried to block the tsunami for Lisa, but too late. Soggy spots appeared on her top.

"Shit!" Wilson yelled. "I'm sorry—those assholes—I tried—"

"It's okay," Lisa said. "I'm waterproof."

"Real mature," a black-eyed girl named Julie told Marc when he surfaced across the pool. Her face shone beneath her sky-blue bathing cap. "Real clever." Marc looked away from her.

The girls gave Lisa a towel and led her off to the girls locker room to clean up. Berry and Wilson didn't see her for the rest of the day.

Afternoon rehearsal came. Mr. Allen almost whispered, as if he stood on a mountainside that speech might dislodge.

He understood all about using surges and ebbs in volume for effect. He made the choir point its feet and extend its necks to hear. Wilson and the cool kids trembled most of all.

"And I saw anew. My soul doth magnify. Let all mortal flesh. Before him stand the. I give you anew. For we like sheep," Mr. Allen breathed.

The choirboys giggled at that last sentence fragment, as Mr. Allen knew they would. His eyes seared them until they shut up. Silence wrapped the chapel in a marble-and-glass towel.

"None of those phrases says much without the stuff at the end," said Mr. Allen. "They all lead up to something important. When I flounder my hands around, I'm trying to make you people think about phrasing. It's the difference between hitting notes and musicianship." Berry had heard this lesson before, but the low voice and Mr. Allen's expression said rage. It made Berry want to giggle or beg forgiveness. He felt terror on either side.

"For now—you guys have a little power," Mr. Allen said after a long silence. "I've got a week to teach you how to harness it and make it count. For once, we have time for stuff besides learning notes. But if you people just want to goof off, please let me know so I can go back to town early. I have other things to do with my life."

Nobody spoke. Berry knew Mr. Allen was just proving he really could play the choir like an instrument. And it didn't matter. Berry still would have thrown himself in front of a runaway grand piano for Mr. Allen, and so would anyone else in the room.

"Frisbee!" Canon Moosehead's voice echoed around the quad on Wednesday. Berry sat under a tree memorizing a Thomas Weelkes anthem. Most of the other boys played Ultimate in the next quad. The Canon's voice cracked like leather on wood, "The church raised $7,432 to send you boys here, money that could have gone to the Bell Tower Fund, and now you're playing Frisbee! Aren't you supposed to be singing?" Berry walked to the quad just in time to see the boys, who'd rehearsed all morning, point at their mouths and mime laryngitis. "And why aren't there any girls playing? We won't have that sort of patriarchal crap with Frisbee, even if we allow it in your choir," said the Canon. The boys just made fake sign language.

Over lunch, the Canon sat at the biggest table and lectured about the importance of gender-neutral prayers and the cathedral's relationship with the city. Marc sat at the next table and made barfing signs as the Canon explained he didn't oppose the Hungry Souls kitchen on principle. "Attracting those sort of people to the neighborhood only encourages urban blight, which is a greater harm than hunger." Then Canon Moosehead asked Mr. Allen what sensitivity training the choir received. "Every one of these doll-faced boys is a rapist in waiting," Canon Moosehead told the hall. "As a feminist, I'd like this male-dominated institution brought into the new millennium."

Marc tapped the pill bottle in his khaki shorts pocket, so it made a maraca noise that only the people nearest could hear.

Wednesday afternoon, three girls jumped Wilson on his way to the pool. "We need to talk to you," said Julie. The other two, Jee and Becky, jerked their heads at the school library. They wore matching tank tops, scrunchies, and sandals.

"Can Berry come?" Wilson asked.

They conferred. Then nodded. "But he can't talk," Jee said.

They led Berry and Wilson to a balcony overlooking the main library. Books on the history of religion and mythology lived in their own alcove, and a couple of study tables perched by the railing. Lisa sat behind one table. She didn't stand or speak when the girls herded Berry and Wilson to seats facing hers. Jee, Becky, and Julie pulled up chairs facing the boys.

"Wilson," said Julie. "We're here to consider your desire to become Lisa's boyfriend. We'll accept that your proposal is in good faith and you understand what this involves."

"Lisa, what's the deal here?" Wilson said.

Julie leaned across the table, red-dyed hair flopping. "You'll talk to me if you have something to say. Now why don't you tell us why you deserve to date Lisa?"

Wilson looked at Berry. Berry widened his eyes. Wilson snorted. Julie smacked gum. Becky twisted her hair around a pencil and then let go, breeding friz. Lisa stared at her hands. Berry scanned the spines of the religion texts. Berry felt trapped in this tiny balcony that smelled of paste. He felt crowded, the way he often did when he was alone with kids his own age.

"Well," Wilson said. "I really like Lisa. I think I could be good for her."

Julie and Becky shared amused looks.

"Yes, but what about compatibility? Are you mature enough?"

"I'm the same age as her," Wilson said. "We go to the same school. I see her at church."

"You may be the same age, but everybody knows girls mature faster than boys," said Jee. "Lisa needs someone older who can treat her special and lend her his jacket on

cold nights and shit. Someone who doesn't still sing soprano, you get me."

"I have a jacket," Wilson said.

"We're just thinking of what's best for Lisa," said Becky.
"We like you, Wilson. If it was up to me, I'd say go for it."

"And let's not even drag in the alky dad," said Julie. "I
heard he does body slams at poetry slams." The other girls
gave Julie a "low blow" look.

Wilson rose and slunk away. Berry stepped around the
girls, snagged a couple of theology books, and ran after
Wilson. He caught up with Wilson halfway across the quad.

"Tell me I'm better off," Wilson ordered Berry.

Berry obeyed.

"Lying fuck," Wilson peeped.

"Girls can be mean," Berry said. "Boys are so much easier to cope with."

Something smacked Berry in the back of the head. A
rocket launcher valentine. He went down on the joints of his
palms, flashes in his eyes. The flying object fell near him,
and through the raver glaze Berry saw a hymnal. It fell open
to "Come Down, O Love Divine," one of Berry's favorite
hymns. Another hymnal careened past Wilson's head. "You
throw for shit," Wilson said.

"Hey Berry, think fast," shouted Teddy.

Berry rolled just in time to save his ribs from a falling
lectern. Its golden eagle head plowed into the turf. Then a ring
of boys stood over him. "Hey, Berry. No hard feelings. Here,
let me help you up," Teddy said. He held out a hand and
pulled Berry to his feet. Then he kicked Berry's legs out from
under him. This happened a couple of times. Berry rolled
away and stood without help. He noticed Wilson walking
away alone. "I gotta catch up with Wilson," Berry said.

"Not now. It's almost time for Evensong, and we need your help," Teddy said. "We gotta distract Canon Moosehead. You're the most distracting person we know."

Berry almost sat back down on the grass.

Berry caught up with Canon Moosehead in the cafeteria drinking coffee. "Hey," Berry said. "I had this book to show you. It's about Christianity without Jesus." He motioned the Canon over to the table nearest the window, where he'd spread out *The Sea of Faith*.

"Can't you bring it over here?" the Canon asked. Berry shook his head.

"The light's better over here." Berry stood by the book at the window. Then the Canon reluctantly walked over, but brought his coffee mug with him. Berry told Canon all about the book's author, a minister who didn't believe in God. "He says God is just an idea we invented to, uh, explain why we need morals." Berry used up all his words. He mumbled something else.

Berry stopped mid-sentence. A hymnal flew past the window. Smoke streamed behind it, and crimson flame rose from its pages. It was probably the same hymnal that had left an anthill on the back of Berry's head. "What the . . . What was that?" the Canon barked.

"Um, I think it was the Hymnal 1982," Berry said. "The Hymnal 1940 has a darker cover."

The Canon ran outside, leaving his coffee. Teddy and Marc sprinted in. "You suck at distracting people," Marc told Berry. He poured blue pills on the table. "How many? Three or four?"

"Just hurry," Teddy said.

Marc crushed four pills under a salt shaker. He swept the results into the Canon's coffee and stirred. Then he and Teddy ran away, leaving Berry with his book.

Canon Moosehead returned a moment later. He had soot on his shoes and hands. "Your fellow choristers aren't studying theology," he said. He swigged. "The amount we pay to rent this school, you'd think they'd supply decent coffee," he snarled. He chugged some more. "Anyway. What was it?"

"Does Christianity need God?"

"Saying that God's only purpose is to inspire ethics is putting the buggy before the mule," the Canon said. He guzzled coffee. "Ethics exist for the same reason you and I wear robes and prance: to bring people to God. When people start thinking of God in terms of Thou Shalt Not or Thou Must, they get turned off." He raised the mug. "My aim is to turn them on," last sip, "to God by being more relevant to the twenty-first century. Does that help?"

"I think so," Berry said. "Morality and cassocks, means to an end."

The choir didn't have enough hymnals to go around. Guess whose hymnal had been hurled, set on fire, slingshot across the quad, and stomped? Berry stared down at the crumbled parchment-colored pages, half of which no longer held notes. His head throbbed and his vision blotched.

"You shouldn't have abused your hymnal," Mr. Allen told Berry.

Rehearsal ended after a thousand Benjamin Britten runthroughs, and Evensong came. Canon Moosehead wore his least flashy robe, a stark black hooded cope that matched the carpet in the Peterman chapel. The Canon walked easily and smiled at everyone.

"He looks normal," Teddy whispered. "How do we know if it worked?"

"Wait," Marc said. "And see."

The choir sang hymns and a short Byrd piece. Then Canon Moosehead got up and looked around at the assembled boys and girls. Most of the girls had skipped the robes and wore miniskirts. Julie and Becky, on either side of the big aisle, crossed their legs and dangled their platforms in the middle of the chapel.

"Welcome to another Choir Camp," Canon Moosehead said. "I can see you've been taking advantage of your time here to get in to all sorts of mischief. But the real reason we're here is to bring honor to the Cathedral of St. Luke's. When I look around at all your impertinent young bodies, I remember when . . ." The Canon's eyes traveled around the chapel. He paused. His eyes lingered in the aisle. They swept the boys and girls again. As the Canon met her eyes, Julie winked. The Canon tried to speak again, and it came out "But—but—you must—" Then he moved strategically behind the lectern that had nearly maimed Berry. He took a deep breath. "But we must harness, we must bind, I mean capture . . . we must use that wellspring of youthful, of . . . of . . . energy and make it service . . . uh, a greater purpose." He took a deep breath. "In the name of the Father, etc." Canon Moosehead sat in a hurry and kept his legs crossed.

"Shortest damn sermon he ever gave," Marc said afterwards. "Recruiting Julie and Becky to show some skin was a great touch. And next time, back at the cathedral, we get the altar boys to help. They bring him coffee all the time."

"Next time?" Berry said. "Wasn't once enough?"

"Not when it was that cool," Marc said.

Canon Moosehead didn't show up at dinner. The next morning, he left early and drove back to the city alone.

Wilson didn't talk to Berry the next day. Berry wandered alone when he wasn't in rehearsals. He felt almost as lonely and empty as he had all summer. He felt like he was falling naked from an airplane in the desert. Even if he survived the fall, the ground offered nothing.

The last evening of camp, Saturday, the choir had a big bonfire out in a field near campus. Someone played hip hop on a boombox, and the kids roasted marshmallows and hot dogs. Nobody sang. Berry sat too close to the fire, so his cheeks smarted and the back of his neck tickled. Wilson came and sat next to Berry. "Hey," Wilson said. "Our last summer."

Berry nodded. "This time next year, we'll all sound like dirt roads. We'll be into skateboards or pro wrestling or something. All our skills, gone to shit." He couldn't explain, but he knew Wilson knew: sugar turning to chalk, the ground slipping away. Berry's eyes stung from smoke exposure, or tears seeping out. He knew the others could never see it, or he'd be smacked into next year.

"That's nature's plan," Wilson said. "Personally I'm glad I get puberty before I die."

Teddy came and sat on the other side of Berry. "Hey," he said. "No matter what, we've kicked some major booty together. And we'll always know we were in the coolest treble section on the fuckin' planet. We mixed blood on that tampon, and that makes us brothers."

Berry was so preoccupied with sucking any tears back in through his eyes that he couldn't reply, only nod. Through his not-crying blur, he noticed a glistening in the other boys' eyes, too, but it was probably just a trick of the fire.

3.

Back to school. New pair of jeans. Black binder with an easy-peel label. Brand new groove. Hey kids, you're upper-classmen now. Just remember, with hallway privileges come maturity and respect.

Every eighth grader seemed to have doubled in height over the summer except for Berry. He walked among evil giants and watched his back in the boys' room, where class-mates pushed his head in the toilets. The other choirboys who went to Orlac Junior High pretended not to know Berry there.

Last year, Berry's class was divided into two sections, the Swans and the Geese. The Swans were the smarter kids, but you weren't supposed to say so. This year, the names were gone, but the sections remained. Now, if you tested too low on a standardized test, you copped an "intervention." The scratch-bubble failures who received "interventions" turned out to be exactly the same kids as the Geese.

Berry's mom had lobbied hard to get him accepted as a Swan, and Berry had gone along because the Swans hit less hard. But even though Berry read years ahead in English, he'd scored puny in math and science. In the end, the school had put Berry into the Swans (or "intervention"-free group) for half the day. This hadn't helped him make friends, but he hadn't expected to.

Berry nicknamed this year's teachers Toad and Rat, maybe because he'd read *Wind in the Willows* over the summer. Toad taught the Geese in a haze that reminded Berry of the year Marco had gotten hooked on muscle relaxants. It took Ms. Hawthorne ten minutes to explain how the sun radiated energy. Meanwhile Rat, who taught the Swans, was a lively man with sharp features. He carried a buzzer that rasped every time one of the Swans broke grammar. Berry hated both teachers and didn't see much advantage in Swanhood. For a week, his mom had driven him around pointing at people on the street and saying either "Swan" or "Goose." A man in a suit with a cell phone was a Swan, said Judy. The newspaper seller and the guy rooting in the garbage were both Geese. Berry had almost died when Judy had marched him through the mall pointing and barking, "Goose, Goose, Swan, Swan, Goose."

Berry had turned to a middle-aged woman in a velvet coat (a Swan) and muttered, "It's a game."

Judy had spun and bugged. "It's not a game. If this is a game to you, then you've already lost, like your father." Judy took paralegal classes when she wasn't working as a company librarian.

Berry's existence as a half-Swan half-Goose misfit might have seemed okay if he'd found the Swans anything like his image of those birds. But the real-life Swans seemed as evil as the Geese, only with nicer clothes. Berry sometimes wished he went to Quaker Day with Wilson and Lisa. Berry held his breath every moment in those airless halls.

He let it out on Wednesday. He ran out of Goose class before the bell sounded and was on the school steps before it choked. Then he waited twenty minutes for the bus to St. Luke's for midweek rehearsals. The gravel alley and choir room were empty. Canon Moosehead had managed to ban choirboys from local shops and restaurants on rehearsal days.

Berry was about to give up and find a place to read when Teddy came out of the cathedral's office building. "Hey," he told Berry. "We're down in the Twelve Step room, it's our new hangout. We're all beating up on the new kid, Jackie."

Berry nodded. They headed for the church office basement, down one flight of stairs to some offices, the soup kitchen, and the Twelve Step room, a hole coated with cigarette ash, coffee- and piss-stains. The carpet looked like a lice condo, but the boys wrestled on it every day anyway. A couple of couches and some folding chairs faced the huge board outlining the twelve steps. One cartoon showed the Higher Power holding hands with a strung-out man. A single fluorescent light and a sliver of window at ceiling level lit the room, which smelled of chemicals and animals.

"Altar boys gonna spike Canon Moosehead's coffee on Sunday," Teddy said on the stairs. "Same pills, same dosage." By the bottom stair, Berry and Teddy could hear violence from the dark hallway's last door.

As soon as Berry and Teddy walked into the Twelve Step room, the banging noise stopped. A pile of boys looked up at them. The wriggling mass almost reached Berry's shoulders. A tiny head poked from the bottom of the pile. Pale eyes stared out of Jackie's pie face. "Please," he chirped. "I've had enough. Please. When do I learn about Orlando Gibbons?"

• • •

Sermon by Canon Simon Moosehead

Ninth Sunday of Pentecost

May the words of my mouth and the meditations of my heart be acceptable . . . So. It's no accident Paul compares the Church to the bride of Christ. This passage riles many feminists understandably in fact because it speaks of wives submitting to their husbands as the church submits to Christ. To some extent, this is Paul reflecting the values of his day. Marriage as an institution has evolved since then, and so has the church. Society no longer expects wives to kneel before their husbands and . . . and . . . I mean . . .

Well. Isaiah says God's church will have a name that is closer than son or daughter, and many scholars believe that name is wife. Now, our church isn't a frowsy hausfrau in muumuu and mules, the way some people seem to think. She doesn't spend her time playing bridge and lugging children around the bargain aisle at Target where the kids undoubtedly grasp at everything Nerf or Nintendo no matter how many times they're told to keep their mitts inside the shopping cart kiddie seat. Oh no. Today's church has a gym membership and takes care of herself, and so instead of spending all her time on child care she's busy creating a life of spiritual and material abundance that's the best gift one spouse can hope to share with another, along with a firm toned supple body . . . uh by which of course I mean a newly restored bell tower once we reach our financial goals. Where was I?

Marriage. Yes. God created wedlock to domesticate our urges. Paul says the wife has no power over her own body, but the husband's. And likewise, the husband doesn't have any power over his own body, except for what his wife shares. In other words, we're all weak in the flesh, and can easily be tempted to, to . . . and Paul says that those who aren't married should stay celibate, but that it's better to marry than to burn . . . to burn. To burn, and what's interesting here is there's this parallel involving the church being the bride of Christ. Because these days it's easy to channel our spiritual urges into secular things, New Age trinketry, politics, what have you, and what Paul's saying is there's the proper receptacle . . . receptacle . . . I'm sorry, lost my place.

We're all burning, searing with the desire for spiritual fulfillment, it's eating us alive, we're plankton in its mouth, and yet we don't go to the one place that God has ordained for us to achieve satisfaction, spiritually speaking, instead we wander the streets in a twilight sweat feeding on our own spiritual hunger until we wind up in some dark hotel room with our ecumenical undergarments hanging off the minibar and the backs of our necks slick with some substance that is not the blood of the Lamb and, and what I'm trying to say here is that my notes are totally out of order. So as you honor the bonds, the bonds of marriage, I'm saying you should treat your membership in the church as a sacred bondage, I mean channel your spiritual desires into the fold. The word of the Lord. Thanks be to God.

• • •

You can control every move your body makes but not your body itself.

Berry practiced sitting and standing, breathing and projecting every second he wasn't doing anything else. You can practice breathing in the shower, in class, on the bus, while your parents argue beside you, even in your sleep after enough practice. You can carry it with you. He would

Charlie Anders

breathe in pure song vapor and Mr. Allen would scrub away the dead-skin dissonance and replace it with bell sounds. Berry might imagine himself naked from the outside in, and Mr. Allen's eyes probing his lungs for bad breaths. Every time he raised his voice he worried he'd get nodes on his vocal chords, which were like burns or poison ivy on the surface of your voice. The least scream could tear you down.

Berry had recently had a kidney stone, but he hadn't understood what it was except that a pointy object put pressure on his willie from the inside and he hadn't put it there, until Marco explained that Berry had to pee really hard to get it out. *Lord let me know mine end.*

Berry felt that same jagged clog, only in his chest, when he imagined that the bellows inside it would gnarl. Every time his voice wavered or his throat felt uncomfortable, Berry worried he was starting to change. He drank lots of water and did voice exercises every day. But he still feared his voice and his self-esteem could shatter at any time.

Berry caught his dad in a good mood. "How did you deal with losing your voice?" Berry asked.

Marco looked startled. "I never lost my voice. See? I'm talking." Marco had shaved his scalp but had a head's worth of hair on his upper lip. Marco had a free-form career as gardener, house painter, spiritual advisor, and sometimes stockbroker.

"No, I mean your singing voice. Your treble one. When did you lose it?"

"Dunno. Thirteen. Maybe fourteen. Your age, more or less."

"I don't want to change. I wish there was some way I could keep my voice the way it is."

"Oh no, Berry. You should be excited. It's a rite of passage to have your voice change. It's like when a sumo wrestler reaches four hundred pounds or an opera singer grows horns of her own and no longer needs her helmet."

Berry's dad had a way of trying to sound whimsical that came across unbearably heavy. Something dragged Marco's flights of fancy into the muck. Whatever it was, it made Berry cringe even as he knew he was meant to admire his dad's quips. Berry listened to his dad talk endlessly about menstruation and some obscure West Indian tribe that proved manhood by removing one testicle. If the boy didn't scream, that proved he was a man. If not, then wave goodbye to the other ball as well. Actually, Marco said, that was one surefire way to keep your boyish voice, "although I wouldn't recommend it. It's a lot to give up just to sound pretty. But back in Renaissance Europe, they used to have singers called castrati . . . But anyway, do you have any questions about sex? I've been meaning to have a talk with you about it."

Berry told his dad he had no sex questions. Marco wanted to have the sex talk anyway, using words like "yoni" and "tigerlily," so Berry stalked off and rode the elevator down to street level. It was Saturday, that non-school non-church day where kids with televisions watch cartoons. Berry talked to homeless people for a while, then went back to his apartment.

"Umm . . . I want to use the computer," Berry told Marco. "I need to do school stuff online."

"You're too proud to learn Sex 101 from your old man, but you'll suck forbidden knowledge off the Web," Marco whined.

Berry opened a chat window with Wilson and hit a search engine. On a whim, he decided to search for "Roland Montreux," the name Lisa had mentioned.

The Wilson chat window sprang to life, slowed by the Jurassic laptop's modem. Wilson squirmed in the same Saturday boredom trap as Berry. Marco looked over Berry's shoulder.

WILSON3874: god shoot me now

BERRIBOI: bad day?

WILSON3874: dad had hard work week. he's hittin whiskey and Keats

BERRIBOI: sounds sucky

Roland Montreux's first hit on the search engine came from a Canadian site about "reptilian aversion therapy." Berry skimmed psychojargon. "Do you understand any of this?" he asked Marco, who pretended he did but didn't.

BERRIBOI: my dad's looking over my shoulder now

WILSON3874: hi mr. s

"Hi," Marco said. "So anyway it's all about the Id."

BERRIBOI: dad says hi. i can feel my pipes turn to shit

WILSON3874: we're all halfway to voice death

Marco asked if Berry was listening to him. Berry said yes and opened another page about Roland Montreux. The second site showed designs for a water tank, with lots of arrows and odd notations showing where "the subject" could float in a state of psycho-evolutionary neutrality.

WILSON3874: lisa won't talk 2 me @ school

BERRIBOI: ask her about reptilian aversion

Marco huffed. "I thought you were going to be looking for forbidden sex. This is boring." He smacked his palm.

● ● ●

The next morning Berry giggled in rehearsal. It started from something Teddy whispered, but it wouldn't stop even after

Mr. Allen's eyes stabbed him. The giggling jolted his insides, guttural like a baritone on nitrous oxide, until the laughter left but the shaking stayed. He couldn't stop. Teddy led Berry outside and pushed him against a chunky wall not too roughly until the motor ran down on Berry's jitters. Teddy told Berry to pull it together like a man. Berry nodded. They went back inside.

The choir stumbled over the same dumb psalm tune over and over, a jerky chant and antiphon called "The Lord of hosts is with us: the God of Jacob is our stronghold." The boys ought to have learned it in their sleep, but they straggled and rushed, went up too much or not enough, and made mistakes out of impatience. Mr. Allen first growled and then raged, but by the time the choir got that jingle straight, there were only seconds to brush up the day's offertory, Howells's "Like As The Hart." "I could train monkeys to replace you all—the choir would improve a million fold," Mr. Allen yelled. Berry hung his head.

"I called Lisa last night," Wilson said as he donned his cassock. "She freaked when I asked her about the reptile invasion or whatever."

"Maybe it's from a horror movie," Berry said.

In the service, the readings, collects, and prayers all blended with Berry's obsessive thoughts of the next winter, from which spring couldn't follow. Bible talk wove with Berry's inner chatter. One reading, from Paul's letter to the Hebrews, said, "In your struggle against sin, you have not yet resisted to the point of shedding blood."

At one point, Berry could have sworn he heard Canon Moosehead and Dean Jackson whispering from their big chairs. "Do you really think sexuality is a gift from God?"

Canon Moosehead asked. Dean Jackson nodded. "Then why did He booby-trap it?" the Canon said.

This week, Dean Jackson gave the sermon. The Dean was the main defender of Hungry Souls and had encouraged Mr. Allen to search the inner city for singers. The Dean used his sermon to defend his pet programs. "When people all praise you, that usually means you're doing something wrong," the Dean said. "Being the person you were meant to be is often the hardest work of all."

The service ended. Organ music purred to silence. Berry hung out with Wilson and the others for a while. Then he found Mr. Allen, who was peeling off his black robe in the empty choir room. Mr. Allen shut the door on himself and Berry, then lit a joint. "Scarlatti always makes me crave weed."

"Sorry we sucked so bad today," Berry said.

"No monumental deal," Mr. Allen said between drags.

Mr. Allen always said most European choral music was written to be sung by boys in the upper registers, not women. Mr. Allen spent hours training each boy to polish his voice like silver, until he could sing more like a bird and less like a reject from a local production of *Annie: The Musical*.

"Doesn't it piss you off," Berry asked Mr. Allen after a while, "that us boys lose our range just when we've learned enough to be rock steady?"

Mr. Allen shrugged. He looked the most relaxed Berry had seen him, leaning back in his chair with his feet up on the desk in his cubbyhole. His shoes rested on a pile of Elgar anthems.

"I get a few good years out of most of you," Mr. Allen said. "And some of the better kids stay on and use their training as altos, tenors or basses. But I have to admit, it's nice to focus on my organ sometimes—knowing the pipes won't suddenly relocate on me." Mr. Allen didn't have much to say on the subject of castrati, except that just between him and Berry, he'd gladly have gelded a few of the cockier boys if he hadn't thought he'd get in trouble with the diocese. "You could always train as a counter tenor. They're coming back in a big way," said Mr. Allen.

Berry went to the library instead of home that afternoon and found several books on castrati. He couldn't find much on counter tenors, who sounded like tenors faking it as trebles. But the castrati fascinated Berry, they'd lived like pimps, covered with gold jewelry and surrounded by posses. Crowds had massed to hear the strange purity of the castrati's voices. The choir boys had giggled once at stories of eunuchs who'd guarded the harems of the sultans, but these eunuchs had partied like sultans.

Marco had a carrot peeler and was seeing how much skin he could skim off each finger before he drew blood. Judy came home from a study group and had expected Marco to cook dinner. Marco threw the carrot peeler at her. It left a plaster gash in the wall. Berry poured cereal and went to his room.

After his parents had argued themselves to sleep, Berry got up and wandered into the kitchenette of their apartment. City sounds answered each other like psalm verses. He wanted a glass of juice, but a bread knife on the counter caught his eye. He looked at it a long time. The light made its serrations glitter.

Berry pulled down his pajama bottoms and hefted the knife. He found the testicles that he'd first noticed a few months earlier and pulled at their nest. They seemed far from his body. Hatching venom. It would take only a quick slash to cut them loose.

He stood straight and parted his legs a little. His free hand pulled his balls from his thighs. He held the knife to the stringy top of his scrotum and slid it until it jabbed. He imagined a lover's caress instead of metal. Teddy had brought a porn film to the Twelve Step room and the choirboys had watched it with muted sound on the church TV/VCR. The male porn star's advent candle-sized dick had slid in and out of his co-star's vagina.

Berry imitated that motion now with the bread knife over his balls. He fucked himself with the knife. It was the first time Berry'd touched himself down there other than to pee that he could remember. The blade rocked back and forth. Berry sawed until the knife bit skin, then gasped, trying to keep his sobs inaudible to Marco and Judy.

The next pass of the knife seared all the way into Berry's stomach. He felt he'd hit a suspending worm. Blood sprayed his legs and then he couldn't keep the shriek inside. It sounded louder and fiercer because he'd held it in so long.

As he heard his parents stir and dropped the knife, Berry had two thoughts close together. The first: he'd hit that note, way up the windy scaffolding above everything, that nobody could reach at the end of Stanford's "Te Deum" in C major. The second: Berry had failed the tribal test and wasn't a man.

4.

Giants with ADD had ripped up a square mile of the North end and started to build, only to lose interest before they found structures to cover foundations. Occasionally, a few stores sold baseball cards or beauty supplies out of half-empty shopping centers next to vacant lots. Late summer baked the cement residue and turned the tar rancid. Gravel skittered under the old Toyota as Judy pummeled the accelerator. She explained her mistake in letting Marco raise Berry while she advanced. Berry watched the never-finished buildings through the back seat windows. Unfinished construction isn't the same as ruins.

Unless Berry thought about abstract things, his crotch killed him. The bandages chafed his thighs and his balls grew rawer every second. Pills didn't help. Berry couldn't get anyone to sign his bandages, he could only sit with his legs as far apart as they went. Berry felt a kick between his legs whenever he shifted.

" . . . going to be some changes around here," Judy said.

The rubble became lawns. Berry spotted a smoothie store. It made him thirsty and need to pee all at once. It also meant they were reaching their destination. A flock of office buildings came after the smoothie place.

Emergency rooms at three AM aren't the glamorous places Berry had seen on television. You carry in a boy with a blood-soaked crotch and whistles from the gunshot-and-overdose crowd will be your quickest response. Loss of blood, and Marco and Judy's tormented whispers, had worn Berry out before a doctor had said hey.

Listening to Judy's voice without taking in her words, Berry thought of one of the sixteenth-century misericordias or Kyrie Eleisons he'd sung a lot of recently. It rose and fell, got going again just as it seemed to be dying down, swung between pitiful and vengeful. "It's obvious the reason Berry hates his manhood is you're not a real man, Marco. No wonder your son wants to castrate himself."

Marco said nothing.

When one brick office building among dozens caught his eye, Marco spoke up. "This one." John Tamarind, MD PhD, had his office in a two-story block with magnolias out front. The trees sprayed blossom scent everywhere and left white petals along the cement paths. Marco held the door open for Berry. He had indigestion face. Judy said she'd wait in the car, so Marco alone led Berry up to the second floor and a walnut waiting room.

They waited together for five minutes, then just as Berry was about to scream or laugh a neat-bearded man with a lean face opened the inner door and turned his lazy eyes on Marco and Berry. "You must be Berry. Pleasure. And you, Mr. Sanchez. You don't have to bring Berry from now on, if he can get here by bus. It tends to make things more casual if there isn't a parent hanging around the waiting room. Berry, please come in." Marco looked around the waiting room, as if wondering whether the chairs would burn him if he tried to sit again. Then he nodded and walked out, back to the wife and car. Berry realized he'd have to take the bus home this first time as well.

Dr. Tamarind's office had framed pictures of guys in wigs and frills, alongside diplomas and shelves of heavy books. Heavy drapes blocked daylight.

Berry told Dr. Tamarind he wanted to stay a choirboy and admired the castrati. Then he'd said all he wanted to. Dr. Tamarind spent the next forty minutes or so asking questions and hearing shrugs and grunts in response. Why did Berry value his voice so much? Was his the voice of God? Or a gift from God? Did voices tell Berry to cut himself? What did Berry think Jesus would say about self-mutilation? What did Berry think about when he imagined being a man? Did Berry have any sexual fantasies he was aware of?

Berry couldn't believe the sun still shone when he finally escaped Dr. Tamarind's office. He half-ran out of the brick cell block and then he had to stand and feel the sun. He felt logy as if he'd hung upside down. He staggered to the bus stop, then saw a bus coming and had to run to catch it, surgical tape scratching.

Berry trudged up to his apartment, each step a killing effort. When he reached the right floor, Marco opened the door and stepped aside to let him in. Judy sliced eggplant and mushrooms in the kitchen.

"How'd it go?" she asked.

"Did you get a lollipop?" Marco asked.

Berry would never speak again. It wasn't a decision, just something he knew for sure. It was a waste of breath. The less Berry explained himself, the more mysterious he felt, and the more a perfect sacrifice to God or music or something. Berry sat on the couch facing the dead TV and heard his parents' screaming with the distant ear he used for school and sermons. Eventually Marco and Judy yelled at each other instead of Berry. Berry ate eggplant and went to bed.

Charlie Anders

A week later, Berry walked like a guy again. His crotch still roared with pain, but you couldn't see it in his walk. His first day back at choir was a Wednesday rehearsal—first the boys by themselves, then men and boys. Berry arrived early because he was still missing school. Teddy and Randy were the next to show up.

Teddy and Randy whassupped Berry and said they'd heard he was sick. Berry nodded without letting their eyes out of his sight. He saw no sign they knew he'd gone blade-crazy. Luckily nobody tried to wrestle Berry in the pre-rehearsal scrum.

Mr. Allen gave Berry a hard time. "I hope you haven't forgotten how to sing during your little vacation." All the boys stared at Berry, who said he remembered how to sing. Then Mr. Allen gave Berry his first ever solo, in Sunday's piece: "This Is the Record of John" by Orlando Gibbons. People kept asking John the Baptist whether he was Elias, or the Prophet, or the Messiah. He kept saying no, no, no in a tender stream of grace notes. The music lilted, but sadly, maybe because these people couldn't figure out who John was.

Finally, Berry as soloist defined his own identity in the sweetest part, "I am the voice of him who crieth in the wilderness. Make straight the way of the Lord." When Berry sang it the first time, Wilson flashed him a thumbs up.

During the dinner break, Wilson talked about race cars and sports cars. "People talk about the Jaguar or the Ferrari but they're fools. They don't know what real power is. So on Sunday I'm gonna catch up with Lisa and just ask her out myself once and for all. No other girls, no grown-ups, just her and me. Wish me luck."

The next day Berry went back to school with a note excusing him from PE. Rat expected him to have done a week's worth of readings and asked him a question about Jane Austen. Berry mumbled. Toad showed a film about microbes then asked questions about it. Berry hid in his seat. Between periods Berry heard one of the Goose girls whisper that he'd overdosed.

After school, Berry took a long bus ride past the bleak North side to Dr. Tamarind's cinderblock. Marco had promised Berry an ice cream or something if he went to Dr. Tamarind under his own steam. Berry thought about skipping therapy and lying about it, but he figured Dr. Tamarind would call his folks if he didn't show up. So much for confidentiality.

Berry walked into the shrouded cavern. Dr. Tamarind looked up at him from behind his desk, his face pale from the light of his single lamp. Dr. Tamarind talked. Berry stood facing the desk, deciding whether to sit. Then instead he opened his mouth and music came out. He hadn't decided to sing in therapy, but once it happened it seemed a good thing. Once the trained voice flowed, Berry felt in control of the situation for the first time. Dr. Tamarind stopped halfway through a question about testicles and communion wafers. The shrink just stared as Berry filled his musty office with the Glory. He ran through several hymns and the anthems of Stanford, Howells, Byrd, Mozart, and Bruckner without leaving much pause between. Finally, R. Vaughn Williams's, "Yea, the sparrow hath found her a house, and the swallow a nest where she may lay her young . . ." After a while, Dr. Tamarind just leaned back in his chair and closed his eyes. Berry wondered if Dr. Tamarind had fallen asleep, but he didn't care.

"That was very lovely," Dr. Tamarind said quietly after half an hour or so of singing when Berry paused for breath. "You have an amazing gift. I can see why you want to keep it."

"I didn't do that to please you," Berry said. But he felt delight in spite of himself. The rest of the session, they talked like friends about music and families. Berry left Dr. Tamarind's office chuckling.

Someone in the waiting room threw a magazine over his face as soon as Berry emerged. Berry only glimpsed Canon Moosehead for a moment. Berry walked over. The Canon held his copy of *Rolling Stone* over his face as if inspecting the Yeah Yeah Yeahs up close. Berry peered over Jem to make doubly sure. The Canon cringed behind newsprint. Berry recognized the meaty face and soft beard, even without a collar. The Canon looked up at Berry, his eyes a plea.

Berry turned and stalked out. It came to Berry what was going on: Dr. Tamarind wanted to spy on Berry, so he was recruiting within the church. Canon Moosehead had obviously come to report on Berry's movements. So much for Berry's victory.

Berry took his time getting home. He no longer wanted an ice cream.

But Marco didn't have an ice cream for Berry anyway. He had "something better, a surprise. Come on." Marco dragged Berry back out of the apartment. Then they walked a few blocks and waited for the downtown bus. They rode south through darkening streets. Berry's paranoia sliced deeper. If Canon Moosehead and Dr. Tamarind could plot against him, what could his dad be up to? The neighborhood got nastier around him as they lunged into the darkness. "I told your mother not to wait up for us," Marco said. "Guy stuff." Berry wanted to run away, but he wasn't sure he could find his way home.

Marco led Berry to a big wooden door with a tiny window in it. He pulled the door open and revealed a stone staircase into a brick cellar lined with a bar on one side and small booths on the other. "Surprise," Marco said. He pulled out a small rectangle and handed it to Berry. In the cellar bar's gloom, Berry could hardly read the shiny little card. But he recognized a picture of himself from a choir photo, looking serious and mature. And he made out a date that overstated his age by eight years. "It's not a driver's license. I didn't want you to get any crazy ideas about driving," Marco said. He ordered two beers and handed one to Berry, who held up the fake ID to the bartender. The bartender barely glanced at it. "After this, we'll go to a strip joint. You're growing," Marco said with a smile. Berry started singing, very softly, so only he could hear.

The beer smelled like the woods around the Peterman school after a torrent.

"Drain it," said Marco. Marco acted scary-jolly, the way he did after one of his rages. Berry stared into his beer. After he drank enough, Marco fulfilled his threat to take Berry to a strip bar. They huddled at the side of a rounded stage with a fire pole at its front. Berry wondered whether a fire station somewhere was missing its pole and the firemen had resorted to jumping downstairs. As the night stretched and woman after slender woman came out and whipped around the pole, Marco put his hand on his son's shoulder and drew Berry's head into his chest. Berry watched the women dance from under his dad's arm until he fell asleep. Then his dad roused him and they took the bus home.

Berry slept through Judy's first two attempts to wake him the next morning. "You can't miss school so soon after your big absence. Now get some clothes on."

Rat sensed Berry's half-awake state and made him stand in front of the class and explain why Mr. Darcy might be a good match.

At choir rehearsal, the boys overheard Berry telling Wilson what had happened. He started out describing it as an ordeal. "It was ass-dark down there and that beer was so big." Then Berry noticed the other boys gathering around. They started giving him thumbs up and hooting when he told about the strip club. Berry soon realized this story was best told as a victory.

"Oh man," Teddy said. "Can we trade dads?"

Berry described all the impossibly top-heavy and skinny women in greater and greater detail, until the boys accused him of making it up. Luckily, Berry had pocketed a strip club matchbox.

Berry sat at the cool boys' table at dinner. Teddy and Randy kept stroking the curves of the matchbox stripper picture. After dinner, the full choir rehearsed in the cathedral for acoustics. Berry saw Canon Moosehead staring at him from the balcony at the cathedral's far end. After rehearsal, Berry passed the Canon in the hallway, but the Canon wouldn't meet Berry's eyes.

On Saturday, Marco took Berry for a "nature walk" in the basement of their apartment building. "Look, a bug. And there's some stuff growing under that leaky pipe. And I think I just saw something furry in the corner."

Sunday's sermon, by Dean Jackson, was called "The Church is Your Gang." Hoping to reach out to the inner city, the Dean compared different denominations to rival gangs. "We wear different colors, but we all run with the same crew in the end. We are all homies in Christ."

When Berry's solo came, he reached down deep to fill every part of himself with breath. He sang not just from his diaphragm but from his hurt scrotal sac. Berry breathed so deep he could imagine his ball sac puffing like a balloon. He focused on the pain, then released the voice of him who crieth in the wilderness. Mr. Allen looked amazed.

Teddy brought Berry a cookie after the service and said his solo had rocked the party. Berry took the napkin full of crumble and said thanks. Then he saw Wilson making his move on Lisa.

Berry caught up to Wilson. Both of them still wore cassocks and surplices. Berry never wanted to take his robe off. In regular clothes, he saw the rust that would swallow him eventually. But every time he caught his reflection in robes, he felt permanently stainless like the knife he wasn't thinking about.

Lisa stood with her mom outside the cathedral steps. Lisa and her mom were a few inches taller than Wilson and Berry, but Lisa's mom was way heavier. She wore a thick woolen jacket and skirt, even in the September heat. Mrs. Gartner kept talking to Lisa, even after Wilson approached.

"Hello Lisa. Hello Mrs. Gartner."

"He should be here," Mrs. Gartner said without acknowledging Wilson. "He's rationalist about everything except being on time."

"That was some sermon, huh?" Wilson said. "I guess Confirmation is like a gang initiation."

"Don't forget we need dill if we're going to marinate those mushrooms. Remind me to tell your father."

"So Lisa, there's this dance next week, and I was wondering if you'd like to, uh . . ."

A black Lexus pulled in front of the church in a smooth arc. Mrs. Gartner stomped to the passenger side and got in front. She immediately started gesturing at the driver, who was probably Mr. Gartner. Lisa got in the back seat without saying goodbye to Wilson and Berry. The car pulled out and ran a yellow light escaping the cathedral.

"I wonder why Lisa's dad doesn't come to church," Berry said.

"So Lisa's mom and her friends all hate me," Wilson said. "It's obvious she should date me. It's the most rebellious thing she could do."

Berry asked Dr. Tamarind about Canon Moosehead in their next session together. Dr. Tamarind merely sighed and changed the subject. Berry could tell it wouldn't help to keep asking, so instead he went back to ignoring Dr. Tamarind's questions and attempts at conversation. About halfway through the session, Dr. Tamarind seemed to run out of energy or ideas. The two of them sat in silence for twenty minutes or so. Berry watched the sunlight redden in the window and imagined it was the glow of stained glass.

Berry's mind wandered and he thought of Lisa mimicking her mom's deaf act after church. "What do you know about Roland Montreux?" Berry asked Dr. Tamarind.

The question jolted the drowsing therapist. "Why do you ask? No, of course. You ask the questions around here. He was a psychologist who made a splash, pardon the pun, in the early seventies. A kook. Tried to salvage the Skinner box."

"What was that?"

"Long story. Basically, Montreux believed the maturation process for children recapitulates evolution, from oceans to land. He was into underwater birth, and he thought children misbehaved because their reptilian, or aquatic, brain got out of control. He wrote this book called *The Shore of Reason* that told parents to submerge their children in water until they behaved better. Sort of aversion therapy. You relive the aquatic existence and progress beyond it. Not a very popular theory any more."

"I saw a diagram of one of his tanks on the Internet."

"I hope your parents aren't thinking of experimenting with his ideas."

"Nah. My dad's all about Rousseau. My mom sometimes talks about Ayn Rand." Then Berry shut up before he said too much or sounded too smart.

"You know," Dr. Tamarind said, "maybe it's time we got your parents in here with you."

Berry shook his head slowly.

"Why not?"

"They'd just fight."

Dr. Tamarind tried to draw Berry out some more, but Berry shut up. The more Dr. Tamarind probed him, the more nervous he got. He still wasn't sure why Canon Moosehead had been there.

When Berry finally lurched out of Dr. Tamarind's office without saying goodbye, he found a beautiful woman in the waiting room instead of the Canon. She had long hair the color of altar linen. Her square face shone with natural glamour and cosmetics, and jewelry glimmered from her neck, ears, and wrists. Her jeans jacket and denim skirt showed off a body almost as sleek as the strippers Berry had seen the week before. She gave Berry a starlet's smile.

"You look frustrated," she said. "I can't blame you. He's such a pill miser. Takes that whole 'gatekeeper' thing way too seriously."

Berry nodded without grasping anything.

"You think you're ready, right? You sure look ready. It would make passing a whole lot easier, I can tell you. But he doesn't care. I wish I hadn't started with him. You know, there's a much easier way of getting what you want."

Berry nodded again. He waited for the woman to make sense. She definitely sounded encouraging. But just then, Dr. Tamarind chose to poke his head out and say, "Maura, come on in." The woman got up, waved at Berry, then disappeared into the spymaster's lair.

Berry got halfway to the bus stop when he decided he couldn't go home without understanding what the woman, Maura, had been talking about.

He turned and walked back to Dr. Tamarind's office building. It had two exits, so Berry had to go upstairs and stand outside the suite door to be sure of catching Maura. He waited around there for half an hour, before Dr. Tamarind and Maura walked out together. They were talking about surgeons.

Berry hid behind a large red donut sculpture. Dr. Tamarind and Maura disappeared into the stairwell. Berry waited a moment, then crept down after them. But by the time Berry reached the ground floor, he couldn't find his therapist or the mysterious woman. He walked around the building twice, but they'd both disappeared. Berry screamed. Then he ran to catch the bus home for a late dinner and parental questioning.

Maura turned up a couple of weeks later, after an extra unpleasant session with Dr. Tamarind in which the therapist actually sang to Berry. "You see, a grown man can still have a wonderfully mellow and lilting voice," Dr. Tamarind said between renditions of "Mr. Tambourine Man" and "You've Made Me So Very Happy." Berry squirmed.

In the waiting room, Maura wore a really short red skirt, go-go boots, and talon-like press-on nails.

"Listen," Berry said. "I need to know about the stuff you were talking about when we met before. What did you mean, there's an easier way? Please tell me."

Maura agreed to meet Berry after her session. He took her for a beer at a nearby karaoke bar, using his allowance and fake ID. Berry drank cola and realized being a man had advantages. He could go to places like this bar, buy drinks for people like Maura, and listen to sophisticated grown-up conversations. It proved to be a big change from sitting around the Twelve Step room swapping fart jokes with the choirboys.

"God, Dr. Tamarind is such a nut case," said Maura. "It drives me crazy that people like that are in a position of power over people like us."

Maura wore rhinestone barrettes in her fuschia hair and a shiny black lycra dress that stopped mid-thigh. Nobody like Maura ever came to Orlac Junior High or St. Luke's.

"So why do you keep going to him?"

"Well, that's the point. If it was just for the pills, I'd probably go one of the other routes. But I can't let go of the idea that I'm going to want the surgery eventually."

Berry felt he was supposed to know about pills and surgery. It was probably one of those things that came along with adulthood, a body of knowledge that uncoiled in your late teens. So he probed: "What makes you think you'd want surgery?"

"I don't know." Maura took a big swig just as a woman in a leather cowboy hat and chaps got up and sang "Macho Man" by the Village People. "I guess I just want to be real."

"I know. I think about being real a lot." Berry tried to project his weekly choirboy image onto the plain boy he saw the rest of the week. Even on Sundays, Berry didn't feel enough like the harbinger he made others see.

"Have you started with the pills yet?"

Berry shook his head. "I'm not sure which pills you mean," he finally admitted.

Maura shook her head. "Huh. Well, for most people it's a combination of synthetic estrogen and progesterone, plus a whopping dose of testosterone blockers. It pretty much nukes the masculinity machine and lets that inner woman come out." Berry nodded.

"I tried to castrate myself. That's why I'm seeing Dr. Tamarind."

"Girlfriend!" Maura slapped her forehead. "You are hard core. It takes balls of steel to do that. But, mama, that is so unnecessary. You don't have to kick out the house guests until you're a hundred percent sure. I mean, the pills do pretty much the same thing. It's way less messy."

"Really?"

"Nobody would know looking at me that I still have them."

"You're a man?" Berry jerked back in his chair and almost knocked over a dancing lesbian.

"Sit down."

Berry sat.

"You are confused, aren't you?" Maura put her hand on Berry's. "Just relax. Yes, I was a man. Emphasis on 'was.' Goddess, what has Dr. Tamarind been doing with you in those sessions of his?"

"Singing to me."

"Now I know he's a quack. Listen, I know a place where you can get started on the pills. Your singing shrink won't even have to know, for now." Maura raised her Corona bottle. Berry clanked his soda against it.

That week the choir worked on a trippy Benjamin Britten piece for the big concert in October. Mr. Allen growled at the boys when they started sharping on some of Britten's weirdest riffs. The whole time, Berry thought about Maura's advice—to get the pills, even from the easy-going people at the Benjamin Clinic, you had to say you hated your body. This shell doesn't represent me, I'm making my way through this world in a false case.

Canon Moosehead gave the sermon that week, and he actually talked about people who hated their bodies. Cutting off your right arm, plucking your eyes out, casting out pig-demons . . . the "secular world" was just coming around to an idea Christians had known about for millennia: your mind, your essence, wasn't separate from your body. Rather, the two were intertwined. But did that mean you should go around lopping off body parts that behaved awry? Wouldn't we all end up mutilated? Maybe instead we should reopen the lines of communication between thumb and brain, try to adjust our self-image to reflect our physical selves? What would Jesus do? Maybe give us the mind-bogglingly contradictory and dictatorial advice to war with our bodies' urges while simultaneously owning up to their essential "us-ness." And repent, repent, repent, of course.

After that, the choir had a sleepy anthem by Herbert Howells, who probably never worried about whether he was his body. After church, Lisa vanished before Wilson could speak to her again.

That week, Berry showed up early for his session with Dr. Tamarind. He heard a voice coming from inside, which he identified after a moment as Canon Moosehead's.

"I've tried so hard, so horribly hard, to control it. But it won't obey. The other day it rose up during a meeting with the Downtown Association. I had to stay behind my desk, even when they started getting up to go. I mean, for years it hasn't stirred since Ronnie left me. Now this. What's it coming to?"

Berry couldn't hear what Dr. Tamarind said. Maybe he sang to Canon Moosehead. If so, the song was short. Soon, he heard the Canon again. "But this is all I know how to do. I'm a man of God, and a damn, sorry, a really good one. What if you had to quit therapy just because you got a stiffy every time somebody talked about his Oedipus complex? Well, whatever. I don't care if you're a Jungian or a lesbian."

Before Berry was ready, the door opened and he had to dash for the sofa and hide behind a Reader's Digest. Canon Moosehead stalked out, apparently too upset to notice anyone.

"Why does Canon Moosehead keep coming here? Is he giving you reports on me?" Berry asked Dr. Tamarind in their session. Dr. Tamarind said no, but he wouldn't say anything else. Berry found that pretty unsatisfying. "He probably spies on me because he's jealous. The other boys and I look much better in our robes than he and Dean Jackson do in theirs. And we actually know how to sing. You're lucky you've never heard Canon Moosehead try to do the whole Cantor thing. Yuck. The truth is people just sit through their boring raps to get to our music. So what is it with guys who want to be chicks?"

The sudden change of topic startled Dr. Tamarind but didn't upset him, since Gender Identity Dysphoria was a topic he knew something about, unlike religion. He explained about the smorgasbord of anxieties that makes people born one sex want to take another. "Imagine if the way people looked at you and treated you felt all wrong. And you couldn't wear the clothes or act the way you wanted," he said. "You'd do anything to change."

Berry reflected. "Suppose I wanted to be like the game show babe who stands by the big wheel or holds out one palm towards the picture of whatever vacation or appliance the person has won? Would that make me gender dysphoric?"

Dr. Tamarind said Berry might not have grasped the whole "smorgasbord of anxieties" concept.

Berry walked out of his session and saw Maura in the waiting room again. "Okay," he told her. "Tell me where to go." She handed him an address.

The Harry Benjamin Clinic was a mile south of downtown in a former noodle-stretching factory. It offered hormones and other treatments for young transgender people on a sliding scale basis, nobody turned away for lack of funds—depending on whether it had funding this week. "Medicaid won't touch trannies, but if you're 'at risk,' there's a safety net made out of old drawers," Maura explained. Being "at risk" sounded sort of like a Goose intervention.

Berry called three times before he got an appointment, on a Friday afternoon. Even sprinting from school, Berry barely had time to visit the clinic before rehearsal. Berry almost missed the steel door set in one cement wall, with its tiny sign. Inside, a man at a bulletproof window took Berry's name and glanced at the fake ID. Berry sat in a tiny waiting room where the television buzzed and the plastic bucket seats crunched his butt and made him glad he had no ass. All around him sat men with leather gear and swastikas tattooed on their heads and arms. Berry folded his arms and closed his eyes.

Maura had coached him on what to tell the triage nurse. "Just remember, you hate your manhood. Your body blows chunks. You were born the wrong shape. You want to live as a woman and wear the pretty. And if they don't give you the hook up, you're gonna get silicone injections from Tijuana." As long as Berry said all that stuff, they'd give him the pills.

It only took a few moments of recitation before the nurse scheduled him for a "psychosocial intake." Then the social worker, Marsha Joyce, listened blearily as Berry recited his spiel. "Blah, blah, blah, wrong body, black market, etc., etc." Marsha nodded a lot. Then she started asking how long had Berry felt like this and did he know what these pills would do. Lots of unsafe sex questions. She scribbled notes. Then she made an appointment for Berry with the clinic's staff physician, who weighed him and took blood and urine samples.

It took a few weeks before Berry clutched scrips for spironolactone and some other pills that Maura said were pure horse pee. "They get a mare pregnant so she's pumping female hormones like a fucking faucet, then they collect her piss and use it to make these pills. No lie. Then they give her an abortion and start the whole shitty process all over again." Maura stuck her tongue out. "But my boobs are worth a horse's pain."

To fill his prescriptions, Berry had to ride the bus even further south, to City General again. The waiting area had a floor that smelled like the Twelve Step room the time Jackie had drunk communion wine mixed with toilet cleaner and thrown up on the Temperance Shroud. Berry waited on a sticky chair, surrounded by people who looked homeless and who Berry imagined were there for HIV meds. Another collection of tattooed punks and skinny girls in Hot Topic knockoffs. He had to take a number and wait at one window to place his prescription. They wrote down stuff from Berry's fake ID.

Then he had to wait at a second window to fork over his choir stipend. Then back to the first window to turn over the receipt and pick up a paper bag full of pill bottles. Berry thought the bag looked like a take away bag from a fastfood joint, except for the receipt stapled to it. He took the first set of pills with drinking-fountain water that tasted rusty, then ran to church.

Charlie Anders

5.

Berry masturbated in his bedroom and stared at his poster of the choir of King's College, Cambridge, England. As he worked his grip on his half-hard dick, Berry imagined joining the incandescent boys in their frocks. Berry's cock twitched slightly as he imagined a chapel full of people shivering in their seats, breathless and raw with the urge for Berry to sing some more, to make a joyful noise unto the Lord.

Berry didn't realize he was singing until he'd reached halfway through the treble solo to Edgar Bainton's "And I Saw A New Heaven." He projected, pushed his voice into his "mask," the space between his eyes, and focused.

"And God shall wipe awaaaaaaay all tears . . ." The world ended. Lovely sorrow orbited mere space. Berry's voice soared through flaking paint and eroded brick. It had the chime of a good treble voice, but also a gospel warble on some high notes. "And there shall be no more pain, neither sorrow nor dying . . ." Berry lost himself in his vocal crescendo as his orgasm built. He slathered his now-erect dick with his own spit. In Berry's mind, he stood out front in an enormous cathedral. Swathes of light bathed him from stained glass windows and a congregation gazed at him.

Berry's voice splintered like a toothpick. That worried him until he saw pearl soup splash onto his stomach. Berry had been so focused on the sound of his own voice, he'd almost missed the intensifying pleasure when he came. His voice wasn't breaking like George's. It was okay. The drugs were working. Berry's heart sounded like a metronome on top speed, either because of his orgasm or because of the fear for his voice. He stewed in sweat, sperm, and rallentando.

Berry wiped himself off with last Sunday's church program and pulled on a sweatshirt and jeans. The sweatshirt more than hid Berry's chest buds. When Berry came out the front door of his parents' apartment, Mrs. Franklin came out of the next-door apartment beaming. She'd obviously lain in wait for his approach. Her gray hair hung loose and she wore a big apron. "Your voice is so lovely, Berry," she said. "You're like a little angel." Berry looked down at Mrs. Franklin's bunny slippers and smiled. He mumbled something.

Mrs. Franklin talked a bit more, but Berry was too busy thinking about that word "angel." All of a sudden, it was like all his hopes and fantasies crystallized around that one word. Berry desperately wanted to be an angel. Berry decided to tell Marsha Joyce at the Benjamin clinic he'd been called an angel. She'd like that.

Berry skipped into his follow-up interview with Marsha Joyce and talked to her about his life in the choir: "Mr. Allen said I had to look at him when he's directing me. Mr. Allen liked my posture and intonation. Mr. Allen kept yelling at me for coming in late and finishing early." It was only when Marsha started asking questions that Berry realized she thought Berry was a prostitute and Mr. Allen his pimp.

"Does Mr. Allen want you to be happy?" Marsha asked. She wore granny glasses and had her blonde hair tied back around a number two pencil.

"Mr. Allen wants me in tune," Berry said.

Marsha knew that Berry lived with his parents, and that Berry's parents didn't know about the hormones. Marsha spent a lot of their second session prodding Berry to tell his parents the truth. "You have to be able to live as your new gender, and that means being honest with the people around you," Marsha said. Berry nodded without promising anything.

Two days after his second session with Marsha Joyce, Berry went back to Dr. Tamarind. He didn't tell Dr. Tamarind about the pills or the tits he was growing. Dr. Tamarind talked about "staring your destiny in the face and making choices. You can't will yourself to stay dulcet and hairless forever." Berry jerked his head a lot and hoped it looked like nodding. He wished he could lock Marsha Joyce and Dr. Tamarind in a room together and go for pizza.

The first few days on spironolactone, Berry felt woozy and like he needed to pee all the time. He'd felt panicky, either because of the estrogen or because of the new secret. A couple of times he felt like he'd throw up and pass out at the same time. But he only felt really woozy when he ran fast, and that made his crotch lacerations angry anyway. He hardly talked most of the time, so now he hardly moved either. He just stayed close to the boys' room between classes and squirmed through Rat and Toad's lectures, until finally the hot bladder cooled off after a couple of weeks.

Berry folded his arms or turned his back whenever people paid attention to him. He slid down so far in his chair at school that his chin grazed the speech balloon of desk. The girls at school used tank tops and tubes to display their own personal growth, which didn't look much bigger than Berry's. He hunched his back in the school hallways. In the locker room, he avoided showers and cringed whenever he had to change into gym clothes. The locker room air felt stickier than summer.

Wherever Berry went, boys talked breasts. They compared the different girls' developments. Marc said Jee was a "fucking milk cow already," but Lisa was "stuck with slivers." Randy liked to cup his thick hands over his own chest and jerk them up and down. None of the girls had jugs like the strippers Berry had seen.

With only cassock and surplice to cover them, Berry thought everybody must be able to see his buds. On Sundays, he had to walk upright and tilt his chest slightly. He looked up at the cathedral's ceiling fans as he marched into church. His music folder didn't cover anything. Everyone in church must be staring at Berry's chest. The thought sickened and thrilled him. Berry felt hazy, pee-blinded and alarmed, like the night he'd drunk a three-liter Coke before bedtime.

Finally he had to ask Wilson, after a service where he'd hardly been able to read notes. "I gotta know. Has anyone noticed?" They leaned against the cathedral wall watching for Lisa. Berry's question came in the middle of Wilson's lecture about NASCAR.

"Noticed what?" Wilson scratched his head.

"Nothing." Berry grinned like a puppy.

"Yes, Berry, we've all noticed you're a retard. Anyway, the point is full-face helmets are for wusses."

One day after school, Berry didn't have choir practice or a session with one of his two therapists. He met Maura at a juice bar downtown. She perched on a stool, pastel clad like the world's smoothest virgin piña colada. Berry wondered if Maura ever got sick of people looking at her, or whether it would bug her if they stopped.

"You keep hugging yourself and bowing like a chilly geisha," Maura said. "Are you all right?"

"Side effects. Dizzy. Plus, umm . . . these spook me." Berry unfolded his arms and straightened enough to show contours.

"Trust me, nobody will notice unless they get way bigger. Maybe not even then. People don't see what they don't expect. And you can always bind them—get bandages at the drug store. I've known trannies who hid breasts C cup and over. And once you look female enough, you can go stealth. Most folks aren't used to wondering if somebody's what they seem, so as long as no alarm bells go off, you're fine."

"Do you think truth is beauty?" Berry was studying Keats for Rat's class. "I think you have to believe in the beauty of truth if you present a game show, even more than you have to treasure the prizes and getaways."

Maura just shrugged.

"I just can't keep track of who people think I am any more." Berry slurped his banana-mango smoothie. "Marsha at the Benjamin Clinic thinks I'm a ho."

"What would be wrong with that?" Maura suddenly sounded upset. It was the first time Berry had seen her anything but breezy.

"What? What did I say? I'm sorry! I didn't mean to hurt your feelings . . . What's wrong?" Panic opened Berry's arms wide, spilled his secrets into his shirt.

Maura laughed.

"I guess I'm still kind of defensive about it. But seriously, didn't you ever wonder what I did for a living?"

"I thought you were a student."

"I go to Hoochie Mama U. I learn on the job," Maura giggled. "Seriously, I like my job. It's nice to be appreciated for being different, instead of hated. And I get to meet interesting people and fuck them." She gave a too-much-infor-

mation laugh and tilted her styrofoam cup to let the obsti-
nate clump at the bottom slide down her long, canted neck.

• • •

"Show me what you got," Marco ordered Berry the next
afternoon. "I never hear you sing anymore."

Berry had his back to Marco, who sat on the couch with
his legs spread and his shirt half open. A Rolling Rock
sweated in his hand.

Marco sang, in the shower, along with TV commercials
before he broke the TV, when he drove Judy's car, and when
he summoned spirits for a client. In the right light, Marco
could look like an Italian tenor. He swore his voice had
sparkled once. Now it grumbled like a deep fat fryer.

"You never come to church," Berry told the mandala on
the wall.

"Fuck church. I wouldn't be able to tell anything from
hearing a million people singing," Marco said. "I want to
hear your voice by itself."

"I don't feel like singing," Berry mumbled.

"Aw, come on. Anything from Bach to Sinatra to those
Backdoor Boys. I'm not picky. I just want to hear your pipes
before they get all rusty like mine."

Sometimes Berry fantasized he'd had an older sister
named Sylvia or Mary. Berry's imaginary sister had been a
delicate maiden with hair a shade redder than Berry's. Her
eyes had shone like pulled-over cop car lights—now
white, now blue. Sylvia/Mary had looked after Berry
while his mom was never home and his dad abnormaled.
But then Berry's dad had scared her off/upset her/thrown
her out. Sometimes Berry actually believed Sylvia/Mary

had existed and imagined her speeding-ticket eyes watching Marco and him.

"Sorry," Berry said. "Gotta save my voice for church."

"Okay." Marco stared at his son's slender back for a few minutes. His beer went flat against one thigh. "So you want to do something? I've got a few hours until my next client. She's a twofer."

"What kind?" Berry watched some younger kids play in the empty lot below the window. One boy found Berry's family's old ice cream maker and threatened to throw a handful of rust-coated ice cream residue at the other kids.

"Investment and spiritual. She wants to cherry-pick genomics stocks and find her animal guide. We ditched the word 'totem' because it makes everybody think of sequoia trunks with Larry King carved into them."

One of the kids threw the ice cream maker at the wall. Berry remembered when he and his parents had played with that machine, vying to see who could invent the silliest flavor. The winner, Berry's pistachio anchovy bubble gum, had clogged the works beyond cleaning. Some time later, Marco had thrown the machine through the window mid-tantrum. Berry's parents had fixed the glass but not the appliance.

Berry glanced over his shoulder at his dad, guessing what bribe the old man would offer. He was torn between what he wanted and what he knew he should want. Teddy would have told Berry to demand porn or another visit to a strip bar. Berry wanted to watch the new Disney movie. He knew he was too old for Disney, and it was better to skew old than young in his tastes. He tried to envision what a grown-up Berry would want. It made Berry sad.

"Take me to the mall," Berry told the mandala.

Berry and his dad went to the big shopping center a few miles out of town. They parked Judy's rusty Corolla between SUVs and walked half a mile to the Citadel on the Hill shopping center. "It's like a church," Berry told his dad. He looked around the two-tiered structure heaped with clothing stores, accessories, shoes, and game show prizes. Berry imagined getting a makeover here. What would it take to make him look like Maura? Berry pictured continents moving, seas vanishing, to make his face a girl's. Berry wondered if his dad would consider a makeover male bonding.

"This place doesn't have any of the things that give a church meaning," Berry's dad said.

"Church has meaning because it's pretty," Berry said without thinking.

Berry's dad laughed and said millions of people in history had killed each other over whether that was true. But Berry shouldn't say that prettier churches meant more than plainer ones or people who went to the plain churches would get mad. Berry sometimes felt his dad still talked to him like a kid. He resented and enjoyed it.

"Do you ever miss being a choirboy?" Berry asked his dad.

"I miss singing. I've thought of joining a group. I don't think I could deal with church. Anyway, I still sing sometimes." Marco swept his arms wide, as if about to serenade the food court.

"Lots of people sing," Berry said. "Only a few are choirboys." They were silent for a while. Berry pictured a photo he'd seen of his dad three decades earlier—a tousled blackhaired boy with a ruffled collar, robe and white mantle, a soulful look in his deep-set eyes.

"I guess I miss it a little," Marco said.

Berry dragged his dad into the Warner Brothers store. He picked up a pewter Wonder Woman. "Grown men don't get too many chances to dress up and act fancy."

"Unless you become a minister. Preachers get to wear pretty things and get all the attention," said Marco.

"That's true. They can't sing, though. But yeah, it must rock pretty hard to be a minister. If I were a dean or a bishop, I'd just have fun and wear the sharpest robes all the time." Berry's voice, now boyish, now grown, chirped happily. Wonder Woman languished, forgotten, in Berry's left hand as he imagined a life of high church fashion. "I wouldn't worry about anything."

• • •

"It sounds ludicrous," Canon Moosehead's oratorical voice came through Dr. Tamarind's supposedly soundproof door. "You seem to think Jung is the solution to all my problems."

Berry had rescheduled his appointment with Dr. Tamarind at the last moment, from Thursday to Tuesday because he was being a Pickled Boy in a local production of Britten's "St. Nicholas Cantata". So he'd ended up right after Canon Moosehead once again.

Dr. Tamarind spoke too quietly for Berry to hear, then the Canon again: "I know spirituality and sexuality are connected, but . . . no. No. No, I don't think my anima is overwhelming my animus. I don't need a what, an anima enema. Yes. Yes, I get your point. I'll try and think about Jung's ideas next time I feel my . . . getting out of hand. I mean, I've tried everything else."

Berry went downstairs and hid so he wouldn't be there when Canon Moosehead's session ended. He wasn't sure if he did this to spare the Canon or himself.

Berry returned late for his own session. Dr. Tamarind wanted to talk about ritual. "It's what being a man or woman is all about, the performance, the pageantry, signs and symbols, tokens and types blah blah blah. Tell me, Berry, what do you know about ritual?"

"It's kinda like the word Ritalin, which is when you can't pay attention to anything people say to you," Berry said. Dr. Tamarind talked some more and Berry stared at his feet, which looked too large for his body. After a while, everything Dr. Tamarind said sounded like "biffle."

That night, after dinner, Berry touched himself again. Instead of staring at the King's College boys, he closed his eyes and tried to wake sleeping porn images. The magazines he'd seen blurred together, and everything he'd blocked out all day flowed into their place. Rat and Toad, Dr. Tamarind, Marco and Judy all gestured and opened their mouths amid nipples and crotch fuzz. Berry couldn't stay hard. The images of happy naked people kept fading out.

Then Berry imagined himself undressed in church. He stood by the communion rail and everyone brushed against his chest as they went to receive Eucharist. For some reason, the Berry in the fantasy couldn't move from the communion rail. This image made Berry spaz and shoot in seconds.

Jackoff fantasies can speak like dreams. The next day, Berry cornered Wilson in the boys' room.

The choir had its own bathroom, at the bottom of a winding staircase from the back of its rehearsal room. Berry figured the toilet was right under the altar. The tiles on the walls fractured into tusks. The one stall had no door and the toilet inside had no seat. Three urinals flowed into a trough. Berry watched Wilson pee. Wilson talked about Lisa. "You'd think she'd get tired of being so stuck up."

"Hey," Berry said. "I got something to show. I got to show someone or I'm about to go nuts." Wilson finished peeing and turned to look at Berry.

Berry unzipped his poncho and lifted his T-shirt.

"What the hell?" Wilson said.

"They're still small." Berry gestured with his free hand at the bumps. "But they're growing fast."

"That's freakish. How did you get these?"

Berry explained about the pills. Wilson whistled. He brought his face near to Berry's left nipple. Berry squirmed. Nobody who wasn't a doctor had ever looked so close at a part of his body, and this part still didn't feel like his. He shimmied until Wilson told him to hold still.

"Jesus," Wilson said. "Mary and motherfucking Joseph."

Wilson's breath huffed Berry's nipple. "This is the first breast I've seen up close since the whole teeth and hair thing. Weird weird. Can I touch?"

"I don't know."

"Come on. Just curious."

"You have to promise not to tell anyone about this."

Wilson drew back as if he balked. Then he raised a sticky hand. "Okay. I'll keep your secret." He prodded Berry's nipple with one finger. Berry jerked. Wilson reached with both hands and squeezed what flesh would separate from ribs. Berry felt his hatchlings stretch.

"Ow," Berry said, not loud enough to attract anyone else down to the men's room.

"Shush," Wilson murmured. "I'm imagining you're a real girl. I'm feeling your breasts and rounding the bases and it's all so perfect that luscious doesn't begin to describe and then I lean in close and put my mouth on yours and . . ." Wilson's lips touched Berry's. Barely a touch at first, then so hard Berry felt Wilson's teeth. Berry pushed Wilson off with both hands.

"Hey!" Wilson held his hands out and jumped back. "That wasn't anything. I didn't kiss you for real, okay? I was just practicing like you were a girl. You practically are. Holy fuck, you a faggot or what?"

"Wilson, calm down."

Berry pulled his shirt back down and zipped up his poncho. Wilson already had his hand on the swinging door that led up to the choir room. Berry ran upstairs after Wilson. By the time Berry got out into the choir room, Teddy and some other boys were greeting Wilson by the piano.

"Hey," Teddy said. "What were you up to down there?"

"Just peeing," Wilson said without looking at Berry.

Berry tried to make eye contact with Wilson all through rehearsal, but Wilson always looked at Mr. Allen or his music. Every time Berry closed his lips, he felt the imprint of Wilson's. After a while, Berry left his lips apart.

"Look at Berry," Mr. Allen said. "He's always ready to sing. If you keep your mouth open all the time, breaths come and go without any effort."

Berry took food to his room and avoided his parents. The next day at school, he decided to pretend he really was an angel as Mrs. Franklin had said. He walked the hallways looking upwards and trod slowly. Berry didn't really think about Jesus that much, but he thought of the music and stained glass, and all the candy lights, of a Heaven without brutality.

Berry might as well have pinned a bull's-eye to his back. He got "faggotted" twice just walking from Toad's biology class to Rat's composition. During afternoon recess, three Geese hung Berry by his ankles from the jungle gym until the blood in his head fogged his eyes. He felt the bandages in his lap pulling and his lunch fighting its way up his throat. He was grateful when they let him fall head-first onto the dense sand.

In the late afternoon, Berry met Wilson, Teddy, and Mr. Allen for Pickled Boy duty. They robed up and jumped into Mr. Allen's rusty Subaru.

Heavy metal jangled from Mr. Allen's tape deck. Wilson claimed the front passenger seat so Berry and Teddy sat in back. "A butcher chops you up," Mr. Allen said and steered. Metallica sang "Enter Sandman." "Don't ask me why. He's like a food service serial killer. He slices you into little pieces and puts the chunks into jars of brine. Then he puts all the jars in a room and puts up a wall to hide them."

"So we sing about being in jars behind a wall?" Teddy asked. "Sounds lame."

"Not quite. Your moms run to Saint Nicholas in distress. He sings a long prayer and then you bust out of your jars. All the boy parts pull together again and come back to life. Then you smash through the wall. That all happens off-stage. Then you come out hand in hand and sing Alleluia over and over."

"I'm not holding hands with Berry," Wilson said without turning.

The city's Symphony Choir had rented the big chapel at the local community college. It had wooden walls and a pink painted ceiling, but no stained glass. Rows and rows of men and women in white shirts and black skirts or pants clustered around the altar in a semicircle. Mr. Allen greeted

Charlie Anders

a man in a tuxedo with a serpent's tongue in back. "I brought you some boys," Mr. Allen said.

The adults in black and white rehearsed for a while without the boys, and Berry had a chance to hear women sing soprano. It confirmed all his prejudices about vibrato and impure sounds, but their voices also had a luster all their own. Wilson sat a few yards away from Berry.

Teddy rehearsed the part of the newborn St. Nicholas, the hero of Britten's Cantata. The choir sang that Nicholas was born in answer to prayer, and then Teddy jumped out of his mother's womb and sang "God be glorified" a few times.

The tenor soloist who portrayed St. Nicholas had a goatee and receding hair in a ponytail. His solo sounded like opera. Someone whispered this guy was a minor star, but his voice reminded Berry of wood that was all grain and varnish. And Berry didn't think he sounded like a saint praying for boys in jars, more like a fat guy thinking about pasta.

But the blustery tenor solo only heightened the stillness after, when Berry and Wilson busted loose, flanking Teddy. In the actual performance, Berry and Wilson each held a candle in their free hands. They floated, not too quick, up the aisle and sang a haunting thanksgiving that God had turned preserved meat back into bodies.

After the rehearsal, Mr. Allen took the three boys to a Chinese restaurant and fed them fried noodles so crispy you could comb your hair with them. When nobody was looking, Wilson spat a mushroom at Berry.

• • •

Berry mentioned The Kiss to Marsha Joyce. "Wilson's a friend of mine," he added, so Marsha wouldn't think

Wilson was a client. "Ever since then, he's acted psycho."

Marsha sighed. "Transphobia is *so* hard," she said. "It sounds like he has his own issues to deal with. But he's a grown-up, he'll work it out." Berry didn't correct her. He met Maura at the Benjamin Clinic's rear entrance when he emerged. "Do you have an appointment here?" he asked her.

"Nah. Just hanging."

Berry got the impression Maura had been hoping to run into him. He walked with her to his bus stop, and told her about the St. Nicholas concert. "It was really cool when we actually walked out into a chapel full of people and the only light was our two candles and we sang that tune over and over again. People were on the edge of their pews."

"I should go to your church," Maura said.

"What?"

"Sounds like you spend a lot of time there. I want to see where you strut your stuff, Mama Chula."

A massive hand poked its fingers between Berry's ribs. He tasted stomach stuff. "Uh," he said. "I don't know if that's a good idea. They're pretty conservative there. They don't know about all this." He glanced at Maura's outfit for the day: a latex miniskirt and sequined stretch top, plus knee-high boots.

"Don't worry," Maura said. "I had a good Christian upbringing. You won't know I'm there." Maura smiled in a way that was probably supposed to ease Berry's mind.

6.

Randy decided to teach Wilson and Berry to hit. Randy held out a palm. "Punch," he said. Wilson made a fist, looked at it and unmade it. Then he recreated it, knotted tighter around his thumb this time.

The three boys stood in the gravel lot behind the cathedral on Sunday morning. Breakfast spills sheened their blazers and ties. A posse of choirboys had hit the Grease Spot for trucker food before church, and now it was about rehearsal time. Berry had stuck to toast and juice to protect his voice.

"Come on," Randy said. "Hard as you can." Wilson put his fist into the soft hollow between fingers and heel. Randy's hand barely moved. "Come on," Randy said. "Harder. Give me what you got. Put some weight into it." Wilson hit several more times, until he shook his limp hand.

Randy looked patient but amused as Wilson pummeled to no effect. For years Randy had beaten on both Wilson and Berry, but now he seemed protective.

"Your turn, Berry," Randy said. "Use your shoulder."

Berry aimed for Randy's love line. He heard a spanking noise and Randy's hand fell back. Randy laughed. "Not bad. But more follow through this time." Berry's arm started to hurt after the fourth punch.

"We'd better get inside," Wilson said. He sounded pissed that Berry hit harder than he did. Wilson usually did a better job of being one of the guys than Berry.

Now that Wilson and Berry had seniority and almost membership in the inner circle, they had to mess with the younger kids and sometimes each other to stay cool. Wilson had given Berry a thermonuclear wedgie a few days after Berry had showed Wilson his breasts. It had seemed to give Wilson the creeps—he'd snatched his hand home as soon as he'd hiked Berry's waistband high enough.

Berry and Wilson grabbed their music just as Mr. Allen made loud piano bench noises and started playing chord progressions. After the choir warmed up, it sweated over a couple of pieces by C.V. Stanford, the nineteenth century composer. The centerpiece of the day's service was Stanford's "Te Deum," which ends with two choices for trebles. They can hit either the high note Berry reached with a knife in his scrotum, or the one an octave below.

Mr. Allen banged the piano lid down with a scowl. "My God—a chain-smoking James Brown impersonator with one lung could do better than you boys. This is a lyrical declaration of faith—not 'Cum On Feel the Noise.'" Mr. Allen had Berry, Marc, and Teddy sing the pleading middle section alone, with a few men. It's a sweet surprise tucked in a thundering anthem, like a kitten hiding under a truck.

Then the choir sang to the end, and Mr. Allen pushed his bench away from the piano like a sailor in a hurry to embark. He stared at the boys as if chasing the sources of sounds he'd just heard. "Berry—you're the only one I hear hitting the last bar. Why don't you sing it for everyone?" The entire boys' section threw murderous glances at Berry.

Berry nodded, glad he'd stuck to toast while the other boys had eaten sausages. He sang shyly, but with clarity. When he hit that final high note perfectly. Mr. Allen clapped. "Now, do the rest of you think you can come within a hundred yards of what Berry just did?" Nobody replied. "Why don't you all just drop an octave on that last note, and let Berry hit the high note alone?" That settled, Mr. Allen drilled the choir on Stanford's "Beati Quorum Via" and some hymns. Then he told everybody to get their cassocks in gear.

Berry saw Mr. Allen, robed and groomed, heading for the side entrance to the cathedral to begin his organ prelude. Mr. Allen nodded at Berry and paused by the door. "You're a talent," Mr. Allen said. "You should consider training—to develop that voice to adulthood."

"What if there was another way?" Berry asked. "If my voice didn't have to age?"

Mr. Allen looked startled. "There isn't—I wish there was." He swooped into the church to grind out Bach. Berry turned to find the choir and line up for the big entrance. He took one step and fell face first on the rough-stained floor. His taped breasts cushioned his impact. He looked up and saw Teddy, leg outstretched. He and Marc stood over Berry. "Whoops," Teddy said.

"Leave me alone," Berry said.

"You think you're hot shit, don't you? Mister fucking high octave. Don't want to be a team player, huh?"

Berry looked up at the tousled avengers. "We gotta go, guys. There's no time for this." The Bach or whatever reached something like a climax.

"We'll talk later," Teddy said.

In all the excitement, Berry's breasts had gotten loose from their bindings, so he had to hold his music folder tightly against his collarbone to keep his chest on the down low. Wilson turned and squinted at Berry.

The hymn started and the choirboys parted the velvet curtain over the stone arch. It was one of those Charles Wesley confections that trills you into submission. Berry saw the rich up front as the choir entered from the side door. They wore nice suits and floral dresses that snagged Berry's eye for a second. Then the procession passed to the middle rows, where the poorest parishioners mixed with middle class suburbanites. Berry wondered how the church let people know where to sit according to income. The procession reached the back rows, where stragglers clustered.

Berry spotted Lisa Gartner a split-second before he saw whom she sat next to. Maura leaned over in her pew and told Lisa a joke—a dirty one, Berry guessed. Lisa giggled. Berry saw no sign of Lisa's mom. Berry wanted to run and hide among the homeless, but he couldn't break rank. When Maura hadn't shown up for church the previous weekend, Berry had relaxed. Now he watched Maura and Lisa laugh together and bristled with dread. He could imagine Maura telling Lisa, *Look at the baby tranny in the wine-colored drag.*

Wesley won't let you brood. Berry had no time to digest Maura's presence until Canon Moosehead tried to lead a chant. Maura wore the longest dress Berry had ever seen on her, lemon tulle over floral web hose and black boots with finger heels. Every time Maura leaned into Lisa's ear, Berry felt queasy. He scripted in his head dozens of ways Maura could destroy him with Lisa.

Pretty soon it was Stanford time. Mr. Allen positioned a mirror so he could play the organ and conduct with his head. Berry tried to look into the enormous dancing eyes, which saw through him even from a reflection. The parts started in unison, and then Berry knew why he took so many pills. The four parts scattered and the trebles peaked. The boys cried "Holy, holy," and the blue pupils swung left and right in the organist's mirror, guiding Berry into the piece's sudden vulnerable heart. Before Berry knew anything, he reached the end and his voice alone nailed the final peak.

Before the Te Deum, the choirboys on the other side of the church had passed a note. When the choir came together for the anthem, the note moved to Berry's side. Soon it reached Wilson and Berry, who read: "Delivered the payload to Moosehead. Same as last time." Berry looked over at Canon Moosehead, who squirmed in his gilded throne next to Dean Jackson. Soon after, the Canon rose and walked to the lectern.

"In this week's gospel, Jesus says there's nothing that goes into you, like food, that can make you unclean. It's only things that come out of people, like sexual licentiousness or violence, that sully us. Jesus was talking about dietary laws and hand-washing, but He was also making a larger point. Even back then, they had wine and drugs that could change how you acted. So why does Jesus say those things don't make us 'unclean?' Maybe being clean is about self-control. Is it actually possible to have self-control, or is control just an illusion because our bodies are alien to us? Remember, Jesus also says having adulterous thoughts is the same as committing adultery. Are we all doomed to be unclean all the time? How do we ask forgiveness for involuntary sins, or for sins we can't even describe or put a name to?" Canon Moosehead shifted more and more in his pulpit, always keeping his crotch hidden behind its lip.

Berry glanced over at Dean Jackson, who watched Canon Moosehead with a gut-punched expression. The Canon went on, "It's so much easier to control what goes into you than what comes out of you, unless you're a compulsive eater or someone is forcing something into your throat. I mean . . . but . . . Jesus must have understood that our bodies constantly recycle and secrete, churn fluids and impulses in an electrified stew that drives us to incomprehensible extremes of convulsion and . . . Jung . . . Jung . . . Jung!" Canon Moosehead sounded as though he was calling a lover's name. "Jung teaches us our unconscious is the playground of ineffable forces. We all share the collective unconscious, which means whatever comes out of me is really coming out of you as well. It's coming out of all of us and getting all over everything and we have to find some place to put it so it doesn't leave a stain. In the name of the Father, the Son, and the Holy Ghost." Berry could hear jaws crashing open around the church.

Then it was money time and the choir sang again. At least the nervous-breakdown-disguised–as-sermon had distracted Berry from Maura and what she might be telling Lisa. And maybe Maura would decide this church was too weird even for her.

As soon as the service ended, Berry ran back to the choir room and stripped off his robes. Every second he waited was another second that Maura could be telling Lisa bizarre and possibly true things about him. Berry slammed into Wilson in the hallway.

"Ow," Wilson said. "I'm trying to catch Lisa." It was the first time he'd spoken to Berry in ages.

"She's with a friend of mine," Berry said. "No sign of her mom."

"Her mom's outta town for a few weeks. No mom, no friends. She may actually be talking without vetting. I'm hoping for un-vetted bliss."

Wilson ran back into the congregation, which voided through the cathedral's front door like a clogged sink. Canon Moosehead stood by the entrance shaking hands and explaining his sermon, even to people who tried to escape him. Wilson pushed through the throng waving the church patch on his blazer like a police badge. "Choir business, coming through." Berry gave up and ran back to the side exit. He reached the front of the cathedral just as Wilson pushed out onto the steps. Wilson shook his head and raised his hands.

Berry saw the hem of Lisa's floral skirt around the cathedral corner and heard Maura's cackle. He grabbed Wilson's arm and led him.

"Hey Berry," said Lisa when the two boys approached. She smiled at Berry and he tried to label it knowing or innocent? "I met a friend of yours." Lisa's lean body stirred under loose cotton.

"Wilson, this is Maura," Berry said. "She and I, uh . . ."

"Berry and I do volunteer work together." Maura took Wilson's hand in two fingers and a thumb. Her blonde locks caught the sunlight just as she drew Wilson's eyes into her own. Berry heard Wilson's breath falter. Then Lisa said hi to Wilson almost as an afterthought, and his attention swung back to her.

"Berry, your cathedral is so fun," said Maura, slurping church coffee. "I'll never look at a naked man nailed to a phallus the same way again. That sermon, especially, so trippy. And you gotta love that holy diva shit you all wear."

Wilson tried to talk to Lisa but she stared at Berry. This made Berry dizzy and channeled voltage through his guts.

"So do you mind if Lisa comes to lunch with us?" Maura asked Berry. "I was really enjoying hanging with her."

"I don't have to get home for a couple hours," Lisa explained.

"Uh, sure," Berry said. "Can Wilson come?"

All the Sunday brunch spots burst with church crowds. The four of them ended up at the Convincing Rye, a deli with wooden high chairs and tiny round tables. Families clustered all around the two boys in navy blue jackets, the peony-covered girl and the beauty in neon yellow.

Berry didn't understand why Lisa was looking at him and ignoring Wilson. He worried that she was trying to fit him into whatever fantastic story Maura had told, and hunted for something else to occupy her mind. "I read up on that guy you mentioned, Roland whatsisname," he said.

"Montreux," Lisa said.

"He sounds majorly Koresh."

Lisa stared at the cartoon Hasidim on the wall holding a plate of knishes. She didn't answer Berry. The robed Jew had a long beard and the caption "Oy! Gott in Bagel." Wilson heard the silence and talked to Lisa about sports cars.

Berry turned to Maura. "So . . . do you think you'll come back to church sometime?"

"Oh sure." Maura glowed. "I feel a very warm energy there."

Lisa cut off Wilson's turbo engine rant. "So what kind of charity work do you do, Berry?"

"I kind of work with poor street women." Berry looked at Maura to make sure he'd given the right answer.

"That's just so heroic and amazing," said Lisa.

"I've worked with street women too," said Wilson. "Just the other day, I gave someone half a sandwich."

Lisa ignored Wilson. "Your skin is so soft, Berry. What do you use?"

"I wash. I mean, I use pads and stuff."

"I wash too," said Wilson.

"I just bet you do," said Maura, brushing Wilson's chin with one finger.

Berry saw sandwiches on the counter and jumped off his chair without waiting for an announcement. He whisked the plastic tray back to their table and started unwrapping wax paper.

"This looks weird," Wilson said of a beet-red meat within the folds of cabbage and bread.

"You stole my tongue!" a woman screamed from in front of the counter. Berry rushed back to the counter with the tray he'd grabbed and apologized piteously. By then, his group's actual sandwiches were ready.

Maura somehow managed to eat a pastrami sandwich daintily and flirt with Wilson. She seemed fascinated by Wilson's rambling about cars and youthful death. She stared into Wilson's eyes, straw seductive in her mouth, while he explained how to ensure a deadly car crash instead of just a paralytic one.

Berry only realized halfway through his reuben that Maura might be distracting Wilson as a favor to Lisa. "You sounded good today," Lisa told Berry.

"The choir's been working hard," Berry said. He wished he'd ordered more food so he could get up and fetch it. "We're a suped-up high-octane singing machine. Wilson would probably have a better engine metaphor."

"It's okay," Lisa said.

Berry bit his sandwich and looked up just in time to see Lisa giving him a smile that came from everywhere in her lithe face. Her tied-back blonde hair, agate eyes, and slender mouth made something more of that smile. Berry almost swallowed without chewing.

"My dad's a poet," Wilson told Maura. "He works at an ad agency, but that's not what he does. You understand. Like my mom's a sculptor even though she does medical billing. Nobody does what they really do."

"I do what I do, but I don't let anybody know I do it," Maura said.

"Are you really going to be student body president at your school?" Berry asked Lisa.

"I go to a small school," Lisa said. She ate potato salad one chunk at a time.

"Anyone can make a fast car," Wilson told Maura. "It's all about control and handling."

"Oh yes. Handling is everything." Maura ran a hand along her daffodil hip and Wilson swallowed.

"My mom says I'm too young to hang out with boys," Lisa said. "I guess it's okay with a chaperone."

"And this is practically religious because we came from church," Berry said.

After lunch, Lisa borrowed Maura's cell phone and called for her ride home. Soon after, the Lexus pulled up outside the Convincing Rye and honked. Lisa kissed Berry on the cheek, hugged Maura, and waved goodbye at Wilson. Then she ran and got in the front of the Lexus next to a stern man in a turtleneck.

"So," Wilson said to Maura. "Have you got a boyfriend?"

7.

Michael Dukakis and Lloyd Bentsen hit town fleeing technical glitches. Someone hacked the mainframe for their party convention. Mailings went nowhere. The campaign sputtered. At four in the morning local planning for the Dukakis visit still struggled with grassroots tangles. Marco met a firebrand girl when they both reached for the last half cup of coffee in the predawn craze. "You drink it," Judy told Marco. "I'll feed off your energy."

After Dukakis came and went, Marco and Judy brunched together, their first or second date depending on what they counted.

Marco described a Cold War courtship to Berry. He and Judy had discussed Kremlinology for hours at the dawn of their love. It had turned competitive. Looking only at the latest translation of Pravda, which of them could tell more about the state of the Politburo and the Soviet power structure? Both Marco and Judy had fussed about geopolitics, Marco in a big-picture way, Judy in a detailed wonky way. What if Perestroika melted down or the cowboy stumbled on the button on his way out? These questions had dominated Marco's flirtation with Judy. Before they'd met they'd both been poli-sci junkies and geopolitical wonks. They'd married two years later.

Berry soaked up his parents' outdated knowledge scraps. He considered Kremlinology a metaphor; the world had divided into two halves, facing each other across a wall. They had resorted to the crudest divination to gloss the images of Dynasty and Dallas, Pravda and Tass. Now it was harder to make clear divisions. Berry wanted to be a Kremlinologist when he grew up.

Rat stared at Berry as he chattered about Uzbek unrest and problems with the ninth five-year plan. Berry realized all the Swans were giving him "nerd" faces too. He shut up.

"I think that's the first time you've ever said multiple sentences in my social studies class," Rat said. "I'm glad someone here can remember the weird old days." He spent the rest of the class talking about Sputnik and the Cuban Missile Crisis. "We really thought we were going to be nuclear wintering on the slopes of Hell," he said almost fondly. Berry felt his interest in school evaporating again. He was getting used to the idea that excitement could easily melt.

Friday evening after choir practice Wilson and Berry went out with Maura. They went back to the karaoke bar where Berry and Maura had met the first time. When Wilson went to the bathroom, Maura told Berry he should wear women's clothes when they went out together. "I only wish I could pass as easy as you," she said. "You bleach that mustache, you'll look like a girl no problem."

"Why would I want to look like a girl?"

"You have no idea how much fun you can have. It's like movie star fascination. People just swoon. I could take you to the Booby Hatch and they'd love you. It's even better than people thinking you're grown thanks to that fake ID of yours. I mean, I wouldn't want you to go pro or nothing, but if you ever did you'd make so much money. But you're too young, you're jail bait and all."

Berry didn't understand why he had to become so many fraudulent things just to stay one true thing a little longer.

Wilson came back and Maura changed the subject. "I mean, I could get the operation as soon as I scare up a mess of greenbacks, but then my earning potential would vanish up my new hole. Men don't want a post-op the same as a pre-op." Maura laughed and rocked the table. Wilson lost his place in the song book. He planned to sing "I Want Your Sex."

"Not to mention it's easy to get a botched job," Maura said. "I'd hate to end up with labia that detach themselves without warning and fly across the room like a drunken butterfly, see what I mean?" Berry and Wilson both nodded, though Berry could tell Wilson didn't get it. Maura looked earnestly into Wilson's wide blue eyes. Wilson sipped his beer nervously, playing with his striped choir tie with his other hand.

"Oh sure," Wilson said. "I can totally get with that." Berry wasn't sure if he should explain to Wilson what Maura was talking about. But Berry wasn't a hundred percent sure he knew the details himself, and he didn't want to weird Wilson out again.

"I mean, it's something you only do once, right? And most people don't even do it once. It's something where you'll totally want the absolute best job possible. You want a Cadillac, not a Yugo."

Wilson perked up. Here was a subject he knew about. "Well, yeah. I mean, people always talk about the Cadillac as a great car. But if you're talking raw engine power, you want something with a few more cylinders, along the lines of a Lamborghini or Corvette. Actually *Motor Trend* magazine says . . ."

Maura interrupted by putting her hand on Wilson's in a delicate gesture of confiding. "Wilson, I gotta know. If I get the operation, will you still . . . like me afterwards? Will you still think I'm sexy and interesting? I know Berry here will accept me no matter what."

"Sure," Wilson said. "I mean, you'll still be able to walk and everything, right?"

"I sure hope so. If I couldn't walk, that'd sure be a shitty operation."

"Well, then I don't see what's the big deal."

Maura suddenly leaned over and kissed Wilson. Not on the cheek, but on the lips. No tongue, but still. Berry watched Wilson's eyes widen, then close.

"Oh Wilson," Maura said. "You're so sweet. You have no idea how many guys lose interest in girls like me once we no longer have that 'something extra.'"

Wilson promised on a stack of beer coasters that he'd adore Maura no matter how many operations she had or what kind. Maura glowed. Later, Maura took Berry and Wilson back downtown to wait for their separate buses, then left. Wilson leaned over and said to Berry, "I don't understand why she's making such a big deal about an appendectomy anyway."

Berry shrugged. "Some people are sentimental about organs," he said. He decided it was best if Wilson never learned the truth about Maura.

Berry got home at 9:47 PM, terrified he'd find a scowling mom on the phone with the cops. Instead Berry found Marco in his big recliner shredding a fat book a few pages at a time.

"Oh hey." Marco glanced up at Berry. "Good day at school? Hey, would you mind stepping out for a few minutes, then come back in? Say fifteen minutes. I'm in the middle of something. Just, you know, walk around the building a few times."

Berry went downstairs into the October chill, walked for a few minutes and bought a hot chocolate at the café on the corner with the last of his allowance. He saw a couple just going out for the evening and imagined all the two-fisted hard-drinking adventures they were set to have. After he'd finished the chocolate, Berry trudged back up to his apartment. Marco wasn't around any more. Berry looked in the trash to see what Marco had been shredding. The trash was empty, but in a tied-off plastic bag behind the sofabed, Berry found a bundle of scraps including a cover that had read, "Divorce Made Easy."

Berry knew about divorce from his classmates and choirmates. It sounded like a vacation, only with more shouting, frequenter bathroom breaks, and better food. Especially if your parents shared custody, the result tended to be more toys than rules.

The next day was Saturday, but Maura had to work. "I make my own hours," she said. "But Saturday's my best night."

Berry saw his mom twice over the weekend, so apparently she still lived there. She worked long hours and slept most of the time she was home, so Berry could never learn much from her seldom appearances. She was like a Soviet Premier.

Berry wondered if "jail bait" was like the lumps of food they put into roach motels to seduce bugs in. He pictured himself hanging in the doorway to the county jail, wearing a white robe like his choir surplice. Maybe they'd lash his hands and feet to the corners of the doorway. Then when some dumb roachy person came to grab Berry, he or she would fall through a trap door into the darkest cell. Everything about that fantasy excited Berry: the bondage, inspiring a doomed desire, even luring someone into shame. But even as he stroked himself at the thought of it, it troubled him. It seemed like the flipside of his true role, enticing people to God. When terror shook the breath out of Berry, as it did in the middle of the night and a few times a day, the idea of becoming a mockery scared Berry as much as people finding out about the pills.

Berry didn't understand why Maura wasn't worried about Wilson being "jail bait." Maybe she was just toying. The next Sunday, Wilson told the other choirboys to look out for his girlfriend in the congregation. "She'll be wearing a purple and black jumpsuit and gold ankle boots. She told me. Right after she said I was cute." The choirboys oohed. Berry realized Wilson and Maura had hung out without him, or at least talked on the phone.

But after they all got a good look at Maura during the opening hymn, Teddy wrinkled his nose in the choirstalls. "I don't know. She looks nasty." That last word had all kinds of furrows.

"Nasty is a good thing right?"

Nobody answered. Berry studied the day's music by Bruckner. Dean Jackson talked about grace. The choir struggled to drape reverence over the congregation. Canon Moosehead stayed out of sight when not dispensing wafers.

Lisa sat with some of the other choirgirls, and left right after church. Wilson went with Maura and Berry to lunch. "Teddy is like hotness impaired or something," Wilson told Berry when Maura was out of earshot. Berry wondered what Dr. Tamarind would say if he knew Maura was flirting with a barely teen boy. He wanted to mention it in his next session, but he didn't want Dr. Tamarind to know that he knew Maura. Berry wondered if all of Dr. Tamarind's patients knew each other one way or another. Maura had mentioned bitch sessions with other trans girls about their shared shrink.

Dr. Tamarind had led Berry into a world of masks and toys. Sometimes he made Berry wear a Polynesian scowl, sometimes a Thai grimace. "Who are you when you wear that mask? What do you feel?" Dr. Tamarind would drag out figurines of elephants or birds to represent Berry's parents, teachers, or peers. "Act out a scene with the elephant and the snake." Berry always did his best, just like at school. Not having the answers, he took the questions to heart. He wouldn't do homework for Dr. Tamarind, like keeping a journal or taking pictures, but in their weekly sessions he played whatever games the therapist called for.

The more people tried to figure out what was going on with Berry, the less he could explain it to himself.

• • •

The senior choirboys hatched a plan to steal the Christmas punch from Bishop Locke. The Bishop's punch of legend fermented from August until December. Nobody knew the ingredients for sure, but every churchgoer who braved the Bishop's Christmas Eve party complained later of sore heads and hazy memories of games of "name that Bible story" with the loser shedding clothes to an organ version of "Night Train."

Anyway, rumor said the casks of by-now-lethal punch sat in a vault behind the Twelve Step room. Teddy sent Jackie, one of the youngest boys, to distract Sandy the pedophile

Verger while Marc stole the basement keys. A stash of killer booze was excitement enough. But the second part of Teddy's plan was to convince the girls' choir to attend, partake, and maybe loosen up. Teddy sent Wilson and Berry to the True Love Waits group with a note inviting the girls to a "sleepover" in the Twelve Step room Friday night. "Everyone knows the juiciest girls go to True Love Waits meetings," Teddy said.

The group met in the auditorium where the boys stole cookies and punch on Sundays. A dozen kids, almost all girls, sat in folding chairs in a semicircle. Canon Moosehead faced them, wearing his "regular guy" uniform: jeans and a sweatshirt.

"Well, personally," said Wilson, oozing sincerity, "I just can't picture sex without the bond that can only come from his-and-hers face towels. I can't get my mind around it."

Berry glanced at Canon Moosehead, who coughed and tried not to look at anybody. Canon Moosehead fidgeted a lot these days. During the Canon's worst fit, Wilson handed his note to Rebecca, the girl to his left, and indicated she should pass it to the other girls whose chairs faced the Canon in a semicircle.

"But what if you marry some guy, and he has elephantiasis or whatever it is that makes your weewee act weird?" asked Lisa. "I mean, say you've never seen one before and you think it's normal for his thing to look for peanuts and drink water? What if he does that thing the Bible talks about and spills his seed on a pillar of salt?"

While Lisa spoke, it was Berry's turn to cringe. She'd brightened when he'd shown up at the TLW meeting. He still didn't know what Maura had told Lisa. The fact that a popular girl wanted to talk to Berry struck him as a scourge.

Bad enough that she talked about obscure French perverts to him. Worse that she seemed to flirt.

Canon Moosehead uncrossed his legs, crossed them again, gripped his knee in both pink-knuckled hands and pulled it up to his ribs. "Well," Canon Moosehead said, "Many married couples face . . . That is to say, back when I was married, we . . ." He actually managed to pull his knee to his chin, so it covered his mouth for a moment. "Jung! I mean, if you look at what Jung said . . . And yet St. Paul . . ."

Berry raised his hand. Ten girls, Wilson, and a flustered minister turned. Canon Moosehead nodded for Berry to speak. He realized he had no clue what to say.

Berry tried to imagine Marco and Judy, their marriage, and how it made sex better, worse, or nonexistent. "Sex can be scary as well as fun," Berry said. "All kinds of bad things can happen. But it's easier and nicer to deal with that stuff if you're married. Married people work together and keep each other safe and stuff." Everyone smiled. Wilson gave Berry a thumbs up. Lisa's smile cast approval or lust, Berry wasn't sure. Eloquence in the cause of abstinence might actually get Berry laid.

The "sleepover" note made the rounds with no trouble. One or two girls giggled despite themselves. Afterward, Canon Moosehead came up to Wilson and Berry and put his hand on Wilson's shoulder. He avoided Berry's eyes. Wilson and Berry were late to meet Maura. "You were both great," the Canon told them. "I'm really glad to see nice young men here in TLW. I wish more choirboys would show up and take an interest. Sex is a wonderful thing, a God-sent fulfillment, but . . ." The Canon trailed off, as if distracted. "I mean, Jung."

The boys finally escaped the Canon and ran to their "date" with Maura. She sat, pleated miniskirt fanned around her thighs, in a coffee shop. Several coffee drinkers stared, and one guy drew her portrait, but Maura paid no notice to them. "Berry! Wilson! How's it going?"

"Pretty good," Berry said.

Wilson seemed nervous about something. Even after all his boasting about his "new girlfriend" he seemed a little hostile to Maura. Finally, when Maura went to the bathroom, Berry asked Wilson what was up. "Uh, nothing," Wilson said.

"Seriously, man. What's bothering you?"

"I made the mistake of mentioning Maura to my parents. Now they want to meet her."

"So what's so bad about that?"

"I know they'll totally freak out if they see her. My mom's totally uptight and my dad's a wreck. And she's . . ." Wilson made a gesture with his hand. "Nasty."

When Maura got back, Wilson started talking about his future, aggressively, as if building a wall in a hurry between him and Maura, and maybe Berry too. "I'm probably off to boarding school for high school, then I'm shooting Ivy League. Columbia maybe, or Brown." He'd major in English and public health, then a masters in journalism. Soon, Wilson would be writing great disease books or fascinating articles for glossy magazines. He acted like he had it all worked out, but Berry could tell his plans were half made up on the spot, half stuff his parents had fed him. After all, Wilson had told Berry often he expected to be dead by college.

"I'm going to have my operation and marry a rich guy," Maura said. "He'll be a surgeon who'll sculpt my body into his ideal, and we'll travel around the world rescuing endangered species and building the world's biggest lizard sanctuary. You know, everybody always wants to save cute birds or baby seals, but what about all those lizards and insects that are fizzling to nothing? So, we'll buy a Pacific island nobody lives on and fill it with every type of lizard. Finally, I'll write a book about all the lizards we've saved and it'll become a major motion picture starring me." She leaned back, satisfied she'd trumped Wilson.

"How are you going to find this wealthy lizard philanthropist? Is he going to rent your ass and fall for you, like in *Pretty Woman*?" Wilson said. Apparently Maura had told him what she did for a living.

"I don't know," Maura said. "You can't plan these things."

"That's because they don't happen except once in a million years. What happens is people grow old and ugly and die," Wilson said. "Or they just die period."

"Wilson, shut up," Berry said.

"I guess you read that somewhere," Maura said. "Or maybe your folks told you. I should ask them when I come over for dinner."

"Both of you, cool it," Berry said.

Wilson bit his lip and looked down. "Please don't," he said.

"Don't what?" Maura said. "Don't ask about your morbid world view, or don't go to dinner with your parents?"

Wilson shrugged.

"Can we change the subject?" Berry asked. "I got a new robe the other day."

"Don't worry," Maura said with a laugh that reminded Berry of Judy mocking Marco. "I can tell you don't want your precious parents meeting me. I'll stay away. From them and from you. I prefer Berry here anyway. At least he's accepted himself. You're a bigger freak than he is, but you keep it under wraps."

Maura got up and stalked out, way speedier than Berry would have expected on her high stilettos. Berry and Wilson watched her go, then sat in silence for a few minutes. "Again with the hella weird," Wilson said at last. "What did she mean, I'm a bigger freak than you?"

"I dunno," Berry said. "Want some hot chocolate?"

8.

The powers at Orlac Junior High chose to have Sex Ed and Career Day on the same day. Because Berry had Career Day in the morning and Sex Ed in the afternoon, he ended up with a Swan's career prospects and the sexual knowledge of a Goose.

Berry settled uneasily in his desk chair, dead center in a classroom full of Swans in khakis and Skechers. Some of the kids had neat little plastic binders marked "Career Goals"—the kids who made a binder for everything, probably even PE. Berry had no binder, nothing to put in a binder. He imagined metal coils clutching air. He thought of Wilson's career plan.

Rat announced the class was lucky to have a professional motivational counselor, Gray Redman, come talk to them. Gray wore Gap just like the kids facing him. He had starch-fed middle-aged features and a neat hairline that started on the top of his skull. Gray Redman didn't give a speech. Instead, he just asked the kids, "How would you like to stay sitting where you are for the rest of your lives? Raise your hands." Nobody raised a hand. "You sure? Those little desk-chair things sure look dope to the max." When Gray Redman tried to talk like a kid, it came out sounding like he'd recorded a sound bite from VH1 and dubbed it over his own voice. "All righty then. Anybody who doesn't want the crappy chair and wack view for the next fifty years needs a career plan."

The kids had to write five adjectives that described their good qualities, five verbs they were good at or enjoyed, and five nouns they hated. Berry stared at his pad nearly the whole time, then wrote five adjectives that jumped into his head from music he'd sung.

That left verbs and nouns. For verbs, Berry wrote, "sing." Then, "chant, descant, process, bathe." For nouns, Berry wrote: "teacher, psychiatrist, bear (he was thinking of the investment bears Marco complained about), testosterone, secrets." He looked up just as Gray spoke again.

"Sweet. So, act like you know. You want a job where they value those five qualities about you. You want to do the things you like. And you want to avoid the things you hate, at all costs. Those fifteen words are your keys to destiny if you know how to read them. Now who wants to read theirs aloud?" Hands rose, except Berry's and a few other kids'. Gray called on Sabine, a girl in a turquoise cashmere sweater, leggings, and a hair-twist.

Sabine breathed in. "Well." She folded her hands in her lap and glanced only briefly at the paper on her desk. "My adjectives were: organized, motivated, playful, creative, and focused. My verbs were: write, draw, power-jog, conceptualize, and empathize. And my nouns: pessimists, dead weights, slackers, phoneys, and bureaucrats." She smiled wide and tight, leaned back.

"Great list, Sabine. You could be a career counselor yourself, and I totally mean that as a compliment. So what are some other jobs Sabine could have?" People offered advertising, creative writing, journalism, court reporting, and some other things.

Hands climbed again. Other Swans recited their fifteen defining terms. Berry sank deeper into his desk-chair. That shyness grabbed Gray Redman's attention. "Why don't we call on someone we haven't heard from yet? How about you there?" He pointed at Berry. "The brown-haired kid in the baggy sweater. What's your name?"

"Berry." It came as a whisper. Already, several Swans giggled. Brandon, an athletic straight-A student, snuck a text message to his friend Todd.

"So Berry. Tell us your five adjectives."

"Um. The first one was 'goodly.'"

The class detonated into laughter. Gray laughed a little too, then waved his hand. "Hey, let's not be mean, here, huh? Goodly. I like that, yo. It's creative and, you know, unusual. I'm not sure if it's a real adjective or what. But it's cool. What else you got?"

Berry's voice, which could fill a cathedral, barely carried. "Uh. Humble. Uh. Fruitful. Contrite. Many-eyed." That last word had come to Berry in a final moment of desperation, from an anthem about cherubim and seraphim dancing in Heaven. By now Gray Redman's half-hearted attempts failed to staunch the laughter hemorrhage.

"Hey," Gray said. Nobody heard. "Hey. Hey. Kids. It's good to be different."

Berry covered his face with his notebook and prayed for Redman to move on to someone else. Berry wasn't sure he believed in God, but at this moment he would have pledged anything if the supreme being would just step in. If God turned the Swans into locusts, Berry would believe forever. Or if Berry had any real faith, at least this pain would be a martyrdom.

Gray seemed determined to finish Berry's "life assessment" before he picked on some other loser. "So hey, what

Charlie Anders

kinds of careers could our special guy aim for with such a great list?"

A voice from the back of the class piped in: "The exciting world of toilet-bowl cleanser."

Gray shouted over the laughter. "Hey, come on. That's not funny, guys. I mean, there are as many exciting careers out there as there are people in this room. How about tech support? Or teaching?" More laughter. Berry had already stood and walked halfway to the door. It was nearly time to turn into a Goose anyway.

Berry hung around the hallway and stared at anti-drug posters for half an hour or so. Their smudgy black-and-white photographs of wan faces gave drugs a fascinating glamour. School made Berry feel as though he'd taken some not very good drugs. He had all the attention-sapping side effects, but without any happy brain fur.

The bell rang. Berry was just about to head for lunch when Gray Redman tapped him on the shoulder. "Hey, kid. I'm really sorry about the career thing. Listen, here's my card. You need any motivational counseling or anything, give me a call, okay?"

Berry nodded. He shoved the card—gray with red letters—into a jeans pocket. "Thanks, I guess. I already know what I want to do, and that's be a choirboy." Berry waited for Gray to laugh at him.

"Are you a choirboy now?" Gray asked instead.

"St. Luke's," Berry said.

"You may not be able to keep doing that forever, and it's hard to feed a family on choirboy wages. But, hey, maybe if you figure out what you like about choirboying, you can look for that in another job."

"I like the radiance." Berry wished people would stop telling him he couldn't do what he did forever. "I don't worry about anything when I sing in church."

Gray smiled and patted Berry on the shoulder.

Berry ate lunch alone. The kids from Swan class watched him and laughed. His fifteen words had obviously become a major topic. Berry had attracted ridicule and sometimes violence before. But this was different. His stomach sank to the root of his still-sore testicles. Berry sensed a turning point.

The other choirboys at Orlac didn't exactly let the choirboy relationships carry over at school. Randy had once stopped a bunch of Geese who were beating Berry—after they'd already bruised a few ribs and knocked the breath out of him, but before they got around to dislodging teeth or cracking fingers—on the grounds that he'd had enough.

That's not to say Berry had no friends in the Geese classroom. He did sometimes chat with Marc from choir, and Zawa, a boy who was deaf in one ear and invented clothing out of paper, cloth, and scrap metal, would pass Berry half-nonsense notes. And some others acted friendly on occasion. Junior High social life seethed with uncertainty. Someone might be friendly one week, neutral the next, and hostile a week after that.

"Hey, how was your career thing?" Marc acted surprisingly friendly. "I found out I could be a food service worker or self-destructive gambler. Randy could be a bus or taxi driver."

"That's great," Berry said. "I wasn't sure what they ended up deciding for me. I think it's a mystery."

"I'm going to be a metal bird," Zawa scribbled on a notebook page.

The adulthood double-whammy of careers and Sex Ed had the Geese acting more like kids, clowning and tussling. Randy used another kid's butt to erase the blackboard, holding him by his belt. Berry found a seat in the magic middle but close to the window.

The other theme of the day seemed to be Teachers' Day Off. Toad introduced two volunteers from the Sex Ed Council, a local non-profit, and practically sprinted for her break room.

A tall, skinny guy in a too-small sports jacket, tie, and jeans talked about diseases, while his colleague, a short, round woman with curly hair, listened. "Insanity, heart problems, brain damage, and death. Sure, gonorrhea is treatable if you catch it in time—just look out for a foul discharge from your opening—but a lot of people don't know if they have it until it's too late. And then there's chlamydia. Chances are somebody in this room will have it in the next few years."

Berry liked diseases and gruesome stories of limbs that rotted off or brains that failed. But the Sex Ed man's disease talk was too boring, it was all pill bottle stuff: side effects and symptoms in dry words. Berry imagined a voice like the stentorian tenor from the start of "Let All Mortal Flesh Keep Silence" by Bairstow intoning that a plague of genital warts came upon the people and they wailed in the depths of despair and the Lord said unto them: "True Love Waits."

The woman was better than the man. For one thing, she was kind of cute—she had Maura's sensuality, but without the live-wire energy. "Abstain doesn't just mean a spot on your stomach," she said. "It's a way of life." Nobody laughed at the "ab stain" pun. She talked for a while about ways to say "no," because you respect yourself too much, or because virginity is not just the potential for something else, but a promise in itself.

The last bell approached and Berry heard laughter in the halls, the machinery of clean young violence clattering to life. Berry felt needles stab his gut. He suddenly knew he wouldn't get away from school without serious beating. What if Brandon and some other Swans just wanted to crack some of his ribs, but then they found his breasts? What if his pills fell out of his backpack? Berry pictured his neck snapping against Brandon's quarterback knee.

He jumped up before the last bell even sounded and ran for the exit. Berry ran a few blocks until he felt he'd out-paced anybody who wanted to kick fifteen kinds of shit out of him. Then he headed for the cathedral. If Randy and Marc ever heard of Berry's big moment, they'd already forgotten about it by the time rehearsal started. They were too busy getting jazzed about that night's sleepover in the Twelve Step room.

Four girls turned up for the sleepover, but no Lisa. Rebecca and Jee both had been at the True Love Waits gathering. They gave Berry warm head-tosses when they arrived at the pizza joint where the gang had agreed to gather. Berry knew Julie from Choir Camp, but didn't know the fourth girl, Betty, at all. All the girls wore little backless blouses tied with strings in back, petal skirts, and platforms.

Berry studied the girls for clues. Mr. Allen and the older choirboys drilled the younger boys endlessly on how to walk, sit, and stand. How to look skyward and keep up with your music. The right facial expression. How to kneel or take communion. But Berry couldn't see any such choreography in the girls' movements. One moment they'd belch and giggle like guys, the next they'd strike exaggerated poses, legs just so, chins tilted, eyes a little wide. It was like Rebecca and pals kept forgetting to give a performance.

"You would have gotten a lot more girls," Jee crunched garlic bread and scattered crumbs on her wavy rainbow stockings, "if you'd done this anywhere but that Twelve Step room. It smells down there. I don't think they cleaned the carpet after that drunk guy threw up on the facilitator."

"We won't sit on the carpet," Teddy said.

"None of us had a house cool enough to host something like this," said Wilson. "And we wanted to have it at the church. It's central and people could tell their parents they were going to a church thing without lying so much."

"My mom nearly called the church to find out more about this thing," said Rebecca. "I had to tell her it was being organized by some people from Omaha who were on the road doing youth events and the cathedral wouldn't know about it."

"Omaha?" said Teddy.

"Hey, bullshit pump not primed."

"As long as that creepy Canon or that weird Verger don't show up or something," said Jee.

"The Canon's out of town at a conference," said Teddy. "And this is the Verger's night to sneak around the skating rink."

"What is the deal with Canon Moosehead anyway?" asked Julie, the non-choirgirl. She had a big hairband, frizzy dark hair, and cat glasses.

"Julie and I bailed from his True Love Waits thing when it turned into True Love Drools," Betty added.

"He's been under a lot of pressure," said Randy. Teddy snorted behind his hand.

"I heard he puts this metal clamp on his . . . thing to keep it from getting hard," said Marc. "I heard it has spikes and stuff so it hurts if he starts."

"Dude, that is so gross," said Julie.

"Cock spikes," said Marc. "I kid you not."

"A crown of thorns," said Teddy in between snorts.

"Poor guy," Berry mumbled. "I mean, he didn't ask to have his thing start acting up." Everybody ignored him.

Finally the cathedral and its offices were dead enough to let the six boys and four girls sneak back in. Randy produced copies of the Verger's "borrowed" keys. They went back across the street and down to the dark hallway under the cathedral offices. Nobody could see more than a few feet past the bottom of the stairs. "Fuck," said Randy. "Where's the light switch?" Marc stumbled over a huge crucifix.

"Find candles," Teddy said.

They stumbled for a while. Berry stepped on someone's foot. A girl's, judging from the high "eep" that followed. Berry thought he heard a rat. One of the boys started singing some hymn about being in the dark and going astray. Teddy shut up whoever it was.

"What if we're trapped down here in the dark? Anybody got a cell phone?" one of the girls asked.

"I can get us out again," said Randy.

Finally, Marc lit a giant candle. "We've got a couple of them," he said. "It'll be cool to do this by candlelight anyway. That way you won't even see the stains."

Randy found the right key to let them all into the Twelve Step room after some trial and error. He left them with one candle and took the other one in search of the Bishop's punch. Teddy found a censer and some incense among all the random stuff in the hallway. He loaded up the canister with incense and swung it around until smoke flowed around the room and the candlelight streamed between its fingers. The smoke and candles made cool patterns on the wall.

"Great," said Jee. "Now it smells like perfumey smoke in here."

"It's romantic," Teddy said.

"I guess," said Rebecca, "in a Satan's armpit way."

Randy rolled in a big barrel. "I think this is it," he said. He opened a big stopper in the top and poured some of the contents into an empty three-liter Coke bottle.

"Careful," Teddy said. "Like we really want to leave the Twelve Step room smelling of punch."

The punch smelled sort of vinegary, but Berry still took a big swig. He wondered if the punch's secret ingredient was actually communion wine that had been left out too long. Mixed with extra fruit juice and/or water, it might have been drinkable. Maybe. "Gross," said Becca.

"Good for your small intestine," said Teddy.

A second empty Coke bottle showed up for the traditional spin-the-bottle game. Every lurch of the bottle made Berry jumpy. He was terrified the bottle would point at him, but also that it wouldn't and he'd be left out.

Apart from "no gay stuff," whoever spun had to kiss whomever the bottle pointed to. Then the recipient had to spin. Teddy kissed Becca. Becca kissed Wilson (who looked flustered). Wilson kissed Julie. Julie kissed Randy and then the bottle rolled to a stop facing a pair of huge, shredded Reeboks that belonged to no teen.

"Can I join in?" asked a tobacco-wrecked woman's voice.

Randy grabbed a candle and held it up. Marge, one of the homeless people who hung around the cathedral for the Hungry Souls and other services, had joined the circle. The candle light made the many lines on her face look infinitely deep. Even in an incense cloud, she smelled of sweat. Marc, whose parents knew Marge, hid his face in the shadows.

"What are you doing here?" Randy demanded.

"Sacking out. Or I was until you guys made all this noise. What are you guys doing here?"

"What does it look like?"

"Hmm. Judging from the bottle and all the lipstick on the boys' faces, I'd say Yahtzee. Or Monopoly. Speaking of which, aren't you girls young for lipstick?"

"Oh, fashion tips from a bag lady," sniffed Julie.

"I heard *Skank* magazine needed a new columnist," said Jee.

"Hey," said Marge. "You think I wasn't a teeny bopper sneaking into the church after dark once? You think I was always old and trashed and sleeping outside?"

"Like I've given your life story so much thought," said Jee.

"Look," said Randy. "Neither of us is supposed to be here. So why don't we just leave each other alone, and we won't tell if you won't?"

"Fair enough," said Marge. "But if I were you guys, I'd move on from spin the bottle. Gets old fast, won't get you into anyone's pants. You run through all the combinations pretty quick. Now Truth Or Dare, that's a player's game."

"Thanks for sharing," said Teddy.

"Trick is, make the questions really personal and unpleasant—nothing about menstruation, mind—and the dares deceptively easy at first, then raunchier and raunchier. You'll have 'em down to bra and panties in an hour, sucking twinkies in two. Of course, you got all night, right?"

"Thanks. See ya," said Teddy.

"We'll try not to disturb your rest any more," said Wilson.

After Marge finally ambled off, the ten kids sat around the candles in silence. Berry felt the punch eat his stomach and the incense jerk his gag reflex.

"So," said Teddy. "Wanna play another game?"

Jee had a cell phone in her hand. "How much do you think a cab would be from here?"

"I'm in," said Julie. "I got ten bucks."

"Who wants punch?" Teddy asked desperately.

Nobody wanted punch. Within fifteen minutes, the girls had a cab. The boys sat a spell, watching the candles burn down. Then Randy stood. "I'll put the punch back. Get this mess cleaned up, nobody'll know we were here. With luck, we'll catch the last bus." Berry and Wilson were the last to stand up.

"Sorry it didn't pan out," said Berry.

"Hey," said Wilson. "I got to kiss two girls." He gave Berry a hand up.

9.

The wind baited Berry. It found every path into his robes
and chilled his head. His cassock and surplice barely protected him. He hadn't had time to grab his blazer from the
choir room. The further he got from St. Luke's, the dumber
he felt in his robes. People eating burgers or pumping gas
kept turning to watch him tread the sidewalk. When Berry
tried to walk the way a choirboy should, Maura or Lisa
pulled his sleeve to speed him up.

Maura and Lisa flanked Berry and swung their outer
arms. A lily scent came from one or both of them. Berry felt
escorted, mostly in a good way. Sunlight brightened Lisa's
muslin dress and turned it transparent. Lisa looked like a
twenties Parisian girl whose picture Berry had masturbated
over, even down to the pointy shoes and round hat. Maura
wore a black cleavage gown and kept talking about going
on an adventure.

"I want to go back and change," Berry said again.

"You'll fit right in where we're going," Maura said.

"I don't look like someone who should be where we are."

Berry looked straight ahead, only partly to avoid seeing
the stares. Lisa kept smiling up at him. He didn't know what
kind of look to give her back.

Lisa chattered about her weekend—she'd gone to a glassblowing shop where actors in historical costumes formed
vases and bottles from goo—and the day's service, especial-

ly the crimson stain Berry had left on Canon Moosehead's crotch. Berry fidgeted whenever the communion wine spill came up. Berry's clumsiness had made him a minor hero to the other choirboys.

"You should have seen the look on his face," Lisa said.

"It was an accident," Berry said for the millionth time. Then he changed the subject and asked Maura where they were going. Maura had led Lisa and him to one of the neutral parts of the city, one that bordered the "bad" part of town as well as the shopping drag.

"We're going to the Botanical Gardens."

Berry had never heard of any Botanical Gardens in the city. Maura led them down back streets, past ancient houses with windows nippled by the passage of time or artisanship Lisa could barely explain after her visit to the glassblowing place. Passing men in baggy beltless pants and muscle shirts in front of a liquor store, Lisa grabbed Berry's hand. He wasn't sure what to make of the gesture until he remembered her dad drove a Lexus.

Berry was about to ask if he could wander the streets in regalia some other time when they found the gate.

Vines almost covered it, heavy with dust instead of fruit or flowers. A hand-painted balsa sign read: "The Wasteness." The hand-twisted flourishes of the wrought-iron gate sagged with rust. Decay and plant anarchy had eaten the fence too. If this had been a public garden, it had long closed. The air smelled spore-heavy.

"They couldn't decide between 'Wasteland' and 'Wilderness,'" Maura explained, pointing at the sign. "So they compromised."

"Why not 'Wilderland?'" Lisa asked.

"Because that sounds like a real word," Berry guessed.

Beyond the gate, Berry could make out a pebble walkway which dead leaves and grass had almost dispersed. Tags on sticks proclaimed places along the path to be the territories of orchids or rare African blooms, but bracken and wild roses swarmed. On the left, dandelions had made a kingdom where a herb garden had sheltered.

"It's amazing," Lisa said. "What happened to this place?"

"Whatever the opposite of urban renewal is," said a man in a Bishop's outfit beyond the gate. "Every now and then they fight over whether to turn this place into a parking lot or a mall or another park. But they can't all get behind one plan, so it stays wild. I think it fell apart after Black Monday or Beige Wednesday or some other color-coded financial disaster day."

Berry stared. The man wore a mitre and shining vestments, but not like he'd seen on Bishop Locke or other bishops visiting St. Luke's. For one thing, the V-shaped overhanging part of the robe was bright lavender. For another, a UV neon light bulb glowed inside the mitre. Even at noon, the effect said raver. Then there was the curling mustache and goatee.

"Berry, Lisa," said Maura. "This is Bishop Bacchus." She gestured at Berry. "We just came from church."

"Seems we have a lot in common," said the pseudo-bishop, "being men of the cloth." He yanked a chain off the gate and swung it open.

"The difference is I'm a real choirboy," said Berry.

"Hey, I'm a real bishop. Got my ordination papers from the Church of Ungainly Joy," said Bishop Bacchus.

"How many members does that church have?" Lisa asked.

"A handful," said the Bishop. "But we're really sincere."

The Bishop led Berry, Maura, and Lisa along overgrown paths. Weeds and the hardiest flowers had called a truce and colonized. At one point, Berry and the others had to climb over a bonsai tree that had gone lopsided; a massive elephant trunk blocked the path while its other side remained delicate. They came to a Japanese-style bridge over a stream steeped with algae.

"Friends and flock," the Bishop said. "I bring newcomers!"

Twenty people clustered around the bridge. Many of them wore costumes. A few men wore women's clothes, including one bearded guy with pigtails and a calico dress. Others wore tie-dyes or turtlenecks. Bottles of champagne and weirdly shaped water pipes littered the bridge ends. Berry immediately looked at Lisa to see if she was okay. She nodded at Berry and smiled, she was pocketing some fear but it was fine for now. She was still holding his hand.

"These are some of my friends," Maura told Berry.

Here, Berry stood out less than on the street, but felt further from the people around him than ever.

Someone handed Berry a basket covered with linen. Inside he found muffins, fruit buns, and pies. "Brunch," a pixie in a leotard explained. Berry took a muffin and handed the basket to Lisa.

"My dad doesn't know where I am," Lisa said as if it had just occurred to her.

"Is that a problem?" Maura said. "I'm sure someone has a cell phone."

Lisa shivered. "Nah. I guess it's okay."

Berry and Lisa munched buns and looked down into green-and-white swirly water. "People are weird," Berry said. A middle-aged woman in a big fairy skirt approached the two of them and smiled. She wore heavy make-up around her eyes and big red circles on her cheeks. "Hi," she said. "I'm Anna Conventional. Welcome to our weed party. We're all weeds here, one way or another." She turned to Berry. "I love your costume."

Berry decided not to bother telling her it wasn't a costume. "Thanks," he said instead. "How often do you guys do this?"

"Once every couple months. But there are often fun little gatherings of some sort on Sundays. Us nonconformists gotta stick together, you know."

Berry wasn't sure whether he saw nonconformists or just conformists in costumes. "Can you tell me five verbs you hate?" he asked Anna Conventional. She thought about it.

Berry and Lisa watched a man in a white jumpsuit teaching Scottish country line dancing to a woman in a sari. Some other costumed people were doing some kind of Pagan ritual. Berry wondered what had happened to Maura. "I'm glad we got to hang out," Berry said tentatively. "It's nice just the two of us."

Lisa took both Berry's hands and kissed him lightly on the lips.

The kiss felt like the first time Berry filled his eyes and nose with sound and breath. It felt like that sweet spot choirboys struggle to reach. He had a sudden rush of energy to his diaphragm. You stagger your breaths, so nobody ever hears you breathe, the music just comes from nowhere, like this did. He thought: *So that's what they're all so excited about.* "They" meant the choirboys Berry's age and a little younger, with their porn stashes and jokes.

Berry hadn't felt this way after kissing Wilson. It had been too rough and Wilson had acted weird before and after. The kiss with Lisa felt romantic, even though Berry didn't know what romance was supposed to feel like.

Charlie Anders

"Uh," Berry said. "I'm not sure . . ." He had a million things to say and no way to say any of them. Was he Lisa's boyfriend now? Were they supposed to have sex right away? Or soon? What would the popular people who hung out with Lisa at school and sometimes at church say about Berry? Never mind what Lisa would think about having a boyfriend with a swelling chest.

"Don't worry." Lisa smiled. "We're still just friends and everything. I like you a lot, that's all."

Now Berry was really confused.

They stood on the bridge and held hands for a while. The air cooled and the plant smells deadened. "I hope my dad's not worrying," Lisa said. "He's totally rationalist but he freaks easy."

"He's not religious?" Berry said.

"Nah. He lets my mom drag me to church and stuff. In return, she goes along with his ideas about how to bring me up."

Berry remembered the French guy. "Underwater therapy?" He tried to make it sound light and friendly.

Lisa nodded. "We have a swimming pool."

Berry guessed it would be dark around five or five thirty, and it was probably already four. "Where has Maura gone?" he asked the river scum underfoot. He looked around and saw fewer people than before. Anna Conventional walked through a semi-clearing near the bridge. Berry waved at her. "Hey."

"Dictate, mutate, criticize, betray, befoul." Anna Conventional saw the blankness in Berry's eyes. "My five verbs I hate," she explained.

"Oh, okay," Berry said, uneasy. "Have you seen Maura? She was wearing the black dress with the sequins on it."

"Not lately," Anna Conventional said. "A bunch of those guys went into Darkest Arboretum to do some mushrooms an hour or two ago. They could be wherever by now." Anna laughed and pirouetted so her skirt billowed.

Lisa suddenly looked terrified. "I really gotta get home."

"Maybe I could give you a ride," Anna Conventional said.

Berry expected Anna to drive a beat-up old Bug or Pacer, two cars Wilson often laughed at. Instead she had a gleaming Mercedes van. Anna Conventional put Berry and Lisa in the back and then went to find her boyfriend Robbie. This took a while. Berry and Lisa sat in the back separated by a big empty space where a third person could sit. They held hands in silence.

"Don't worry," Berry said. "I'm sure your dad won't mind. Just tell them you had a church event to go to. Anyway, you'll be home before dark."

Lisa nodded. "What about your folks?"

Berry shrugged. "They go through phases. Sometimes they worry about me. But right now, they're on the we-have-no-son trip. It makes getting around easier."

"I'm sorry," Lisa said.

"Don't be. They're mostly cool, and it's not that they don't care. My mom works really hard and my dad does . . . stuff."

More time passed. Eventually Anna showed up with Robbie, who had a long brown ponytail and white-flecked stubble. He wore a Dear Abbie Hoffman T-shirt. "So where do you live?" Anna asked. Lisa told her a neighborhood way outside the city loop. Berry started to feel hungry. He'd only eaten a few rolls, and that had been a while ago.

"We'll have you home in a jiff," Anna promised. A while later she announced she had to stop for gas. They found a Circle K with pumps. While Robbie pumped, Anna took

Lisa and Berry inside the shop and bought them gumballs. "Which do you think is the prettiest color?" she asked, holding a bunch in her hand. She started juggling the balls and dropped a couple on the floor. "Three second rule," she said, scooping them and putting them back in her plastic bag. Then Robbie wanted a hot dog. He had to microwave it because no one wants a tepid convenience store Oscar Mayer. Berry got a hot dog too and shared it with Lisa, but didn't microwave it.

Finally they got away from the Circle K, Anna wearing a big straw hat she'd bought and brandishing a CD of "Trucker Gold" from the store's bargain rack. Robbie didn't want to listen to Anna's new CD and the two grown-ups argued while Lisa and Berry huddled behind them, a girl in a brandy-brocade muslin dress and a choirboy.

Anna screamed at Robbie, then pulled over in someone's driveway. "Why don't you respect me? You resent me because my portfolio is still worth something because I stuck with blue chips because I didn't get carried away thinking a Jeff Bezos shat money because I'm not an unemployed Web designer with a tweaker's attention span because you've never dealt with your childhood fear of being taken serious-ly." There were a few more "becauses" in that sentence. Berry mentally charted the sentence structure the way Rat had taught him. It was all subordinate clauses.

It was fully dark. Lisa and Berry hugged. Lisa put her head on Berry's shoulder. Berry stroked her hair. It felt like the velvet knee cushions at St. Luke's.

Finally Anna and Robbie made up and Robbie confessed about his stock portfolio and his fear of being taken serious-ly, and said he'd try to pay more attention to Anna and buy a no-load long-term-oriented mutual fund. They pulled out of the driveway and set off again. Robbie needed to buy flowers to make up to Anna.

By the time Berry and Lisa got to Lisa's house the dash clock read 7:52. Berry walked Lisa up the flint path to her two-story house, which had trimmed hedges all around it and a big wreath on the door. They hesitated at the door, then Lisa used her key.

She hadn't turned it in the lock before the door opened from the inside. A lanky man with boxy glasses and a shirt buttoned all the way up with no tie looked down at the two intruders. "Lisa," he said. "Do you know what time it is?"

"I had church stuff," Lisa said. "I . . ."

"Church ended hours ago. I called. Nobody knew where you were." The man's Adam's apple throbbed, but his voice stayed even. "Lisa, it appears someone has thought with her aquatic brain again. Child development, like evolution, contains many throwbacks and dead ends." He gripped Lisa's arm.

"Please don't," Lisa said. "I'm too old for that. I—"

"Leave her alone." Berry stepped forward and placed his big purple sleeve between Lisa and her father. "It's my fault Lisa's late."

Lisa's dad looked down at Berry. "And who is this?" he asked Lisa. He smelled smoky. He wore flannel pants and a horseshoe belt buckle.

"This is Berry," Lisa said. "He's from the church choir. He got me home."

"You were supposed to take the bus," Mr. Gartner said.

"I'm very sorry," Lisa said.

"The pool should be warm," said her dad. "We'll talk once the reptile has tasted its element."

"Leave her alone," Berry said again.

The man grabbed Berry's collar frill and pulled hard enough to choke. Mr. Gartner lifted Berry off his feet. "Get out of my house," he said. Then he stepped onto the stoop and threw Berry onto the lawn. Berry landed on his back and his breath rushed away.

Berry relaxed his chest to let air flow back in. It took a while. The door to Lisa's house closed.

Anna Conventional and Robbie were gone. Maybe they hadn't understood that Berry also needed to get home. Or maybe they hadn't cared.

Berry shivered. The freezing day rolled over him like the sludgy river, and only his robes kept him a little warm. The darkness doubled his stranded status and the night sky and satellite dishes all around proclaimed the wrongness of his being here in these vestments. He might never see the city again. Hopelessness kept him down longer than breathlessness had. Maybe if he stayed flat on his back long enough, the lawn would swallow him, robes and all.

Finally Berry sat up and resolved to make sure Lisa was okay. He walked around the back of the Gartners' house until he found an outdoor swimming pool set among flower beds, hedges, and porcelain statues. The pool had a flat plastic dome over it. At its highest point in the middle of the pool, the dome only reached about a foot above water level. Berry couldn't see through the dome. He worried Mr. Gartner could see him from the house. All of its lights seemed to be on, including a big porch light over a glass door. Behind the door, Berry could see a yellow kitchen with bookshelves and racks holding pans, mugs, and implements.

Berry crawled, getting more stains on his white surplice. He tried to find a handle on the plastic dome. He couldn't see anything. He pushed on the dome but it didn't move. "Lisa," he whispered. "Are you there?" He heard nothing.

He crawled through some rose bushes to the other side of the dome. He added dirt to his grassy cassock and pricked his fingers. Finally, at the deep end of the pool, Berry found a handle with a clasp on it. It only opened from the outside, but had no padlock. Berry slid the bolt out of its rings. Then he could raise the dome, which creaked. He managed to lift it a foot, but wasn't sure what to do then. It seemed to be on hinges. It probably flipped over onto its side. Berry found a cinderblock to hold the dome ajar. He could just stick his head and one arm inside. He touched the water. At least the pool felt warm enough. He couldn't see inside. "Lisa?" he whispered again.

"Berry?" Splashing. The sounds came closer. Berry saw Lisa tread water at the deep end of the pool. "What are you doing here?" Lisa still wore her prim muslin dress. It fanned into jagged wings around her waist. Her hair threaded the surface. The water covered everything but her face. She could barely tread water and talk.

"I wanted to make sure you were okay," Berry said.

"I'm fine." Lisa swallowed water and coughed. "Please go." She coughed some more. "If my dad finds you here . . . he'll kill us both."

Berry tried to argue, but it just sparked more coughing. He waited until Lisa said she'd reached the center of the pool, then pulled out the cinderblock. He lowered the dome slowly and resealed the bolt. The dome would barely let Lisa get her head above water. He wondered how Lisa, as a little girl, had managed to tread water in the pool's center, which must be too deep for a smaller girl.

The driveway to the Gartners' house led to a small court, which led in turn to a street with sparse houses and big lawns. Berry walked and tried to remember how Anna Conventional had driven there. The endless cross-hatching of driveways made Berry feel tiny. He had to find a phone, call home, and hope Marco or Judy answered. They'd probably have another 'sode, but at least they'd rescue him.

Lisa's dad had mentioned a bus, but Berry wasn't sure where to catch it or whether it ran this late.

Berry walked along the suburban road. Everything blurred into boxes and lawns. Berry could tell one block of his neighborhood from another in his sleep, but here he could hardly tell when a block ended and another started. Berry hadn't seen any cars in ages. Finally, Berry reached a junction with a big street where a few cars passed. Berry turned right and walked a while. He wondered if Lisa was out of the pool yet.

Berry felt he could barely keep walking. He tried to think marching thoughts like a soldier, but all that came to mind were the Pickled Boys in jars behind a wall. For all Berry knew, his costume would attract Satan-worshippers to slice him up.

He reached a gas station/convenience store like the Circle K he'd visited with Lisa and Anna Conventional, it seemed years ago. The clerk stared at the muddy, grassy robe and kept one hand under the counter. "I just need a payphone," Berry almost sobbed. The clerk jerked a hand at the corner of the store. The payphone hid between racks bearing condoms, lip balm, and greeting cards for every occasion except all the ones Berry had lived through recently.

Berry had almost no money in his pockets. Maybe he'd left it in his choir blazer, hanging in his locker back at the St.

Luke's rehearsal room. He realized he'd also missed a dose of his pills. But he found a few coins in one pocket's lint ball. He popped two of them into the phone and dialed home. It rang a long time. Eventually Berry heard Judy's voice on tape: "You've reached the answering machine of Marco and Judy. Friends and clients can leave a message after the tone." The message sounded normal enough except for a low cackling, probably Marco's, throughout. Just as Judy said the word "tone," Marco said "ow" loudly and Judy put an extra emphasis on that last word, either to cover Marco's pain or to emphasize whatever she was doing to him. Berry left a short message saying he'd lost his friends and gotten stuck in the suburbs.

After Berry hung up, he realized he should have kept talking for a while. If Marco was at home but not answering the phone, he might have heard Berry and picked up. Berry looked through his change, but didn't have enough to call home again. He sat on the floor of the convenience store, at eye level with a clump of gum and Fritos in the aisle leading to porn. Berry stared at that clump. He studied its contours as if it were a clue or a city. Berry heard a sound and realized the clerk stood behind him looking down. Berry stood up unsurely, the way homeless people at the cathedral often did. He felt his legs melt like swizzle sticks in cocoa. "I'm just thinking who to call," Berry said.

"You want to think outside?" The clerk wasn't much older than Berry, but he had a mustache and attitude. Past his best-before date, like everything else in this mart.

"It's okay," Berry said quickly. "I've figured out who to call." As if he had a million options. He dialed the operator and asked to place a collect call to Wilson Fennimore. What was Wilson's dad's name? Berry thought for a moment.

Charlie Anders

"George Fennimore," he said. "Collect call to George Fennimore." The clerk watched suspiciously. This was the kind of collect call where the caller gets a chance to speak for fifteen seconds before the recipient chooses whether to accept. When his chance came, Berry blurted: "I'm Berry, a friend of Wilson's. I need some help. I'm in your neighborhood." Mr. Fennimore accepted and Berry explained a little more. "I got separated from the others in my church group and I think each van driver thought I was in the other van." Mr. Fennimore asked where Berry was. Berry asked the clerk, who gave the information like a death threat. "It's not far," said Wilson's dad. "I'll be there in a few minutes."

Berry dreaded seeing Mr. Fennimore. He'd only met Wilson's folks once or twice. But Wilson had always described his dad as a scary drunk and angry poet wannabe. Wilson's mom just sounded violently disappointed.

Mr. Fennimore surprised Berry. He wandered into the convenience store in a T-shirt and jeans, big smile between shy hairline and weak chin. "Berry," Mr. Fennimore said in a casual tone, "you're looking very ecclesiastical today. This must be the longest recessional hymn you've ever had." He swatted Berry on the shoulder and led him to a VW Rabbit.

In the car, Mr. Fennimore wanted to talk to Berry all about the relative merits of Palestrina and Gibbons. Mr. Fennimore talked for about ten minutes about passion and sinew, infrastructure and melody. Finally, Berry said in a dry-bone voice, "Gibbons rules. Palestrina sucks."

"Oh. What about R. Vaughn Williams?"

"Sucks."

"Stanford?"

"Rocks."

"I see." Mr. Fennimore was actually quiet for a moment. "You know, I wish Wilson was more like you. I sent him to that choir to learn about music and all he ever talks about is cars. He's never once expressed a musical opinion."

Berry wasn't sure if he was supposed to defend Wilson or agree his friend was an assbag. He thought it must blow to worship cars and have a dad who drives a Rabbit. Berry couldn't remember being so tired.

Wilson's house was way less nice than Lisa's, and on the inside it smelled of damp animal. Every surface held books, including the sofa and the kitchen counters. Mr. Fennimore barely shut the door before he grabbed a bottle of whiskey and poured a drink. "Would you like anything? Food, juice, a copy of my book of poetry, self-published but acclaimed?"

Berry was about to say no thanks, but then he remembered he hadn't eaten since that half hot dog hours ago, so he made himself a sandwich. He ate it in seconds, then waited for Mr. Fennimore to finish his whiskey. At last, Wilson's dad handed Berry a sleeping bag and led him upstairs to a door with a poster of two robots fighting and a banner that said "Nerd Free Zone."

"Wilson," Mr. Fennimore said, knocking. "You've got a visitor."

"Huh?"

Wilson didn't get out of bed or open both eyes. Berry got out of his trashed robes, then stripped down to his briefs and climbed into the sleeping bag. It smelled pessimistic. "Hey. So what happened to you today? I didn't see you after church."

Berry started in on the whole long story, but exhaustion wrong-tracked the details. He wasn't sure how much to tell about Lisa's dad and the swimming pool, and anyway,

Charlie Anders

by the time he reached that part he'd gone over to rambling. "And her dad was like, psycho killer qu'est que c'est, and I had to leave and by the time we'd had our scene the car was gone . . ." Berry realized Wilson hadn't heard anything he'd said.

"You kissed Lisa?" Wilson sat up in bed, both eyes open at last and mouth cocked.

"Well, sort of. Really she kissed me. But it was more a sort of friendly how-ya-doin' kind of kiss. More like the chocolate than that heavy metal band."

"It was as good as chocolate!"

"No. Yes. Sort of. I thought you didn't like Lisa any more."

"You have no idea how long I've lusted after her."

"What about Maura?"

"What about her? She's a loser. That whole lizard millionaire thing was just the end."

"Anyway, you don't have to worry about me and Lisa."

"I know I don't, because I'm going to tell her you've got Pam Anderson jugs." Wilson's voice sounded like his dad's, but way rougher.

"Aw no. You promised. You said you wouldn't tell anyone." Wilson didn't reply. "Besides, she'll never like you if you go spreading dirt about other people."

"Maybe you're right. We'll see. Anyway I gotta get my sleep. My dad wants me to raise my grades and I've got three tests tomorrow."

Berry lay in the sleeping bag and shut his eyes, but he couldn't sleep. His body felt meat-packer tired, but his head kept turning over and over. He'd lied to Wilson: that kiss with Lisa had been heavy-metal-band good, not just chocolate good. It had been white greasepaint and black eye makeup, torso sweat and guitar-on-fire good. Not that

Berry listened to seventies metal, but he heard it in Mr. Allen's car. Berry thought about Lisa trapped in her swimming pool, drowning a mythic reptile. He imagined Wilson running around his Quaker day school telling Lisa and whoever else cared that Berry had a chick's upper half. By the time Berry slept, the sunlight animated Wilson's race car curtains and flashed their headlights.

Wilson's dad had to drive into the city for a mid-morning meeting. He dropped Berry off near home. Berry wore his white shirt and gray pants but not his choir tie and ruined robes. He gingerly opened the apartment door and crept to his room. He just wanted a shower and a change of clothes.

"Where have you been? Where were you last night? Why aren't you at school?" Judy wore a tracksuit and headband. She'd obviously taken a day off and stayed home to study or wait for Berry. She held a book about law in one hand. She'd told Berry paralegal school was about the same thing as being a librarian, making connections between subjects and fitting pieces.

"Hi mom. I was at a sleepover. I told Marco. Didn't he tell you?" Judy threw her hands up in the air and made an unoiled door noise. "When does Marco tell me anything?"

"I wanted to get to school, but my ride from the sleepover messed up. This is the first day I've missed since . . . that thing, and anyway I'm pretty wiped."

Berry remembered at the last moment to fold his arms over his breasts, which jabbed under his white shirt.

Judy didn't seem to notice. "You're going to school now. I'll drive you."

"'Kay. Just give me five minutes to change."

Judy nodded. "Five minutes."

In the car, Berry asked "So what's going on with you and dad? I haven't seen you home lately. And he's acted stranger than usual."

Sigh. Click lip against teeth. "I've been taking a break. Studying hard. Staying with a friend." Jingle keys in ignition. "I'm sorry I haven't been around for you, Berry. I care about you. I love you a lot. I'll try and do better."

"No problem," Berry said. He glanced at the dash clock and realized he was late enough to miss Swan time and go straight to Goose. "Just keep learning what you're learning." It sounded wise in Berry's head but dumb when he said it.

10.

Say you listened to religious music sung in another language or without voices, and you didn't think of God. Say you decided Mozart's "Ave Verum Corpus" expressed lust or racism. Who knows what Mozart thought of when he wrote it. He may have been thinking about his cable bill, or how he wished he'd composed last month instead of playing Xbox, and then he wouldn't have all these deadlines.

Berry asked Mr. Allen about this before Wednesday's rehearsal, while the other choirboys practiced knife-throwing in the Twelve Step room. "It depends—on whether you think of music as signal or carrier," said Mr. Allen.

"Huh?" said Berry.

"I mean, does music convey something? Or is it enough for music to convey itself? Maybe there isn't any information or ideas in music—like emotion or whatever—there's just patterns and relationships between notes."

Berry liked talking to Mr. Allen about this stuff even when Mr. Allen didn't make sense. "But if music doesn't have to say anything besides its own stuff, how does that make it Goddy or whatever?"

"Goddy?"

"Goddish. About God."

"Maybe the listeners make it Goddish. If nobody in the choir does anything to make them think of something else."

In the rehearsal, Mr. Allen started the boys on stuff for the upcoming fall concert, some Gabriel Faure, some Britten, some Harold Darke. Berry noticed Teddy looking at him weirdly, then Randy gave Berry a thumbs up.

"Heard you got a girlfriend," Teddy whispered between canticles. "Heard you and Lisa got to third base."

Berry wasn't sure which base was which. But he was pretty sure he hadn't gotten to any bases with Lisa. He started to say so, but then it was too late and Berry realized a denial would just make things worse.

Halfway through Bruckner's "Locus Iste," Berry felt something land on his head. He knew without looking up it was the Mack Hat, at a player's angle. The other boys had never let Berry wear the Mack Hat before. Berry sang "inestimabile sacramentum," this place is inexpressibly sacred. Voices crested over a place of hushed grandeur and the Mack Hat quivered with Berry's passion for Bruckner's sacred and maybe meaningless awe.

Break time came. "The Mack Hat," Randy said. "Wear it well, my son. For you are a man." The Mack Hat bristled with fine green and brown herringbone. A feather, mostly a bare spine, stuck out from its silk brim. The boys had found it in the closet near the Twelve Step room.

"Thanks," Berry said. "I don't know, I mean Lisa and I aren't necessarily a thing . . ."

"Understood," said Teddy. "You get some, you get gone."

Berry nodded. The Mack Hat nearly fell over his eyes.

"Just make sure you break the third base barrier before you hopalong Cassidy your way out of there," Teddy added. "Get you some home runs under your belt."

"Home runs," Berry said. "Got it." He saw rage in Wilson's eyes from across the room. Berry was relieved when rehearsal started again. Between Randy's tips on female orgasm and Teddy's urging him to go all the way, Berry couldn't take the stress.

Berry wondered as he sang who'd told the boys about his kiss with Lisa. It could only have been Wilson or Lisa, and Wilson seemed too jealous to mention it. The idea of Lisa going around telling people, at school or at the girls' choir, about the kiss freaked him out. What did Lisa think was going on?

Whatever. It was obvious Berry should avoid Lisa for a while.

"Berry?" Lisa stood at the door to the choir room as rehearsal ended and the boys walked out. "I wanted to talk to you. I told my dad I had a church thing. He's picking me up in an hour." Lisa wore a scarf, sweater and long denim skirt. Her face glowed pink like a newborn gerbil.

Several choirboys punched Berry on the shoulder or high-fived him. "What's their problem?" Lisa asked.

"Uh, nothing. Come with me." Berry wanted some privacy for his hour with Lisa. At least he'd lost the hat. He led her down the dark, shit-and sperm-sprayed alley next to the cathedral office building, then through a little window that the Verger never locked. On the other side, a small office nestled below ground level. "We can talk in here."

The room had a big sofa and a ton of books with titles like *Blow Off Divorce* or *Peter Pan's Concrete Overshoes.* A carpet covered half the floor with gullies and whorls of fraying weave.

"Why were the choirboys acting weird?" Lisa asked.

"They heard somewhere you're my girlfriend."

"Huh." Lisa's eyes and lips seemed too much lushness in one place, like the rare blooms of the Wasteness growing into gorgeous turf wars.

"Mr. Allen says music doesn't have to mean anything, that it can be signal and not carrier," Berry said to fill the silence.

"I'm sorry things were weird the other day. Sometimes my dad's like a Teletubby with a busted vacuum tube. Actually, he's okay most of the time, when he's not tripping on rebel brain iguanas and stuff."

"It's cool."

"But thanks for trying to help."

Berry lowered his head.

"I really like you," Lisa said. "You're not like the other boys I know. You're sweet and smart and don't smell like a cheesesteak."

"I'm kind of unusual," Berry said.

"I figured," Lisa said.

"I mean really unusual. Look, I gotta show you something. Wilson's going to tell you about it anyway."

"Is that the only reason you're showing me? Because of Wilson?"

"No." Berry thought a moment. "But I might have waited longer otherwise." Then before he could lose his nerve Berry tugged up his sweater and then his T-shirt. Berry made sure the curtains covered the window and the door was locked, then unwound the Ace bandages under his armpits. He didn't look at Lisa until he was done. Then he watched her face. Her eyes widened like a spill.

"Oh shit. Holy fucking shit." She stared for a while. "Are those real?" Berry nodded. "God, that's weird. I mean, you're a boy, right? From the waist down."

Berry nodded again.

"Oh man!" Lisa bent until her eyes almost grazed his chest. Berry shivered. His nipples felt raw from the draft and Lisa's gaze.

"Fuck me," Lisa said loudly. "Yours are bigger than mine."

"Really?" Berry said, almost proud. "Can I see?"

Lisa unwound the scarf from her neck. Berry held his breath. His head buzzed by the time Lisa pulled her blouse up and off and worked on her bra. Berry let out his breath as the bra fell to the exposed cement floor.

"Wow," Berry said. "Can I touch them?"

"If I can touch yours."

Berry's breasts really did dwarf Lisa's a little. But hers felt nicer. The curve of their undersides made a crevice like a closed elbow. The texture, from sloping top to rib cage, with that fertile seed mid-swell, captivated Berry. Lisa's breasts must have still been developing. Berry probably had a bigger jolt of estrogen in his body than she did.

"Lisa," Berry said. He felt his privates twitch. "I really, really like you too." He ran his hands over her breasts, and she over his. "I hope this doesn't freak you. There's this whole complicated explanation I can't get into now. But all you gotta know is that I haven't become, I mean, I'm not turning into—"

The door opened. Canon Moosehead broached the doorway, nausea in his eyes. He stared at the two topless teens with their hands on each others' breasts. "What in the name of Jesus . . . I mean, Jung! I mean . . . Oh shit." The Canon jumped back into the hallway and slammed the door.

Berry grabbed at his bandages. "We'd better get out of here. Please don't tell anyone about this."

"Okay."

Charlie Anders

"Maybe we could hang out on Saturday. Downtown or something."

"I'll talk to my dad. I'll call you."

Berry had his bandages on and his sweater pulled over his head. Before he even had an arm through a sleeve, he opened the window and pulled a chair over to it. "I'll go first and catch you on the other side."

"Okay."

Berry caught Lisa in the alley but the force of her landing threw him against the church wall. He held her tight and her impact grafted their bodies together. They stayed like that for a moment, holding each other in the alley. Then Lisa looked at her watch. "Shit. My dad's probably here. Don't let him see you. You're not his favorite person."

Berry waited in the alley a few minutes. Then he walked to the alley's mouth and looked around for signs of Lisa's dad. Nothing.

"Yo, way to go." Teddy stood at one side of the alley.

"What do you mean?" Berry looked at the head choirboy and bit his lip. Berry had assumed Wilson would never tell his secret to the choir, especially since then Berry would tell about their kiss.

"Man, I heard everything. She said, 'fuck me,' and then 'man, it's so big.' Canon Moosehead went down there and then ran back upstairs with that look he always has lately."

"We kind of had to leave in a hurry," Berry said. He felt sick at the idea of Teddy and the others anointing him studly for all time.

"No kidding. Fucking in the Canon's office. That's pretty bold. Where you gonna do it next time? On the altar?"

"Naw," Berry said. "Too hard. I like cushions."

"Like that big sofa. Gotcha." Teddy high-fived Berry again.

"Um. Gotta catch my bus."

"Sure thing. See ya."

"Right."

Berry wished Judy hadn't picked this week to make sure he actually went to school. At least he noticed no difference in the Swans' scorn the next day, but the Geese noticed Berry anew. Obviously Randy and Marc had spread around that Berry had a hot girlfriend. People whispered "No way" or "I can't believe it" during class.

At afternoon recess, Guy, a jock in his Goose class, loped up to him. "Berry. They say you're dating a babe. I'm like, she has to be hideously deformed under her clothes. Or secretly a guy. Am I right?"

Berry stared into Guy's turnip face and didn't say anything.

"So what's the deal? She straight? You banging her or what?"

Berry wanted to make a clever answer but had none in his head. Eventually Guy tired of taunting Berry and went away.

Berry sometimes wondered how he'd get through another four years of this. The high school near Berry sounded as terrifying as Orlac Middle, only with more drugs and veteran bullies. Wilson had told Berry he had a better chance of going to an Ivy League college from public high school than Wilson would have from his prep school, because the Ivies have quotas for each private school and only get one or two applicants per public high. "Don't worry," Berry had said, "I won't take your slot."

At day's end, Berry ran for the exit as soon as the bell sounded, but he wasn't quick enough. Guy and a few others intercepted him near the big staircase to the exit. Berry went limp the moment they seized him. They dragged him to the school cafeteria and pitched him into the big can of food waste.

"Maybe we should take a picture to send to his girlfriend," one of them barked.

Berry sat in the can for a few moments until he was sure they'd gone. He then climbed out and went to the boys' locker room, where he cleaned up the best he could.

He had to run to the Benjamin Clinic. In the waiting room he looked around but ignored the neo-Nazi tranny punks. He tried to imagine this place bursting with steam, the bustle of people in coveralls and the sound of machinery eeking every extra inch out of noodles. Covered in cafeteria leavings, Berry tried to feel clean.

Marsha Joyce looked Berry over from scalp to shoes and frowned. Berry worried at first the food trash bugged her. "Tell me about your transition," she said. "I don't see you making much effort."

"What do you mean?"

"You're supposed to be living as your new gender. That's the reason for the hormones, to make it easier for you to pass and wrest acceptance. The changes in your body are a means, not the end in themselves."

"I know that," Berry protested. "I'm doing way better. I've had a bunch of solos lately, and Mr. Allen says I'm using my head voice more than ever."

"We're not doing this to please Mr. Allen. He's just using you. This is about you and who you want to be."

"Yeah, yeah. Right, of course." Berry hunted for news. "I told my girlfriend the truth. I showed her my new self and stuff."

"That's great. How did she take it?"

"She thought it was cool. I think."

"So why bind your breasts?"

Berry looked down. "Oh." He'd forgotten to undo his bandages before the Benjamin Clinic appointment. "I guess I still haven't gotten used to them."

"They're here to stay."

"Sure. I guess, with my parents and all . . ."

"Do you want me to talk to your parents?"

"No. I'll be talking to them. It's just that they're going through a tough time right now. I think they're splitting up."

"That's too bad. But they still deserve to know about you. Their problems are theirs, not yours. Berry, what I see happening here is your body changes but not your life. If that goes on long enough, it becomes progress in the wrong direction. We want to keep you focused."

Berry looked down. "Feels like I'm racing already. But I'll try to move faster."

This was the first time anyone had told Berry his breasts were "here to stay." Like rock'n'roll. Berry had always thought they would shrink like a bump on the head if he stopped the pills.

"Maybe if I let Maura teach me," Berry said to Marsha. "She wants to pimp my ride."

"Sounds like a great leap forward to me. Berry, we used to make people like you live as women, full time, for a year before we'd dole out hormones. It was a punishment to face female life without breasts or body softness. Now we've done away with that. But we still expect you to make an effort."

Berry promised that the next time he showed up at the clinic, they'd see a major change.

Berry hoped to see Maura at the clinic entrance when he left, but for once she wasn't hanging around. He hadn't seen her since she'd left Lisa and him in the weird garden.

Someone had made a pile of cassettes and CDs in the living room of Berry's apartment. Berry vaulted over the soundtrack to Marco's and Judy's relationship. One hand-labeled tape atop the quasi-pyramid read "Love and Nuclear Nonproliferation." Berry felt defeated, as if by the flu.

It hadn't been that long ago that Berry had grasped at magical explanations for his life. He'd believed his dad was a warlock trying to save his mom from a curse, or struggling with a curse of his own. Another month, Marco had seemed a mad scientist growing brilliant snakes in the basement. Marco had talked about scheduling a "drain-snaking." Berry had feared his dad planned to let the creatures loose in the sewers.

Now Berry needed to disappear into mystery more than ever, but he'd lost the ability. He blamed Marsha and Dr. Tamarind, who both asked too many questions.

Berry decided to call Lisa and see how she was doing. He held his breath lest Mr. Gartner pick up. Instead, a woman's voice said, "Hello, Gartner residence."

"Hi, is Lisa here? It's one of her friends from church. No, no. Nothing like that. I'm just in her Bible study group and I had a question."

Berry had guessed right. Mrs. Gartner, the religious one, was back from her trip. "I'm glad to hear she's keeping up with her Bible study. Hold on."

It took a while, but Lisa's voice came. "Hey," Berry said.

"Oh, hey," Lisa said. She sounded drained. "I can't talk right now."

"Okay," Berry said, feeling his legs turn to scaly tentacles. "Is everything okay?"

"Sure. Yeah. Everything's fine." Translation: No, everything's fucked and I can't talk about it.

"Are you creeped out by yesterday? By me?"

"Gee, I dunno," Lisa said with too large cheer. "I guess it's one of those passages that could mean a few things. But hey, we can talk about it more in Bible study on Sunday. Bye now." Her voice turned to noise, then Berry heard a bright chord.

Berry sat on his bed and stared at his choir posters. It was almost eight and he hadn't eaten dinner. No parent seemed to be home. Berry hunted in the fridge and found three dried out chalupas, which he panfried. While he ate, he searched through his stuff and dug up the paper where Maura had written her number. It rang and rang.

Berry dug out his *Choral Fugue State* CD and sang along with the Trinity College Choir on Bach while pondering how to clean his robes by Sunday. He wondered if they'd go in the bathtub, maybe with some of Judy's moisturizing shampoo.

Berry heard a noise in the sitting room/kitchen area when the tub was half full. He rescued his robes and ran out. There stood Marco and Maura. Marco wore a checkered silk shirt, unbuttoned to his waist, jeans, and cowboy boots. Maura wore a pleather mini-skirt and skintight tube top.

"Berry," Marco said. "I'm glad to see you. I've got something to tell you. This," he gestured at Maura, "is your new mother."

Berry stared at his dad and his friend and didn't know what to say. So he threw his shampoo-soaked robe at his dad. Marco didn't react, until the shampoo got in his eyes and they blinked and watered.

"I've never seen this guy before," Maura said. "I was looking for you and he let me in. This is where I dropped you off one time."

"He's my dad," Berry said.

The purple robe covered half Marco's head and ran down his back, sloping over one shoulder. He stood still and then shook himself like a dog. The robe landed on the pile of tapes and CDs. Berry retrieved it.

Maura searched for something nice to say. "He's very Pearl Jam."

"He's usually more .38 Special," Berry admitted

"I wanted to apologize for Sunday. I totally screwed up. That Bishop guy is a dork. They all are in that gang. This one guy started hitting on me. I didn't mean to leave you guys alone so long. Then I heard you got a ride."

"Yeah, sort of. They told me you'd done mushrooms and wandered."

"Only a little."

Maura and Berry sat on the sofa. Marco wandered off to his and Judy's bedroom. They heard some thuds, then silence. "I hope he's okay," said Maura. She looked more exotic than ever on Berry's sofa, a halfling concubine in red.

They didn't talk for a while. Berry didn't trust Maura, but didn't want to be alone with Marco. Finally, Berry mentioned about Lisa and how freaked out she'd acted.

"Maybe she's not ready to think of herself as a lesbian," said Maura.

Berry jumped out of his seat. "A what?"

"I tried to warn you," Maura said. "If you become a girl, then any girl who dates you gets a visa to queerland. There's nothing wrong with it. It's pretty cool."

"Look," Berry said slowly. "I just showed her my chest. I didn't say she had to start calling herself a lez! I think she was pissed because my tits were bigger than hers. She said they were. Maybe I should call back and tell her I'm sure hers'll grow out."

Maura squeezed Berry's arm and didn't let go. "I don't think you should bug Lisa right now. She probably just needs some time to figure stuff out. She's a really smart person."

"But I need to explain—"

"Later." Maura held onto Berry's arm and dragged him back to the couch. "She needs space, girlfriend."

"I'm not your girlfriend!" Berry's raised voice provoked shuddering stumbles from Marco in his bedroom.

"Look, I know it's tough to be doing this so young," Maura said. "But you've got a great head start on the rest of us. And you're going to knock 'em dead."

"Whatever." Berry chewed his thumb—not the nail, the flesh—until he swallowed blood. "Hey. I need your help. Can you turn me into a girl?"

"Sure. I thought you didn't want that."

"Marsha Joyce wants me to make 'progress.' Whatever that means."

"Gotcha. So you want to strut into the clinic looking like a monster debutante."

"I guess."

"No sweat," Maura said. "You're already more of a hottie than I'll ever be. Bleach the fuzz on your upper lip, unleash those boobies and you'll look killer. Maybe a little makeup and some nasty girl gear. Oh, baby."

"Uh huh." Berry did the twist in his seat. Maura still held his arm prisoner while she plotted to make him a hideous beauty.

"I said it before, you should come to the Booby Hatch. Baptism of fire. Or rather baptism in hot sticky syrup. They'll eat you up."

"I don't want anybody to eat me up."

"Girl, you can't hide in that shell forever."

"How 'bout just the next decade or two?"

"That's not what you want. You love being the center of attention. I've watched you in your choir, with your prancing and solos. You're a big supermodel-wannabe."

"It's not the same thing at all." Berry had started to explain when the door opened. Judy entered, body rigid except for her shoulders, which swung as if she wanted to push someone.

"Berry." Judy grunted. "Why aren't you in bed? Who's this? Where's your dad?"

"This is my friend Maura from, uh, from church. It's still kind of early for bed and all. And dad . . ."

Judy took another look at Maura, and it became a stare. Maura still gripped Berry's arm, but under Judy's gaze she let go and folded her hands in her mostly naked lap. Judy saw Maura's outfit and her mouth screwed tight.

"This is my mom," Berry said.

"I thought I was your mom," Maura said.

"She met Marco just now," Berry explained. "He's in your room, pretty wasted."

"Oh." Judy didn't seem to respond to Maura's comment. "Nice to meet you, Maura. I'm afraid it's Berry's bedtime."

"Sure," Maura said. "I oughta get going anyway. Busy social calendar. You know how we do." Maura kept babbling until the door closed behind her.

As soon as Maura left, Berry stood up. "Guess I'd better head bedward."

"Wait." Judy's voice stopped Berry before he reached the hall. Berry returned to the couch and sat again. "We need to talk, obviously," Judy said. "What has your dad told you about what's going on with us?"

Berry spread his hands.

"Oh." Judy breathed deeply through her nose. "I don't know what to tell you. I still hope your dad and I work things out. He seems to have gone into a 'sode. Obviously, the lack of stability at home is having an effect on you." Judy jerked her head at the door where Maura had just left.

Judy stood akimbo over Berry. He considered telling her everything. For a moment. "Aw, no. Maura's fine. I've known her for ages. I was just counseling her on cultivating clean living and all, when—"

"Maybe you should make friends your own age."

"Maura's only a year or two older. I'm too mature to hang out with people my own age."

"You're sounding like Marco." Judy finally got tired of standing in judgment. She perched on the coffee table facing the sofa, a drained look on her face. "Do you have any friends your own age?"

"The choir," Berry said.

"Do you see people from the choir outside of choir stuff?"

Berry shrugged. "Sometimes."

"Maybe you should spend some more time with them."

"Okay." Berry got up to rinse his robes out and go to bed. This time, Judy didn't hold him up.

Berry sleepwalked through school and thanked his angels nobody messed with him. But he watched his back anyway, and when school ended he sprinted away.

After school on Friday, Berry reached the cathedral early. He found Mr. Allen in no mood to talk music theory. In rehearsal, Mr. Allen had it in for the choir from warm-ups on. His blue dinner plate eyes seemed to watch each boy at once. Berry didn't understand what had upset Mr. Allen until he mentioned "the record" in passing.

"The record!" Teddy said.

Nobody had said anything about a record since the boys had lost George.

"We kind of let the idea of putting you guys on a disc slide a while ago—when our lineup changed," Mr. Allen said. "But now we've got an honest-to-God record company interested." *Choral Fugue State* 2, a British import, had made bank in the States. So the record company behind both *Choral Fugue States* CDs wanted to record an American men-and-boys choir in the Euro tradition. A couple execs had visited the previous Sunday's service, featuring Berry's solo and his dousing of Canon Moosehead with wine, and had liked what they'd heard.

"Not a done deal yet," said Mr. Allen. "But we're going to cut a demo and see how it plays. If everything goes right—we could be the next Tallis Scholars or Chanticleer."

Mr. Allen might as well have said "the next Rolling Stones." And Berry's solo had helped launch them. Playing the Benjamin Clinic's dress-up doll seemed a dirt-cheap price.

"Hey stud," Marc whispered. "Heard your girlfriend dumped you."

Hunting for the next piece of music, Berry wasn't sure he'd heard Marc right. "Huh?" He found the score and got it to the front of his folder just in time. He sang through "I Give You a New Commandment" with most of his mind on what Marc had just said. He managed okay with the notes, but when he saw Mr. Allen wave at him frantically he realized he was blasting forte on the piano passages. He shushed and Mr. Allen nodded.

"What are you talking about?" Berry whispered as soon as the piece was done.

"Lisa was telling everybody at her school you weren't her boyfriend, she doesn't have a boyfriend, and she'd kill whoever mentioned you."

"Oh."

The men showed up for the last forty-five minutes before the dinner break. Berry watched George, now a bass, palling with Maurice. George never looked at the boys.

For once, Mr. Allen whaled harder on the men than on the boys. The men were supposed to learn their parts in advance and to be experienced singers. Tonight, they were all over the map musically and their dead-muffler vibrato clashed with the boys' clean sound. Worse, they didn't seem to care.

Berry would have died if Mr. Allen had roared at him the way he was doing at the men, and the other boys would have treated him like a traitor. The men looked bored. Berry thought the worst part of being a choirman instead of a choirboy must be losing that awe of Mr. Allen. When your heroes are the same size as you, it makes you smaller.

Mr. Allen stopped yelling. He shut the piano and looked up at the men's section. "I can do with fewer of you." It was almost too quiet to hear. Then he let the choir go to dinner.

Berry pined for Lisa to show up at the choir dinner, where some choirgirls came to flirt and smirk at alto fashion disasters. But she wasn't there.

A bunch of the older boys sat together, including Wilson and Berry. Wilson didn't talk to Berry and barely glanced at him. The other boys were mostly too busy basking in the potential record deal and stardom to say much about Lisa punting Berry's ass to the curb. In line to get some barely identifiable stew, Teddy did say it was "too bad, but that's the pimpin' life."

"Ain't sharing a dressing room with the rest of you losers," said Marc. "I want my own. Wet bar and leopard fur walls."

"Get real," said Teddy. "Nobody's getting a dressing room, even if we do lay some tracks. We're talking Tallis Scholars, not Boyzone."

"And anyway," Wilson spoke up, "we'll all be men by the time any CD ever comes out. Maybe still in the choir, maybe not." He looked into his stew again.

"How long does it take after recording to put out a CD?" Berry asked.

"Who knows?" Teddy said. "Gotta be six months or so. Mr. Allen must be shitting himself. If we record this thing with this lineup and then half a dozen of us 'graduate' before it comes out—he'd never replace us."

Berry shrugged and didn't say anything more.

After dinner, Mr. Allen repeated to the men what he'd told the boys about recording the choir. That made an impression on the men. They seemed to have woken up since dinner and left out some of the gravel and potholes. One of the pieces Mr. Allen started them on after dinner was Handel's "Dixit Dominus," a chattering masterpiece with an ornate treble solo. Berry coveted it like a purse snatcher who spies Prada. This piece was sure to go on the record, if it happened, and there was no way Berry wouldn't shine on it. Mr. Allen said he'd do auditions to choose the "Dixit" soloist. For now it rotated.

On his turn, Berry pleaded for love, or at least freedom from abuse. He made the same demand in every solo he sang. Just love me, or treat me gently enough to let me pretend you love me, Berry sang to nobody in particular. The exposed treble voice flowed into the knife-dance of voices answering each other in Latin.

11.

Pentecost ripened. It flooded the cathedral with melancholy, the sense of seasons without change. The only way to tell late spring from early fall was sequence, the air turning colder or warmer. Pentecost swallowed both times of year and kept swallowing. It spelled moody anthems that reminded Berry of Wilson in his morbidest space.

"I want to be buried in my choir blazer, if it still fits." Wilson put a sports drink nipple to his lips. Green drops leaked on his chin. He sat on the front steps of the cathedral looking across the street at the Sunday-becalmed office buildings. He did look sharp in his choir blazer and bright red tie, tawny hair parted on one side.

"I thought you weren't talking to me," Berry said. He didn't sit next to Wilson. He studied the latest church leaflet in a holder next to the front door. It didn't mention Canon Moosehead.

"I'm not," Wilson said. "You're a faggot."

"I thought you were mad because I kissed Lisa."

"A fag can date girls to trick people."

"I guess." The leaflet had the choir doing two pieces it could sing in its sleep, "Wash Me Thoroughly" by S.S. Wesley and Palestrina's "Sicut Cervus," which the boys called "Seek out her cervix." The big October concert was Wednesday, and Mr. Allen wanted to use every rehearsal to run drills for it.

Berry had his robes in a big shopping bag, pinker than the others after the bathtub laundry. He hoped nobody would notice.

"Do you think we're going to pull off this record?" Wilson asked, suddenly friendly again.

Berry shrugged. "The choir's never sounded so good. But you never know when another of us is going to open his mouth and let out a Jimi Hendrix solo."

Wilson nudged Berry's leg. "Except you."

Berry twitched. "We'll see."

"You know, you got the rest of your life to think about, even if you make this last another year or two," said Wilson.

"Two years is a long time," said Berry. "You're supposed to be dead in four, right?"

Berry felt less and less sure of his choices lately. The costs seemed higher than he expected, and the better he sang, the scarier it all went. All of a sudden, his voice was a public concern. Teddy brought water and asked him how the pipes were holding up. Randy and Marc let the Geese know that bullies could do what they wanted to Berry and he was under nobody's protection, but if anyone made him scream or damaged his singing ability, they'd suffer. This made life easier for Berry in some ways, but it also made him seem more delicate and a prime fucking-with target.

Berry missed Lisa. His bandages chafed under his armpits and around his rib cage, and his crotch still stung sometimes. Every time Berry went to the locker room or crashed into someone in the hallway, he cringed at the fear they'd learn the truth. The moment where he put on his washed-out robes and lined up with the others still made it all worthwhile.

Maura and Lisa sat apart in the congregation. Lisa sat with her mom, who was grim in a drab suit and tight-but-large hairdo. Lisa wore a long, navy blue dress. Maura sat alone among the most distinguished parishioners, laughing with one hand over her mouth. The young man in a suit next to her laughed too, hand over mouth and eyes askance.

Berry took all this in while singing the first hymn. When he got to the choirstalls at the front, he noticed Canon Moosehead wasn't there.

The service went smoothly for once. Mr. Allen conducted from the organ bench by jerking his head in his mirror. Dean Jackson gave a sermon about the end of the world. He said humanity still schemed to erase itself, but in any case worlds ended all the time and we should see these "mini-apocalypses" for the moments of truth they were or the real end of days would catch us flat-assed. Berry shot Wilson a glance. Wilson yawned dramatically.

After church, Wilson didn't want to talk to Maura, who loitered out front. Berry didn't mind talking to Maura, but he really wanted to catch Lisa. He and Wilson both found Lisa studying the church bulletin board as if bingo or Hungry Souls revved her pulse. "My mom's just gone to the ladies," she told Berry and Wilson.

"Haven't seen you lately," said Wilson.

"Been kinda grounded," Lisa said. "Long story." She kept her eyes on the bulletin.

"Sorry," said Berry.

"Not your fault," said Lisa.

"So. End of the world," said Wilson.

"Did that make any sense to you?" asked Lisa.

"Sort of. You've got a religion based on an apocalypse that refuses to happen," said Wilson. "So you have to redefine your terms. Maybe the end already happened a bunch of times and nobody noticed."

Berry really wanted to talk to Lisa alone. But Wilson wasn't about to leave. "We're going to record the choir," Berry told Lisa. "Big high-pressure make-or-break star-is-born event."

A clot of churchgoers further down the hall broke up to let a burst of sequins, rayon, and nylon pass. One member of the Downtown Association stayed against the wall long after Maura passed, as if afraid she'd come back. He glanced at his friends, as if mourning the fact that Canon Moosehead hadn't kept his noodles long enough to save the cathedral from riffraff. Maura ignored the glares and kissed Berry on both cheeks.

"Oh great," said Lisa. "The 'shroom queen."

"Hey," Maura said, as if she hadn't heard Lisa. "How you guys doing?"

"Not bad," said Berry. He thought of something his mom had said: Why does someone so much older want to hang with you? Isn't that weird or sad? He thought about all the times Maura had hung around the clinic waiting for his appointment to end, or showed up for church.

"I'd better find my mom," Lisa said.

"What's with her?" Maura asked after Lisa left.

"The whole being stranded in the overgrown slum garden thing," said Berry. "She's having a hard time putting it behind her."

"I'd better steal cookies," said Wilson. He left too.

Maura leaned against the wall next to Berry, taking her weight off her high heels. "Haven't seen you."

Berry pulled away from her. "My mom told me not to hang with you. I'm trying not to piss her off. Things are all *Girl, Interrupted* at home. Anyway, don't you have any friends your own age?" Berry demanded.

"Sweetie, I have friends of all ages," Maura said. "You've met some of them. But this is different."

"Why?"

"Let's take a walk," Maura said. "Don't worry. We won't go far, you won't get lost, and I'll have you home for milk and cookies."

Berry saw few other people. Even on the main drag where restaurants slept, shops locked and dark in the afternoon sun. Berry pulled up the collar of his choir blazer to keep the wind off his neck.

"You have to understand," Maura said. "I went through six years of Hell before I started hormones. I ran the whole teen obstacle course as a boy. My body changed and kept changing. All for the worse. Hair where I didn't want it, big arms and shoulders and hands, big ugly feet. Every spurt, my body said 'fuck off and die.' Meanwhile, I suffered adolescence in a boy's body. We brawled, we yelled, we sported, we jostled for girls. I had to act like a maniac to survive. Changes happened that I can never undo." Maura held her hands, knuckles out, in Berry's face. "Show me how to shrink these."

"I don't know," Berry said. "They're not so big."

"I can't imagine living for decades as a man before making the change," Maura said. "Six years was eternity enough. Baby, you have no clue what's coming. The worst you've endured so far is squat. Fucking nothing. If I can save you from some of that . . . help you go all the way and become a girl . . . I promised myself to save others if I could."

"That's your way," Berry said. "Not mine." He thought *The world ends all the time, in secret.*

"It's yours too. You chose, now you have cold feet. You're me, seven years ago. I didn't know what I wanted back then either."

"Even if I wanted to, how would I become a girl? Everyone would know."

"You could start high school as a girl. Where they don't know you, or just explain to your classmates this is who you are now. People tolerate us more and more."

"And I'd help them learn to tolerate others by being a big public deal and getting sliced," said Berry.

"You could go stealth. Like I said, find a school where they don't know you. Get that M changed to an F on your transcript. Nobody will know."

"Except I'd have a dick."

"By high school, it could be gone."

Berry didn't know what to say to that. He stared down at his crotch for a few moments. He couldn't imagine being dick-naked, blank between his legs, and thinking of it made him feel like he'd drunk the Bishop's punch. Finally he said, "My balls would look pretty weird without a dick over them."

"They'd be gone too."

They passed a fast-food joint that miraculously served customers in the weekend-narcoleptic downtown. Berry suddenly wanted a milkshake. He turned and entered. Maura trailed, examined leaflets about the nutritional content of burgers and fries. "Only 59 percent fat," she called after Berry.

Berry got a coffee milkshake. Back on the street he said, "How would I nuke my privates anyway?"

"I've told you before." Maura borrowed Berry's shake and slurped some. "Dr. Tamarind would prescribe it. You just need to convince insurance or someone else to pay for it. Or you raise the money somehow."

Berry thought he knew how Maura expected him to raise the money.

"I don't think I could convince Dr. Tamarind to order that surgery," Berry said. "He doesn't even know about all the pills I've been taking."

Maura dropped Berry's milkshake on the ground. It spilled, but few inches remained. She grabbed the messy wax-paper cup and held it out to Berry, who shook his head.

"Damn! Sorry about your drink, but damn! Girl, what do you talk to him about, anyway?" Maura dumped the milkshake cup in the trash and wiped her hands.

"Uh . . ." Berry thought. "Fish, cars, stuff. The influence of Phoenician traders on classical Greek culture. Books I've read. My weird parents. You've met them, there's lots to say. Singing. Vibrato. The right tempo for 'Beati Quorum Via,' some people rush it. You know, all that stuff. But I don't want him to know about everything that's going on with me."

Maura shook her head. "You don't want anyone to know you. You're a bundle of secrets."

Berry felt as if he'd been called a bundle of worms.

"Berry." Maura put took Berry's free hand in both of hers. "Give me a chance to show you. What life is like as a girl. You've never even tried it."

Berry said he'd think about it.

When Berry got home the apartment was empty. A big sombrero full of candy sat on the sofa, where Maura had death-gripped Berry's arm the other night. Berry tried one of the chocolates but it tasted weird and bitter on the inside so he spat it into the trash. Berry read some of *The Man*

Without Qualities and then looked over some of the music they were readying for the big fall concert.

The phone rang. Berry almost let it go, figuring it was one of Marco's gardening/spiritual clients. Then he grabbed it on the third jangle. "Can I talk to Berry?" Lisa said.

"Hey," Berry said. "I'm uh glad you called."

"Hey. Like, uh . . . You know I'm . . . sorry I acted all Mariah today and lately."

"Sure."

"My friends gave me shit for hanging with you. And my parents have been acting extra amped. Mom keeps having struggle sessions with me. That's where they pray over you, it can be intense. And Dad . . ." Berry heard silence, or not exactly silence. The creeping of telephone circuits, the music of switchboard traffic.

Berry wondered if the chocolates in the hat were really Mexican jumping beans and whether he'd die from eating one. It hadn't jumped in his hand. "Berry," Lisa said. "I really like you. A lot. And I think it's great you're so brave and don't care what people think of you and stuff."

Berry sat next to the sombrero. He wasn't sure what Lisa was talking about.

"I'm not that brave," she went on. "I just want to be popular. When people thought you were my boyfriend, it got . . . intense. I was trippin'."

"I never told anyone I was your boyfriend."

"I know. I really want to be friends. At church and hanging out and stuff."

"That's cool. I really don't want a girlfriend right now." Berry felt like he'd sweated out a fever.

"Cool. Friends?"

"Friends."

"I'm only half grounded now. Can you get to the big mall out near Farming Hill?"

Berry looked at the clock. It was a little after three. "There's a bus," he said. "I don't know how often it runs. And I gotta be back here for dinner."

"I could get my mom to give you a ride home if we met at the mall."

"I thought your mom didn't like me."

"She doesn't like me going with boys period. It helps if I say you're from church, but . . ." Long spell of silence. "What would really help is if you weren't a boy."

"What?"

"She'd never know. Just don't hide what you got and you'd be a total girl."

"What if I see someone I know?"

"At the mall out here?"

"I have a mustache."

"You have fuzz. Lots of girls with your coloring have worse."

First Maura, now Lisa. Berry felt gangbanged. "What would I wear? I don't have any girl stuff."

"Dunno. T-shirt and jeans. That's what I'll wear."

"I don't know." Berry wondered if they lynched people at malls.

"Nobody will know. I promise. If you do this, we can hang out all the time. I would be so thrilled."

"I thought the whole me having breasts thing was, like, freaky to you."

"A boyfriend with breasts would be wack. But all my friend friends have titties."

"Do you like being a girl?"

"I'm not sure. I guess. I don't really have anything to compare it to. Look, just ride the bus to the mall with your boobies all bandaged, and then you can unwrap in the bathroom when you get there. I totally promise you nothing bad will happen."

"Okay. Maybe. I'll see you there." They arranged to meet at the food court around four. The whole time on the bus, Berry drummed on his knees. He felt as though he hadn't blinked in a week, hadn't swallowed in a month. The bus quivered as it took Berry away from his neighborhood into the suburbs. When he arrived, Berry almost caught the bus home.

Berry stuffed his bandages in his knapsack then studied himself in the boys room mirror. In his baggy jeans and a tight T-shirt, he could be a wannabe J-Lo dancer. Nothing had changed but the shape of his chest. His neck-length hair, his soft mouth, his small hands, all could play female. But Berry still felt like an imposter waiting to be spotted. Then he realized he was standing in the boys room with his tits loose. He ran out and lost himself in the crowd, circling to erase any connection between the girl he was now and the boy who'd entered the boys room.

"This is Berry. Like the fruit."

Lisa's mom didn't recognize Berry from church. Instead she just wrinkled her nose at the PARTY MOB T-shirt. She agreed to meet them in an hour and a half back at the food court.

"The first thing you need is a bra," Lisa said as soon as they'd left her mom behind.

"I don't have any money," Berry protested once Lisa and he were alone.

"It's cool," Lisa said. "I'll spot."

Lisa led Berry to one of the big department stores and found the junior misses department with rows and rows of denim skirts and skimpy tops that said, Hey, I've got a rack. Berry's huge-seeming chest fit into a B cup bra. After trying a few, he found one that he and Lisa both thought would be okay. Berry sang under his breath. Every second he expected to see someone from church or school. A lot of church people did live near here and the mall attracted people from all over, but nobody seemed to notice two more teen girls shopping.

"We don't have to buy a ton of stuff today. But you should wear the bra so my mom doesn't get a coronary. Just kind of look around and see what else appeals to you." Lisa kept running from rack to rack in junior misses. Every few moments, she'd whisk hangers aside to make a new gap and show off some discovery. Berry tried to pretend that he wasn't doing this, but also that he did this all the time.

Berry found a dark concord skirt that felt churchy, with some white frills around the hem. He also found a slightly frilly white blouse that could almost have been a boy's shirt. Some of the other stuff he noticed looked just like boys' clothes.

Berry didn't spend every moment in the department store feeling his fingernails itch with the feeling someone would notice a boy in the wrong place. That feeling came and went, but so did excitement. Trying on one dress, Berry twirled and giggled at his reflection.

Berry and Lisa only bought the one bra at that store. Then Lisa wanted to go to another store and look at jewelry. "We're just talking a few bangles," she reassured Berry. He shrugged. She thought he looked really nice with a big pink hoop around his neck and some plastic bands on his wrists. "It's too bad your ears aren't pierced." Berry let her try stuff on him but not buy anything.

Lisa and Berry held hands and it was okay because they were two girls at the mall. They went to the bookstore and looked at *Sixteen and a Half* and *Teeneurosis* magazines together. "Hey look: 'Eight Great Looks for Winter. Bad girls wear wool too'," Lisa read.

Berry asked Lisa what she thought about Canon Moosehead's absence from church that morning. "He was always a big jerk, but then he got spastic," Lisa said.

"I think it was the pills," Berry said. He flipped through page after perky page of girls whose hair and skirts spilled into text columns.

"What pills?"

"Oh, you know. The Bob Dole pills the altar boys spiked his coffee with. I never actually saw his willie rise in church, but he definitely went wiggy after that. He talked about Jung a lot. I mean, I've read some of Jung's works and I'm not sure I get the link between the collective unconscious and the possessed pigs running off a cliff." Berry stopped, afraid he sounded brainy *and* dorky. Anyway, Lisa wasn't listening.

"What pills, now?"

Berry explained again.

"That's so cruel. Making him think he was a nut or a perv."

"I guess. I mean, he was anti-homeless people and hated the choir."

"And you knew about this all along?"

"Well, I knew about the pills. But for a while I thought he was acting weird because this guy my parents made me visit told him to spy on me, and . . ." Berry realized it sounded dumb.

"And you didn't do anything about it?"

"Well, not really. But—"

Lisa dashed the teen magazines back on the racks. "We've got to save him! He needs to know what's been going on! Then he can get his job back and everything will be all right."

"Are you sure? I mean, he'll kill everyone if he finds out."

"He's a man of God. That means he's obligated to forgive our trespasses and all that shit. Plus, he's learned an important lesson from this and he'll be grateful and all."

"What lesson?"

"Who knows? I'm not a reverend. Come on!"

Lisa grabbed Berry's hand again and they sped out of the bookstore. They ran to the food court, only to stand around the Entrailer Park restaurant soaking in the smell of frying intestines.

"I don't know why we hurried," Berry said. "Your mom won't be back for another half hour."

He bought Lisa and himself Cokes and they sat in the food court.

"We need a plan," Lisa said after a long silence. "If we just tell the Canon the truth he won't believe us."

"We could tell the Dean," Berry said.

They sat a while longer. Eventually Lisa's mom came and found them. She was in a good mood because she'd bought some scarves. She drove a town car with calfskin leather on its cavernous back seat. Berry and Lisa held hands, so Berry didn't think Lisa could be too disappointed in him. She said she'd call him and let him know about their project. Berry wasn't sure which project she meant, but he just nodded.

Berry got home before his parents. He dashed to his room and resmushed his breasts. Then he called Maura. "I bought a bra today."

"Great," she said. "How'd it feel?"

"Okay, I guess. Like shopping."

"Where did you go?"

"To the mall. With Lisa."

"I'm glad you're friends again. What did you talk about?"

"Bob Dole."

"The reason the mall thing didn't rock your world was because you didn't go all out," Maura said. "You bought like one bra, right? You could have so much more fun if you'd let me show you."

Berry's parents came home and he had to hang up. Marco and Judy seemed unusually cheerful. They both laughed a lot, and Judy even danced. They'd been to a party and brought food home to Berry.

"Everything's going to be different now," Marco told Berry as he unpacked the doggie bag of General Whoever's chicken and broccoli. "We got our shit together."

Marco and Judy put on music and danced like movie newlyweds or two of the ten most romantic people in *Teeneurosis* magazine. Berry left them and fell into bed. The moment before he fell asleep, he felt the kind of pain in his crotch and chafed torso that's comforting instead of disturbing because it means things are healing as you rest.

12.

The choir drilled nonstop until the day before the Fall Concert. Then everybody had the day off with orders to rest his voice. Berry didn't talk for nearly forty-eight hours between the Tuesday evening rehearsal and Thursday's pre-concert warmup. He would just nod and maybe smile if people tried to talk to him. Marco and Judy tried to bond with Berry now that they'd sewn things up with each other. He just blessed their remastered relationship in silence.

At school, Berry pretended to have laryngitis. He got through a whole morning with Rat and the Swans without making a sound. This wasn't too hard since Berry seldom spoke in class. Rat wanted to have a lively free-floating discussion on Shakespeare and called on Berry, who mimed his opinion that Rosalind was a cocktease who deserved to be stuck in the woods forever reading dumb tree-poems. It took a while for Rat to decode this input.

In the afternoon, Berry had a rough moment with Toad, who really wanted Berry to explain some of his answers on a biology quiz. Berry just shook his head when Toad demanded to know why Berry thought all birds photosynthesized except for pigeons. Berry shrugged and pointed to his throat with a karate-chop hand until Toad gave up. Some of the Geese wanted to beat Berry up for his mute act, but Randy and Marc let it be known Berry was extra off limits today. Nobody even chased Berry home after school. He enjoyed walking slowly.

Berry's Trappist day broke when Lisa called. "Hey," she said. "Guess what?"

"Can't talk," Berry whispered.

"Then listen. My mom really, really liked you. As a girl, of course. I think she thinks of you as a project I've taken on—no offense, it's just the way her brain works. Anyway, she wants me to take you under my wing in a big way and make sure you never lack for training bras."

"Um." Berry managed to convey doubt, confusion, annoyance, and hunger in a syllable.

"Don't worry, no struggle sessions for you. She saves that stuff for me. Probably no bake sales in your honor, either. But she's very much for us hanging out."

"Um."

"My dad won't recognize you even if he does see you. You guys only met once, it was dark, and you wore that robe thing which totally distracts the eye. So anyway, when's our next girl date?"

"Dunno. Fall Concert's tomorrow night."

"I know. I'm there. Speaking of which, I figured the solution to the Canon Moosehead sitch. I wrote an anonymous note to him and Dean Jackson saying what happened. I said if they needed proof, they'd find a pill bottle under the wine cabinet in the vestry."

"How did you know they'd find it there?"

"I put it there. Stole my dad's."

"Oh."

Lisa talked a while longer, about the cruelty of making Canon Moosehead doubt his own mind. You don't get to be a minister without spending a lot of time in your own head, and the Canon had probably felt comfy there until somebody had sprayed sewage inside. People could be so cruel, especially in religious contexts where you'd expect otherwise.

Berry wanted to know exactly what Lisa had written on that note, but didn't want to use his voice. He tried asking the question in the form of a cough, but didn't even break through her flood.

"Sometimes it's good to be able to live inside your head. I know you know what I'm talking about. In class. Or when I'm stuck in that swimming pool with just my nose above water, sometimes I imagine I'm swimming back to a warm beach or something. I mean, inside your head you're safe from the mean people, except if they find a way to get past the plastic cover into your airspace. You know, Berry, you are possibly the only person I've met with no cruelty in you. That's one thing you'll have to learn about real girls, they can be meaner than soldiers. Girls have to cut each other down. You'll get the hang of it. I mean, I know you don't want to, but you'll pick it up either way. But that's kind of the point. The cruelest people are often the ones who live in their own heads the most. I could be deadly mean and not know it. But you'd tell me, right?"

When Lisa was ready to hang up, Berry whispered, "Bye." She wished him luck on the big day.

Thursday went harder. Rat called on Berry a few times and he had to gesture his disdain of Courtly Love, romantic heroines, and that "mewling, puking" speech. Then Toad wanted him to get up and do a presentation on the periodic table. Berry tried to whisper that he'd lost his voice. Toad asked if he had a note. Berry shook his head. "Then you have a voice," Toad said. Berry got up and pointed at different points on the elemental chart while whistling and making other sound effects by blowing

Charlie Anders

through his clasped hands. Helium was a bunch of whistles and clicks. Argon was a duck call. Oxygen was the sound of Berry rubbing his palms together very quickly. Toad scowled but let Berry sit down.

Then after school Berry had to run uptown to Dr. Tamarind's office and sit for an hour, then run back downtown for the pre-concert rehearsal. It wasn't strange for Berry to give Dr. Tamarind the silent treatment for a whole session, so he figured this time would be no challenge. But Dr. Tamarind seemed determined to make Berry talk at all costs. "Do you know how much your parents are paying for this? Your dad is having to take on extra gardening work part time to pay my fees. Your parents really care about you. Do you think they'll divorce for real?"

Berry shrugged. He hadn't told Dr. Tamarind about his parents' reconciliation.

"You know, maybe your problem is just that you're not such a good singer," Dr. Tamarind said, eyes on Berry's face. "Maybe you like to pretend you have talent because it gives you pride. But in reality, you're just not very good. I mean, if you really were good, why would you want so much to hold on to your fleeting moment? You could bask in it while it lasted. But maybe there's nothing to bask in. Maybe there's just a fantasy that you're hiding behind and the reality is too hard on you, not to mention other people's ears."

"Solos," Berry whispered.

"What? You've been given solos to sing? That's great news. When is that?"

"Tonight. Concert at cathedral."

"Congratulations! I take it all back. I'm sure you're excellent. So the concert's this evening? Around eight? I might be able to go. Would you mind? I won't disturb you."

Berry shrugged.

Dr. Tamarind switched back to needling Berry about his parents and their dismal relationship. By the time Berry escaped he felt as though he'd spent a year under torture.

Berry tried to forget Dr. Tamarind's goading but it scratched at the underside of his skull as he rode the bus back downtown. If he really wasn't any good, what the fuck was he doing? The cost of saving his voice grew higher all the time, and he couldn't bear to think it could be for nothing. Berry knew Mr. Allen liked him. Berry was the only boy who sat and talked with Mr. Allen outside of rehearsals. Maybe Mr. Allen was giving him solos to be nice to him. Berry pictured the others grimacing every time they heard his voice. Maybe the choirboys laughed behind their hands or sat around the Twelve Step room when Berry wasn't there and joked about his squawks.

But two days of not speaking seemed to have done wonders for Berry's voice, which Tuesday's marathon rehearsal had left demoralized. He felt and heard the difference as soon as Mr. Allen started with some scales. His "head voice" sounded as trumpet-like as it ever had. For a moment, Berry forgot his doubts from Dr. Tamarind's session and sang right into his mask, making it light up.

But the fears returned when they started in on some of the hardest parts of the concert. Berry could tell for sure he was hitting the notes. And he was using every technique Mr. Allen had taught him. He breathed from below his ribs and sang into the space between his eyes and around his nose. He kept his mouth and eyes open, his posture straight. But maybe his voice shrilled instead of chiming? What if he was just good enough instead of great? When Berry's solo came, he took a deep breath and sang. All of a sudden, his voice sounded harsh in his own ears. The notes were off a hair, he was sharping, no, flatting. His high notes crunched like one of Marco's vinyl albums. Mr. Allen waved his hand halfway through the solo. "That's fine," he said. "Let's move on and spare Berry's voice." The rest of the rehearsal, Berry trembled and tried not to hear himself among the other voices.

"Berry, what in Hell's best hotel room is going on?" Mr. Allen asked once the rehearsal ended.

"Nervous," Berry said with a shrug. Then, as Mr. Allen turned away, Berry touched his arm. He swallowed and said, "Am I really a good singer? I'm not just, you know, okay?"

"Berry much as I like you—I put the choir and my own career above all else. I'd never give a solo to anyone who wasn't the best kid for it. And there are some very good trebles in this choir besides you right now. I wouldn't want you to get a swelled head, but you're probably the best treble to come through here in the last few years, if not longer. I want to keep training that voice—even after it changes. We need to think about your future as a singer."

The choke-hold went away. Berry felt power coming back to him. He couldn't keep the good news to himself, it just poured out. "Don't worry! My voice is unbreakable. I've been taking pills, hormones and stuff. I'll sound this way forever."

"You what? You—" Mr. Allen's eyes swelled and he leaned against his piano, like a crutch guy whose bus had jerked forward. For a moment, he looked lost in his own house. "Are you joking . . . no, I can't believe . . . Berry, what have you done?"

Mr. Allen stared at Berry, then jolted back to the moment. All the others had their robes on and had lined up in the hall. "We'll talk after," he said.

Berry had no time to worry about Mr. Allen's weird spell. Fear also left him. His mind felt as empty as it did during Toad's chem lectures, but with a difference. He felt calm and focused. He could hear his own voice in his head and tune it to perfect. He could blend with everyone. Berry had noticed more and more boys "leaning" on him lately, following whatever notes he sang. Occasionally he led them all off a cliff. But mostly Berry got it right.

The procession seemed to pause in the hallway leading to the cathedral's side entrance for a million breaths. Wilson and Berry traded nods.

Mr. Allen played and the choir advanced. After that, time sped from legato to super-allegro. Singing without breaks for prayers or sermons gave Berry a rush. Berry never once took his eyes off Mr. Allen, even though he made the token page turns on his music. His mind and voice knew where to go.

A piece by Gabriel Faure opened the concert like a shameful velvet purse. It wasn't even about God as far as Berry knew. They'd walked through the words one day, some passionate French poem about yearning and joyful attenuation. Its gooey sweetness had stuck to Berry's fingers in rehearsal, but now it felt brilliant, like kissing Lisa topless and touching each other's breasts, only this was in front of everybody.

Then the Faure morphed into religious music after all, "In Paradiso" from Faure's Requiem, the haunting song about Heaven. From French into Latin, and all of a sudden Berry glided to the stone rafters, and the forbidden desire of the previous piece became the reward for all good Christian soldiers. Berry felt the cleverness of Mr. Allen's plan, to meld the world and the Kingdom so you couldn't flee one for the other. It was all sensuality, pulling the pleasure reflex whether the music was about hapless panging or righteous death.

Now Berry not only heard his own breathing, he could hear everyone in the cathedral breathe. The crowd had none of religion's fidgetiness. As "In Paradiso" gave way to Darke's "Peace I Leave With You," the mood went fully Goddish. But Berry had a sudden flash of knowledge. Maybe the way he felt right now wasn't about marching in formation, wearing fancy robes, and looking pure.

By the time "Dixit Dominus" and Berry's solo came, he'd almost forgotten about it. For a moment, Berry's mind was so blank he felt paralyzed, and then his mouth opened. The solo came seamlessly out of the music that came before, and Berry didn't have to think except to breathe. Then the solo was over and Berry fell back into the group. Berry noticed George giving him a look of pain, resentment or admiration. George's eyes half closed as if he'd just been napping, but his mouth gaped of course. His eyes slowly moved back to Mr. Allen.

After that, the concert moved really quickly, even through the tough Britten piece. After the choir filed out of its usual place into the wings, the audience kept cheering for a few minutes. Berry realized it felt strange to have the congregation applaud. Finally Mr. Allen led them back out front for an encore, Palestrina's "Sicut Cervus," which the choir did with the kind of gentleness that comes from power under control. The Palestrina piece starts quiet and never leaves its meditation behind. It's way harder to pull off than the more brilliant colors of Faure. Some of the younger boys, who still didn't know how not to blare, sang in a whisper or not at all. After the high-energy concert, it was almost plainsong.

By the time the crowd stopped applauding the second time, the choir was back in the rehearsal room and half unrobed. Berry suddenly remembered about his unfinished conversation with Mr. Allen. It terrified him. "We've got to record this group," said Wilson, "before it's too late." Everybody was thinking the same thing. It scared them to know they'd brushed awesomeness for the first time, maybe the only time, in their lives. By luck or somebody's will, they were part of something way better than themselves.

George approached Berry as he buttoned his blazer. "Man," George said. "You kicked ass." He held out a hand and Berry shook it.

"Thanks," Berry said. He wanted to apologize or something. George looked a foot taller than Berry. Wisps of mustache and goatee had settled around his mouth. George looked happy. Maybe he couldn't even remember who he'd been. He was still part of the choir, as a mediocre bass instead of a supertreble.

Mr. Allen entered and waved for quiet. "You guys were amazing. If we can sound this good for the microphones, we'll be made. I'm going to try and get some mikes in the cathedral in the next couple of weeks—whether or not we get the label on board. Berry, I need to talk to you in private."

Everyone cheered. Berry asked Mr. Allen if he could get some cookies before they talked. Mr. Allen said yes.

Berry walked with Wilson across the alley to the office building. "We just got to defluke tonight and get it on tape," Wilson said.

"Toad, that's my science teacher, says anything that happened once didn't happen. Only things that repeat under the same circumstances actually happened as scientific events," said Berry. "I told her that if a giant asteroid crashed into the Earth once, it would still have happened." Now that his two-day silence had ended, Berry couldn't stop talking.

Upstairs from the Twelve Step room, the big reception hall had tables covered with cookies and punch and milk and things that seriously fuck your vocal chords if you plan on singing. The boys covered napkins with cookies so high that doughy fragments fell everywhere. Even Berry shut up so he could fill his mouth with sugary butter balls. He'd forgotten to eat dinner.

Sugar and relief made the boys more hyper than usual. They ran around the hall and up and down the stairs and onto the stage at one end of the hall, twenty crazed kids in blazers and ties and gray worsted pants. The floor made bat sonar noises as their rubber soles skidded. Randy shrieked about Nimrod the Mighty Hunter and gave one of the younger boys a Holy Noogie. One of the boys found a teeny elevator that led down to the kitchen across from the Twelve Step room and the other boys put Jackie into it and sent him up and down in it. The adults, meanwhile, gulped wine and high-fived Mr. Allen. Jamal, one of the youngest boys, ran gangly-limbs-first into Canon Moosehead.

The Canon looked down into Jamal's face. His eyes bulged and his mouth opened and closed, as if he struggled to say something or hold something back. He lifted a hand.

"Sorry," said Jamal. He smiled hopefully, eyes wide and nose wrinkling.

Canon Moosehead took a deep breath. He looked over at Dr. Tamarind, loading up on bread and cheese. Then he smiled. "No problem," he said. "Just watch where you're going." Jamal nodded and sped off.

Canon Moosehead wandered over to Dean Jackson and muttered to him. The Dean nodded but looked worried. Berry tried to move as close to them as he could. "I agree we need to make changes. For one thing, I'm changing the locks on that vestry and keeping it locked. And nobody gets at the communion wine, especially after the incident with that homeless gentleman. But let's not go overboard," said the Dean. The Canon said some more inaudible stuff. "Look, what happened with those pills, if true, was reprehensible and horrible. But that has nothing to do with the Hungry Souls or the choir, and I'm sure the parish council and the diocese will . . . Look, let's talk about this later."

The Dean walked off. Berry felt someone touch his arm. "You're the superstar of the night," Lisa said. "Everybody loves you. Now would be the perfect time to tell everyone your secret."

"Leave that to me," Berry said. "What did you put in that note?"

"I just said, 'Viagra in Canon's coffee and diet Slice. Check under shelf in vestry for pill bottle. Yours in Christ, etc.' Except I didn't sign it."

"Canon Moosehead is totally ballistic. They're probably going to kick out all the homeless people and kill the soup kitchen. And the choir's going to be shredded."

"Berry, I'm sorry. But I couldn't let the guy keep suffering."

"Who are you talking about?" Maura wore a crushed velvet jacket with puffy ruffled sleeves and a long straight skirt. A bunch of men, from the choir and the audience, stared as she glided over to Berry and Lisa.

"Canon Moosehead," Berry said. "He got dosed with Viagra."

He was about to explain the whole story, but Maura squealed "Oh my!" and ran to the Canon, who stood in the corner, studying the floor.

"No!" Berry threw a cookie at Maura's head, hoping against hope to stop her. The butter cookie missed, flew across the room, and struck Jackie in the forehead as he climbed out of the food elevator. Jackie fell on the floor and cried. Berry felt his insides wring. He ran over to Maura, who had just tapped the Canon on the shoulder with a conversational smile.

Lisa took Berry's hand. "You can't do anything," she said. "Go over there and you'll just get sucked in."

"I gotta stop her," Berry said. "She's insane."

The Canon's face filled with blood like a well-fed mosquito. His eyes engorged. Maura held her palms a half foot or so apart. "She's actually comparing Viagra experiences in church," Lisa said. "When did she ever use it?"

"With clients," Berry said. The Canon's mouth opened and a strangled cry came. Maura stopped laughing and frowned. She shrugged and said something philosophical. The Canon barked something angry. His hands scrunched into fists. "Oh my God," Berry said. "He's going to hit her."

"Ministers don't hit," Lisa said.

Maura shrieked, whether with laughter or horror Berry couldn't tell. Maura put her hand on the Canon's shoulder, and he brushed it off. By now, the interaction of the gaudy bitch and Canon Boner had a crowd. Berry noticed Dr. Tamarind hovering, watching his two best clients. In the confusion, Berry got close enough to hear what Maura and Canon Moosehead were saying.

"For the last time, I did not use that substance recreationally! It was given to me against my wishes!"

"Oh, I know how that goes," Maura said. "Demanding wife. Long dry spell. Tired hubby gets a boost he never saw coming. Huh? Where's the wife? I have some suggestions for her about other ways to rouse the rooster."

"I've been divorced for five years."

"And she still makes you take that stuff? Fire your attorney, your divorce settlement sucks butt. No offense."

The Canon raised fists and clubbed his own ears. Dr. Tamarind had told Berry he had a rule against socializing with patients or seeing them outside of sessions. Berry wondered if it would apply if one patient was murdering another.

Maura talked about special massage techniques she knew. Canon Moosehead gripped her shoulder so hard she yelped. She looked up at him, suddenly terrified. He let go and stepped back. "I'm sorry," Canon Moosehead said. "I didn't mean to startle you."

"That's okay," Maura said.

"It's been a disturbing time. Do you know who did this?"

"Just heard someone talking about it," Maura said.

"I've been to Hell," the Canon said. "Hell is where the flesh rules the spirit instead of the other way around."

"Come with me," Maura said. "I think you need someone to talk to. Really, I promise I won't laugh any more."

Maura took Canon Moosehead's arm and led him out of the room. They disappeared around the corner and Berry heard them walk down the big stairs to the exit. "Where are they going?" Berry asked nobody.

"Berry." Mr. Allen tapped Berry's shoulder then folded his arms. "We still need to have our talk." He looked way smaller than ever before. No rehearsal or service, however grinding, had ever crushed Mr. Allen so hard. Several boys stared at the two of them. "Let's go."

Berry and Mr. Allen went back into the cathedral and sat on his big organ bench looking out at the deserted pews. "I just wish you'd told me sooner—before I started planning a big recording date. I don't think you can be in the choir now," Mr. Allen said. His voice echoed.

　　　　　　　　　　　　　　　　　　　　　Charlie Anders

"No, wait," Berry said. "I'm not changing. I mean, I am. But I'm doing this to not change."

"I thought I knew what was going on with you. Why couldn't you confide in me, Berry? Or whatever I'm supposed to call you now. Are you going to be wearing dresses? Is there a timetable?"

"Please listen," Berry said. "I just wanted to keep my voice from going like George's. So I took the female hormones and other stuff to put my voice on ice."

"You can join the girls' choir if I clear it with the Dean," Mr. Allen said.

"I don't want to join the girls' choir," Berry said. "I've been meaning to tell you for a while. I didn't know how to explain. When George's voice changed, I got scared. If I'm not this . . ." He gestured around the cathedral. ". . . I'm nothing." He explained about the kitchen knife and the clinic. "But now I've changed a lot and I don't know what's going on," Berry said.

"Have you talked to a doctor about this?" Mr. Allen said.

"Nah, just the people at the clinic. They think I'm older."

Mr. Allen breathed the wrong way, too quick and from the shoulders. "So you're taking all these pills. And you don't know what they all do, except you've developed breasts and your voice hasn't changed. So far."

Berry nodded.

"Who knows what you're really doing to your body taking all this stuff at your age?"

"Everything seems okay," Berry said. "They check on me at the clinic."

"So some of the pills are to stop your testosterone from working. And some of them are to give you female features," Mr. Allen said. Berry felt weird talking about this stuff in the empty cathedral. The big statue of the crucified Jesus stared down at them, its eyes asking, "Is it nothing to you?"

"I guess so," Berry said. This was an idea he hadn't thought of before. "I could just take the anti-testosterone pills but not the estrogen and stuff, huh? Is that what you think I should do?"

"I'm just trying to understand your situation. I'm not giving advice."

"I really want to stay in the choir and make the record. Please let me." Berry squeezed one hand with the other.

"I don't know. People will blow donuts when they hear of this. Especially on the heels of the whole Canon Moosehead thing—"

"Nobody needs to know!"

"What kind of position are you putting me in? Are you trying to destroy me? I have a shot at everything I've killed myself for these past dozen years. All the church politics— the blood-thinning rehearsals—the organ grinding for a congregation of monkeys. You have no idea how many dues I've paid in how many currencies." Mr. Allen looked around the massive stone shell. "This is not the life I had in mind when I left Juilliard. But I am not willing to lie or help you cover your secret for my chance at the brass ring."

"If I tell everyone the truth, can I stay in the choir?"

"I really don't know. I'll fight like hell to keep you in. My political capital has never been great—but people liked this concert a lot—at least until the Canon's psychotic break. As long as nobody thinks the choir had anything to do with that . . . I don't know."

"I can stop taking the pills," Berry said. "But then my voice might change. And it can't change back. And besides . . ."

"Besides what?"

Berry looked into Mr. Allen's bubble glasses and could hardly bear what he saw behind them. He wanted Mr. Allen to be happy no matter what. "I don't know. Since I started on the pills, I've been . . . jazzed. I like feeling not like the other boys. I've never really wanted to be a man, I guess. The only thing I like about being a boy is the choir. I know I don't want to grow up like most of the men I know. I just . . . I don't know."

"So maybe you do want to be a woman."

"I don't know. I don't know what I want to be. Maybe there isn't a word for it."

"Oh." Hush stilled the cathedral, like the moment of silence during services when people pleaded inaudibly for the recovery of sick loved ones. "Sounds like you've got some thinking to do," Mr. Allen said. "This is what I'm going to do. I'll let you stay in the choir on one condition: you show up for rehearsal with a note from your parents saying they know what's going on and they're okay with it. As long as you call yourself a boy you can stay with us as far as I'm concerned. If you dress female or call yourself Betty, you're out. That's the best I can do."

"So I don't have to tell everybody?"

"Just your parents."

Berry thanked Mr. Allen and, though the thought of telling the newly "together" Marco and Judy all about his recent activities started the dark satanic mills in his chest, things seemed clearer. Maybe there was a way he could stay on just the pills that saved his voice without all the others. Maybe there was a way he could be himself without becoming whoever Maura wanted him to be.

Judy had been too busy at school to attend the concert, and Marco had promised to show up the way he promised all kinds of things. But both parents sat in front of the newly repaired television when Berry got home. They looked as domesticated as Berry could remember.

"Did you know the pygmy shark eats its own young unless they disguise themselves as fecal matter?" Marco said. "It's an adaptation they made to survive."

"Really?" Berry said.

"No," Judy said. "He's being a nut. Tell us about the concert."

Berry told all, stressing his triumph and inevitable choral idol-hood. His parents congratulated and cheered and all that good stuff. "Mom, dad, I've got something else to tell you. I've been taking these pills, mostly to keep my voice from changing, but they've been turning me into a girl, which is kind of a by-product, but I'm not one hundred percent sure how I want to end up and for now I just want to stay a choir-boy, so I need a note from you guys saying it's all good."

Marco and Judy stared. A documentary told them about the disappearing rainforest. Berry twitched while his parents froze. "Um," said Berry. "I think there's paper in the kitchen drawer, and I saw a ballpoint pen on the table. It doesn't have to be a long note."

"Pills," Judy said. "You're hooked on pills. What kind of pills are we talking? My son's a pill addict. I knew I should have been around more. Show me your pupils. Are your pupils dilated?"

"You haven't been listening," Marco said. "He's a drag queen. Our son's a drag queen."

"Well, if you marry a repressed homo, I guess you get what you pay for."

"Who's a repressed homo? I took him to a strip bar. This is not my fault, Miss Cunt of Steel."

"Um," Berry said. The television talked about endangered lizards, the kind Maura would save once her sugar daddy arrived.

"You took him to a strip bar?"

"Male bonding. He needed one parent who took an interest in his life."

"Did you take him to your pusher as well? Is that how he got into pills?"

"Please," Berry said. He found a piece of paper and a pen and held them up.

"I don't have a pusher, you bitch. Not since that Green Anteater incident, which I still think was all your fault."

Berry knew from experience his parents were five to ten sentences away from throwing shit and breaking appliances. Ordinarily he'd have run to his room and locked the door. He had a whole ritual for blocking out these storms, using Choral Fugue State and candles. But this time was Berry's fault. He couldn't prevent Maura and Canon Moosehead from visiting the Weird Zone together, but this he could prevent. "Shut up!" Berry screamed at the top of his lungs.

Marco and Judy stopped yelling and looked at Berry. He seized the TV remote and squashed POWER. Silence gathered, a smaller and less perfect stillness than an empty cathedral. Car sounds and neighbors' lives broke in.

"I am not a druggie or a drag queen, and I wish you guys would listen to me for once."

Judy looked down. "Just tell us what's going on."

"I'm taking some pills, okay? They're not drugs or anything. They're more like hormones and stuff. I started taking them because I didn't want my voice to change. Now I'm not sure what I want. Some of the pills are turning me female, which I don't know what I think about."

"Son," Marco said slowly. "You only have one body and you need to treat it with respect."

Judy looked sharply at Marco's flab and drug-fuddled gaze, and snorted. "Berry," she asked, "do you want to be a woman?"

"I don't know. I just know I don't want to grow up like . . . ," he didn't look at Marco, ". . . like most guys." Then he glanced quickly at Marco, who looked like he'd just taken a knife to the gut.

"It's official," Marco said. "I really do suck."

Judy took Marco's hand for a moment, then let it drop. Neither of them looked at the other. Berry still held out the pen and paper, but neither parent took it.

13.

The sound of hammer blows woke Berry, a percussion regular as assembly lines. Berry lay on his bed, still wearing his
concert clothes from the night before. He pulled off his jacket and shirt, unwound his bandages, and put on a T-shirt.
He no longer needed a torso disguise at home.

Judy chopped a cucumber into pieces of almost identical
width on a cutting board. "You're not going to school," she
told Berry. "Dr. Tamarind has a slot free at eleven and we're
going to drive you." She attacked the cucumber so hard
Berry feared for her thumb.

"I just saw Dr. Tamarind yesterday," Berry said. "Twice,
even." Berry's voice still felt torn down from explaining
himself to his parents half the night, staring through sleep-
less lids at their grainy shadow selves. The facts had looped
and his parents had nodded as he'd talked pills and changes.
Then they'd asked the same dumb questions until Berry had
given up and slept.

"You've got a lot to tell him," Judy said. The door opened
and Marco brought in a paper bag of bagels and cream cheese.
Nobody wanted cucumber slices on their bagels except Judy.
"Greek salad tonight," she said. She was bagging work.

Nobody talked on the drive to Dr. Tamarind's and Berry
wondered when would be a good time to bring up the fact
that choir rehearsal was tonight and he needed that note. He
figured after his session.

Dr. Tamarind hopped like a grasshopper around his office long after Berry sat down. The therapist couldn't stop clucking. Berry hadn't seen him this giddy.

"Business is good, huh," Berry said. "Have Canon Moosehead and Maura been here yet today?" Dr. Tamarind just bounced and chuckled. "Ya know, Canon Moosehead was head-fucked long before someone dosed him. And no, I don't know who did it."

"We're not here to talk about Canon Moosehead," Dr. Tamarind said. "Lovely concert, by the way."

"We stomped the motherfucker in the name of the Lord. They gotta re-roof the cathedral."

"Speaking of mending roofs. Berry, why are you here?"

"Question I've asked myself since session one." Berry heard aggro in his own voice. He leaned forward in his seat and counterattacked for the first time in therapy. Suddenly he wanted to pin that grasshopper to a cork board.

"I mean, why are you here today?"

"Today's no different than other times. Why am I here? So you can study me? So I can try and explain what it's like to have a gift with an expiration date?" Those were the most words Berry had spoken in therapy. "The reason my parents brought me today is I've been solving my problem on my own."

"Tell me about your solution."

Berry told. Dr. Tamarind finally sat down and listened, eyes closed, the way he had when Berry had sung in therapy. When Berry finished, Dr. Tamarind stayed like that: asleep or thinking.

Finally, Dr. Tamarind woke up. "You know, Maura may be right about you." Berry started to argue, but Dr. Tamarind raised a bony hand. "Gender Identity Dysphoria isn't an exact diagnosis most of the time, even though we pretend it is. Sometimes people feel depressed or disjointed and decide their gender is part of it. The reason I often keep people in therapy a long time before I greenlight hormones is because I want to be sure."

"Yah. Maura said you were a pill miser."

"One thing's for sure. You won't get any more pills if you're not really transgendered. Not from me, not from that clinic. We can't prescribe without a clear diagnosis. GID is a diagnosis. 'Wants To Stay A Choirboy' doesn't show up in the DSM-IV."

Berry jumped from his chair to lean over Dr. Tamarind's desk. "That's not fair. I knew you wouldn't understand! You're just trying to blackmail me like everybody else."

"Nobody's blackmailing you. Berry, there's an old saying, 'therapy is looking your destiny in the eye and saying, No.' It seems to me you've already done that. Look, I've had to piece things together about you while you gave me the silent treatment all this time. This could explain a lot."

"Like what?"

"You don't want to grow up like your dad or other men. You want people to perceive you as," Dr. Tamarind waved his hands. "As bright and delicate."

"I'm a choirboy. It's different." Berry watched the sliver of daylight through the tight curtains, the one glimpse of outside Dr. Tamarind allowed.

"I kept asking what it was about being a choirboy you needed so badly. Maybe now we know. Have you ventured out as a girl?"

"I went to the mall and got a bra."

"That's a start. Maybe you need to try it some more."

"You don't think I'm too young to make this decision?"

"Maybe. But you've started and it might be wrong to turn back. They're starting people on hormones younger and younger. I know of a few fifteen-year-old TSs. Only a couple years older than you. The younger you start, the greater the effect the hormones have."

"What about choir? I can't stay in it if I'm a girl. It's all I care about."

Dr. Tamarind sighed. "I understand." He fussed with the bridge of his nose where his glasses chafed. "Give yourself some time off choir. We'll talk about it more next week. Meanwhile, I want you to try life as a girl."

"It's all I care about," Berry repeated.

"Nothing lasts forever," Dr. Tamarind said. "You find new things to care for. Maybe you already have. There's only one way to know."

Dr. Tamarind led Berry out to the waiting area. His parents sat on chairs instead of the sofa. Judy had a gardening magazine unopened in her lap. "I think Berry's a transsexual," Dr. Tamarind said, as if announcing the sex of a fresh baby.

Both parents nodded. Marco asked if this was his fault.

Dr. Tamarind pinched his chin and bowed from the waist. "It's not a question of fault. It happens. There's nothing wrong. But now Berry has to choose whether to finish what he started. He's confused."

"I am so not going to school as a girl," Berry said.

"Probably not a good idea right away," Dr. Tamarind agreed.

"If he becomes a woman, can he still have kids?" Judy asked.

"We could freeze some of his, um, her sperm in case she finds someone she really wants to inseminate. But that's a long way off. We're not talking about surgery now, just continuing with hormones." They talked for half an hour more. Dr. Tamarind convinced Berry's parents to let him hang out with Maura, Lisa, and whoever else wanted to aid Berry's immersion in girl soup.

Marco and Judy took Berry to lunch at a Tex Mex/Tibetan restaurant. Marco had ice tea with yak butter in it and Momos Rancheros. Berry had curry tofu ribs.

"Of course, we're going to support you no matter what." Judy picked at a salad. "I mean, short of human sacrifice or heroin. We just want you to be happy."

"We do?" Marco sounded like he'd missed a memo.

"I was happy," Berry said, "in the choir."

Berry got tired of staring at pictures of yak herders in cowboy hats and yurts with cacti out front. And tireder of Marco's brooding and Judy's tries at putting a brave face on things.

"Basically I got a week to figure it out," Berry said. "Not a ton of time." He called Mr. Allen from a pay phone and left a voice mail saying he'd told the parents, but no note yet.

He went back to his parents' booth. "Everything will fall into place," Judy told the arugula on her fork.

"Tell me about Kremlinology," said Berry.

The question startled Marco and Judy, but Judy finally had an answer. "It was a sort of religion, like understanding the precepts of a really obscure sage. Or the rituals of a lost faith. Every day, state newspapers came out of Moscow, along with speeches and promulgations. What they didn't say mattered more than what they did, and you sort of peered through all those gaps to catch the real meaning."

Marco joined in. "And so then once the USSR was dead, you could hear what was really going on from people who were on the inside, and find out how wrong we'd all been."

Berry asked Marco and Judy to drop him downtown. "There's somebody I need to see. I have a lot of stuff to work out." His parents argued with him, but helplessness won out over their responsibility. They dropped Berry near the bus depot. From there, he walked to the business district. He'd left Gray Redman's card at home, but remembered the name of the building and the street it was on. He walked around for an hour or so, past men in suits and women in pressed skirts and jackets. Berry wore a jeans jacket, T-shirt, and black sweat pants. He had no idea whether he looked like a boy or a girl to these people. Either way, he wasn't one of them. Here all the buildings had upward-sloping glass walls. Pigeons danced around Berry's feet. Berry wondered if he'd miss more than one day of school. That'd be something. People in business wear came from lunch or went to meetings. This was the world that had defeated Marco, and that Judy strove to join.

Finally, Berry found the right building and scanned the illuminated list of names and office numbers. A security guard in the lobby stared at him. No "Gray Redman." Finally, Berry spotted Inspirational Vocations, which rang familiar. It was on the fifth floor. Berry got to the elevator just as the guard lifted himself from his chair to hassle him.

On the fifth floor, Berry stalked the hall twice before he spotted the glass door next to the men's room labeled "New You Electrolysis and Inspirational Vocations." Berry pushed the door and found himself in a small room stacked with boxes. Two doors, both closed. Berry knocked on one and a Asian woman in a blue smock opened it. She wore gloves and a nose/mouth mask. She told Berry Gray Redman worked in the other room. Berry knocked on that door and a voice said to come in.

Gray Redman had his feet up on a desk in a small room with one other chair. He had a computer with ergonomic keyboard. He wore suit pants, a blue and white striped shirt, and a yellow tie, but Berry couldn't see a jacket anywhere. "Berry," Gray Redman said. "I'm so touched you decided to give me another chance."

"No problem," Berry said. "It wasn't your fault. I've got a lot of stuff to crunch. I need to know about work."

"Work sucks. Why do you think I became a consultant instead of getting a real job? But doing what you love for money is aces," Gray Redman seemed to recite rote phrases.

"Uh huh."

"Most people work. A few lucky ones practice active dreaming. But you're young. It's never too late to start finding that dream job, unless it's ballet dancer. But it could be too early in your case. Most kids your age have no clue. I've talked to enough classrooms full of kids who think they'll be doctors when they'll really be Amway reps. So what's the rush?"

"You offered to help. And I have deadlines."

"Deadlines are for dead people. Finish your work early and hit the beach. Or do more work, if it's your dream job."

"I already have my dream." Berry told Gray Redman about the choir and his pills. "If I became a woman, what would I do?"

"Get a mammogram every year after forty. Oh, you meant careerwise. I don't know. Much the same as if you stayed a guy. So right now you have this awesome gig with Gloria and Hallelujah and Kyrie and pass the collection plate."

"Yeah."

"Religion is big business. Ten billion last year." Berry didn't ask ten billion of what, and Gray Redman didn't say. "So you're a child star, sort of. What you need is a mentor."

"I have a ton of mentors," Berry said. This started to look like a waste of time. "They all say different things."

"Mentors are like that. Okay, kid. I need to do some leg-work. What you need is someone who has the kind of job you'd like to have. Then he or she can tell you how to get there." Berry started to protest that he didn't know what job he wanted, but Gray Redman waved a hand. "We'll try a few things, huh? Opera singers, torch singers, wedding singers. Whatever. We'll have a mini career day for you, introduce you to some people. Check back on Monday."

Berry thanked Gray Redman with as much happy as he could force-feed his voice. He'd let himself think the con-sultant would have some magic solution. Instead, it sound-ed like they'd fumble in the dark until Gray's guilt stopped fucking him.

Berry wandered the city for an hour or two. He didn't feel like calling Maura, and Lisa was still at school. He wan-dered into a magazine stand and looked at *Sixteen and a Half* and *Teeneurosis*, the magazines Lisa had shown him. The articles on makeovers and boyfriends in *Sixteen and a Half* bewildered Berry and the magazine seemed too old for him. *Teeneurosis* looked a little easier to figure out. It had makeup stuff that made sense, Berry could see himself using eye shadow and eyeliner to draw attention to his dark eyes. He mentally twirled in one of the magazine's fall dresses, a gray number with pink trim. Berry found an advice column called "Girlfriend, You Better Deal" by Gwen Indoubt.

Gwen seemed to handle mostly boyfriend problems. He won't kiss me, he wants to go all the way, he treats me weird around his friends. But she also answered questions about other stuff: I'm too fat, I'm a tomboy, I don't like boys, I'm too nerdy. Gwen gave every question the same cheery tone. She didn't scorn the fat protodykes any more than the girls who wanted to be seen with the popular boys but not touch them. Her answer to everybody was the same; do what shakes your tree the most. She seemed way nicer than the sarcastic columnist in *Sixteen and a Half*, Greta Clue. Greta dissed everybody.

The saleswaif at the magazine store seemed not to care if Berry read a whole magazine twice without paying. Berry noticed that the masthead said *Teeneurosis* had offices downtown, not too far from Gray Redman's. Berry used a toothpick to scratch the address into the back of his left hand, where it soon faded.

Berry tossed the slightly dog-eared *Teeneurosis* back on the rack and ran to the street, where he struggled to recall the address. It took him a while to find one slanty glass building among a dozen, and then longer to figure out that Advantage Point Publishing meant *Teeneurosis*. He ran up the stairs to the third floor and arrived at the carpet-walled suite still gasping.

"I'm—huh—looking for Gwen Indoubt," Berry panted. The woman at reception stared at him through cat glasses. Her jet black hair squirmed in a bun. She looked nothing like the *Teeneurosis* girls. "My name's Berry. I'm thirteen years old and I need advice."

The woman reached under her desk and handed Berry a list of resources for teens in the area, including GLBT rap groups and services for the homeless and drug-ragged. "This is what there is."

"I just wanted to ask Gwen. I won't bug her."

"There is no Gwen. It's a pen name. Whoever leaves the most dishes in the office sink writes the column each month. But feel free to send a letter and—"

"Berry! It's Berry, right?" A blond head with red streaks poked through the office door behind the desk. It took Berry a second to recognize Anna Conventional in a suit. She'd almost have blended in with the people on the street, except for the dye job and sun-and-moon earrings. "What are you doing here?"

"Looking for Gwen Indoubt, who doesn't exist. What are you doing here?"

"I work here. Actually, I write most of Gwen's material. I'm a slob in the office kitchen."

"I thought you were an accountant or something."

"Managing editor and staffer."

"Jane, do you know this kid?" the receptionist said.

"Berry's the cutest choirboy this side of Vienna. So what did you want to ask Gwen about?"

Anna Conventional held open the inner door for Berry to follow her into a maze of fuzzy walls you could see over if you stood on tiptoe. A woman in tartan threw a pencil at Berry when he craned over her wall. The walls curved around tiny ledges holding computers and phones, and chairs nestled inside the nooks. In some of them, people talked and typed.

Berry didn't trust anyone whose name changed so often. (Anna, Gwen, or Jane?) But he let the woman lead him into her small windowless office and plunk him on a stool with a view of the grilly back of her computer monitor and her poster of the city at night. "I can't believe you write dating advice," Berry said. "I've seen you and your boyfriend."

"Ex-boyfriend." Anna Conventional laughed. "It's easier to give advice than to live it. Did you have fun at the Wasteness?" Berry shrugged. "Everybody liked you, especially Bishop Bacchus. You're pretty connected in the alternative scene for a choirboy."

"I don't know if I'm still a choirboy." Berry started to cry from who knows where. He hadn't cried in years, and hadn't expected to. Once he started he couldn't stop. His face soaked. He wondered if the girl pills had turned him rawer inside. Anna/Jane gasped, grabbed a box of tissues, and thrust it at Berry. He took one. She threshed his hair with a few fingers.

"Hey," Anna/Jane said. "Hey."

"Sorry," Berry sniffed. "I never do this."

"'Sokay. You should see the freelancers when I kill their stories. So what's the sitch?"

For the umpteenth time, Berry told his story. Anna seemed fascinated, especially by the "gossip" about Maura. "I always knew that girl was a freak recruiter," she said.

When Berry was done, Anna Conventional threw her hands up. "Shit, kid. Clueless equals me. If you wrote all that in a letter, I'd wash my dishes on time for a whole month. Look, as far as I'm concerned you ought to be able to have everything you want while you're young, because the world shrinks when you get older. Be a choirboy. Be a diva. Be a football star. Whatever. I get so sick of hearing from kids who think they have to pick one clique or self-image."

Anna Conventional didn't sound as peppy as Gwen. Berry must have looked disappointed, because she tried to cheer him. "So Maura wants to pretty you up and take you out. Well, I know she can be kind of intense one-on-one, and I have a lot of free evenings since Robbie took off on his underwater tantric vision quest. Hang on, I'll see what she's doing." Anna Conventional had Maura on speed dial. "Hey. It's me. I got your boy here. How many boys you got? Berry. Duh. No, he's not a girl. Not yet, anyway. Dude. Dude. Listen to me. Dude. You're in bed with who? Whatever. Listen, what are you doing tonight? Cancel. We'll meet you at the Metro K. You and Berry. I'm playing buffer. Yeah. Yeah. See ya."

Berry protested, but Jane—acting more and more like Anna Conventional every moment—shushed him. "What's your parents' number?" Berry told it. She dialed. "Hi. Is this Berry's mom? Great. Great. This is Jane Willbury, managing editor of *Teeneurosis* Magazine. That's right. Yes. I'm a friend of Berry's. He didn't? I'm sure he has lots of friends. Yes. I know all about that. That's why I'm calling. I'm giving Berry some pointers. No, he won't be in the magazine. He probably won't be back tonight. I have a pull-out bed. Don't worry. Really. I'm a trained advice columnist. No. No hard drugs. No human sacrifice. I promise. Right. You'll see him tomorrow, a happier and better-adjusted Berry. Fine. Okay. Buh."

After she hung up, Anna Conventional turned to Berry. "They're fine. Oh, and I want some before-and-afters of the makeover. No biggie. You won't have to sign a model release, they're just for my stash." Berry blinked. "So what's this about Maura being in bed with a minister?"

Anna Conventional got off work early and donned a fake leopard skin coat and pink fuzzy hat over her business drag. Maura wore a black tube dress that started below her armpits and went to mid-thigh, plus a shiny belt. Berry couldn't tell what held the strapless dress up. Maura's hair flowed up in a big swoosh around her rhinestone bow.

Anna Conventional and Maura bought Berry dinner at the Metro K, a yuppie-ish after-work joint with sandwiches and salads on its menu, named after famous actors or old noodle-stretching tycoons. Berry had a burger and fries. "You're lucky," Maura told Berry. "You can eat anything at your age and it doesn't live on your ass." Both Maura and Anna Conventional ate salads.

The entire dinner conversation consisted of Berry's makeover. "I'd say some gel for her hair," Anna said. They both used the female pronoun for Berry after a while. "Maybe some red highlights, they'll wash out. Luckily there's almost no body hair."

The two women could go for ten minutes saying nothing but names of beauty products.

"Colorbust by Lavienne!" Anna exclaimed.

"Lustrelash by Cosmetique!" Maura shouted back.

Berry just ate his burger and fries and let the product litany go by. Maura turned to him and said: "Hon, your eyelashes are going to be longer and thicker than your intestines. That's a promise."

"Eating," Berry mumbled.

Dinner was over too soon. They sped him back to Anna Conventional's apartment, a converted warehouse loft. Anna's apartment was bigger than Berry's parents' but he saw no sign she shared it with anyone. The front room had a sofabed, where Berry would crash. It had a nice glass coffee table with glossy mags, mostly Anna's, on them. Every wall and some of the ceiling showed off paintings by artists Anna Conventional knew, including one huge painting by Bishop Bacchus of a warrior clown impaling a sacred prostitute on the spike of a condom-shaped umbrella. Anna Conventional and Maura hustled him to the bathroom.

"What's first?" Maura said.

"First she bathes. Kid's gotta smell nice and have soft skin. Berry, I want you to take a long bubble bath and use every single one of the oils and gels on my shower caddy. Okay? Don't skip any. In the meantime, where'd I put my bong?"

Berry did what Anna Conventional said. As the bathtub filled, Berry felt in his joints the fact that the choir was rehearsing without him. What had Mr. Allen told the choir? That Berry was sick? That he had a schedule clash? Or that he was mid-change into a freak of science?

Berry poured a finger each out of a dozen bottles into the tub, including shampoos and exfoliants. He sank in up to his hair. The smell reminded him of the incense-and-booze-doused Twelve Step room during the coed sleepover a few weeks ago. A bottle spun in Berry's mind, not stopping for anyone, spinning forever until the people around it blurred, boys and girls, into an unkissable mystery.

"Well, I'll be fucked to bleeding. She fell asleep. Kid, did you fall asleep?" Anna Conventional sounded less alert than earlier.

"Not asleep," Berry said. "Just thinking."

"Can you think and wash your hair at the same time? Moisturizing shampoo, then a little conditioner." Anna Conventional didn't seem too interested in Berry's naked-ness under all the foam. She picked over several shelves of beauty stuff while Berry showered, rinsed, and conditioned.

"You're lucky I'm here," Anna Conventional told Berry as she did his hair with gel, a hot curling iron, and a blow dryer. Berry's hair had never looked so big. His head had exploded. "If it was just Maura giving you a makeover, she'd go overboard with the cosmetics. Don't tell her I said that. She thinks if one layer is good, ten must be better."

"I heard that," Maura said.

Berry dried off and wrapped himself in a fluffy bathrobe. Maura didn't see Berry naked, not that it probably mattered. For the next hour or so—it felt like fifteen million sermons—Maura and Anna Conventional worked on Berry's face with brushes, pads, and fuzzy pipe cleaners. Berry's job was to look straight ahead, or up, or to one side, to open his mouth, or close it, as they directed.

"You know," Maura said. "Canon Moosehead is a great guy. I found him sensitive and caring, and a hell of a kisser."

"You kissed Canon Moosehead?" Berry jerked forward. Anna Conventional restrained him with one hand while brushing with the other.

"No moving," Anna Conventional said.

"He was very upset," Maura said. "We talked it over. He's a wronged individual, I gotta tell you. So I comforted him."

"How . . . how much comfort did you end up giving him?" Berry smudged his lipstick.

"Oh, a fair amount. You gotta save something for the second date, ya know."

"Second! You mean—"

"Sunday night. He gets so strung out after services."

"Does he know . . . that you're . . . about your . . ."

"Ya know, not sure. You think it matters?"

Anna Conventional puffed flour in Berry's face. He sneezed. "Hey, watch that. No olfactory responses until your face is in place." Berry tried to hold his breath. "So isn't this Canon guy some kind of pew-kisser? So he should be Reverend Tolerance, right?"

"Uh," Berry said. "Before he started busting stiffies, Canon Moosehead was pretty uptight."

"Maybe he's mellowed out. Trouble broadens the mind. I gotta say, Maur, your life thing is really trippy, it's like the ultimate life as art trip, or maybe art as life. I dunno," said Anna Conventional.

"Speaking of art," Maura said, "you think she's about done?"

"Give me a few more minutes," Anna said, concentrating. "God, I wish I could put this in the magazine. We'd win a Pulitzer for makeover-related journalism."

"They have a Pulitzer for makeovers?" Maura said.

"Or maybe it's just a Nobel Prize. I forget."

Berry just resigned himself to being putty and letting the two of them work on him. He didn't go back to sleep, but he did drift into a space where nothing mattered. Makeovers seemed to be haircuts times ten.

Finally, Anna Conventional nodded to Maura, who grabbed a mirror and plunked it in front of Berry. The image looked unlike anything Berry had seen in the mirror before. It was like that moment, a year after Berry joined the choir, when he'd first figured out the tiny face he saw was his own, and that he was a separate person like the other people he saw everywhere, and not some disembodied vantage point. Except, this time, he saw an alien supermodel instead of himself.

"Oh my God," Berry breathed.

The person facing him had fascinating dark eyes and proud cheekbones, a pouty but not bratty mouth, and feathery black hair. As a boy, Berry could never approach a girl like the one he saw. The hormones had furnished the raw material for this candy face, not just tits but also softer features.

"Nice," Maura said. "Definite Pulitzer material."

"I went for subtle," Anna Conventional said.

"Hey, my third or fourth middle name is subtle."

"Now it's just a matter of clothes," Anna Conventional said. "We want something that shows off that bust and those hips, without necessarily making too much of a big deal out of his doohickey."

"I don't suppose we could tuck it," Maura said. Berry wasn't sure what that meant, but it sounded hideous. He and Anna both shot Maura dirty looks. She tossed up her hands. "Fine, fine."

They made Berry try on a few trillion of Anna Conventional's dresses and blouse/skirt combos. He got twitchy by the time they settled on a purply-blue stretchy dress with a low-cut front, leading to stretchy lycra over the tummy and then a foofy gathered skirt made of some kind of tulle. "Yes," Anna said. "Yes, yes, yes, definitely yes. I haven't worn this since Bush the first. You gotta be skinny to pull this baby off."

Berry stared at the debutante in the mirror in the frilly low-cut dress and bare feet. She looked glamorous and untouchable, but also vulnerable. Shy and anxious for someone to shield her from the world. A soft minx whom some man could, should, come and possess. Berry felt inadequate to take care of the girl in the mirror. She needed a powerful man, not the boy who blinked at her loveliness. Where had Maura and Anna found the lushness they'd grafted onto Berry's skin?

"Wow," Berry said. "I can't believe this is me. I mean, wow. Gotta admit, I'm impressed. Blown away, even." Anna Conventional took a bow. "So can I take it all off now?"

"Are you insane?" Anna Conventional laughed, scandalized. "We must take you out on the town. You had your snow tires fitted, now you gotta be road tested."

"She's just nervous," Maura said, stroking the back of Berry's neck. "God, I've waited ages for this. It's Okay, Berry. It'll be fine."

"Nerves have nothing to do with it," Berry twirled in front of the mirror despite his reservations. He practiced tossing his head with a smile. "If someone from school or choir sees me like this, I'm fucking dead." The girl in the mirror pouted. Berry wanted to kiss her.

"They wouldn't recognize you anyway," Maura chortled. "All they'll see now is a hot mama chula with perky tits."

"Anyway, we'll go places nobody knows you," Anna Conventional said. "Think we could sneak her into Merry Queen of Scotch?"

"She's got a fake ID," Maura said.

"Wow, kid, you get around."

"My dad's a failed role model," Berry explained.

"Flawed heroes are the best kind," Anna said in an artistic pronouncement sort of voice.

"Uh huh," Berry said uncertainly.

Maura really wanted to take Berry to the Booby Hatch, the city's tranny hangout, but Anna Conventional vetoed that for now. "It's just a little overwhelming. Lots of your fellow, er, professionals tend to congregate there, and so do a lot of would-be clients."

"I hate you artsy fartsy types," Maura said.

Berry wasn't sure whether Anna Conventional and Maura really liked each other. They both focused a lot on Berry.

Merry Queen of Scotch was darker than the karaoke bar he'd gone to with Maura and Wilson, and it had a line out front. It had fewer tables and chairs than the strip joint Marco had taken Berry to and no stage. Swords and kilts dangled around the bar. But the bar also had purple neon strips behind it, and a pirate hung over the pool table.

When Berry and friends got there, it was already past Berry's normal bedtime. The club was just starting to fill up. Maura got Berry a virgin daiquiri with a big umbrella.

Clubbing turned out to be boring. The club was a crowded place where speech died in the rumble of music. Maura and Anna Conventional seemed to enjoy standing around and sipping drinks. Occasionally someone they knew would drift past and they'd make a huge pantomime of waving and smiling. Then they'd go back to standing and making signs at each other or shouting in each other's ears.

"Hey," Anna Conventional told Berry. "That guy thinks you're cute." She pointed at a man standing in the corner who wore a nice suit and blue tie. "Of course, you're jailbait, but he doesn't know that."

Berry could hear Anna Conventional if she stood right beside him and shouted. Berry wasn't sure how he was supposed to feel about the random stranger checking him out. He definitely was, though. Berry looked into the stranger's eyes and saw something like reverence.

"It just shows we did a good job," Anna Conventional said. "People find you hot and a convincing girl, which I never doubted. We had good raw material. This is what it's all about."

"We're hanging out, just the girls," Maura shouted, as if labeling the situation would make it appeal to Berry. "We're having girl talk. We're sharing feminine mysteries. We're girlbonding. We're *doing girl stuff*!"

"Uh huh," Berry said.

"Why don't you try giggling?" Maura said. "It's a wonderful feeling, a release. Here, we'll all giggle together. One, two three . . ." On three, Maura made a rattling cans noise in her throat. Anna Conventional made a half-hearted attempt to join in. Berry just watched them as if they were insane.

"You didn't join in," Maura accused.

"Look, I really appreciate the girlbonding and all. It's just that I feel a little weird. This is all kind of new to me, and I'm really not used to acting like a grownup. I mean, what do girls my own age do?"

"Giggle," Maura offered.

"Play with makeup. Obsess over their weight. Masturbate in secret. Listen to bad bubblegum pop. Write inane letters to magazines about how they like this boy but can't tell if he likes them back, or how some boy likes them but they just want to be friends," said Anna Conventional.

"Sounds great," Berry said.

"It pretty much sucks to be your age no matter what sex you are," said Anna Conventional.

They went to the karaoke bar, where Berry could relax and sing a song he liked by Christina Aguilera. The crowd loved Berry, and he liked what he saw in their eyes. By the song's bridge, he stalked like the stars on MTV and urged the audience to shout "Ho!" at intervals. He hit some impossible high notes, Mariah-style, and the crowd shrieked. When he got back to the table, Anna and Maura hugged him. "You were amazing! You're getting into it!"

"That was fun," Berry admitted.

"You just found your inner vamp," Anna Conventional said. "I'm thinking big head-dress or tiara. I'm thinking rhinestone bustier and sequin gloves."

"I love to sing," Berry said. "Everything else is just show."
Another guilt wave about the evening's missed rehearsal.

"Enough of this trifling," Maura said. "Can we please hit the Booby Hatch now?"

"I dunno," Anna Conventional said. "What do you think, Berry? You up to descending to the tranny underworld?"

Berry yawned nakedly. "Dunno. Depends if it'll be more interesting than the clubs we've hit so far."

"Don't be a jerk," Anna said without heat. "We'll go for a little while, just to see what we think. Unless we're rapturous, we'll head on back. That's why God made cars."

The Booby Hatch was a mile or two away from downtown, in a run-down area of warehouses and massage parlors. From the back seat of Anna Conventional's SUV Berry watched the neighborhood slide downhill as the car moved further north. "Hey," Berry said. "Thanks for taking me under your wings and stuff. I know it's a pain dealing with me."

"You kidding?" Anna Conventional said. "This is the most fun I've had in weeks."

"This is a blast," Maura said. "I just wish you were enjoying it more."

"I am enjoying it," Berry said. "I'll try harder."

"We're here!" Maura pointed at a golden awning with a white neon sign that said "TBH" in cursive letters. The "B" looked like cleavage. A bouncer and a few women loitered outside. Anna Conventional found a parking spot right away.

The Booby Hatch was as dark as the other bars, but with textures of shade on purpose. The women in the room seemed to thrive on near-darkness, like anti-plants. The moment the trio entered, Maura rushed off the street. She kissed cheeks and hugged everyone in sight. Most of the girls there wore more makeup than Maura and they glistened shyly as if rapid movement might dispel their womanhood.

"They're all jealous of you," Anna Conventional whispered to Berry.

Berry couldn't believe her. All these women looked so perfect and sophisticated, their hair in place and faces etched in strong lines. They looked realer than most women. They all socialized amongst themselves while they waited for someone/something else. How many of them were workers like Maura?

Something disturbed the equilibrium of Berry's ass. Fingers thrust into the cleft under his skirt and squeezed. "Hey, stop that," Anna Conventional swatted a man's hairy wrist. He'd emerged from the gloom without Berry noticing him. He pulled his hand away, but the move upset the delicate balance Berry had striven for all night on his three-inch chunky heels. He'd been on tiptoe for hours.

Berry pitched forward, one knee bent and hands flailing. He knocked over one of the lacquer-headed goddesses standing by the bar and she fell face first into the puddle her own drink created as it landed. "Oh God!" Berry cried. He teetered and tripped on the downed girl, then flew himself into a full-on belly flop. Maura's arm lunged and grabbed him at the last minute.

"Jesus!" Maura said. She pulled Berry to his feet. "Maddie, you all right?" The woman on the floor groaned and nodded. She raised herself slowly and with difficulty, then staggered to the bathroom to rebuild her face and hair. "Jesus!" Maura said again. "Berry, you have been drinking virgins haven't you?" Berry nodded. "Everybody, this is

Berry. She's still finding her T-legs!" Maura introduced him to all the bright figures. He wondered if their makeup glowed in the dark like the stars on Wilson's ceiling. They all smiled at Berry. One or two of them shook his hand as if they wished him the Peace of the Lord.

Once Berry's pupils dilated enough to suck light from every meager source in the room, he saw that Maura and the others weren't alone. A dozen or so men crouched in the corners and at the fringes of the bar. They all looked older than the women there, and stubble clouded their faces. Most wore casual club gear, but one or two wore suits. They all sat nervously or patiently, Berry couldn't tell which, and watched the women mingle. The men didn't talk to each other. One of the women standing near Berry made eye contact with one of the men and smiled as if greeting a best friend. After they locked smiles, she went and sat on his lap. He bought her a drink and soon they sat skin-to-skin from neck to thigh.

Berry found Anna Conventional at his elbow again. They held hands. "Having fun?" Anna Conventional asked.

"I guess so," Berry said. It seemed he'd aged decades since his parents had dragged him to Dr. Tamarind this morning. Weariness turned to a hatred of everyone around him, even Anna who clutched his hand. Berry had never felt so hostile. It frightened him, more alien than the hose and lipstick he wore. The costume he could try on and discard just as easily. The anger was inside him, a previously unknown organ. Was this what Marco felt like? Or Mr. Allen?

Bar music faded and way louder beats started. A large woman in a tight dress and huge wig got on a small stage in the corner that Berry hadn't noticed before. She pranced around the stage, cracking wise at the girls who waved dollar bills at her. Then she lip-synched to the song "You're So Vain" by some ancient songstress Judy used to put on the CD player before Marco "accidentally" broke the speakers. The memory of Marco slapping a hammer down, again and again, into the paper around the speaker's woofer until it only farted, made Berry wonder what Marco and Judy were doing tonight.

The large lip-syncher finished, her dress stuffed with bills. Another woman got up and mouthed Debbie Gibson. "I don't understand," Berry said loudly. "Don't these people know how to sing?" Maura shushed him.

When they finally left, Berry was exhausted and raw. Maura kept talking about how great it had been and how much everyone had liked/envied/admired Berry. Berry stayed silent, then finally blurted, "Is that all there is?"

"What do you mean? What more do you want? Some people look forward all week to going out and showing off at the Booby Hatch. And for others, it's where they make the rent."

"That's not all there is to transgender life," Anna put in. "A lot of people don't go clubbing at all. This is just one subculture."

"You didn't like it?" Maura said, hurt.

"It was pretty stupid. I mean they had some nice outfits and stuff. It was just kind of lame and boring. I mean, how can you like places like that after you've been to church?"

"What's so great about church?"

"Everything. The music, the costumes—we don't just move our lips there, we make actual sounds. It's culture and spiritual stuff and dress-up all rolled into one, and that's why it's way cooler than any of that clubbing crap."

"Perhaps a minority view among teens," Anna muttered.

"You are such a little bitch!" Maura yelled. "I can't believe how ungrateful you're being after we went to all this trouble for you! You've had all these opportunities and you just act spoiled and jaded!"

"Go fuck yourself," Berry hissed.

"Now that sounds like a teenager," said Anna.

"Oh yeah, the big teen expert," said Maura. "Why don't you enlighten us? What would Gwen do?"

"Who the fuck knows. Depending on how much caffeine I get, Gwen would say be yourself, listen to others, or don't be a brat."

"I'm just really tired," Berry said. Then he closed his eyes, and the next thing he knew, Anna Conventional was leading him upstairs to her sofabed.

14.

Berry woke to guilt. He lay tangled in the flannel covers of the rollaway bed. His neck throbbed from the unnatural posture his heels had kept him in all evening and dryness stung his mouth. But much worse was the image of himself as a spoiled debutante mocking Maura's haunts. He wouldn't have thought himself capable of being either so lovely or so mean, let alone both at once.

Berry drank scant saliva and vowed never to be in a position to disappoint anyone ever again.

Anna Conventional saw Berry awake and offered coffee, but he took OJ and ibuprofen instead. It was almost noon. When she took his glass to refill it Berry thanked her and mumbled that he wasn't usually such an asshole.

"Did you lose your bitch cherry last night? Congrats."

"Thanks, I guess." Berry drank a second glass of OJ. "Any ideas how I get it back?"

"The bitch cherry, once popped, never restores. But you can choose not to exercise those muscles. Anyway, Maura kinda had it coming. She expects too much of people and then flips when they fall short."

"What about you?"

"I had fun helping you explore. No pressure."

"Thanks. Shit, gotta call my parents."

"Phone's inside the papier-mâché walrus. How are they coping with this?" Anna Conventional waved a hand at Berry's chest, barely hidden by the T-shirt he'd slept in.

"Not sure. They seemed pretty creeped yesterday."

"Hey, you need a place to crash . . ." Anna nodded at the sofabed.

"Thanks. That's really nice of you." Berry squinted. "What makes you think I'll need somewhere to stay?"

"Hopefully you won't. But I don't think you know how much shit you're letting yourself in for if you go through with this."

Berry looked at this cool friend who suddenly wanted to suffocate him with warnings. He almost yelled at her. Then he shook his head. "Thanks. Hope you're wrong. But thanks."

The phone rang for a long time at Berry's house. Then he heard an answering machine, a new message in Judy's voice. It simply mentioned the phone number and said to leave a message. "Hey. Berry. Everything's fine. Home soon. Bye."

Anna Conventional insisted on taking Berry for waffles with blueberries and syrup. She lent him a nice pair of jeans and a knit top. With his one bra and the heels he'd worn the night before, he looked just like a girl his age. As an afterthought, Anna gave him a dash of foundation, powder, blush, and mascara, just enough to put life on his face. At the brunch place, Berry felt self-conscious, but not as scared as the night before. Femininity started to feel like a second, or maybe third, skin.

By the time Berry got home, he felt soothed, the way he did when performance jitters gave way to confidence. He'd get his parents to sign the note before tomorrow's services, and be back in business in time for the recording. Once the choir laid tracks there'd be time to decide on girl or boy or what.

On the car ride back to Berry's place Anna Conventional seemed a little startled that he didn't live in suburbia with Lisa. "Want me to go up and explain to your parents about last night?" she said.

"Nah," Berry said. It sounded tempting, but he didn't want her to see his place. If his neighborhood had disappointed her, what would his apartment do?

"Fine. You've got my home and cell phone numbers." Anna Conventional kissed Berry on both cheeks, then drove off leaving him to climb to the sixth floor alone.

Berry was glad Anna couldn't see the Sanchez apartment. It took him a while to take it all in. One chair sat on its side. Books and old vinyl records covered much of the floor. A vase had hit one wall, full of water, then fallen and broken. Flowers and shards littered the floor and the wet spot on the wall showed the impact had happened recently. Berry hadn't seen the place this bad.

Neither parent was home. Nor was there any sign where they'd gone or when they'd be back. He almost called Anna Conventional's cell phone, but changed his mind. He needed time alone anyway and might need her help way more later. Plus, Berry needed to talk to his parents and get that note for Mr. Allen.

Berry took off the high heels. He felt like he'd just unsnapped the jaws of two poisonous snakes from his insteps.

The television seemed broken again. Berry started to listen to *Choral Fugue State*, but that just made him more anxious. Finally he called Lisa. Her dad didn't recognize Berry's voice from their confrontation. He'd heard about Lisa's friend from church.

"How's it going?" Berry asked Lisa when she picked up.

"Not good," Lisa said. "Been swimming."

"Oh."

"How are you doing?"

"Not great. Went out last night with Maura." Berry told Lisa about clubbing.

"I wish you'd let me give you a makeover instead," Lisa said. Berry wasn't sure if he wanted another makeover, but he wanted to see Lisa. "Do you want to hang out tomorrow after church?" she asked.

"I don't know if I'm going to church tomorrow." Berry explained about the note.

"Well, if you can't go with the choir, you can go with me. I'll sneak you in as a girl. Nobody'll even know you're there."

"I don't know. I . . ." Berry heard door sounds. "Shit. Parents. I'll call back."

Berry ran out into the desolate living room/kitchen area. Marco had a bandage on his left hand and stitches under his right eye. Behind him, Judy closed the door and put away keys. Marco wore a T-shirt that said "Old Fart." He smiled when he saw Berry.

"Son. How's tricks?" Marco asked.

"That's not our son. That's our daughter," Judy said.

Marco rammed a fist into Berry's chin. Berry fell on his butt. His jaw thrummed and his sore neck spasmed again.

"That's our son," Marco said. "Get up, son. Say howdy to your old man."

Berry stood up. Marco punched him again. This time on the nose. Berry felt blood dribble into his mouth. He fell like a flag on a pinball table. He landed on something hard, which jabbed an inch from his spine.

"What are you doing?" Judy asked.

"Just roughhousing," Marco said. Berry tried to get up and Marco split his lip. "With my son."

Berry stayed on the ground, hugged himself. "Little friendly father-son wrestling," Marco said. He pounced, bear-hugged Berry's neck with both arms. Berry cried out. Marco pulled Berry by the throat.

"Stop it!" Judy yelled. "I just got back from patching you up! Let her go!"

Marco let Berry go. Berry huddled against the kitchen table, sobbing despite himself.

"Hey, son," Marco said. "Your turn. Free shot."

Berry peered over at his dad, whose arms crossed behind his back. Marco sat on the floor against the wall waiting for Berry to hit him. He beamed. "Pop your pop one. Come on. Kisser or gizzard, your choice."

"I don't want to."

"Marco, leave your daughter alone—"

Marco grabbed Berry's shirt and hauled him vertical, shoved him hard against the wall. "Hit me, goddamnit! Hit me, you little fucking queer!" His face blocked everything. His dark eyes looked bloodshot and bulged. He smelled of antiseptic, coffee, and stomach acid. "Now, you shit!"

Berry fell forward or lunged, he wasn't sure which afterward. Either way, his forehead crunched Marco's face. He felt the impact just above his right eye. It hurt Berry worse than any of Marco's blows. The sudden sharp pressure above Berry's eye made him see flashes.

Marco roared and let go of Berry. Berry staggered backwards into the kitchen. He looked up to see Marco, hands on his stitches and agony stretching his mouth. "My son is evil," Marco said. He turned, one arm gesturing. Berry flattened against the wall, near the trashed chair. "We can't close our eyes here, he'll murder us as we sleep. He tried to gouge my eyes out. You saw it."

Judy said nothing. She and Berry just crouched at opposite ends of the room and waited for Marco to make a move. He raged and raged. Then he paused and looked at his wife and kid. "Not that it matters what I think," he said. Then he walked down the hall to his and Judy's bedroom and shut the door.

Berry listened for sounds from his parents' bedroom, but didn't hear any. He stayed on the floor, too drained to get up.

"Sorry about that, Becky," Judy said. "Is Becky okay? Or what should I call you?" Berry looked down at the blood on his shirt. "Your father's just having a tough adjustment. He seemed fine at first, but he couldn't let go of the idea all this was a judgment on him somehow."

"Why didn't you tell him it wasn't?" Berry said.

"I didn't know what to tell him. I mean, you went and left us to absorb this information by ourselves, and we kind of reached our own conclusions. Don't worry, honey. I'm not mad. I understand you had some things of your own to work out."

"That's good. I guess."

"You know we haven't been close. Maybe now that you're my daughter we can be." Judy acted like she'd been elected student body president. Like Berry had chosen her over Marco.

"I guess. You know, this whole girl thing isn't in stone, I mean . . ."

"We'll just take it one step at a time."

"I mean, I don't really know that I want to be a girl. That's just what I told people to get the pills so I could keep my upper range."

"Dr. Tamarind said you were confused."

"Has he ever actually helped anyone? I know two of his other patients and they're both insane."

"I'm sure they were worse before they started seeing him, Becky."

"Berry. Call me Berry."

"Okay. It's kind of a weird girl's name."

"It's kind of unisex." It hurt Berry's jaw to talk. "Listen, I really need that note for Mr. Allen."

"What note?"

"The one that says I can stay in the choir."

"I thought the choir was boys only."

Berry explained again. "He just needs a note saying I'm still a boy in spite of . . . everything."

"But that would be lying."

"No, it wouldn't. I'm tired of explaining to people, I'm not a doll to play dress up with and buy accessories for. I want to live my own way."

Judy's student body president face melted. In a moment her face became more liquid than solid. "Oh, Berry . . ." She sobbed, violent in-gusts followed by long outward sighs. "Why are you doing this to us? I don't understand what's going on. Your father and I were patching things up, and now he's worse than ever. I can't play your games right now. Tell me this is all worth it because you're becoming something beautiful. Fighting to be yourself I can understand, but not all these riddles. Berry, please."

"Mom. I wish it was that simple. All I need from you right now is that note."

"I'm sorry. I can't."

Berry screamed and explained about the big recording date. "After that we can make a quilt together or pick flowers or buy bras. Two weeks. That's all."

"I don't understand. You should go forward, not backward."

Berry screamed again.

"Please don't wake your father," Judy said.

"I want to wake him," Berry said. "Maybe he'll write me that note."

"Berry. Look. Look at me. I just want to support you. Do you want me to take you shopping? Do you have enough girls' things? And then there's the question of where you'll go to school once you're full time. I've been reading up on it, see. Maybe you can transition when you go to high school."

"This is all weird." But the idea of going to high school as a girl fascinated Berry. Maybe it was just the idea of being in the girls' locker room when they all undressed. Or maybe Berry liked the idea of a new life. He couldn't imagine high school anyway. The little he'd heard so far sounded like a non-stop rave of hurt—worse than Orlac, if that were possible. "I don't know. Maybe life would be better as a girl," Berry said slowly. "Maybe it'd be easier to get girls as a girl. Maybe I'd be under less pressure to get girls, too. Maybe it could be fun."

Judy seemed relieved to hear something positive from Berry. She started clearing some of the living room debris, making piles of records and books.

"Just explain something," Berry said. "You haven't taken an interest, a real interest, in me since bed-wetting. Why now? Why this?"

"I'm sorry if I've been kind of absent."

"Understatement."

"I left it up to your dad, and maybe expected too much from him. You're obviously a special person, Beck . . . I mean Berry."

"That makes me sound like a cerebral palsy kid doing the fifty yard freestyle. I'm serious. Lately everybody wants to help me. Now you. What's up with that?"

"I don't know about the others." Judy thought. "But you're . . . I already said special, right? I don't know what to say. You seem to want this a lot. You went to all this trouble, the hormones, the hiding. Okay, there is something else. You're such a sweet kid. Until today, you've never raised your voice except to sing. I always thought you'd have been a lovely girl. And you're at that age when sweet boys turn into brutes. I'd love to see that not happen to you."

Judy took Berry shopping. "I have so much to share with you. I wish I'd been there for your makeover. Do you curl your hair? I bet curlers would do miracles."

Berry turned sullen. He stopped paying attention to his mom and stared out the window at all the people and dogs on the late Saturday afternoon.

Judy bought Berry a couple of blouses and a few shirts, plus a few more bras and some panties. "I don't know if I'll wear this stuff," he said.

"Well, you can't wear what you don't have."

They didn't go to the big mall Berry had visited with Lisa. Instead, they went to the big outlet mall across town, where the irregular and discarded ended up. Then Judy took him to a shoe store to find some cute sandals or platforms. "I just don't know why this can't wait two weeks," Berry grouched. Judy shrugged and handed Berry a pair of Mary Janes to try on.

Back at the apartment, Marco stalked back and forth. "I was your active parent." He jabbed a finger at Berry. "I taught you everything." Judy didn't speak, just stood with her arms folded. She definitely looked as though she'd won some unspoken war, one she'd never expected a shot at. Judy went and cooked nut cutlets. Marco walked closer to Berry.

"Please don't hit me again," Berry said.

"I'm not going to hit you. What kind of monster do you think—you're the monster, you know—I always tell my investment clients and spiritual disciples to beware the false path, the disguised ogre. But I never thought."

Berry ate as fast as possible. Then he went to his room and shut himself in. He tried masturbating but couldn't get hard. That squicked him. They'd mentioned that side effect when he'd started the pills, but it hadn't sunk in, maybe because Berry hadn't had so many erections before that. He stared at the Kings College poster but nothing happened. He zipped up, went out and found Marco.

"Dad, I need your help. You're the only one who understands. I'm not a girl, you know. Please write a note to Mr. Allen telling him that and saying I can go back to choir."

Marco didn't look up. "If I do that, you'll drop all this? Stop taking those things?"

"I need the pills. Some of them, anyway. For my voice."

Marco didn't answer. Finally, Berry's dad got up and walked away.

"I should stop the female hormones and just take the pills that kill testosterone," Berry told Lisa on the phone. "That way I lose the breasts and stay a boy. The only problem with that is getting more pills once my prescription runs out next week. They won't prescribe unless I'm a wannabe girl."

"It's too bad," Lisa said. "You look so cute the way you are. But maybe you can get the pills you want off the Internet."

"Time's not on my side," Berry said. "If I stop the estrogen, I don't know how soon it'd be obvious. And I felt something weirdly awesome when I was all done up last night. It's nice having my mom pay attention to me, and you, and Anna Conventional. You've been really great. I feel important, sort of like a foreign dignitary only with fewer sashes and more fuzzies. I feel awesome when you guys girl me up and stuff."

"See? You could get to like this."

"I don't know. Maybe. It's like I have two voices in my head all the time. One says, 'Wash me throughly from my wickedness,' like the anthem, and I imagine myself all clean and pretty like a girl. The other just says 'False!' over and over again."

"Take your time," Lisa said. "Make up your mind at your own pace. But come to church. And hey, I wanna see your new irregular clothes."

"I can't go to church. No note."

"Come with my mom and me. Just please come as a girl, or my mom's brain'll melt."

"I'll come as a boy, then meet you and your mom afterwards at the pizza joint across the street dressed as a girl. She won't see me in the boy stuff. Okay?"

• • •

"Then Job answered the Lord: 'I know that thou canst do all things, and that no purpose of thine can be thwarted. "Who is this that hides counsel without knowledge?" Therefore I have uttered what I did not understand, things too wonderful for me, which I did not know.'" (Job 42:1–6, 10–17)

Berry hid from the choir as they marched in. They sounded good, but Berry heard something wack in the hymn, a trick of the throat as the melody passed from mid-to-upper treble. Finally they reached the stalls and he didn't have to crouch in his pew any longer. He watched them giggle, put on beatific faces, then lapse back into giggles. The blessing mask resumed, then slipped again. He'd never realized how glaring it was when the choir goofed off.

Then the choir settled. Canon Moosehead stepped up and blessed the congregation. He preened for the first time since Easter. He waved hands above the congregation as if parting a sea and intoned that the gifts of God were for the people of God. He didn't twitch or stammer or ramble about Jung or try to shield his crotch behind a rail.

The anthem by Tomas Luis de Victoria sounded polished, but with the same cracks Berry had heard earlier. Even as he dissected the performance, Berry started to cry. Every lilt, every clear high note sliced Berry's breast. He soaked his linen shirt.

Berry waited for the kind of disaster that made church fascinating and fun to gossip about afterwards. But, instead, the service went smooth. Maybe the Dean and the Canon had cracked down in the wake of Bonergate. Even Sandy, the kid-loving Verger, was on his best behavior. Canon Moosehead gave a sane sermon about the healing of the blind man in the reading from Mark's gospel. He dwelled on the idea the beggar's own faith had healed him and managed to turn that into a comment on the Hungry Souls soup kitchen. "Sometimes the greatest charity is to put limits on charity, so people may heal themselves."

Then the offertory, then the Eucharist. Berry stayed hunched in his pew through the wafers and wine, then ducked out as soon as the recessional hymn started. He wished he could say hi to Wilson and the others.

Instead, he went to the pizza place and got a soda. He got the bathroom key and locked himself in the boys' room.

The bandages unwrapped in moments (Berry had practice) and then he slipped on a bra and a red scoop-neck blouse from the remainder store. He didn't bother to change his slacks or shoes.

He came out of the bathroom and slurped his soda until it made ice noises. He wondered if he should get a pizza slice or wait to eat with Lisa.

"Fucking insane! I heard it but I didn't believe." Teddy stood in the door of the pizza place. He stared at Berry's chest. "Boy got a rack. Fucking weird. What is that? You a C cup yet? How could you do this to us? You were a star, now you're one of the people too strange for us to pray for by name."

"I did it for the choir," Berry said. "Ask Wilson."

"Wilson says you're a faggot."

"That's not true. I'm not anything. I just wanted to save my voice." Berry wondered where Wilson was.

Teddy grabbed Berry's blouse-scruff and dragged him out of the pizza place and onto the sidewalk. Marc and Randy came and watched. "Look at the fag with jugs. God damn," Teddy said. "I can't believe this. We almost hung out with you. Now look at you!" Teddy kicked the back of Berry's legs and he fell onto his hands and knees. "Cock sucker," Teddy said. "No wonder you hit the high notes we couldn't get."

"Better ask somebody," Randy said.

"It's twelve hours too early for the freak show," Teddy said. His voice had a new gruffness. He lifted Berry and threw him against a lamp post. "Maybe if you were less pretty, you'd be smarter."

"Your voice," Berry wheezed. "It's changing." He covered his face with both arms and pulled his knees up. His ribs stung and his face felt raw all over again.

"All our voices," Marc said. "Plus Wilson's."

"All but you, cocksucker." Teddy kicked Berry again. "You got no balls, so I guess you won't care if I kick below the belt."

"Excuse me," a voice said. "But what the fuck do you *boys* think you're doing?" Berry unshielded his face to see Lisa with her arms folded. "Is this a church activity that I missed between the knitting social and the Bible study for the blind?"

Teddy kicked Berry in the shin, then turned to Lisa. "You want everyone to know he's a friend of yours? I thought you were like popular girl."

"I don't care who knows I'm anti-thug. Don't you boys have a gang war to fight with the Lutherans or something?"

"Later, fairy. Later, fag hag." Teddy led the boys back to church.

"Whew." Lisa dusted Berry's outfit. "Too bad. This blouse looks like it kicked booty. Pretty color. I like what it does for your skin. So now I've seen two sick things in one day."

"What was the other one?"

"Canon Moosehead and Maura face-gluing behind the cathedral after services. Tongues, groping, the whole revolting, guacamole-heaped enchilada."

"No way."

"Way. On church property. I'd show you, but I bet they've got a room by now."

Berry sighed. "I'll take your word for it." He could see the cathedral across the street, quiet except for stragglers and some younger choirboys playing in traffic. Off limits. "My life is over."

"I have that feeling a lot."

"I mean it. Over. No hope."

Lisa hugged Berry. "It's gonna be okay."

Mrs. Gartner took Berry and Lisa to lunch at a big sit-down restaurant with a plastic sign that said "The Golden Trough Tours Welcome." Berry had a plate of home fries and pancakes. Mrs. Gartner and Lisa both tried omelettes. Mrs. Gartner talked about the service after lunch. She praised Canon Moosehead in particular. "He's so dignified and mature. He understands the difference between charity and being made a fool of."

"I thought you were supposed to be a fool for Christ," Berry said.

"Now, that's referring to all the silly repeat-after-me business in church. We're supposed to be a good flock, and you never see sheep giving their wool to the other sheep. Anyway, the Canon looks so much happier and more collected than in ages. Maybe he's found a way to restore the dignity of the church."

Lisa didn't say anything. Berry stopped challenging Mrs. Gartner and let her ramble. Berry liked church to be nice and pretty, but didn't understand what that had to do with the homeless. When Berry tuned out Mrs. Gartner, though, he could only think about all the people he'd hurt, like Maura, Mr. Allen, and his parents, on his way to a goal he could never reach.

"I feel sick," Berry said. He wasn't lying.

Mrs. Gartner and Lisa made comforting noises. He went and sat in the girls' room for a while. He stared at the bathroom stall and read every spider leg scribble on the walls. Josie is a slut. Mara and Lee 4 Eva.

"Hey," a voice said outside the stall. "You okay?"

"No," Berry told Lisa.

"Sorry. Look, this is going to work. You're going to shine a new way." Berry rocked on the seat and didn't reply. "Really, you're going to have a new life with people who care about you," Lisa wheedled.

Berry flushed the toilet for no reason. He and Lisa went back to the table where Mrs. Gartner talked about righteousness. Berry randomly said, "I'm not sure I'll ever believe in anything again," during one of Mrs. Gartner's brief pauses. "I mean, it's all just shapes and voices. Nothing means anything."

Mrs. Gartner looked at Berry as if he'd spoken in tongues.

"Sorry," Berry said. "Bad day."

"We all have dark times and doubts," Mrs. Gartner said. Then she talked about her personal relationship with Jesus.

Back in the Gartners' car, Lisa and Berry sat in back. "Can we go home, mom?" Lisa asked. "Berry and I want to try on clothes."

Berry watched city surrender to freeway, and freeway to grass and gas stations. But his eyes saw only Teddy screaming at him for deserting choirboys and boys in general. Then his dad howling. Lisa talked to Berry softly about the clothes they would try on. Berry had brought the stuff his mom had bought him. Lisa murmured about the bottle of perfume hidden under her dresser, the teen fashion mags, the Barbie dolls, and the dolls' clothes.

When Lisa mentioned magazines, Berry told about Anna

Conventional working for *Teeneurosis*, and more about their night out.

"Wow. Do you remember what they used on your hair?"

"Sorry. My head is full of music I'll never sing again. No room for hairspray."

When they got to Lisa's house, they ran upstairs without stopping to talk to Mr. Gartner, who was building a spice rack in the kitchen. "Hi dad," Lisa called from the top of the stairs. Then they went into Lisa's room.

Lisa's room had a big mirror with light bulbs around it and a Barbie house with a dog-sized plastic corvette parked out front. Posters of boy bands and bubblegum girl singers hung where Berry's wall celebrated choirs. A few school books sat in the corner, but no bookcase supported heaps of literature like the ones in Berry's and Wilson's bedrooms. Lisa's bedspread was pink with white hearts. A heart-shaped throw pillow nestled against her real pillow. She kept her room neat.

Berry pulled out the plastic remainder store bag from his knapsack. He dumped the contents on Lisa's bed and she went through them. "This one's not bad. I don't think peach is your color. This one you could get away with if you had the absolute perfect skirt. Hang on."

Lisa abruptly pulled her frilly pink church dress over her head. "Let me see this on you," the cloth hump said to Berry. She yanked it all the way off and handed it over. Her bra and panties sported butterflies. Berry obediently took off his clothes, including his bra but not his panties, and pulled the dress over his head. "We're about the same size, but your hips are like negative space to the max. Turn around."

Berry obeyed and Lisa zipped. Then she gestured for him to spin, which he did. "Not bad," she said. "Maybe a touch too pink for you."

She tried another fancy formal dress on Berry, with gathered skirts and a low-cut front and a big ruffly collar and sleeves that started puffy and got skinny. "Too 'Dr. Quinn Medicine Woman'," Lisa considered. Berry giggled.

Lisa found a cute stretchy top that said "Power Fem" on it, and Berry tried it on still with no bra. "Wow, like stare-o-rama. Man." She found another top, a plainer black shirt with a scoopy neck. "Not bad." Lisa took off her own bra and tried on the Power Fem shirt, which stretched, but not as much as when Berry wore it. "See, I can't do that Britney tits thing."

They tried on clothes for an hour. Berry started to cheer up and relax despite everything. Lisa found some outfits he looked ridiculous in, but others he looked thrill-hot in, even to himself.

"Okay. Now swimwear. It's only about six months until summer, you know." Lisa, who never swam, found four bathing suits in her closet. She shucked her panties. Berry stared at her thatch of light brown pubic hair. Lisa covered it with a navy blue one piece with low-cut back.

"Wow," Berry said.

Berry didn't think he could wear a swimsuit without people seeing his privates. But Lisa made him try on a black and white striped bikini. He hesitated, then shimmied out of his briefs. He started to pull on the bikini bottoms.

Lisa looked at Berry's pubes. "Hey wow. Maura told me the pills might make it . . . you know. Does it still, like, work?"

"I think so," Berry said. He nudged his dick, and it nudged back.

"Can I?" Lisa asked. Berry nodded. She reached out one finger and stroked ever so lightly. It responded. It got longer and gained heft. Berry's heart arpeggioed. "Wow. Weird. No offense. First one I've touched."

"I thought you had lots of boyfriends."

"At school. But my parents won't let—"

The door swept open. Mr. Gartner stomped, even before he saw into the room. His daughter knelt naked before a hermaphrodite and touched its erection with her delicate hands. The hermaphrodite's eyes rolled back in its bruised face. Lisa smiled eerily.

Mr. Gartner sucked in breath, but didn't let it out. His face turned the color of communion wafers.

"Dad, I—" Lisa said.

"The reptile nests and controls the host," Mr. Gartner said in a choking tone once he could breathe. "The aquatic brain is in ascent."

He bent and grabbed Lisa's ankle, as if afraid to get any closer to her. He dragged her out of the room by her leg. She yelped as her body bounced down the stairs.

Berry hesitated a second. He saw himself naked in the mirror, nipples and cock erect. This wasn't his family. He'd done enough harm today.

He pulled on jeans and ran downstairs. Mrs. Gartner sipped cocoa in the kitchen. She saw Berry and offered him some. He ignored her. He ran to the sliding glass doors in back. It took a moment to find the unlocked door. The late October air lashed Berry's bare chest.

Out back, Mr. Gartner stood over the pool, where Lisa's head protruded. Her nakedness shimmered under the water. "You'll stay here until after sundown. Until natural selection reasserts itself over the evils under your skin."

Berry ran and threw himself at Mr. Gartner. Lisa's dad fell forward into the pool, a belly flop sonic boom that scattered water a few feet from the pool's edge. Berry fell on top of him, then pushed him away and found Lisa with his other hand. He shook his head to get the water out of his eyes and ears.

"Come on," Berry said. "Get out! This isn't right."

Lisa didn't move. She let him tow her to the edge of the pool and haul her out. By then, Mr. Gartner swam to the edge as well.

"Bring her back here! The primitive cortex owns you both!"

Berry pulled Lisa all the way out and found the huge lid just as Mr. Gartner reached the side. He swung the lid down. He heard a cracking sound as the lid hit something solid. Berry held the lid down. Lisa stared at him.

Berry laughed. Once he started, he couldn't stop. He quaked. "It's okay," he said. "We're free. We're free. They can't hurt us."

Lisa didn't laugh with him.

"Come on," Berry said. "Let's leave this loser and go try on some more clothes."

"Get away from the pool," Lisa said.

Berry let go of the lid. She lifted it off the pool. Her father floated face down in the sickly blue water. Blood dripped from a gash in the back of his head where the pool's lid had struck. His suit jacket flared like a magician's cape.

15.

After the ambulance came, Berry started to wonder how he'd get home. He couldn't wrap his mind around the paramedics struggling to revive Mr. Gartner with every gadget they had. Lisa didn't talk to Berry. She disappeared inside with her mom for a while. If Mr. Gartner the atheist died, Berry wondered, what did Mrs. Gartner believe would happen to his soul? High Episcopalians like Mrs. Gartner didn't stress Hellfire, but there were some hymns about wailing and gnashing. Mostly, the mainstream Episcopalians took comfort in a fluffy Heaven that let in anyone who dressed well and acted friendly.

Berry felt super calm except that his thoughts wouldn't stop spinning and churning. He never quite zeroed in on the thought *I've just killed a man* but it turned up as a sideways half-thought at the fringes of the picture. Like when Berry thought, *Maybe the choirboys will think I'm cool again now that I've popped someone.*

Berry tried to remember the anthem from the day's service but couldn't. It had been beautisplendicool, he was sure, but nothing about the actual music came back to him. Would Mrs. Gartner want the choir to perform at her husband's funeral? It was always kind of cool to sing for funerals, because you got to wear all black and no robes and sing extra solemnly. Weddings or funerals often meant an extra tip for the choir. Berry wished he'd be able to sing at Mr.

Gartner's funeral. He could do that no more pain, no more tears solo from that Bainton piece that always sounded really cool and moving and it would be a perfect funeral piece. Of course, Berry and Mr. Gartner hadn't really gotten along when he was alive, but that didn't mean Berry couldn't sing at his last rites now that Berry had . . .

Berry wondered what you did with a swimming pool where someone drowned. You'd let out all the water and put a good extra batch of chlorine in the water the next time you filled it. But how did you get the lichen of someone-died-here out of the walls and the water, the chill no heater could dispel? Maybe there was a special exorcism for swimming pools. Maybe you just left the pool alone for a while until everyone forgot. Maybe you filled the pool with dirt and made it a memorial garden.

Berry felt the air freeze. He realized he still stood in the Gartners' back yard wearing just a pair of jeans. It had stayed warm until the past few days, but now it was definitely too cold for sunbathing. Berry's nipples sparked. Maybe it would soon be too cold to wear the kinds of outfits Maura wore, too. Did she still wear short skirts but thicker tights? Did she just shiver in summer wear and find "friends" to warm her up? And what would people expect Berry to wear in cold weather, assuming this "trans" thing went ahead? Berry didn't even let himself think about prison uniforms.

He finally tried the back door to the Gartners' house. It was locked. All the sliding glass doors in back were locked. Berry sneaked around to the front and tried that door. Locked. He finally found an open kitchen window. Barefoot, it was a chore to climb up and into the raised kitchen. He tumbled off the counter and onto the linoleum with a thwack. Then he hopped upstairs as quick as he could and found the rest of the clothes he'd worn earlier. He put on his top and socks and shoes. He didn't bother with underwear. Then he scooped up all the clothes his mom had bought him at the remainder store and put them all in his knapsack. He saw the Power Fem shirt still on the floor and grabbed it too. Lisa wouldn't mind if he borrowed it, and having to ask for it back would ensure she called him soon. Then Berry ran downstairs. He wasn't sure how he'd get home.

"Oh, there you are." A woman stood in the front room, holding a pair of keys on a little ring. She looked about the same age as Mrs. Gartner and wore a puffy gray sweater with a long black skirt. "You're Lisa's friend, right? I'm here to take you home." Berry gathered from snatches of the woman's talk that Mrs. Gartner had called her. Berry never learned her name. Berry got in the passenger seat of her Lexus sedan and thanked her for the ride. She asked where he lived and he told her.

They drove silently for a while. The suburbs pulled their disappearing trick and soon industrial detritus washed past. Berry finally asked the woman if she knew what had happened to Mr. Gartner. "I'm not sure. It sounded bad," was all she said. She gave him sympathetic glances at stop lights and exit ramps.

The woman asked several times if it was safe to leave Berry in his neighborhood. Then she let him out by his building and drove off at an illegal speed before he reached the door to his building.

It never occurred to Berry to tell his parents what had happened. Judy was cooking dinner, glad he was home in time. "What did you do with your friend?" she asked.

"Tried on clothes. Swam."

"That's good. Your father's gone to some strip joint to prove his masculinity. I made sure he took only a little cash and no cards."

Berry still remembered the strip bar Marco had dragged him to. "Boring. Not as fun as the mall."

"You really aren't cut out to be male," Judy reveled.

Judy had the TV working. After dinner, they watched mostly sitcoms, plus one police drama about dogged investigators who find the culprit through a mist of intrigue. Berry shivered and his shivers became tremors. His teeth clattered like windows in a storm in a movie he'd seen. Judy noticed after a while. "You okay?" she asked, putting one hand on Berry's shoulder. He nodded.

"Just cold."

Judy wrapped Berry in a blanket.

Berry imagined himself dragged away in wrist and ankle chains. He saw himself in prison shoveling a black tar that made him cough dirty phlegm and coated his hands. Maybe he would start a prison choir, teach all the murderers and rapists the work of Wesley, Stanford, and Byrd. He'd teach all the convicts to sing like angels and become famous, the Songbird of Cell Block A. Word of his musical exploits would reach Mr. Allen, who'd shed a tear at all that could have been and the horrendous wonder of redemption. Berry let himself dwell on the rows of men in striped suits singing Vivaldi's Gloria for a moment, then snapped back to reality.

Berry said he wasn't feeling well and went to bed. He still wasn't going to school while his parents figured out which sex he should be, so being sick would get him nothing but sympathy. He lay in bed staring at flickers from street lights and passing cars.

At some point, Marco came home with a loud plan. He'd found out about an exchange scheme where you could send an American to live with a host family in Burma for a year, and the Burmese would send one of their kids in return. "Just think, we could ship Berry to Myanmar, or whatever they're calling it, and get a normal healthy kid in place of our mysterious whatever-it-is."

"Can I send you to Burma instead?" Judy demanded.

Berry finally slept and saw singing inmates again, but this time they sang off key. The most gorgeous Vivaldi passages shredded to dissonance. Berry stopped them again and again, pleaded with them to sing in tune, to listen to the recording, to run through their parts. But the inmates wouldn't listen, they jeered at Berry. One of them crunched his music score into a paper ball and hurled it at Berry's head. Another one bashed someone with a metal music stand. Soon the rehearsal became a riot. Berry's dream ended when an inmate dropped a piano on him.

Then Berry dreamed he was underwater, trying to sing. The music came out like the whale song Marco sometimes played for his spiritual clients. Bubbles of failed song floated around his head. He couldn't breathe in and he tried to rise to the water's surface, but something held him down. The musical bubbles—they had quarter notes, half notes, and triplets in them—turned into a huge cloud over Berry's head. He swatted at them but couldn't disperse any. Finally, everything faded to chlorine.

Berry wasn't sure how much he slept, but he felt exhausted the next morning. Judy came into his room and dumped brochures for day schools and boarding schools onto his legs. "This is a great opportunity. You can finally become the achiever you were always meant to be. That stupid school always wanted to keep you out of the Swans. We're going to get you into a select school as a girl. Did you know girls do better than boys academically? That's because teachers like girls better and girls are less rambunctious. You'll be trading up from Bart Simpson to Ophelia."

"Can we afford any of these places?" Berry asked without caring.

"That's the hard part. Your father isn't working a lot lately and I'm still in school. But we can get you a scholarship if we tell a good enough story. You did badly in some classes, sure, but that was because you were the wrong sex. Or you can get some kind of singing scholarship."

Berry didn't really believe anything Judy said, but it didn't matter. It comforted him to know he'd soon be locked up. It made the scary future go away.

There was a brochure for a performance school out-of-state which accepted kids only a little older than Berry. "Don't get your hopes up," Judy said. "But they might take you early and let you enter in your new sex. I'll make brunch, you fill out forms." She'd printed out some of the forms from the Web using her daisy wheel printer. Others, she'd picked up somewhere. Berry's hand cramped after a couple hours.

The phone rang at noon. They let the answering machine pick up. "Hey, Berry. Gray Redman. I've been doing some heartstorming, that's like brainstorming only you use your heart, and I think I have some ideas. Buzz me."

Judy wanted Berry to call Gray Redman back, but Berry felt too weary. He promised to call later. "Sounds like you have everything figured out anyway."

Another message a while later: "Hey, why aren't you at school, fairy? I was looking forward to showing everybody your jugs." Berry recognized Randy's voice. The background noise sounded raucous enough for the school cafeteria at lunchtime. Either Randy had coaxed the payphone to accept coins, or one of the Swans had lent a cell phone. Berry deleted that message too.

"So many calls," Judy said. For lunch they were eating couscous with leftover salami and salad mixed in. "You obviously have a lot of people who care about you, Berry. How come you're playing Garbo?"

Berry didn't get the reference. "Whatever they're all expecting from me, they're all going to be disappointed."

"You're being really ungrateful. More couscous? Well, your loss. It's really good this way. A lot of kids your age starve for attention."

"I'd kill to be left alone." *I already did*, Berry thought.

"Getting left alone is easy. Getting people to stop leaving you alone once they start is hard."

Berry put his hands over his ears, like he did when he wanted to block all other singers and hear only how his voice sounded inside the echo chamber of his head. The danger of pressing against the bones that meet your eardrums is that you distort the sound of your own voice with skull harmonics. You drive yourself sharp that way.

Hours passed. Application forms seemed written by the same people who devised the Book of Common Prayer. Judy had given Berry index cards containing stock phrases for him to sprinkle into his short essay answers, and even into the little blanks on the forms themselves.

"I don't really have an interest in multiculturalism that comes out of my choral background," Berry told Judy.

"Compared to most dirt dumplings your age, you're a positive cultural studies guru. You don't watch TV, you read books. Besides, don't drag the old Berry into this. We're talking about the new Berry, who only just arrived." Berry was surprised to hear Rat and Mr. Allen had both agreed to write recommendations.

"And what does 'gender gifted' mean?" Berry asked.

"Search me." Judy flayed the Internet seeking information for Berry. "Ah," she said while Berry was on his fifteenth form. "This Lambda Youth organization has a transgender support group. It's the perfect thing for you, Berry. They'll be people your own age, who can identify with what you're going through." The group planned a meeting that evening at six.

Judy drove Berry in circles for fifteen minutes before spotting the Lambda Youth center, which hid under a big awning that said "The Art Sanctuary." The staircase to the awning's right, below street level, led to a big metal door with a tiny sign bearing a midget triangle and the letters "LY" in even smaller print. Berry hopped out of the car, waved at his mom, and ran down the staircase. He rang the bell and waited five minutes before a shaved-headed man with a pierced septum and tattoos opened the door and said, "Yeah."

"Name's Berry. I'm here to be supported as a young gender queer person."

The skinhead shrugged and led Berry to a clammy room with posters of Nelson Mandela and Brandon Teena. Motley people slouched in folding chairs clustered in a circle. Berry grabbed one of the still-folded chairs by the wall while he checked out the roomful of grown-ups. Everybody there looked way older than Berry. And then he saw Maura out of the corner of his eye. Berry sighed and pulled his chair into the circle across from Maura.

"Welcome to the Young Gendernauts. I'm Zulu No-Gender and I'm the facilitator here. We were just doing personal introductions and affirmations." The speaker looked kind of like Whoopi Goldberg, only with more tattoos and piledriver hands.

"Oh." Berry slumped forward, head to knees.

"My name is Bakka," someone to Berry's left said. "I'm a male-born female. I go to Holy Mystery Technical Institute. My personal affirmation is that I'm a quail." Berry looked up. Bakka was easily six feet tall, with athletic shoulders and hairy arms. She wore huge numbers of bangles on her wrists and a diva's ransom in makeup.

Most of the Young Gendernauts looked like men to Berry. He didn't understand who they were trying to fool. Some of them even wore men's clothes and had beards, for God's sake. Maura was one of the few pretty ones there—nobody else was as glamorous as most of the girls at the Booby Hatch.

Soon the introduction chain reached Berry. "Hey. Berry. Think I'm in the wrong place. Looking for the Transgender Youth Group." Various people assured Berry he was there now. "But you're all old," he said. Maura gave him a javelin stare.

"Don't mind Berry," Maura said. "She's awfully young. She doesn't think about what she says to hurt people. Dearie, everyone in this room is twenty-five and under."

"Oh. Sorry. Anyway, I'm a . . . I don't know what. I'm a kid. Oh, and my personal affirmation is that I killed a man yesterday." It felt good to say it aloud for the first time.

"That's nice," Zulu said. Then she opened the discussion to "free topic." It turned out the guys with beards weren't men doing a weak job of looking like women, but women working to be men. Pretty much everyone felt oppressed, and talked about hegemony and landlords. Their parents didn't talk to them. Their families and friends didn't understand. People threw them out of their homes and they couldn't get jobs because of discrimination. Half a dozen people there were some kind of homeless. In fact, Berry recognized one from Hungry Souls.

"So, Berry, tell us about you," Zulu said.

"Um . . . Well, did I mention I killed someone? Speaking of which, how long does it usually take the police to arrest someone when they've committed murder, because I was kind of expecting the cops to bust in at any moment and save me from having to write 'learning is my wings' for the tenth time on an application form today. Somebody obviously wanted to punish me in advance before they carted me off to maximum security to be an extra in the next Dr. Dre video, speaking of which, Dr. Dre is really weak, there I said it, and speaking of which, music is my life and my life is over even if I hadn't taken a life, and I don't know why I'm here."

Twenty gender outcasts transferred their oppression to Berry with their stares. Only Maura looked concerned.

"Berry," Zulu said. "I understand you're nervous about being here, and we're all older than you."

"Dr. Dre is not weak," Bakka interrupted.

"But let's back up. You're on hormones, right?"

Berry nodded.

"How does your family feel about this?"

"Dad's disturbed. Mom couldn't be happier, now that she's over the shock. She's paying attention to me for the first time since the birth thing. She's really hyped on the 'I have a daughter now' trip."

Several people gasped. "So let me get this squared away," Bakka said. "You have a supportive moms who doesn't push you onto the streets. You've managed to start hormones young. And you're upset *why*, exactly?" Maura gave Berry a look that said, *I told you.*

"So have you transitioned?" one of the other beardless men asked. "Or are you planning on transitioning soon?"

"That's where the wine becomes actual blood, right? I'm Episcopalian. I'm pretty sure we don't believe in that. I always thought it was way gross, even before I spilled it on Canon Moosehead's crotch."

"That stain is *not* coming out, by the way," Maura volunteered. "He's very upset, poor baby."

"Shut up, Maura," said the other girl, whose name was either Sophie or Sojourner. "Transitioning is when you start living full-time as your new sex."

"Oh," Berry said. "I'll probably do that next week, if I'm still walking around."

The other gendernauts decided to ignore Berry's weird non-answers and go back to their own problems. Sophie/Sojourner had lost her job just as she was saving up for her operation, so she had to spend her savings on rent, and her parents persecuted her every way they knew. Another woman traded sex for a couch to sleep on. Berry felt more depressed than ever listening to these stories.

Finally, the group broke up. Everybody shunned Berry except Maura.

"Hey. So you sure you want your pals here to see you talking to me? I don't think they like me," Berry said.

"You're fine. They offend easy here. So, you want to get a milkshake?"

"My mom's picking me up."

They walked out into the dark hallway. "So what was that stuff about killing someone? You on the lam?" Maura asked.

Berry started to answer, then he spotted something. At first he thought he must be wrong, like the time he thought he'd seen Mr. Allen in the supermarket but it was an old lady. But then he looked again, and it really was.

Through the window on the door across the hall, Berry sighted Wilson fidgeting in another folding chair. "What's he doing here?"

Maura leaned into the door and chuckled. "No idea. Could be anything. Maybe it's a bestiality encounter group. I could imagine Wilson with a hamster, they're on the same wavelength."

"Shush," Berry said. Wilson saw the two people outside the door and tried to cover his face too late. The leaflet he used to cover his face said *Young? Gay? OK!* on the cover. "Just a guess, but I think it's a gay group."

"Oh. So much for Wilson's dark secret. Big fucking deal. Everyone's a homo nowadays," Maura said.

Berry tried to see the rest of the room. Like the young trannies, most of the people looked ancient compared to him. There were probably a dozen gay youngsters in there, under a big flow chart showing the relationship between self esteem and self improvement. Wilson finally uncovered his face and sank into his chair.

"Can I gloat? Please tell me I can gloat," Maura said. "Mister I'm so normal and perfect that I'm going to bang some chick at Harvard and spawn two baby brain surgeons . . ."

"Shush," Berry said. He saw something else. A big waxed mustache in rapid motion at the fringe of his view. "I think it's that Bishop guy you introduced me to." He ran out front and didn't see a Toyota Corolla waiting. He ran back in.

"Hey, Maura. Do me the biggest favor on Earth? I don't want to miss my mom in case she's circling the block. Can you go out and wait for her? I really need to talk to Wilson."

"Doesn't your mom still hate me?"

"Why don't you ask her yourself? Please?"

Maura went. Berry kept vigil by the doorway to the Bishop's gathering. He kept away from the door. He heard a shout outside and almost went to look. The door opened and guys Maura's age wandered out in twos or threes. Probably going to a bar. Any youth group whose members could drink booze without fake ID was a sham in Berry's book. Still no Wilson. Berry finally barged into the room, where Bishop Bacchus and Wilson sat with one empty chair between them. Bishop Bacchus had his chair turned around so the back was against his crotch.

"Labels are for sticker guns," the Bishop was in the middle of saying. "Those price gun doodads are the funnest part of retail, speaking from rich personal experience. But you don't have to label yourself until you're ready."

"Hey, Wilson." Berry said. "So I hear you told Marc and Randy I was a fag."

"Awkwardness," Bishop Bacchus said. "Major on the spotness. Friend finds you at strange table eating wild fruit grown under the Earth."

"Underground fruit is called roots. Like a carrot," Berry said. "Hey, Bishop."

"Oh, we've met? Here I go by Pete the Facilitator, or P-Fac for short." The Bishop looked younger in a tank top and jeans, both of them slashed and tattered.

"Got it. So what are you," Berry asked Wilson. "L, G, B, T, or some other letter?"

"Hey yo, label-free zone," P-Fac said. "You seem all wound up, kid. Must be hormones."

"Hormones," said Berry, "are the least of my worries. But I like the label-free thing."

"So you're happy," Wilson said. "Now I'm a weirdo too. At least I still sing."

"Sort of," Berry snorted. "I heard you guys yesterday. Cracks."

"You know that thing where a calm surface hides a horrified chaos lurking beneath? That's the choir right now. We've been nuts. Teddy's basically a man. You're gone. Randy, Marc, and I are unreliable. I don't know if we're going to do that recording session or not."

"If we don't do that recording, it'll be all my fault."

"Hell yeah, it will," Wilson said.

"Hey, judgment," P-Fac said.

Berry couldn't stay mad at Wilson. For one thing, he needed to hear more about the choir. "I think my mom's waiting. You should eat with us."

Wilson considered. "I'd have to call home."

When they got outside, Maura was sparring with Marco. The Corolla was parked nearby. Marco wore his blue parka and Hawaiian turtleneck. His moustache crinkled with rage.

"Hey Berry," Maura yelled. "You didn't tell me your mom was transgender as well. I was just congratulating her on passing so well."

"That's not my mom. It's my dad."

"I thought Maura left already," Wilson groaned.

"Just get in the car," Berry said. He opened the rear door, shoved a box of Steely Dan cassettes on the floor, and turned back to where his dad and Maura argued without making sense.

"I just don't hold with all this and neither does my son," Marco shouted.

"All what? Anyway, you have no son."

"No, *you* have no son." Marco jabbed at Maura with a finger.

"Huh?"

"Dad can we get going?" Berry tugged at the parka sleeve.

"Just a moment, son. My boy's a normal kid. I see myself in him. I'm not even worried about him going to lairs of confusion like this. It'll just help him realize faster that he doesn't fit in."

"Newsflash, Magnum P.I. Your son has a shelf you could balance a bowl of nachos on."

"Thanks for the mental image, Maura. See you later, okay?" Berry opened the passenger side front door and clicked the safety belt home.

Marco jumped in the front side and started the car without wearing his seatbelt. "Finally. Let's move." He pulled the car out of its illegal spot and sped down the street, running a light two shades shy of red.

"So where we eating? I figured the burger joint."

"We're not stopping for dinner, son. I'm kidnapping you and taking you to Vermont. I'm taking you away from all these bad influences and back to nature. We can do home-schooling and herd goats."

"Can I put in a vote for burgers instead of goats?" Wilson said from the back seat.

Marco almost crashed into the on-ramp's metal guardrail. "What the fuck? Who's that?"

"You remember my friend Wilson. You came to his house once," Berry said. "He's just come out as gay or something."

"Hey, label-freedom. Supportiveness," P-Fac said. Berry turned to see both Wilson and P-Fac in back. "Hey, I thought we were going for food," P-Fac explained.

"Peter's the bishop of a really lame religion," Berry told Marco.

"God dammit! I'm trying to abduct my son here!" Marco swerved between two lanes on the freeway, trying to fake out other, slower cars. Several cars surrendered the left two lanes to him.

"Ya know, this whole abducting your kids thing is so old school," P-Fac said. "My church teaches that children nurture their parents and forgive them for their mistakes. Parents give life to their children only once, but the children give life to the parents over and over after that."

"Okay, okay, I'll fucking pull over and let you out," Marco said. "Just don't talk any more." He chose an off-ramp at random, zoomed through the exit and took a hard right into a gas station lot. The pumps looked rusted past the point where anything could flow. The lights were smashed and the lot held no other cars. Across the road was a deserted junk yard, past that some untended fields. "Okay, here you go." Marco stopped the car.

"Where the Hell are we?" Wilson asked.

"North of the Dead Zone," P-Fac said. "A mile or so out of town, but way further than that from anywhere you'd wanna be."

"Good enough for me," Berry said. He lost his seat belt and jumped out. Marco grabbed at Berry's arm, but he shook his dad off.

"Come back here!" Marco screamed. Berry ran toward the gas station. Behind it was a tiny church, the Holy Day Revival Shack. Berry could hear singing and tambourines inside, even on a Monday night. It wasn't European choral music, more like Elevator Gospel, dominated by a cheap synthesizer.

"Your dad's crazy," Wilson panted. He ran right behind Berry.

"Why are you running? He's not trying to kidnap you."

"He doesn't seem too jacked in. I don't want to risk him deciding to take me to Vermont instead."

Berry looked at Wilson running with him in the dark and felt joy out of nowhere that his friend was with him. "So this gay thing," Berry panted. "Did it start . . . I mean, when you and I . . . Did I make you?"

"I started figuring it out before that," Wilson said. "That's why our kiss freaked me out."

They reached a parking lot, beyond which an alley led to a construction site, with a hole in the ground and rusty girders in uneven piles. They ran through the alley and stopped at the edge of the hole.

"Where are we running to?" Wilson asked.

"Not sure," Berry said. He sat down on the border between lot and hole. Wilson sat next to him. "Do you think I could ever get back in the choir? If I don't get dragged to Vermont."

"Maybe," Wilson said. "We've been going over some new music. There's this Schutz piece where we have to divide into two choirs, it's way intense. I think Mr. Allen must have been nuts to give us this piece right after losing you and Teddy. Check it out, there's this part where Treble A comes in and then Treble B comes in half a measure later and the melody gets fucked like a dog." Wilson found the sheet music in his knapsack and spread it on the tarmac. "Yo, I be Treble A, you be Treble B." He counted it off, and

Berry picked it up pretty quickly. It wasn't a fugue, more like two bugs chasing each other or mating. One bug would lunge and then the other one would swoop. Berry squinted at the music under the one lamp hanging nearby.

The second time they sang it, the top two Schutz parts meshed way better. Wilson's voice led, still strong but with cracks. But Berry was right there and they blended, two instruments tuned just the same way and stained with the same brush. Their voices filled the dead construction site like a really dirty cathedral. When they finished, Berry and Wilson sat side by side looking into the hole. Berry felt like he was smiling for the first time in years.

"Thanks," Berry said. "I've missed singing."

"Cool," Wilson said. "Can we get out of here?"

"Sure. Maybe we can call your dad. Or I know this chick who has a car. Listen, Wilson. You know Lisa? I killed her dad yesterday."

"Huh?"

"Mostly by accident."

"Well, she wasn't at school today. But they told us her dad was in the hospital but he was going to be okay. And they totally said it was an accident. They didn't say anything about a killer choirboy."

"Oh."

"Yeah, like get over yourself, fuckin' pimp daddy killa at large."

"I wondered why I hadn't been arrested yet."

It took ages to find a payphone and call Mr. Fennimore. They went through some more of the choir's other new pieces and Berry felt less out of the loop. Finally, the Rabbit pulled up. "I feel bad—this is the second time I've been stranded and needed a pickup," Berry said.

Mr. Fennimore laughed. He wore a blue flannel check shirt and a black tie. "So it must have been a pretty amazing model car meeting if you wound up out here," Mr. Fennimore said to Wilson.

"Yeah," Wilson said, giving Berry a shut-up look. "Long story. We kind of got separated."

"Speaking of which, whatever happened to the Bishop?" Berry wondered.

Mr. Fennimore took Wilson and Berry to a burger joint at last. Berry called home from a payphone. Judy sounded ragged with fear. "Marco said he was bringing you right home. Where have you been?"

"Oh, he tried to kidnap me and Wilson to Vermont. We ran away. He still has your car."

"Fuck! The fucking bastard. Vermont? Why Vermont?" Judy asked a bunch of questions. Berry gave short answers. Just when Berry was getting ready to hang up, she said, "Oh yeah. Mr. Allen is here, from the church. He wanted to talk to me about the choir."

Berry skipped all the way back to his table at the restaurant. Not even Mr. Fennimore's attempts to make Wilson and him discuss aesthetics could damage Berry's high. Wilson just looked down and mumbled as Mr. Fennimore threw out conversational openings about some chick named Edith Stein. Wilson shot Berry a disgusted look as his dad droned. Berry shrugged. Mr. Fennimore was a nice guy, even if he was wound pretty tight and his breath smelled like isopropyl.

Then Mr. Fennimore started rambling about his poetry and how he'd won some award once, and how he was doomed to have no respect in this lifetime because of his day job in advertising, but if only his own son would respect him it would make the whole deal bearable.

Wilson muttered under his breath, "Ivy League. Phi Beta Kappa. Marry a doctor," over and over.

Finally, Mr. Fennimore drove Berry home. Berry said, "See ya soon," to Wilson, then ran upstairs three steps at a time.

The apartment looked clean again. Judy had a glass of wine in one hand and wore a tight-waisted long skirt and lacy top. Berry wasn't used to his mom looking so foxy. It made her slender face and wispy auburn hair look way younger, and her cheeks had a coal-fired exuberance. Berry licked every one of his bottom teeth one by one. When she saw Berry, she ran over and hugged him. He felt the sweat on her arms and chest.

"I'm so glad you're home safe," Judy said. "Vermont?"

"It's almost Canada," Berry said.

She made Berry tell the whole story twice, tense at the first hearing and maniacally giggly the second time. "Oh my God, you couldn't make something like this up. I hope he goes to Vermont on his own. I'm changing the locks first thing tomorrow morning. Vermont. Well, I married him because he made me laugh. Who knew I'd divorce him for the same reason?"

Judy had never mentioned the "D" word before. It felt like the cathedral's storeroom filled with moldy hymnals. "Uh. Are you sure about that? I mean, just a few days ago, you guys had this new lease on love and now . . ."

"A lot happened in the past few days."

Berry could only think of one thing that had happened in the past few days. "Uh. You know that thing where the kids feel responsible for the parents splitting?"

"Stockholm Syndrome?"

"Maybe. I saw an after school special about it before Marco broke the TV. Anyway, I kind of feel like this is my fault."

Judy put one hand, fingers spread like a spider, on Berry's forehead. "Oh, Berry. Even if it was partly your doing, it's for the best. He's such a maniac. And it's worth it to gain such a pretty daughter."

"Oh."

Berry almost forgot to ask how Mr. Allen's visit had gone.

"Oh, Mr. Allen . . . he's a terrific guy."

Berry wished he was watching the DVD of his life so he could switch to the commentary track and understand what Judy was saying.

"I think Mr. Allen's great too. So when do I go back to the choir?"

Judy looked as if a bug had turned up in her wine. "Oh, you're not going back. Mr. Allen and I talked it over and decided it would be totally inappropriate. You need to move on. He was disappointed at first, but he got over it." She laughed.

Berry screamed. He didn't make words, just shrieked at the top of his range. Judy tried again and again to shush him. Finally, she encouraged him instead. "That's right, hon, just let it out, primal scream your pants off, it's the best thing, it's okay to mourn the old life."

She put her arms around Berry again and she felt moist and soft like the warm towelette at the fancy restaurant Judy and Marco had taken Berry to on their twelfth anniversary.

"Oh, baby, my miracle changeling child. This is all so salty and perilous." She breathed loudly. "The ground won't settle beneath our feet, but I know this is right. You've always been more beautiful than any boy should have to live with. Now you're going to live up to it. I'm so proud of you, my sweet girl." She held Berry until his shrieking turned to crying and the crying went dead. Then she let go and made root beer floats.

All that sugar so close to bed made Berry brush his teeth twice. It also meant he lay in bed watching the flicker of outside lights against his choir posters. He couldn't begin to take in everything that had happened. Sometime around three in the morning, Berry still couldn't sleep.

My tears have been my meat day and night . . . Berry hummed to himself. *Would God I had died for thee* . . . He went into the sitting room/kitchen and stared at the television without trying to turn it on. In its opaque grayness he thought he saw Lisa's father, face down in his own psychiatric lagoon, and then, flooded almost to death, laid up in a hospital bed with tubes into every opening or limb. Berry wondered if Marco was halfway to Vermont yet, if he drove all night.

He imagined himself at dinner with Wilson's dad, at the burger joint. He should have warned Mr. Fennimore, "Stay away from me. Don't you know? I'm the father-wrecker. My own dad or other people's, no matter. I'm poison."

Berry took off his clothes and examined himself. His naked body swirled in the dead TV screen. He saw weirdly pasted porno. Tits and a dick at a standoff. Was it any mystery why everything in his life bled shit? Berry felt nauseated, not just by his body, but by the realization that he'd been enjoying himself. He'd kicked and complained, but a big part of him had enjoyed everything, the clothes, the attention. When he'd started to enjoy his freakish not-this-not-that life, he'd cut it all to shreds.

He wished he were looking at his body in a toilet bowl and could tug the flush to send it away forever.

He looked older in the gray image, tired and grime-coated. Maybe he was seeing a twentysomething version of himself, homeless and desperate like the Lambda Youth girls. If he couldn't sing at the cathedral any more, maybe he'd visit the soup kitchen and throw up on the choir. Berry found some lipstick Anna or Maura had left him and drew on his reflection in the voided screen. He put circles around his breasts, for containment. He drew red crosses over his eyes' reflections.

"I miss when I thought I was just going to prison forever," Berry told the television.

Morning loomed. Sunrise would hold everything in place, like an extra helping of gravity. Things that shifted in the dark would be permanent by day. Berry would be out of the choir forever. And his family would be wrecked for good.

Berry ended up in the kitchen again, holding the same knife he'd used to attack his balls last summer. This time he held it to the ridge beneath his breasts. Berry took a deep breath, worth a minute underwater or a long phrase, then he raised the knife to bite at the softness beneath his alien growths. He bit his lip and promised himself to make no sound this time. He sawed until the pain felt like an animal clawing inside him. Then he sawed some more. He used his anger to counterbalance the burning. He felt rivers flow down his stomach to his lifeless pubes. He held the knife in place until his hands lost their strength. Then he let himself fall on the kitchen floor until the cracked ceiling drifted down onto him.

16.

"Self-mutilation as a means of self-expression has certain intrinsic limits, particularly if you resort to it each time life gets hairy. After a time you run out of limbs. I've seen it a few times; psych wards full of fingerless malcontents trying to dislodge their teeth with calculated falls into furniture. It's hard to believe you grew breasts just to gain two extra easels for your art. Okay, so maybe it's not art, art implies technique, which you lack. Unless tormenting others scores as an art form. I can talk all day, you know. That's what these framed papers on my wall attest to: my ability to fill an hour with words. But speaking of psych wards, you're lucky you're not locked up under observation right now. To cut yourself once and all that; but the Wilde reference goes over your head, huh. You know, it's in your interest for me to feel in the loop. I can do a lot for you if I know what's going on. It's not about power. It's not. It's about prudence. I've already gone out on a huge limb for you. Not a huge limb, a very thin and ill-supported limb extending a few feet over a bottomless drop. Allowing sex-changes in barely pubescent kids isn't exactly in the mainstream of psychiatric thought, you know. It's been done in a handful of cases, where the patient seemed especially, I should say suicidally, determined, as you did. But I guess one shouldn't confuse determination with random self-destructiveness. Trying to discern a meaning in the jumper's descent only distracts from the need to position a net. Speaking of suicide. Have I mentioned I'm out on a limb?"

"I'm not self-destructive or suicidal," Berry said. The bandages bear-hugging his chest only covered a scorching pain that made it difficult to think about anything else. The hospital had released him after just forty-eight hours, but Dr. Tamarind could send him back any time. He was on pain pills and antidepressants, and off hormones.

"It speaks," Dr. Tamarind said.

"I'm not an it."

"So what are you?" He tapped a pen on his legal pad.

Berry shrugged. "You talk too much."

The heat beneath Berry's sternum flared as he twisted in his seat as if to escape Dr. Tamarind's deep black eyes. The bandages reminded him of the ones he'd used to hide his breasts for so long. Only now, the new wounds meant Berry couldn't repress his chest for months, if ever.

Berry started to tell Dr. Tamarind about his parents' reconciliation-turned-divorce, his near-murder of Lisa's dad, the discovery his maybe-womanhood had helped turn Wilson gay, and his exile from the choir on the eve of recording. As he spoke, pain flared. It comforted and terrified Berry, because it jarred his mind away from his usual terrors, but also reminded him where they led.

Berry was forever scarred, the doctors said.

Dr. Tamarind seemed to reflate as soon as Berry gristed his machinery. He had a slice of cake with too much fruit and frosting on top to eat chaotically. He had to eat some fruit and frosting to make it less top-heavy before he could scoop at the sides. He started with Wilson. "You don't really think you could have made your friend gay, do you? I mean, you may be attractive, but let's keep a sense of proportion. You may have helped him become more conscious of something that was always there." Then he tossed out a lot of questions about Mr. Gartner's special swimming pool, and whether Berry had intended murder. Then there was the divorce.

Berry's guilt lessened a little, replaced by annoyance. Berry thought a makeover might be fun compared to Dr. Tamarind's droning. "You're missing the point," Berry said in the middle of a long sentence about the difference between thought and deeds, or faith and works. "It's my fault because I was starting to enjoy this." He gestured down at his femaleness.

Dr. Tamarind's precarious cake had turned out to have a delightful creamy center. "So you *have* started to enjoy it all. The clothes, the bangles, the makeup. But the price was too high, eh? The price is always high for truth, often higher than you could know."

"So what do we do?"

"Maybe we went too fast." Dr. Tamarind clasped hands in mid air, then let them fall in his lap. He breathed through his nose. "Okay. So first I need you to promise me no more cutting anything but coupons and paper dolls. Or else it'll be the observation ward for you and night shift at the county bughouse for me. That's number one. Number two: do we keep you on the hormones and geegaws? Going on and off hormones is dangerous, but maybe you should quit for good."

"I don't want to stop." Berry hadn't expected to be so sure.

"Okay. If your parents want to come in and talk to me about it, maybe we can help them through this. Your dad especially. Meanwhile, I'm going to talk to your mom about letting you go back to your choir as a boy for now."

The fire-pins inside Berry swept like pennants. He started to sob and shake. "I'm going to sing again," he let out between gouts of wet air. "If the other choirboys don't kill me for being a fairy."

"You're not a fairy. You're an incredibly brave person, way braver than most kids your age, who should stay away from knives for a long, long time."

Judy had bought a book called *Your Self-Lacerating Teen*, complete with heartwarming pictures of recovered self-slashers and a "Blade-Free Pledge" you could ask your kid to sign. She read it cover to cover several times. From the book, she learned:

• More teenagers cut themselves than people realize.
• If they stay away from wrists, neck or other arteries, this is a Good Thing.
• This behavior usually means something.

She'd gone robotic when she'd taken Berry back to the emergency room. She'd alternated between crisis mode resolve and exclamations like "Oh my God oh my God . . . what are we doing Oh my God . . ." Seeing the terror and crippled emotions in her face, Berry'd felt worse than before he cut himself. But she hadn't scolded Berry. Instead, she'd stroked from neck to collarbone, kissed his nose, and said, "Oh baby, please be okay, please don't do this again, my sweet baby. Please . . ."

Marco had showed up at the hospital on Wednesday, halfway through Berry's stay. Judy had seen someone it was okay to blame. "Come to finish the job, macho kid-rejecting asshole fiend?" Marco glared and would have thrown a telephone at Judy if the nurse hadn't watched him. "Fucking creep, you'd rather beat our daughter than see her as she is."

Marco had left without talking to Berry.

Judy's pattern of alternate panic and dead-eye stillness had continued after Berry'd left the hospital. "Oh Berry," she'd say after staring into the shiny kitchen floor an hour or two, "you're such a perfect blessing and I love you. I wish I'd said that before." She'd hug Berry so tight his stitches almost popped, then return to staring.

Berry felt Judy needed Dr. Tamarind more than he did. The two of them spent an hour together after Berry's session. Berry sat out in the waiting room trying not to think about what they might be saying about him. Instead he leafed through Judy's self-laceration book. For fun, he went through and crossed out the word "not" with a chewed-end ballpoint pen. "This behavior does ~~not~~ mean your child is a Satanist. Your teen does ~~not~~ know what he or she is doing. You should ~~not~~ leave your teen alone with sharp objects." Then Berry felt guilty for his "not" crossings. Anything he did to battle his guilt just made him guiltier.

Judy came from Dr. Tamarind's office looking bloodless. "Hey mom." Berry hid the defaced book behind his back. "You look like you should eat."

"We're having dinner with Mr. Allen."

Once, two years earlier, Wilson's parents had invited a bunch of St. Luke's people over for a dinner party. They'd summoned Mr. Allen, Berry and his parents, and a few others. Mr. Allen had shown up looking like the victim of a beautician's assault. Somehow, he'd sprayed his mane into a neat dome over his head and trimmed his beard, mustache, and eyebrows. He'd swapped his normal thick glasses for a special pair with flared steel rims. He wore a square blue tie with white stripes, a tweed jacket, and dark pants. Berry had dropped his stuffed mushroom on his good pants at the sight of Mr. Allen tamed. Mr. Allen was always the wild musician who played forty men and boys using gentle hysteria as his bow.

But even weirder, Mr. Allen had brought a girlfriend to the Fennimores. She'd been younger than Mr. Allen, a few years at least, with tanning booth skin and bleached hair, plus square glasses. Berry couldn't remember her name, but the other choirboys had called her the Fox. That was the first Berry had heard of Mr. Allen having a life away from church.

Staring at the choirmaster had distracted Berry from watching his parents struggle to act sophisticated in front of Wilson's. Marco had thrown a fit before the party, taking an hour to find a stain-free tie. He'd finally dug out a power tie from his broker days, creased but not blotted. At the Fennimores', Marco had sloshed dip on the Power Tie anyway. Berry had listened to Mr. Allen discussing politics with his mom, and ignored Marco's attempts to impress Wilson's parents. Marco had stayed sober and tried to sell Mrs. Fennimore on one of the Spiritual Growth Funds he'd peddled at the time. (Biotech stocks plus animal guide consultations.) Mr. Fennimore had gotten roaring drunk and shrieked at Dean Jackson about subjectivity. The Fennimores hadn't invited Berry's parents to another party, if they'd held any. Berry had never seen the Fox again.

"So map out the Mr.-Allen-and-you thing for me," Berry said to his mom on the bus. Marco still had the car. Judy had threatened to sic the cops on him to get it back, but she wouldn't mind if he drove out of town and kept driving in one direction.

Judy leaned over and lowered her voice. Across the aisle, a large woman made a show of not listening. "I just enjoy talking to him," she said. "He's passionate about music. And I know he's had a big influence on you. It's nice to have him around."

"So he's my dad now?"

Judy laughed. "Let's not jump the gun."

Berry imagined vaulting over a gun that fired wildly, half-aimed at pubes, legs, or torso.

Mr. Allen was due at their apartment around seven PM. It was Thursday, the free day between rehearsals. Berry realized with a jolt that it was also the original target date for the choir's recording. The apartment looked neat beyond recognition. Judy had thrown out most of Marco's junk. All the wrecked appliances had vanished. The Native American wall rugs sat in the dumpster behind the apartment building, and Judy had vacuumed and polished. "Wow," Berry said.

"I had to do something while you were gone." Judy pulled out the big table and unscrunched the middle section to make a space for place settings and candles. "I'm marinating wings. So would you dress up nice, Berry? Boy or girl is fine."

Berry laid out some clothes on his bed and stared at them. Berry hadn't done boy in ten days. His breasts still hurt like vinegar or hate. It stung just to touch them, and there was no way he could bind them. Hiding them meant layers, or a loose poncho. Berry wanted to make Judy as happy as he could. In the end, he pulled out a pleated gray skirt that Anna Conventional had bought him at Old Navy, a high-necked white blouse, and his choir blazer. The effect was a pastiche of choirgirl. The breasts pushed at the blazer and the skirt made him look schoolgirlish. High white socks and black shoes finished the outfit.

When Berry came out of his room, he found Mr. Allen and Judy making out on the couch. The choirmaster had the same trimmed-everything look he'd brought to the Fennimores' place two years before. He wore a nice flannel shirt and jeans instead of tweed. His hand sat near Judy's lap. Judy had one hand on his beard. Berry coughed. They stopped kissing, but not in a hurry.

"Hi, Berry," Mr. Allen said. "Wow—you look terrific."

"Wow from me too," added Judy.

"Thanks." Berry looked at the glass coffee table. He'd never seen its surface before. "So I'm sorry I messed things up. I know tonight was supposed to be the big recording."

"Don't worry—it's not the end of the world or anything." Mr. Allen smiled and stayed leaned back against the couch and Judy. Berry looked up at the huge blue eyes behind rimless glasses, seeking the lie in his smile. When he found none, it shook his whole image of Mr. Allen, the obsessed maniac who lived for the choir's performance. He'd always assumed Mr. Allen spent every spare moment grinding his teeth over each rushed half note or squeak the choir committed. He'd pictured Mr. Allen walking the streets cursing at his unfocused boys and amateur men. Not sitting with a glass of mineral water in one hand chatting about opera with Berry's mom.

Judy's wings had marinated for twenty-four hours and tasted yummy. But everything else about dinner was awful, and Berry marinated through Mr. Allen and Judy's boring conversation. Judy talked about her car for half an hour, including all the work she'd done on the suspension and winterized undercarriage, and how badly she'd miss it. Mr. Allen said car custody battles could turn just as ugly as human ones. They talked about all the construction on the Downtown Loop and plans to turn some old noodle-stretching plants into nightclubs. Mr. Allen talked about church politics and how Canon Moosehead had convinced the Downtown Association to support a revamped Hungry

Souls program that kept the homeless from wandering onto the main street.

"Canon Moosehead is dating my friend Maura. She's a tranny ho," Berry chipped in. Mr. Allen's eyes went wild and he nearly bit a chicken bone in half. He looked more like the choirmaster Berry knew. "We should hang with her. She's really cool, even if you did get off on the wrong foot with her, mom." Judy didn't remember Maura. Mr. Allen couldn't quite take in what Berry had said. "Maybe you shouldn't mention that to anyone else," Berry said as an afterthought.

Berry cleared up after dinner. Mr. Allen and Judy ended up back on the sofa while Berry washed dishes. Berry sneaked a glance over the half-counter dividing the kitchen from the living room. Judy had her legs up on the sofa and her head rested against Mr. Allen's armpit. Berry felt jealous of each of them getting to be close to the other and a weird resentment on Marco's behalf. The idea of a music scholarship at a school far away tempted Berry.

"Can you tuck yourself in?" Judy started to lift herself. "Mr. Allen and I were planning on going out for a drink."

"Oh," Berry said, looking at the coffee tray in his hands with cups and butter cookies on it. "Okay."

"And hey, Berry," said Mr. Allen. "Hope you can make it to rehearsal tomorrow evening." Judy nodded. Then the two of them donned coats and strolled out.

Berry put the tray down and danced across the apartment. Then he practiced marching back to the kitchen as if it were a cathedral. He rushed into his room and peeled off the skirt so only the blazer and white blouse remained. He considered: how could he squelch the breasts without dying? Then he forgot that question and went back to dancing bottomless around his room, hearing the voices raise within. A thought snagged Berry's brain, what if Mr. Allen was only dating Judy to get Berry back in the choir? It would be really sweet and touching, but not necessary now that Dr. Tamarind had given the go-ahead for him to come back. Berry hoped Mr. Allen treated Judy well if that turned out to be the case.

Berry went to sleep hearing an inner chorus cascading something out of Handel's "Zadok the Priest." He woke at three AM to the sound of Mr. Allen and Judy across the hall—at least he assumed they were the ones moaning and stuttering. Berry felt anxiety crowd out his assurance. His family had warped faster than his body. What would the other choirboys say if they knew Mr. Allen was fucking his mom? That thought took Berry back to the one he'd been avoiding all night: how would he deal with the other choirboys now they knew he was a sex-change case?

Berry sweated and trembled in his bed until the noises from across the hall stopped. He stared at the flickers on his ceiling. Then he finally collapsed into dreams of kids standing over his battered body, kicking his face, his injured breasts, his stomach. "Please not the teeth," he begged in the dream. "I just got my grown-up teeth, I can't replace them." In the morning, Berry felt like a survivor of an ancient war.

"This past week has set me back a month," Judy complained in the morning. Mr. Allen wasn't around. "I'll be lucky to pass my night classes with all I've missed, and they're perma annoyed with me at work. But there's always hope." She'd talked to the principal of Orlac Middle, who might be willing to bend some rules to get Berry back in class.

Judy wanted Berry to return as a full Swan, away from the "rough-housing" of the Geese. Berry could be officially a girl, but wouldn't have to do PE or home ec, two subjects where ambiguous gender could craze people. Judy would make sure Berry got exercise. Hearing about this plan, Berry felt the pain fingers xylophone his ribs. "I won't last a week," he said.

"We're still going to find you a new school for next year, where they don't know you," said Judy. "Mr. Allen has some ideas. But this will work for now."

Before the confrontation with Mr. Hanson, Berry had someone else to see. "At your age, you would be starting an apprenticeship if you were living in the eighteenth century." Gray Redman held up a picture of a boy in a tricorner hat and funny ribbony jacket. "I found this in a magazine. Cute, huh? Ever read Johnny Tremaine?"

Berry shook his head. "A lot's happened. I tried to cut off my breasts and now I'm a Swan."

"That's heavy duty." Gray Redman shuffled folders. "Well, here's what I've found. The fastest growing jobs are all in information. Don't believe what you hear about the dotcoms, it's all just a downtick. Anyway, this is good news because tech companies are way mega tolerant, and soon enough nobody will have a body anyway, we'll just be genderless consciousnesses in cyberspace. You'll be skills and dirty jokes wrapped in a multiple choice identity, dig?"

"So I'm losing what this has to do with me."

"The point being you're not too young to get into the new economy. You're almost too old, if anything. Go work for a web design firm—your musical background will help in some way I can't predict right now—and get on the fast track." Gray gestured at his sliver of window. "This town used to be all about noodle stretching. Then the old economy died. Now this whole area revolves around stretching noodles of a different kind." Gray tapped his head.

"That's it?"

"I thought it was pretty cool. Especially the 'noodles of a different kind' part." Gray looked at the disappointment in Berry's eyes. "Aw man. I'm sorry. I couldn't find anything about how to become an opera singer. I think you have to go to a conservatory or something. Look, there's one other thing. I have this web service I subscribe to. You go there and type in a job and it tells you what other jobs are similar." Gray swiveled to face his monitor and tapped on his keyboard. A web site appeared and Gray typed the word "choirboy" into a white rectangle, then clicked "Go." A few moments passed, then five words appeared: "Priest, opera singer, game show host, politician, singing telegram."

"Hmmm," Gray said. "I'm not seeing the big money here. I'm telling you, the web's where it's at."

"Game show host," Berry said. "I've always wanted to be Vanna White or something."

"Got any connections in Hollywood?"

"Not really. My friend works at a magazine."

Walking into the noon sun downtown, Berry felt happiness flicker over every inch of his skin. He wondered if the hormones caused mood swings. He almost didn't care. "I was glad, glad when they said unto me, we will go, we will gooooooo into the House of the Lord," he sang. He twirled his skirt so it fluttered up like a cocktail umbrella. Then Berry imagined becoming a singing telegram. He tried to make up some messages he could sing. "Sorry I almost drowned your dad, ta dumdumdum, Didn't mean to make you mad, scoobie loo loo, It's just one of those things. The memory still stings. Next time I'll throw in a pair of water wings, dadudadudaduadudadaaah . . ."

"We value diversity here at Orlac Middle," Mr. Hanson said. Berry felt the grilled cheese Judy had fed him for lunch adjust seismically in his gut. "Enough school boards have gone to court trying to bar transgender kids and lost in the past few years. So we have a policy of total non-discrimination." Mr. Hanson wore a tartan shirt, blue sports jacket, and slacks. He seemed the opposite of Gray Redman, who always acted super-hip because he was terrified of not being taken seriously. Mr. Hanson took it for granted he had your respect and admiration, so he could afford to act cozy.

"That's good to hear. I think." Judy sat straight. She'd told Berry she was ready for a fight or tears, whichever might win results.

"Frankly, we're excited, in a terrified and disturbed way. I'm hoping we avoid the screaming school board meetings, like we had with that gay coach a few years back. The more low-key, the better." Mr. Hanson's thick face never really smiled.

"I'm not sure how you plan to get there," Judy said.

"I'm glad you asked that. We have a strategy we call selective denial. We're going to pretend nothing much has happened or will happen. We'll give Berry the same attitude of zero tolerance for harassment we extend to all other students. And we'll try like hell to keep this out of the media. Anyone want to interview you guys, you shut them out. Hopefully it won't be a slow news week any time soon."

"Sounds like a nightmare," Berry said.

"Let's hope not so much," Mr. Hanson said. "I'm personally all about diversity, preferably the non-screaming and burning down school facilities kind."

"So what if I change my mind in a few months?" Berry asked. Mr. Hanson and Judy both looked like he'd swung a very long crowbar and hit them both in the heads simultaneously. "I mean, I don't think I will, but this is all new to me, and I may stop being into it."

"You're not allowed to change your mind," Hanson said quickly.

Judy just glared. Once out of the meeting, Berry said, "I think that went pretty well, huh."

Judy grabbed Berry's shoulders. "What? What did I do? Why are you torturing me? How much do I have to suffer while you toy around? If you don't really want this, that's fine, but stop flipping a goddamn coin. Which is it, Berry?"

Berry just tilted his head and widened his eyes, not knowing how to answer.

"Are you just nuts? Should I have let them commit you or observe you or whatever the fuck? Dr. Tamarind thinks you're sane, but maybe he's grading on a curve. The point is it's not just you now. I've thrown away my marriage and risked losing my mind so you can become the person you want to be. Mr. Allen's taking a big risk letting you sing again. Mr. Hanson's going to get crucified if you go back to school here. So what's it going to be, Berry? What are you?"

"I'm a choirboy," Berry said.

"That's not an answer. You can't hide behind those robes forever. You need to make a commitment."

An empty school bus shuddered at the parking lot's edge as someone tried to start it. Leaves, half-defined and almost dust, scuttled around their feet. The wind plushed Berry's skirt out and made an outline of his arms and breasts under his deliberately loose blouse.

"I'm sorry," Berry said.

17.

Bathroom stalls are amazing. They have acoustics to die for, if you feel like singing on the john. You can shut the latch and live private. The bathroom may invite only boys or girls, but once inside the stall, it's just you and your configuration. Berry wished he could stay in the girls room at Orlac Middle forever. They could slide food to him under the stall door, and he'd sleep there when the school noises became night noises and the neon lights strobed overhead no longer. The only difference in the girls' room was the pink tiles.

"Who's in there?"

Berry heard two or three girls outside his stall and smelled cigarettes. They laughed, coughed, and stomped.

"Whoever it is, she didn't just come out of a class. Somebody's playing hooky in the girls room. Hey in there, come on out and party with us."

Berry didn't move.

"She's shy. Harrup." The last speaker made a noise as she did a chin-up on the stall door. Amy Beckerman looked down at Berry. Her pigtails quivered. Her green eyes widened and she grinned wide. "Hey, wow!"

"Who is she?" someone else asked.

"Not 'she.' It's that Berry guy. In a skirt and in our bathroom."

Berry shrank down in the stall to hide from the green stare and lipstick-coated drool coming down on him. Amy panted at the effort of holding herself up.

"The stories were true!"

As Berry slid further down on the seat to get away from Amy, hands grabbed his ankles. His skirt bunched and his back thudded as it hit the floor. In seconds, the girls pulled him out of the stall. He lay on his back surrounded by laughter, cheap perfume, and cigarette ash. The bathroom had crumbling foam tiles on its ceiling. Sneakers and boots prodded him.

"Eww, he's looking up my skirt! Pervert!"

Berry tried to close his eyes so he couldn't look at anything he wasn't supposed to. He tried to imagine how a real girl would react to this situation. Maybe if he just projected the right persona, these girls would be his friends.

"He wants to be a girl." Amy had her breath back. "We should help him. Berry, has anyone taught you about tampons? They're important in our world. Grab him."

Berry went limp in the girls' hands. He panicked just as the ground whirled away from him. His balance upended. Nausea and terror kindled a scream from deep inside him. Blood soaked his brain. He opened his eyes to see a metal container full of bloody pieces of cloth and plastic. His head descended into the bin and everything fell dark.

"You see Berry, tampons are supposed to be flushable, but they don't let us flush them here because the school plumbing sucks," Amy lectured. "They come in three kinds: junior absorbency, regular absorbency, and super absorbency."

"His shoulders are too wide to go in."

"Push harder."

"I can see his underwear. Oh gross. He's wearing panties and they're all dirty."

Berry's world got smaller than the stall he'd tried to hide in. Sounds went distant. All around he felt garbage bag and cloth. The can smelled rancid. The girls' shoves chafed his injured breasts and started the fire cycle. Heels clattered. Berry tasted stomach juice. He started kicking and screaming. The girls laughed louder.

"Excuse me." The door opened and Judy's voice came from far away. "I'm looking for my daughter. She came in here to use the bathroom a while ago."

"Daughter? I don't think so, ma'am. We're the only girls in here, and we've all got mothers of our own."

Judy apologized. Berry screamed louder from inside the tampon case. He tried to twist his body free, but the girls held him fast. The girls' room door closed. The girls rattled Berry's box. Night doused Berry's mind, made him drunk from suffocation. He was sure he'd die inside this canister and be discarded along with its contents. The box dragged along the ground.

"Time to go," Amy said. Berry felt the box lift and push through the girls' room door and into the hall. The floor bumped his bare legs.

A male voice shouted "Kick the can!" Something rocked then smacked. The tampon canister amplified impact. Berry howled and thrashed his legs. Voices cluttered the air into deafening white noise. Boys and girls laughed all around Berry, and voices took up the chant "Kick the can! Kick the can!" Berry's entombed head rocked.

"Oh my God, Berry!" Judy's voice came again. "What have they done to you?"

Judy pulled Berry's head out of the can. They were in the school hallway outside the girls' room. He blinked at her, then at the ring of impassive kids. Judy dragged him back into the girls' room. He saw smudges on his hair, hands, and face in the mirror. Judy stared at him for a moment, then pushed him over to the sink and scoured him with a paper towel. "We're out of here. You can't ever go back to this death camp."

Berry and Judy went home on the bus. Berry wanted to explain himself more, apologize for how things had worked out. Instead, he just put his head on his mom's shoulder. Judy patted his head and clucked.

At home, Berry cleaned himself up and dressed for choir rehearsal. Judy kept asking if he was sure he wanted to go; wouldn't he rather rent a video or skate? Berry just shook his head.

Rehearsals Friday afternoons and evenings had an informal dress code. After his second shower, Berry looked through all his clothes to find his malest look. Everybody knew the truth by now, so Berry had to show them he could stay a choirboy even if his sex went its own uncharted way. Berry wore something similar to the previous night's outfit, except with slacks.

"Slacks are the new skirt," Judy commented.

A rockslide in the mostly darkness, St. Luke's seemed prone to fall on Berry's head at any moment. Its imitation-Gothic phallic spires waved him away. The city glow reflecting off its dull stained glass warned him off like a lighthouse. Berry looked up and breathed.

"Want me to stay?" Judy asked.

"Why?" Berry said. "I'll be fine. It's just a rehearsal."

Judy nodded, then walked out of the cathedral's parking lot/makeshift basketball court/boxing ring/extra rehearsal space. Judy waved as she reached the cathedral's corner, then became diminishing sound in space.

The whole area looked deserted. Maybe nobody had come yet, or maybe they'd canceled rehearsal. Berry hunted for reasons to flee. Then he walked over to the cathedral office building and into the basement. Three steps from the bottom, he paused. He heard kids' voices from the Twelve Step room. Laughter, percussive noises of heads knocking together, and low weeping.

Berry reached the last step, then paused again. Then he sprinted into the boys' room, ran into a stall, and knelt. He gripped the cracks in the wall over the toilet with both hands and heaved. He tried to throw up but nothing came, not even the stomach acid he'd tasted earlier. If vomit was voice, Berry's had gone silent. He stared into his pale image. The toilet's white hole framed the reflection of his nose. Then he straightened up and left the stall.

Half a dozen boys stood near the sinks and mirrors, including Randy and Marc. When Berry came out of the stall they all moved into combat stances. A few kids blocked the door, and Marc stuck his thumb into his jeans front pocket.

"Girls' choir don't rehearse tonight," Marc said.

"And this ain't the girls room, yo," Randy said.

"I'm back," Berry said. "Mr. Allen said I could sing."

"Can you still sing? Treble, I mean?" Marc asked.

Berry nodded. More boys wandered in, sensing a spectacle. Randy moved closer to Berry, head down. "Your mom's not here to protect you now," he said. "Neither is your lesbo girlfriend."

"I don't need them," Berry said.

"Don't hit the delicate little girl," Marc said in a mewling parody of concern.

"I'm not delicate," Berry said.

"Good." Randy lunged.

Berry hugged himself to protect his injured breasts from the impact. That meant nothing kept him from smacking onto the bathroom floor. His butt near broke. Randy landed on top of Berry, pinning Berry's arms with his knees. Someone pulled off Berry's shoes and socks.

Randy smacked Berry's mouth. "Cocksucker." He smacked again and again, in rhythm. Dotted quarter note, eighth note, dotted quarter note, eighth note.

"Let's put him on the altar and sacrifice him," one of the smaller choirboys said.

"Let's cut him into chunks and put him in the organ pipes," Jackie said.

"String him from the balcony by his legs!"

Choirboys clustered around Berry's half corpse. He looked up at the staring faces and fists. Then he giggled with relief. It was okay. They were hazing him.

"I know," Berry said. "Grind me up into teeny little pieces and sprinkle a little on each communion wafer on Sunday."

"Who asked you?" Randy said. Another tattoo beat on the face.

"Pig pile!" one of the smaller kids yelled. The others took up the chant. Berry closed his eyes just as a knee landed between them. Someone's elbow crushed his pancreas.

"Pig pile in the boys' room!" The yells echoed in the hall outside. The weight on Berry's sore chest and legs mounted. He couldn't breathe. Bodies squirmed all over him. He felt kicks and jabs in his ribs and neck, even his crotch. He yelped when a sneaker jabbed his balls. Someone tried to give him a wedgie, but couldn't reach under him with all those other bodies on top.

Randy couldn't slap Berry with so many other boys climbing on them. Berry closed his eyes and tried to drift away, ignore the pain and helplessness of being at the bottom of so much frenzy. He couldn't have explained how he knew this was different from the tampon box earlier that day, he just knew. When you were hazed, it ended with you being one of the group.

Berry nearly passed out before someone yelled that it was rehearsal time. Boys tumbled off him one by one, until only Randy remained, laying flat against Berry's torso.

"Hope you sing as pretty as you look," Randy said, face a few inches from Berry's. Then he lifted himself off Berry, straightened his clothes, and left.

Berry sat up slowly and looked around the empty bathroom. His chest felt cut up all over again. He took slow breaths and thought about music. This would all pay off.

"I found your shoes in the trash." Wilson held them delicately between finger and thumb. "Your socks are a lost cause."

"That went pretty well, I guess." Berry wiped his shoes with a paper towel.

"Randy still has it in for you," Wilson said. "He'd put you in the ground if he could. But damn, we need your voice. Come on, we're late for rehearsal."

They got to the choir room in time to warm up. Berry took his place in the middle of the right row of boys, facing the piano where Mr. Allen ran through easy vocal exercises. Mr. Allen's hair and beard still looked neater than usual.

Berry felt like he'd starved so long that food could kill him, and here was food.

"So Berry—hope you enjoyed your little vacation," Mr. Allen said with just enough sarcasm to tell everyone Berry was still one of the boys as far as he was concerned. "The rest of us have worked hard while you've been at the beach—think you can catch up?"

Berry nodded.

They worked. By now the choir drilled a lot of Christmas music, plus some stuff they still planned to record in the postponed session. Carols. That "Unto Us Shall Come a Son" bit from Handel's *Messiah*. Some slushy John Rutter stuff. The transition from somber Pentecost to Advent always caught Berry off guard—it was like tuning from an indie-folk-goth station to an easy listening one.

Berry's pipes sounded just like they had before he'd hit the beach, which was more than he could say for the other boys his age. He caught strange glances from some of the other boys. The choir obviously flexed way bigger muscles with Berry than without him. It was weird not having Teddy there. Enough of the music was stuff Berry had covered in previous years or in that abandoned building site with Wilson that he caught up pretty quickly.

For dinner, the cathedral served the choir a defeated stew and stale fish sticks. Berry asked Wilson about Lisa. "She's been quiet at school. There's all sorts of rumors about her. Her dad's a gangster or she's becoming a nun or she fucks doggies. But she still has a clique, and they closed ranks."

"I hope she's okay."

The other choirboys seemed less weird toward Berry now they'd pig-piled him. They had lots of questions. "So what's the deal, are you going to, like, kiss boys and stuff? Isn't it weird to like wear perfume and eat salad?"

Berry said he'd never kissed a boy (slight lie), eaten salad, or worn perfume. He'd never watched a chick flick. "I don't know what I'm going to turn into. For now, I just want to sing."

Teddy showed up again with the other men for the evening rehearsal. It was way strange hearing unsteady tremors from his throat. It went up and down, but Teddy's voice seemed to settle. Wilson, Marc, and Randy limped as trebles, but they found rips in their voices when they relaxed into them.

This wasn't the same choir Berry had sung with for the fall concert. Even though the boys had stopped whaling on him, things felt less comfortable. The choir had changed, but so had Berry and he didn't quite fit his old space. He hadn't expected a best friend's welcome from the whole choir, but he had expected it to feel right to sing again. Instead, it fit him weirdly like a sweater that's been stretched on a hanger and then shrunk in the dryer. Berry's unease only grew as the stained glass on the outer wall grayed. When rehearsal ended Mr. Allen smiled at Berry, but Berry left without talking to the choirmaster.

"Buy Wilson and me milkshakes," Berry ordered Judy when she showed up. "We owe Wilson. Marco tried to kidnap him along with me."

"I'm not sure I can afford to buy Wilson a milkshake," Judy said, chewing a knuckle. "I just lost my job."

"Oh," Berry said. "I'm sorry. Shit." He stared at his dirty shoes. Nobody spoke for a while.

"I've got some leads on jobs. I've got enough school under my belt that I may be good for a paralegal gig," Judy said without taking the back of her hand out of her mouth.

"Hey, I'll get the shakes," Wilson said. "I just got my choir paycheck."

They went to the Metro K and ordered vanilla shakes. Judy explained. "A woman my age is dispensable to the people in power. Unless you work like ten zillion hours and have no life, you're a gimpy working mom. I started taking sick leave and word got around I was a single mom. All of a sudden they were overstaffed. At least I get two weeks to look around, plus maybe some kind of severance package the HR department is working out."

"I'll ask my dad if there are any jobs in advertising," Wilson said.

"Thanks, but my whole background is in coincidences and free-associations."

"I hear the Internet is still big in spite of everything," Berry said helplessly. Wilson slurped.

The next morning, Judy's Toyota turned up on the sidewalk a block from their apartment building. It had a note on the windshield: GONE TO SHAMBALLA OR PITTSBURGH, WHICHEVER I FIND FIRST. SORRY I BORROWED CAR. MARCO.

"We could have walked around for weeks without knowing the car was here." Judy crunched Marco's note.

"Can I spend the day with Anna Conventional?" Berry asked. He explained who that was.

Judy sighed. "Whatever."

Anna Conventional drove Berry out to the countryside and bought him a big straw hat and floral skirt. He reclined the passenger seat all the way and pulled the skirt on while she drove. She surveyed the results with relish. "You look totally countrified."

They drove until the one-lane roads twisted and looped indecisively. Pastures and cornfields flanked the roads.

Finally, Anna found a cemetery she liked and pulled the car over. She spread a picnic blanket over the bumpy grass of a couple of graves, then laid out plates and Tupperware.

Berry munched a cookie while Anna Conventional explained how homophobia caused hangnails. "These youths think long nails make them gay, so they trim cruelly. They chew and bite and pick and clip as if their nails might go limp if they grew. Underdeveloped bonsai hacked by the world's craziest gardeners—I think that's an actual Fox TV show, world's craziest gardeners. Anyway, you can always tell how a man views his masculinity by looking at his nails."

A scream broke Anna Conventional's lecture. Berry's first thought was that a gay-basher was pulling off someone's fingernails. He heard it again, a throat-rending roar, like a zombie from *28 Days Later*. It got closer. Berry heard stalks being trampled as the source of the noise charged through the wall of cornfield next to the graveyard.

"It's an animal," Berry said. He squared himself against a headstone. Violence seemed as inevitable as lunch. Berry felt like screaming, running, or tearing at his own cheeks. But he didn't do any of those things, his panic fell into a bag of cotton balls. People were going to attack, like waves on a shore, and the best you could do was let them pass over you.

The screams seemed near now. "I think it's between us and the car," Anna Conventional said. "Maybe we can lose it in the woods behind that church."

"Too late!" Berry yelled.

A large man staggered out of the woods. He had shaggy black hair over his eyes and a wild unshaven face. Dirt covered his clothes and skin in whorls and stripes. His Universal

Pride T-shirt and sweat pants gaped with a million rips. He made the animal noise again.

Anna Conventional recognized him first. "It's Bishop Bacchus!"

The filthy thing stared at Anna Conventional. Berry saw a sagging mustache that once had been plumed with wax. Dirt ringed the soft mouth and wide green eyes that had looked so placid days earlier. There was no mistaking the shredded sneakers and single hoop earring. Bishop Bacchus shrieked again, then threw himself on the ground at their feet. He breathed hard.

"I can't believe it's really you," he said. "I've wandered here for days," he told Berry. "Since your dad drove us to the middle of nowhere."

"Oh," Berry said. "I'm so sorry. We didn't mean to. I mean, my dad had to find Shambolica or wherever, and—"

"Don't be sorry," Bishop Bacchus said. Anna Conventional pushed a Dixie cup of sangria at him. He guzzled, then held out the cup for a refill. "Is that brie? Anyway, don't be sorry at all. I've wandered through darkness and grime. After I lost you guys, I fell into a great hole in the ground, which I believe to be an entrance to Hell. I heard strange chanting while I was down there, as if to curse me forever. But I climbed. I climbed until I reached level ground. I found a forest and walked a long time. I slept in an abandoned dumpster. Or rather, I thought it abandoned, but then they scooped me and deposited me at the county dump, a few miles from here. Oh God, that isn't hummus, is it? I've been living off mushrooms and nuts, plus that squirrel I caught yesterday. Anyway, this has been the greatest experience. After wandering a couple days with no money and no way home, I felt this amazing clarity. I could feel someone reaching out to me and comforting me, letting me know I wasn't really lost. I heard Jesus call my name."

"Jesus?" Berry said. "Like *the* Jesus?"

"I thought you were a Pagan," Anna Conventional exclaimed. She poured sangria down Bishop Bacchus's throat. "Do you need drugs? I can get drugs. If you're in withdrawal—"

"I had a fevered delusion of Paganism," Bishop Bacchus insisted. "I was raised Baptist and strayed. But the Good Shepherd brought me here to redeem me."

"My dad's a shepherd now?" Berry said. "I thought he was going to be a goatherd."

"Snap out of it!" Anna Conventional snapped her fingers in front of Bishop Bacchus's nose.

"I have snapped," Bishop Bacchus insisted. "Out of it, I mean. I sleepwalked and now I'm awake on my feet."

"He needs to talk to someone. Maybe Canon Moosehead can help," Berry said.

"Good idea. Hanging with a real live Christian minister could scare anyone away from religion." Anna Conventional grabbed her cell phone. "Maur. We need your boyfriend to meet a new convert. Actually, someone you know. You'll see. Don't worry, it'll be fun. One hour, at Carlo's." She hung up and tossed the cellphone in her bag. "Come on, let's get John the Baptist here a shower and some Clinitron skin saver."

They carried the picnic basket back to the car and put the Bishop in the back seat on top of their blanket. "So something I don't get," Berry said. "You were a bishop with the church of insufficient plumbing or whatever. You had those cool robes and got to party with the strange kids. Now you're going to become Christian and get demoted to layperson."

Charlie Anders

Bishop Bacchus just showed palms. "Will of the Lord."

"Don't worry," Anna Conventional said, swerving onto the freeway. "We'll save him. Organized religion would make Jesus a Satanist. You're just lucky you missed Maura's Sacred Prostitute phase a couple years back. She got so busy with rituals and speeches she had no time for partying or actual johns."

An hour later, they sat at a window table at Carlo's. On the outside, the tinted glass greened the grays of sidewalks, suits and sixties office buildings. On the inside, all was walnut and overhead vines mixed with ceiling-mounted conical lights. They sipped lattes—Berry's was decaf—and watched the gray battalions pass. "Do you like your job?" Berry asked Anna Conventional.

"Sometimes. A lot of it is insanely boring and frustrating. We have a beauty writer who doesn't understand the esoteric word count concept and a bunch of advertisers who don't want their ads next to the horoscope or what have you. But yeah. Has its moments."

Holding hands with Canon Moosehead meant Maura had to crabwalk into Carlo's. She wore a V-necked blouse that only revealed a smidge of cleavage and a knee-length skirt. Winter wear, Berry decided. She clutched a small oblong purse and perched sunglasses on her forehead. Canon Moosehead wore a denim jacket and baggy gray corduroys over his black shirt and white collar. They got milkshake-looking coffee drinks and joined the others.

Maura introduced the Canon to Anna Conventional and Peter, aka Bishop Bacchus. "Peter here had a religious experience after Berry's dad stranded him in East Bumfuck, pardon my language."

Anna Conventional nudged Berry and winked.

"I know how that is," Canon Moosehead said. "I got lost once, thought I'd lost my mind. I didn't know where I was or how to get home. I'm still not sure how I pulled through. I found strength somewhere. But it changed me. Everything I cared about before seemed small afterwards."

"That's exactly what it was like! I got changed. I discovered something and now I'm a new person. I'm almost born again, but without the bad haircuts and homophobia."

"You have to reach your lowest point before you can shine your brightest," Canon Moosehead said.

"Yes!" Peter said, clapping his hands.

Anna Conventional and Berry stared at each other. Anna gaped and stuck her chin forward in a "what the fuck" motion. Berry made "don't ask me" hand gestures.

"It's like dying and being reborn," the Canon said.

"It's like losing your luggage," Peter said. They went on like that for a while.

"Road to Emmaus!" Canon Moosehead shouted.

"Road to Damascus!" Peter shouted back.

"If Jesus is the answer, I hope he's multiple choice," Anna Conventional muttered.

"Everything happens for a reason," Peter announced.

"Yeah, it's just that some things happen for really stupid reasons," Berry said. "I mean, I've been transformed and reborn and suffered and whacked. But I still haven't got a clue what I'm doing here or where I'm going and if I think about it for more than two seconds I get so scared I want to throw up."

Maura gave Berry a hug. The whole restaurant seemed to watch them. Berry felt bad that he'd torn down the tent revival with his confession. Expressing his non-stop simmering terror hadn't made him feel better about it. If anything, it was harder than ever to ignore now that it was in the open. He violently hated the Canon and Peter for their easy answers.

"It's too bad you're not Jewish," Canon Moosehead told Berry.

"Excuse me," Anna Conventional said. "Aren't you like über Jesus guy?"

"Sure, sure." Canon Moosehead cleared his throat. "But I'm the first to admit when other faiths offer advantages, and one of the best things about Judaism is it recognizes the stage of life you're gong through right now. You could celebrate it by having a Bar Mitzvah or maybe in your case a Bat Mitzvah. You know, celebrate the new person you're becoming but acknowledge you're a work in progress."

"Jewish people have the suckiest music," Berry offered. "I went to a synagogue once and they couldn't keep a tune if it had a collar and leash."

"But maybe there is something we can do," the Canon said. "For both of you. We're supposed to baptize some babies tomorrow morning at Eucharist. It's a horrid ritual. One of them always vomits on my surplice. But maybe we could work you two in. Berry, is there a new name you'd like to be baptized under now that you're a young woman?"

"Still Berry. Like the fruit, I guess."

An hour later, Peter and the Canon still sparked. They discussed gay priests and the importance of ceremony in W. B. Yeats and WB dramadies.

Berry tried to call home. The machine picked up but the outgoing message was blank. All the breath left Berry and he knew in his gut's heart his mom had followed Marco's example and disappeared. She was halfway to some other city by now, seeking a life without a kid who didn't know what he was.

Berry left a message, including Anna Conventional's cell phone number, then he found the girls room. He balked only a little at the door to the place where he'd suffered so much lately. He forced himself to sweep the door before him. Then he hunched over the sink, crying without moisture. He washed his face several times and tried to decide if "orphan" rhymed with "dolphin." All this religious talk only stoked Berry's dread—you only talked religion outside church when you were in trouble or decorating. Berry saw his own thought patterns circle like drainwater. Always back to the choir and its impossible awe. Dr. Tamarind said the purpose of therapy was to bore you, to help you sicken of your own repetitive thought sequences and obsessions, all the better to discard, edit, renew, accept. Berry realized he'd gorged on his constant thoughts of the choir whenever religion, sex, or self-image came up. Thinking about the choir finally started to bore him. But he had nothing to replace the choir with. He washed his face for the millionth time. He tried to make up a lovely hymn about being orphaned.

"Oh hey. Your mom called," Anna Conventional said when Berry returned to the table. "We're meeting her for dinner at Buffalo Country."

Canon Moosehead held forth about the importance of Aramaic scholarship in deciphering the Gospels and the possible existence of a "Q," or source Gospel. Maura stuck her tongue in his mouth and held it there until he stopped trying to move or talk. Then she brushed his face gently, tongue still in mouth, knees visibly nuzzling his crotch. After a paragraph's space, she pulled her tongue out. The Canon squinted as if he'd never seen her before. He carefully wiped his mouth with a wad of napkins.

"He's a great guy," Maura said to Berry, "as long as nobody gets him talking shop." She drew Berry aside. "Actually, I wanted to ask you something. This is totally hypothetical and who knows if it'll even happen, but . . . Canon Moosehead and I have been talking about maybe tying the knot in the spring or summer, you know how these minister types are, all marry-or-burn."

"You really think he's going to marry you?" Berry said. "I mean, he's always been really political."

"He's changed. Anyway, so we might tie the knot and I'll just pretend I'm a virgin." She giggled. "Anyway, we would be like so totally honored if you'd sing at the wedding if it even happens and now I need to touch wood just for mentioning it. But seriously, it would rule. No choir, just you. You could wear a bridesmaid's dress or choirboy gear or hockey pads, I don't care."

"Wow," Berry said. "Wow. I'm like . . . that's really cool. Thanks."

"Don't tell anybody. I'm totally jumping the gun here. I'm just so stoked at the idea of being a preacher's wife like Whitney."

Everyone piled in Anna Conventional's SUV and drove from one patch of business district to another. Along the way they noticed a group of a dozen or so people toting signs and candles. A single television crew followed the small crowd, one man with a shouldered camera and another with a boom mike. "Now there are some people with nothing to do on a Saturday afternoon," Anna Conventional remarked.

"Wait, slow down," Canon Moosehead said. "I recognize somebody. That's Rodney Gretzen. And there's Anita

Gartner. And . . . and . . . oh my. I recognize all of these people from church or the Downtown Association or both." The Canon's eyes pooched.

Berry spotted Lisa's mom walking out front in a parka and holding a sign he couldn't read. Her jaw clenched.

And there, next to her, marched Lisa herself in a plastic yellow raincoat. Lisa had a candle in one hand. Wax dribbled past its paper holder onto her thumb. She stared at her shoes.

One of the signs swiveled enough for Berry to read: NO DRAG QUEENS IN OUR CHOIR.

Berry said something profane.

"Definitely people with too much Saturday afternoon and not enough imagination," Anna Conventional said.

Another sign turned out to say something about queers, and a third quoted an obscure passage from Numbers about clothing the lamb in linen and the fish in diapers or something.

"I just can't believe it," Berry said.

"Stop the car," Canon Moosehead said. "I want to talk to them." He yanked at his seatbelt and reached for the door handle.

Anna Conventional plunged her foot all the way down onto the gas. "No fucking way. You don't want to make those asslickers feel more important." The SUV sped past the protesters.

"But they're my parishioners."

"You're dating a transsexual," Maura pointed out. "You can't afford to draw attention to your own glass house, hon."

Canon Moosehead squirmed.

"Please just drive, just drive," Berry prayed. He yanked at Anna Conventional's shoulder strap.

"Don't do that! Going as fast as legal," Anna Conventional barked. She slapped Berry's hand and ran a red light. Soon the group shrank to angry, sign-waving flecks.

Berry hated sports. Buffalo Country had sporting equipment everywhere he looked, a basketball hoop next to the bar, a dartboard in the corner, trophies and pictures on every brick surface. Judy and Mr. Allen sat at a table with a big net across its center. Plates of nachos and wings crowded the net. "Sorry we're late," Berry told them. "Got distracted on the way over."

The six o'clock news came on during dinner on the big screen TV behind the basketball hoop. A candlelight vigil at St. Luke's was the third story. The camera made the turnout look way larger than the handful of people they'd seen on the street.

"Everybody saw this," Canon Moosehead said, swinging a nacho back and forth in front of his face by its tip. "It'll be in the morning paper too. When they gather tomorrow morning, they'll have many more people waving bigger signs. This will destroy everything."

"Well, there's no such thing as bad publicity," Mr. Allen said with forced cheer. "I only wish we had CDs to sell already."

"Hear the drag queen sing, in living stereo," Maura said.

"Are you insane?" Canon Moosehead reddened. He hit the table, scattering nachos onto every lap. "Of course there's such a thing as bad publicity. You've just seen it, and chances are you'll see a lot more. This is against all reverence."

Peter saw the Canon's aneurysm waiting to happen and put a hand on his new friend's shoulder. "Hey, dude. Chill out, like turn the other blind eye before you get a mote in it. God will provide and all that."

"Shut up, you fucking moron!" Canon Moosehead brushed Peter's hand away. "This isn't some lark. This is serious."

"Honey," Maura said. "Try to relax and think of the big picture. I love it when you get all rise-above-it-all." She took Canon Moosehead's hand and kissed it. He snatched his hand away as if it burned.

"I am seeing the big picture. For the first time in months. I'm seeing the Bell Tower Fund going down in flames. I'm seeing the Downtown Association turning its back on us. And St. Luke's falling into squalor. All because I neglected my tasks and took comfort with the worst of us."

The Canon stood up and stalked toward the door.

Maura ran after him. "Baby, calm down! I've never seen you wig like this!"

The Canon looked at Maura as if he could barely stand to see her. "Cathedrals don't run on positive vibrations and happy dancing. This is the end of everything!" He ran out the door.

Maura stood and gazed at the shrinking corduroy figure as if deciding whether to follow.

"Don't," Anna Conventional said, grabbing Maura's arm. "Let him go. He needs to be alone."

"I can't believe this," Maura said. "I comforted him when he was all freaked out, and now he just runs off."

"The Bell Tower Fund." Mr. Allen shook his head and whistled. "It's okay, Berry. He can't keep you from singing."

"Is it too late for me to go Unitarian instead?" Peter asked.

"Unitarians don't have bishops," Anna Conventional said.

"This is all my fault," Berry told his mom, who hadn't spoken in some time. "All I've done is wreck everything."

Judy quietly slid the steak knives out of Berry's reach. She didn't look at Berry or say anything.

"Don't worry, Mom. I'm not cutting anything. I'm going to stand up for myself." All of the chattering in Berry's head had stopped. The terror was still there, but he could ride it like an elephant. He felt sure of himself for the first time in ages. "If I can't fix what's happened, the least I can do is try to bring some beauty out of it. I've come too far to let those people shut me out." Then Berry seized some nachos. He felt ferociously hungry all of a sudden.

18.

Judy surveyed the apartment she'd occupied for ten years. Half-full boxes crowded the middle of the room and the walls and furniture looked nakeder than ever. "Most of this junk we don't need. What's not all-the-way broken can travel. Marco gave us the car back. We'll load it up and head out."

"Why? I don't understand." Berry watched his mom pile. "What's going on?"

"Time to move on. Start over. I can't face this town any more. You're about to become the new poster boy for the religious scream brigade. Neither of us has a reason to stay. I lost my job, remember?"

"You still have school."

"I'll transfer."

"I have friends. You still have Mr. Allen." Berry looked at the small pile of kitchen gadgets that had survived Marco's rage. "I think I still have the choir."

"You don't. Berry, listen for once. It just turned poisonous for you to keep singing there. Mr. Allen is a nice guy, but he's not my boyfriend or anything. And he's a fool if he thinks he can still let you sing."

Berry didn't think a few nuts with signs could stop him. "It's late," he said. "I have to get up early tomorrow morning for rehearsal."

The night hissed like the coffeemaker Marco had destroyed. The refrigerator ticked. Berry remembered Lisa, wax slowly coating her hand, face bent away from the people around her.

"I don't think so." Judy crossed her arms and stood by her piles. "I want to hit the road tomorrow morning. We drive all day, we can reach my sister's place by evening. We'll just abandon most of this junk."

Berry heard his mom breathe. Her hands twitched like a hard drinker's. Her neck swelled like a weightlifter's arm. Her jaw could barely unsnap enough to talk.

Berry put his arms around her. "Mom, I know this has been super scary. I've put you through a lot and I haven't always explained. But I don't think running away is the answer. Things are going to be all right now."

"Well, that's sure helpful. Is there room for two in your alternate reality?"

"I should call Mr. Allen. He can talk to you."

"I don't want to talk to Ted. I'll call him from my sister's place."

"What's changed? This was always going to be weird. Now it's going to be weird with signs and candles."

"They'll mobilize at that stupid cathedral and draw so much attention to you that school will be Hell, wherever you go around here. Our only hope was for you to find another school in the area where you could be low-key and people could accept you as a girl. Now you've sabotaged that plan. I'm sure whatever new town we move to will have a girls' choir of some sort."

"I can't run away. I want to stand up before God and my friends and let them see me as I am. I need to rejoin the choir, at least one last time."

"They'll crucify you."

Berry coughed up a depthless giggle. His mom glared down at him. "Sorry," he said.

"Pack your bag. Girl's clothes and stuff a girl could wear. We'll do a Salvation Army run first thing."

"Look mom, if you want us to blow town, I guess I can't prevent it. But just let me go and sing tomorrow morning first, okay? I've been waiting a long time to go back. This means a lot to me. I've taken a lot of pain for this."

Judy sighed. "You're like your hair. Can't style it, snarls every comb, and no matter how short I cut it, it grows like dandelions. It's worse now you're a girl and we're going to want to braid or perm it."

"Anna Conventional says conditioner is like spanking your hair. A little keeps order. Too much makes it sullen and resentful."

"She's a wise person. How do you find them?"

"I have good friends. It's luck or something."

"I hope you don't lose it. Or drive your friends away like Marco did."

Thinking of Marco made Berry's soft palate burn. He still hadn't ever heard the details of Marco's downfall, and he wasn't sure he wanted to. He was sure he'd hear plenty of evil of his dad in the fugitive days ahead. He no longer feared or wanted that information. Something had changed, Marco's collapsed life now seemed Marco's own and not so much a warning to Berry. Berry could end badly, but not in the same way as his dad. "It's not like Marco's dead," Berry said aloud. "He could still turn his life around."

"Maybe," Judy said. Berry kept squeezing her stomach and lower back.

Charlie Anders

Berry wanted to talk more, about his dad, the choir, or the sketchy road trip Judy planned. But he felt too exhausted. His thoughts as he fell asleep in his room for maybe the last time were about God, an entity he'd only thought about in squalls before he'd met the born-again Bishop Bacchus. It seemed unfair for a spiritual experience to be derailed by candle maniacs who hated Berry for something he barely represented. Berry fell asleep before that thought could loop itself.

"The parents' council saw it on television. They called around and got the ex-gays to show. The ex-gays got the Not Adam and Steve people—or whatever they're called," said Mr. Allen. "I doubt any of these people are Episcopalian. It's just your bad luck nobody's tried to perform a gay marriage or ordain a gay minister lately."

"I'm not gay," Berry said. "Although, I think I like girls and if I become one that would make me a lesbian according to Maura. Do you think they'd leave me alone if I said I'd only date boys from now on?"

Mr. Allen shook his head. He, Judy, and Berry sat in the pizza place across from the cathedral, the same one where Teddy had thrashed Berry the week before. Mr. Allen and Judy drank rank-smelling coffee. Berry had a smoothie. The pizza place served donuts for breakfast, but they looked greasy and dry. The three of them stared out the window at the mob—it really was a mob—outside the cathedral.

"I just don't believe it," Judy said. "I mean, I expected nuts, but this is insane." She looked pale and lifeless. She'd been up packing nearly all night. She didn't look to Berry like someone who should drive all day. She wore a too-bright floral dress to compensate for her pale face.

"Something pushed their buttons," Berry said.

"It's the way you threaten to get mud all over their precious pure image," Mr. Allen said. He wore a linen suit and the workaday glasses. "It's like learning that angels like to do it with cherubs." He touched Judy's hand. She pulled hers away.

"I can't believe you're letting him sing in spite of all this," Judy said. "It's like you don't care about anything but the choir sounding good."

The hastily prepared signs said things like AIDS CURES GAY CHOIRBOYS and CHOIRBOYS, NOT QUEERBOYS.

"It's not that," Mr. Allen said. "I can't let these hooligans tell me how to run my choir—it's bad enough when the diocese rides me for having anthems in Latin." He looked out the window. "You don't have to skip town over this, it'll blow over."

"We need to start over," Judy said.

"Just give it a few days first," the choirmaster urged. Berry had heard him threaten and implore sarcastically, but he'd never heard Mr. Allen plead before. Judy didn't answer. "Give yourself a little time to think."

The only sound for a while was the inner edges of donuts curling from their own staleness. Berry watched the protesters. He didn't see Lisa, but it was a decent-sized crowd.

"Who are Adam and Steve anyway?" Berry said at last. "Is it a sitcom I missed?"

Wilson ran into the pizza place, choir blazer over his head as if it rained shit. "There you guys are," he said. "Rehearsal in half an hour, right? God, I'm scared to death. I can't bring myself to walk through that lynching party."

"They won't know," Berry whispered in Wilson's ear. "I haven't told. People will never suspect. You're into cars and stuff."

"I'm supposed to live another three or four years," Wilson protested. "I can't die today. What if they think I'm you?"

"Do you have tits?"

"This is going to make it weird for everyone."

"I wish it were different. I'm not sorry. But I wish it were different."

They heard martial rhythms and brass instruments at odds with each other. Someone had dosed John Philip Sousa with acid and then told him to come up with a new arrangement for "Soul Man." And then the musicians had decided to improvise over his arrangement. Berry ran to the pizza place's door and poked his head out. Just at the crest of the hill where Fairview met Main, a group of men and women in Renfair drag and hippy costumes waved instruments as they marched on St. Luke's. Berry squinted into the early sun and saw a gold lamé mitre at the head of the group. "It's Bishop Bacchus! He's back in uniform! And he brought some people."

"Just what we needed," Judy muttered. "More crazies."

Berry hugged her. He stroked her hair the way she always had when he'd been sick or scared. He kissed her forehead.

"Maybe we'd better get to the rehearsal room before they get here," Mr. Allen said. "I get the feeling it's going to be a zoo soon."

Berry felt the terror he saw on Wilson's face walking through the tall grass between the street and the church. Berry tried to cross his arms over his breasts, but one of the protesters spotted him. "It's the queer freak! It's among us!" People waved crucifixes and tracts in Berry's face. Someone shoved a Bible at him with their finger holding it open and pointing to a particular passage that Berry couldn't make out. Someone knelt and gripped the hem of Berry's shirt and prayed loudly for God to look down upon this unfortunate creature and do Berry wasn't sure what. He'd lost track of Mr. Allen and Wilson, maybe they'd made it through. His mom had stayed behind. On all sides, people in black and white pressed against Berry and screamed. Berry put his hands over his ears and closed his eyes, then he felt a gentle tug on one of his upraised sleeves. He opened his eyes and looked into Lisa's. Contusions surrounded her eyes and her lips pushed inward. He couldn't see her mom. He wanted to say something to Lisa but couldn't make himself heard in the crush.

Berry couldn't even tell what direction St. Luke's was. He could see nothing but much taller people all around him and a little sky. For once, he wished for the mother of growth spurts. He shrank into an acorn of self-embrace, hoping to let the ministrations wash over him.

Then he heard "Beat It" and the "Star-Spangled Banner" play at once over a new set of chanting voices, and the giants encircling Berry turned to face the marching band of Bishop Bacchus. Lisa yanked on Berry's arm again and he gave her his hand and they ran through the orchard of believers to the front door of St. Luke's.

After the darkness at the center of the rally, St. Luke's shone brighter inside than ever. The rays from the stained glass looked still sunny after passing through the likenesses of saints. Lisa and Berry ran up the aisle still holding hands, until they reached the altar.

"Thanks," Berry said.

"You're not a monster," Lisa said. "I should know."

"I'm really sorry about your dad. I didn't mean to hurt him."

Charlie Anders

"For a moment, I thought you'd killed him. Then I was sorry you hadn't."

"I was glad I hadn't."

"That's why I'm a monster and you're not."

"You're wrong." Berry couldn't explain to Lisa why she was wrong. He heard the choir warm up. Scales and exercises, melodies that led nowhere but to the same melody half a step higher or lower. Berry hugged Lisa, then turned to the huge statue of Christ crucified at the cathedral's rear.

It seemed a long walk from the altar around the side and down the hall to the choir room. The vocal exercise had gone up a major third by the time Berry got into the room.

Nobody stopped singing. Berry noticed in the mirror his hair looked disarrayed and his lip swelled after a jab from a protester's elbow. He looked too rough-and-tumble to be a choirboy. Berry wondered, if the Devil offered him five extra years as a choirboy for his soul, would he take it? Maybe once he would have. Berry felt the stares of everyone, from Maurice and ancient Bill in the basses to little Jackie. He took his place in front. Mr. Allen didn't scold him for lateness.

After warm-ups, Mr. Allen closed the piano lid. "This is the part where I threaten to cancel church if you losers don't pull your shit together. Not today. This time nothing could make me yank the plug. We're going to show those fuckers what a professional men-and-boys choir sounds like. I don't give a flying fuck if those shitheads want to outlaw double beds or install close-circuit cameras in every motel room. But when they dick around with my choir— they're asking to get their asses kicked. Now let's make a joyful noise unto the Lord."

The service leaflet called for the choir to perform something Stanfordy. But Mr. Allen substituted "Hear My Prayer" by Mendelssohn, which belongs to a single treble soloist who kicks it off alone. It had been George's centerpiece in the spring concert, and now Mr. Allen gave it to Berry. Berry sensed the choirmaster wanted to rub the congregation's faces in his gift. Berry had never sung the long solo portion before, but he knew it by heart from listening to records and George. It contained few vocal gymnastics, but you needed the purest sound to let the plaintive melody flow through you. It started with a bright tune, which turned into a twisty maze of half steps and then one shocking upward interval. When the choir jumped in and answered the soloist, the piece went frenetic. "Anybody feeling rusty on this piece?" Mr. Allen said. "We've got time for a couple of run-throughs." The choir shuffled in fear of a standing jump back into the piece. George stared at Berry. Berry hummed to himself, inventorying every note in his range.

The mob outside brought its noise around to the alley near the choir room, so it got harder for the choir to hear itself sing.

The second time through the solo, Berry shook so hard the music in his hands blurred. He knew for sure he couldn't go out and sing in front of so many who wished him dead or neutered. He tried to keep his voice even, but it only took on more vibrato, like the women sopranos Mr. Allen disdained. About the time the full choir came in, Berry dropped his music. When he bent to pick it up he felt sick. "Excuse me," he muttered to the boys around him. He made his way past his row, all still singing, then headed for the boy's room. At the last moment he changed direction and ran into the hall-way. He stood there, bent over and hands clasped to face, listening to "Hear My Prayer" and the chaos outside. He could see dark figures through the window at the hallway's end, jostling like gears in a grinding machine.

Berry looked back through wet eyes into stained-glass trails. He saw a figure coming from behind the altar into the hallway. It was tall but hunched over, and it had bandages on its head, partially covered by a cocked fedora. As it approached, the figure crackled like a sick dog.

The creature rasped something that sounded like Berry's name and raised a fist. Berry backed away. He felt for the door to the choir room, but he'd already backed up past it. The monster got between the choir room and Berry. It wore black silk and leather, and its eyes squinted behind its bandage mask. Berry was driven back, almost to the door leading to the alley outside, where the people waited to smother him with prayer. He saw one other door, to his left.

Berry opened that door and ran through a dark space with beams and ropes jutting on all sides. At the end of the dark narrow corridor was the thin wooden spiral staircase Berry had seen on his first day in the choir. The gaps between the steps seemed enormous. Every step up the staircase meant leaping half Berry's leg-span. He heard the rasping pursuer close behind as he jumped from step to crumbling step. The staircase went around and around and over and over, until an enormous corkscrew trapped Berry. Below was space and the masked creature. Finally, the staircase ended at a wooden ceiling. Berry felt around it without seeing any way through. He heard the breathing, hoarser than ever, behind him. He found a metal latch. It was already unsnapped. He pushed upwards and the wooden trap door flipped over. Berry pulled himself into the bell tower. He saw a half dozen big ropes attached to levers the size of his torso. They were labeled with the names of notes.

Lisa stood near the big window, looking down at the sign-waving people far below. Her face glowed red and her hair blew in her eyes. "You can see why Canon Moosehead wants to fix this tower," Lisa said. "I nearly killed myself climbing, and this masonry teeters if you lean on it."

"Please don't jump," Berry said.

"I just came to get some space."

"There's a creature following me. It's got bandages and breathes weird and—"

A gloved hand reached up through the open trapdoor and the monster pulled itself halfway into the bell-ringing area.

"That's my dad," Lisa said.

"I should have known," the thing coughed. "You two gather once again. The lizard cortex directs, the warm flesh dances its choreography."

"You're wrong," Berry said. "No lizard direction here. Just bells and sightseeing and me running from you because I didn't know who you were, not that it would have made much difference."

"Lisa," Mr. Gartner croaked. "Come with me."

"He got water in his lungs," Lisa told Berry. "It sounds worse than it is."

"Lisa." Mr. Gartner advanced on his daughter, who shrank at the window.

Berry saw the stonework fissure behind Lisa, hewn brown chips scatter. She leaned back further as her dad approached. The stonework gave under her weight.

"Leave her alone." For the third time, Berry put himself between Mr. Gartner and Lisa.

"Berry, stay out of this," Lisa shouted over the wind and the marching band and chants below. "If he wants to experiment on me some more, there's nothing you or I can do.

He's my dad and that gives him unlimited weird-science rights over his offspring. Come on, dad. Give me the pool treatment. I love what chlorine does to my hair. Or better yet, just give me a little push and we'll see if I'm a flying lizard. Come on, Dad. What are you waiting for? You know you want to. Push!" On that last word, Lisa hit the wall behind her with her fist. Masonry crumbled. Two big stones dislodged. They fell backwards into the sky. Berry heard shouts and commotion below. The wall trembled as if it might lose more stones.

Lisa looked at the hole in the window's underpinnings and then at her scraped hand.

Mr. Gartner stood for a moment, then turned back to the trap door. "No use. Too late. You're already the thing I worked to keep you from becoming. No sense compounding a failed effort." He turned and climbed painfully down the long spiral.

Berry let out a breath. "You okay?"

"Never stood up to him before," Lisa said. "Canon Moosehead is going to kill us."

"After your dad and those nuts down there, Canon Moosehead can do what he likes," Berry said. "I'm not scared any more."

Berry got back into the rehearsal just as the choir was finishing up the day's hymns. He realized that his blazer and pants had tower dust on them. The other choirboys stared at him as if surer than ever that he was diseased and might be contagious. Mr. Allen nodded at Berry, apparently not concerned, and went to robe up before his organ prelude.

"Where the fuck were you?" Randy asked Berry.

"I felt sick. I feel better now."

"Got your period or something?" All the choirboys within earshot laughed at Randy's joke.

Berry punched Randy without even thinking. His tiny fist used every technique Randy had tried to teach him, and struck the bridge of Randy's nose, thumb couched behind knuckles. More from surprise than impact, Randy lost his footing and fell on his back. He lay on the floor and looked up at Berry. Berry walked away and willed himself not to massage his bruised hand.

Nobody touched Berry or talked to him. He went to his locker and found his robes.

"Shit, man," Wilson said. "You're insane. What kind of a girl are you?"

"A girl who hits, I guess," Berry said. He remembered his mom talking about not losing his sweetness. Maybe sweetness too long kept or too hard protected turned to poison.

Out in the hall, the boys lined up. Canon Moosehead stood near the side entrance covered in finery and holding a huge golden cross. Berry walked over to Canon Moosehead.

"What happened to the bell tower?" were the first words out of the Canon's mouth.

"I don't know," Berry said. "I heard some falling stones. I was down with the choir. I'm sorry about all the crowds and commotion. Do you still want to do the baptism thing?"

"I'm not sure." Canon Moosehead's face was impervious to smiles or scowls. He looked at the dust on Berry's pants. "Do you have a soul? Is there a belief in the infinite somewhere inside that chemical hybrid of a body? Do you ever think of anyone but yourself?"

Berry nodded. "Yes to all."

"Consider that your catechism."

The organ ramped up some polite 1920s hymn about the suffering in their tenements and God's mercy. The doorway leading into the church looked floodlit by the stained glass beyond. "So how long do you think you could do this?" Wilson asked Berry. "Stay in the choir with tits and people who want to kill you?"

Berry looked ahead, readied his hymn book flattened open to the right page. "My mom still wants to blow town. But if she stays, I might sing for another year or two. If this is the last time, at least I'm going out in style."

The choir jerked into church. Berry kept his eyes up and away from the hymn he'd long since memorized. His occasional onward glances showed Lisa, Maura, and his mom in the congregation. Most sign-wavers had stayed outside, but a few sat right up front. Maura gave Berry a big thumbs up and a teary wink. Next to her, Anna Conventional blew Berry a kiss.

When Berry got to his old spot in the wooden choirstalls, he saw someone had carved something into the hundred-year-old oak. Someone else had tried to erase it with a plane or chisel, so only the outlines and a few letters remained. It said PER-E-T and then some scratchings that could have been pictures or letters.

Dean Jackson started the litany by wishing the audience, "The Lord be with you." Berry looked around the congregation. It seemed most of the people had their eyes on him. The Dean also gave the sermon, about miracles—the miracles of virgin birth and resurrection, but also everyday miracles. "Nowadays, science can keep alive those whose hearts have failed and transform men into women. Death and sex aren't beyond our control any longer. But the greatest miracles are still those we cannot explain, those that happen in the human spirit . . ." It was pretty much standard sermon material, except for the shoehorned reference to sex changes. Dean Jackson didn't actually take a stand on sex reassignment, or how it fit or didn't fit into a world of angels and the reliving dead.

Berry felt his mind wander. He imagined a choir made up of all those whose boy voices had coarsened: Dr. Tamarind, Marco, George, Teddy, Mr. Allen . . . They stood in barbershop quartet formation and sang in falsetto harmonies a song that went "We're still beautiful inside." In Berry's daydream, Mr. Gartner did a solo punctuated by wheezes. Then Berry imagined himself on his fiftieth anniversary as a choirboy, a plump grande dame in a fur coat and tiara over his cassock, singing a medley of William Byrd anthems.

Berry's dream ended when they announced the baptisms. Canon Moosehead called forward mothers and babies, asking the mothers if they and their assembled friends would help the babies renounce Satan and embrace Jesus. The mothers and congregation all agreed to take this on. The Canon sprinkled a little water on each baby's forehead.

That done, Canon Moosehead turned to the choir. "And we've got one more baptism to do, someone who can speak for herself. Berry, would you like to come down here?"

Berry looked around at his choirmates. Some smirked and others just stared. He squeezed past the boys in his row, then walked to the baptismal font where Canon Moosehead stood. Up close, it looked gorgeous; white and lustrous, carved with angels and flowers.

"Berry (like the fruit), do you promise to renounce Satan and all his ways?"

"Yes."

"Do you vow to embrace Jesus Christ as your lord and savior?"

"Yes. I do."

The Canon told Berry to repeat a form of words, then put his hand on Berry's shoulder. "You've ruined everything," the Canon whispered. "You're not welcome here." Then he pushed Berry's head into the bottom of the baptismal font. The last thing Berry heard was "In the name of the—" Then his ears broke the surface. He stared into the white shimmering bowl and it seemed to have no depth.

Berry let out his air in a stream of bubbles, but couldn't breathe in. He realized the Canon was holding his head underwater for a lot longer than usual for adult baptisms. Usually, it was just a quick dunk, or maybe one sprinkle each for the Father, Son, and Holy Ghost. Berry forgot which. Water poured into Berry's nose and mouth and flooded his throat. Still the Canon's hand pressed harder at the back of Berry's head.

Lights appeared at the center of the baptismal font. The angels carved on the font's outside reached through the bowl's marble case. They beckoned Berry. He watched the lights dance and grow larger. Star-shaped fingers of joy and acceptance sailed through Berry's pupils and into his retinas. He understood he couldn't be what he had been, but he could shine a new way, like Lisa said.

Berry wondered if someone who drowned in holy water went straight to Heaven. Berry couldn't form thought-chains any more, but he had an image of himself (herself) being born from that light, which was just a pinprick now. He could swim past the hardness in front of his face into a new life. He'd be a mermaid or an oyster-diving girl. The lights darkened. A black oval surrounded the whiteness and then it started to close in, swallowing the light.

Then the Canon hauled Berry's head out. He swatted Berry on the back. Berry coughed water.

"You okay?" said the Canon. "You must have lost your balance. I tried to pull you out. You'll be fine." Then he raised his voice, "I baptize you Berry Sanchez."

Berry couldn't take breaths. He made trapped baby seal noises when he tried. He nearly fell, but the Canon held him up. That black circle slowly widened and framed his vision. It disappeared as Berry staggered back to the choirstalls. He tried to hang on to the feeling of peace, of accepting who he'd become, that he'd felt at the bottom of the baptismal font.

The organ started and it was time for "Hear My Prayer." Six bars of intro, then Berry's solo. Berry felt water on his face, not from the baptism but from his sore eyes. All that would come from his mouth was a rattle. Maybe that was what Canon Moosehead had intended. The organ reached his cue. Randy gave Berry a vicious look without changing his bright-eyed open-mouthed choirboy stance.

Berry's solo was a second away. He still felt as if his lungs were full of water. He wept that his voice could fail him now. He looked at Mr. Allen at the organ, then closed his eyes. He couldn't let it end like this.

Berry took a huge breath through his nose instead of his mouth. He clutched his music tight against his chest and looked up into the cathedral's ceiling. High above, fans circulated and stone rafters interlaced the space teeming with air, enough air for every voice for a million years. Berry imagined himself filled with that light and that air. Not a sick wreck drowning inside himself. The intro ended. Berry opened his mouth.

Charlie Anders

The solo cracked at first, but then it flowed. Joy, glory, terror, the human ability to imagine a millionth pinprick of another being's suffering, filled Berry's voice as he pleaded with God to hear his prayer. His voice cracked, but he didn't let that stop him. He breathed in and his insides sloshed, but he sang. The solo seemed to go on forever, but Berry's voice came surer the longer it went. He sang past the water in his lungs and the piece of paper taped to the back of Randy's music folder facing him which said, FOOL YOU GONNA DIE, and which Randy flashed in Berry's eyes. Past the angry people. None of it mattered.

And Berry knew then that he could keep singing no matter what, no matter what anyone did to him. And that his voice could fill any space, no matter how big or awful, even into the dullest acoustics of despair and ear-blindness, he could keep singing.